™

BY DELILAH S. DAWSON

STAR WARS

Phasma

The Perfect Weapon (e-novella)

THE STRIKE SERIES

Strike

Hit

THE SHADOW SERIES (AS LILA BOWEN)

Conspiracy of Ravens

Wake of Vultures

THE BLUD SERIES

Wicked Ever After

Wicked After Midnight

Wicked as She Wants

Wicked as They Come

Servants of the Storm

STAR WARS

PHASMA

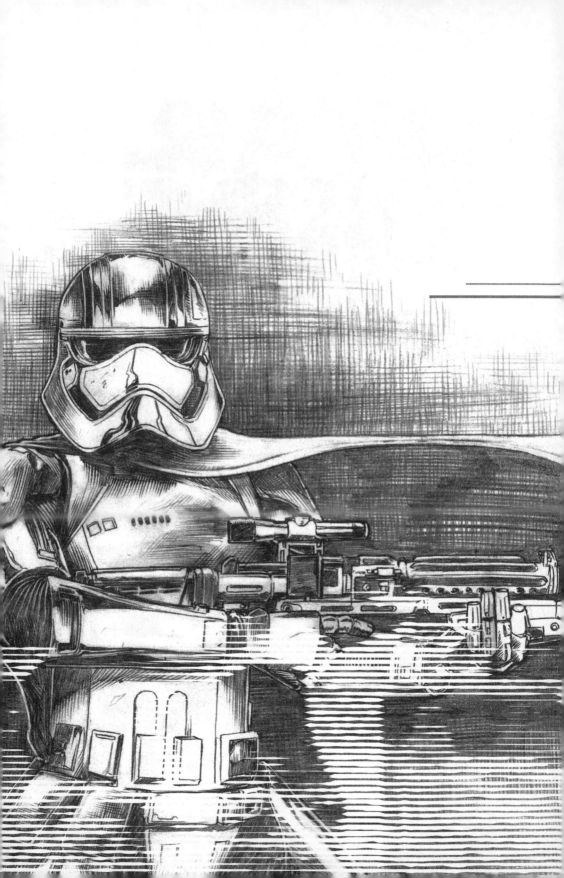

STAR WARS

PHASMA

DELILAH S. DAWSON

DEL REY • NEW YORK

Published in the United States by Del Rey, an imprint of Random House, a division of Penguin Random House LLC, New York.

DEL REY and the HOUSE colophon are registered trademarks of Penguin Random House LLC.

Hardback ISBN 978-1-5247-9750-8
Ebook ISBN 978-1-5247-9632-7

Printed in the United States of America on acid-free paper

randomhousebooks.com

2 4 6 8 9 7 5 3 1

Special Barnes & Noble Edition

Book design by Elizabeth A. D. Eno
Captain Phasma poster art by Larry Rostant
Cardinal poster art by James Zapata

To my sweet husband, Craig: I forgive you for killing me with those Noghri in the *Star Wars* RPG back in 1997.

Mostly.

THE DEL REY
STAR WARS™
TIMELINE

I THE PHANTOM MENACE

II ATTACK OF THE CLONES
THE CLONE WARS (TV SERIES)
DARK DISCIPLE

III REVENGE OF THE SITH
CATALYST: A ROGUE ONE NOVEL
LORDS OF THE SITH
TARKIN
THRAWN
A NEW DAWN
REBELS (TV SERIES)

ROGUE ONE

IV A NEW HOPE
BATTLEFRONT II: INFERNO SQUAD
HEIR TO THE JEDI
BATTLEFRONT: TWILIGHT COMPANY

THE DEL REY

STAR WARS™

TIMELINE

A long time ago in a galaxy far, far away. . . .

STAR WARS

PHASMA

ONE

IN THE UNKNOWN REGIONS

THERE'S SOMETHING COMFORTING ABOUT HYPERSPACE. RUNNING TO OR from trouble, it's always the same. Steady, beautiful, soothing—even for spies carrying highly sensitive intel that plenty of people would kill to possess.

As the stars zip by and Vi Moradi settles into her pilot's chair, she sighs and pulls a bag from the floor. She's been working on this lumpy mess on and off for weeks, knitting the thick, soft yarn into a sweater for her older brother, Baako, a dignitary recently stationed on Pantora, of all places. She's not very good at knitting, but it's relaxing, and Baako always told her she needed to spend less time gallivanting around and more time creating something worthwhile. Of course, she had to use her "gallivanting" contacts to obtain this highly coveted but not "quite" illegal hippoglace yarn. Hopefully the warmth and brilliant azure hue will hide all her dropped stitches. Since she must hide her work with the Resistance from him, Baako still thinks of her as his mischievous, unfocused dilettante of a little sister.

Little does he know.

Her comm blinks, and she sees who's calling and grins at Baako's uncanny way of knowing exactly when she can't talk. Not only because she's elbows-deep in a lumpy sweater, but also because she's on official gallivanting business that he wouldn't approve of and can't know about. Much as she could use a friendly chat to warm her heart after the chill of this assignment, the general is expecting her to check in soon.

"Sorry, brother," she says, flicking the button to shuttle his call to her busy message. "You can tell me all about the new job and lecture me about my lack of focus once I'm done with this mission and giving you this sweater in person. But you'd better meet me somewhere civilized and comfortable, because I'm done with impossible environments."

The comm goes still, and she feels a small ping of guilt for ignoring him. Most ships can't even handle communications at this range, but the Resistance does have some wonderful toys. Vi puts her boots up and leans back in her seat, focusing on the unwieldy wooden knitting needles that look more like primitive weapons than elegant tools.

"It's all about forward momentum, Gigi," she says to her astromech, U5-GG. "Better a hideous sweater infused with love than . . . I don't know. What other gifts do people give their only living relative? A nice chrono? I shall continue to the end, if imperfectly." She spins in her chair and holds up what she's accomplished so far. "What do you think?"

Gigi beeps and boops in what sounds like apologetic disappointment.

"You be nice, or I'll make one for you. A droid cozy to clash with your paint job."

The droid gives a cheerful whistle and turns around as if desperately interested in the hyperspace swirls darting around them. When the Resistance assigned her the droid, Gigi was the factory colors— white and blue—but Vi painted her new friend yellow and copper to match her own bleached-yellow hair and burnished-brown skin.

Vi turns back around and knits furiously. Her hair is cropped short just now. The last time her image popped up on a wanted list, the long dark locks had been far too noticeable, so she'd hacked them off immediately and ejected them into space. Wiry and petite, she's had a hard time finding Resistance uniform pieces that fit her well. The cobbled-together costume she wears now has been altered and shows its long wear in rips, scuffs, and patches. Even the soles of her boots are torn to shreds. Her current assignment has involved some very physical work in a terribly unpleasant place, and she's looking forward to a few days of rest on D'Qar.

Hyperspace lulls her to sleep, and Vi manages a short nap tangled in thick, soft yarn before Gigi beeps and whirs to let her know they've nearly reached their destination. She sits up and stretches as much as the cockpit will allow, wishing the Resistance had provided her with a roomier ship but knowing that for ships, much like for herself, being small and unassuming often means avoiding detection. The ship emerges from hyperspace to float gently in the middle of nowhere, exactly according to plan.

Taking a deep breath, she puts her knitting away and types a long code into her comm. The answer is immediate and, as always, mysterious. They never say more until she's confirmed her identity.

"Copy."

"Starling, reporting to General Organa."

A familiar voice replies, warm but professional. "Welcome back, Starling. What have you got for us?"

"Ah, General. It's always business first, isn't it?"

"When the galaxy is on the line, I have a way of skipping past the formalities of my youth. Let's hear your report." Vi can hear Leia's smirk and likes her the better for it. No wonder they get along.

"Finally found the missing piece of the puzzle, although I had to hunt around. Rough place."

"Everything is rough in the Unknown Regions. So you have what we need?"

Vi shrugs. "Knowing how monsters became monsters doesn't always help destroy the monsters."

"Sometimes it does. Every weapon in our armory has a use, Starling. Now, I know you're due for some time off, but I've got one more set of coordinates, and you're already in the right corner of the galaxy to drop by. Can I count on you?"

Vi looks down at the blue yarn spilling from her bag. She hates putting off time with Baako. They see each other so rarely these days. "Of course, General. That's why I'm here."

"Transmitting coordinates."

On her screen, Vi plots the best route to the general's next stop. Leia wasn't lying—she's already pretty close, and not many pilots have the experience or the guts to explore this shadowy corner of nowhere. She confirms the route and lets Gigi plot the jump.

"Not too bad. I'll be there shortly."

"Good. Just a quick sweep of the area. We've heard rumors of First Order ships there, and it's vital that we know if they're true. If you see anything, be ready to jump. We've had several pilots go missing."

"Bet they weren't as fast as I am."

Leia sighs, sounding every year of her age. "It's not necessarily about speed, but if they come back, you can race them in the Five Sabers. I'll buy you a ship. For now, just a quick sweep and then home. I need those reports."

"Aye aye, General." Vi salutes, wishing they had visual. "About to enter hyperspace. Keep safe, General Organa."

"You too, Starling."

The line cuts off. The starhopper zooms into hyperspace. It's a short trip, not relaxing at all, and she doesn't bother picking up her knitting again. She's jittery now—it's been too long since she's slept. And then they're dropping out of hyperspace again. The long lines of stars judder into pinpoints against a sea of black. Vi's eyes adjust, and she mutters a curse. There should be nothing here, just peaceful darkness and twinkling lights. Unfortunately, there's rather a large something: a *Resurgent*-class Star Destroyer. Leia was right: The First Order is here, big time. Even before she can think the words, her fingers are already typing in new coordinates.

"Come on, Gigi," she mutters. "We've got to get out of here. I hate it when the general is right."

For all her speed, she's not surprised when her starhopper quavers and begins to move. Not forward, like it should, but sideways toward the enemy ship. Whatever new tech they've been cooking up while hidden out here is hard, fast, and implacable. Vi tries every trick in her book, but the starhopper can't break free of the tractor beam. Her firepower is minimal, and she knows they could blow her to smithereens and call it a win. As Gigi squeaks and burbles frantically, Vi considers her options.

"I know, I know." She locks her datapad, encrypts it, and jettisons it into the darkness of space, along with her patched Resistance jacket. The chance of her returning to claim either item is infinitesimal, but every little bit of hope adds up. Reaching into a storage cubby, she tugs out an old black leather jacket she pulled off a dead Kanjiklubber and slips her arms inside. It smells of oil and sand and home, and it did her good on her last mission. Her ship eases ever closer to the cruiser, and she pulls out a small mirror and plucks dark-brown contacts from her eyes, revealing their natural amber hue. What with the hair, eyes, clothes, and fake documents in her front pocket, there's a good chance she won't be recognized.

When Gigi beeps in alarm, Vi settles and taps her temple.

"Don't worry, Gigi. I've got it all where it counts. And they won't break me."

Gigi makes a noise that suggests the odds are against such an occurrence.

"It's okay, little buddy. If I fail, you'll never know."

Swiveling around in her chair, she keys a code into the astromech slot and wipes the droid's memory.

Her earlier comfort and insouciant slouch are gone. This is not the first time she's been captured, and she's got to get her head in the game. She leans back in her chair now, legs spread, arms on the seat's armrests. Every muscle is tense, one foot tapping by the bag of forgotten yarn. Her eyes flash dangerously, her lips set in a thin line.

One way or another, Vi Moradi is going to survive.

TWO

ON THE *ABSOLUTION*

THE ROUGHED-UP STARHOPPER GLIDES INTO THE HOLD OF THE *ABSOLUTION* and settles gently onto the hangar deck. It's a little thing, just big enough to hold one pilot, a droid, and a hyperdrive, and yet it's so dwarfed by the belly of the warship that it looks like a child's toy by comparison, or possibly an insect. Vi feels like that, too—like a tiny, rough, insignificant trifle surrounded by much bigger, more dangerous predators. She goes cold, wondering if this impersonal, black-and-white deck is the last thing she'll ever see, if she'll become just another missing pilot devoured by the mysterious First Order.

Just in case she can defy the odds and find a way out of here, she counts and stores away everything she sees: hundreds of TIE fighters, troop transports, speeders, and even a few walkers. General Organa will be glad to know what kind of firepower they're up against in this new fight. They tell her only what she needs to know to complete her assignments, but considering the intel they were already paying Vi to provide, the Resistance needs every bit of help they can get. At the moment, facing impossible odds, so does Vi.

As stormtroopers surround her starhopper, blasters pointed, Vi's attention is drawn to their leader. She's seen troopers before, of course, but never one like this. His bright-red armor is a strange twist on the regular stormtroopers', but the sanguine violence of the color lends it an air of bloody menace their tidy white just doesn't possess. An armorweave cape falls from one shoulder, and a spherical black droid floats in the air to the trooper's side. Even if this guy didn't look different from his troops, and even if she didn't know who he was, she would immediately recognize his importance. There's an attention there, a level of focus that the grunts just don't possess. She glares at him as one of his men opens the hatch of her ship and points his blaster at her chest. All this time, she affects the look of a regular smuggler caught by hostiles: scared but defiant. She's got to play stupid if she wants to stay alive long enough to escape.

"Get out," the red trooper barks.

She waits a moment, fingers curled over the armrests, before climbing out to stand on the deck of the Star Destroyer.

"Hands on your head."

She obliges him . . . but in return, she's got to test him.

"What are you supposed to be?" Vi asks. "The big red button? The emergency brake?"

He ignores her taunts as he snaps binders on her wrists. "Why are you in this sector?"

"Same reason you are. Enjoying the peace and quiet. At least, I was. Look, I'm an independent trader traveling under legal documents. I have no quibble with anyone. So why the blasters?" Gigi beeps in alarm, and Vi turns to find two troopers digging through her cockpit. "And why are those guys roughing up my droid?" One of the troopers yanks out her yarn and starts unraveling the sweater with his clumsy gloves as if looking for weapons. "Hey, Private Friendly! I worked hard on that. You can't just paw through someone's personal property. And who are you, anyway?"

"Silence," the leader says.

"I asked you a question. Who are you?"

He takes a step closer, and his blaster jams into Vi's belly. "I'm the one in charge. Which means I'm the one who asks the questions."

"But isn't the Empire gone?"

He chuckles.

"We are not the Empire. And you know it."

"Sir," one of the troopers calls from her cockpit. "We've got the logs. The most recently visited planets are Arkanis, Coruscant, and Parnassos."

The blaster jerks against her belly. It's going to leave a bruise. One of those three planets must have set him off, but which one? Not the heavily populated Coruscant. Arkanis or Parnassos, then. Lots of First Order secrets on both planets, but not much else. They'll never let her go now. Good thing she picked up this junker two hops after D'Qar, because that's one planet these monsters don't need to know anything about. They're going to be suspicious now, but she's got to act normal, which means belligerent. Just because she knows who he is doesn't mean the red trooper knows who she is.

"What you're doing is illegal," she shouts at the troopers tearing the starhopper apart. "That's my ship."

"Not anymore it isn't. Search the ship and turn the droid in for parts, then report to your stations," the leader instructs his troops. "I will handle this interrogation personally."

"Personally, huh?" she says.

He spins her around and jams his blaster in her spine, which is a pleasant enough change from her belly. "Walk. I know who you are, Resistance spy Vi Moradi, and I would be all too happy to shoot you."

"I don't know who that is. I'm just a trader, and my boss isn't going to like this."

"No, she isn't."

Her heart sinks. He knows. She can almost feel his finger on the trigger. He wants to pull it so badly. Sweat trickles down her neck as she watches him over her shoulder. She had hoped this was just a random grab, just the usual First Order business. See a ship where it shouldn't be, claim it, dispose of the inconvenient person inside. But if he knows her name and he knows who her boss is, what else does he know?

He glances up at the control room, almost nervously, it seems. When he nudges her with the blaster, she moves.

"Bosses can indeed be a problem," he says. "Now walk."

Vi was trained to remember every detail when it counts, but even she can't keep up with the labyrinthine twists and turns of the enormous Star Destroyer's guts. Long hallways end and intersect, and turbolifts up and down make it impossible for her to recall their route. It's one thing to see pictures of ships like this one, but it's another thing to really understand the enormity of their enemy's resources. As he guides her into another lift, the man in red stands in front of the panel so she can't see which level they're headed to.

"Your place or mine?" Vi asks, hoping to goad him into moving aside.

But the man in red is silent, the gun always rammed into some soft place on her body and the spherical droid floating by his side. Her leather jacket has built-in armor plating, but it wouldn't do much to stop a fatal shot at this distance. Thing is, she knows he's not going to shoot her. But she has to play along. When she slowly begins to take her hands down, he clicks his tongue at her.

"Tsk. Hands on head. You know how this works, scum."

The blaster shoves into her kidney, and her hands go right back up. "Look, I'm not scum. I don't know who you think I am, but I'm just a trader. Maybe I smuggle a little, but who doesn't? And wouldn't that be the New Republic's jurisdiction, anyway? Did I travel back in time? Shouldn't I be in a cell, waiting to speak to some cadaverous bureaucrat in a jaunty hat?"

The lift door slides open, and he shoves her out into a hall that's downright dungeonous. They didn't see anyone farther up, and Vi is willing to bet that's due to a combination of this trooper's knowledge of the ship's rigorous schedule and his droid's meddling, as it sometimes pushed ahead to lead. But down here—well, it's clear nobody goes down here. Except people doing things they shouldn't be doing.

The lighting is dim and flickering, and there's something dripping, maybe runoff from the vent system. They're deep in the bowels of the Star Destroyer, then, in an area that's generally off-limits or beneath notice. And that's not good for Vi. Even the First Order has rules, and the red trooper is breaking them. If this guy kills her, he won't even have to do datawork. She'll just be another load of garbage sliding down toward the incinerator.

Great. The Resistance doesn't know much about the enemy they're facing, and the New Republic doesn't consider them a threat, which means Vi hasn't been briefed on the protocol these people generally follow. She doesn't know what to expect. She's been trained to resist interrogation, but she also doesn't know what new toys this guy in red might have. A chill trickles down her spine. She might be in over her head.

"They put you in the penthouse, huh, Emergency Brake?" she says, because she always babbles when truly worried. "Top-notch accommodations. Can we get room service?"

The blaster doesn't leave her spine. Her captor gives her directions—turn here, turn there—but doesn't respond to her taunting. Finally, he presses a long code into a control panel on the wall, and a door slides open far less smoothly than Vi would expect in what's obviously a new ship. The room inside is colder than it should be and smells of moisture, metal, and, no point in denying it, blood. The spherical droid hurries inside first and turns off the cams, one by one. Vi pauses on the threshold, but the trooper finally touches her, shoving her hard with a gloved hand so that she stumbles to her knees, her fingers curling into a rusty grate set in the floor.

"Get up."

"You really know how to treat a girl right."

He reaches into her jacket's collar and hauls her to her feet, spinning her around. She staggers into the wall, putting her back against the cold metal. The room isn't large, maybe three meters by four, and it clearly has only one use: interrogation. Well, two uses, if you count torture. Three, if you include the inevitable death promised by the fact that she's not going to give up any intel on the Resistance. The space is dominated by an interrogation chair, and the only other furnishings are a simple table and two rickety metal chairs, a place for the bad guys to sit down with a cup of caf and go over their notes while their victim bleeds out, probably.

"I hope the linens are clean."

He shakes his head like he's disappointed, grabs her jacket lapels, and drags her to the interrogation chair. They call it a chair, but it's actually like a gurney standing on end with metal pincers to restrain her head, chest, and wrists as she stands on the metal lip. As part of her training, Vi was shown dozens of images of such machines ranging back from the days of the Empire's Inquisitors to more sophisticated units currently being manufactured for Hutts and other thugs with too much money and a need to get information while keeping their slimy hands clean. This unit, she's sad to notice, has life-support capabilities and a mind probe, which means her captor can bypass discussion and go straight to her brain. Vi has been trained to withstand fists and weapons, but no one has yet found a way to evade direct attacks on the nervous system. She contemplates the poison tooth implanted in the back of her jaw for the first time, running her tongue over it as her captor snaps the metal manacles closed around her arms and torso.

She won't bite down yet. There's still a way out of here. There has to be. With everything she knows now, surviving will mean major strides for the Resistance. They'll have a better idea of what they're truly fighting, in numbers, technology, and enemy mindset. But that means she's got to find a way to live through this interrogation with her mind and body intact. And that means she's got to stop focusing on her own predicament and start paying attention to her enemy and what makes him tick.

Luckily, she knows a lot more about him than he knows about her.

After strapping her in, he checks the panel monitoring her vital signs, flicking it with a finger.

"Your heart rate is up," he notes.

"Yeah, well, I'm strapped into a torture chair, standing on somebody else's dried blood. Seems like a natural response."

"You've got something to hide."

"Who doesn't?"

His red helmet tips, just a fraction, conceding the point. As she watches him, he moves around the edges of the room, double-checking the cam feeds his droid already shut off, as well as what she'd guess is the comm system. The droid hovers ominously beside his shoulder, and he makes the rounds slowly, as if giving a warning.

This is not official.

This is off the record.

No one else is watching.

There will be no interruptions, no reprieves.

This is not how the First Order does things.

"So this is personal," Vi notes.

"We shall see. It's up to you. We can do this the easy way or the hard way."

Vi wiggles, testing the strength of her bonds. "Letting me go would be really, really easy. Besides, you can search me all you want, but I don't have anything useful. Let your boys tear my ship apart, deconstruct my droid, unravel my sweater, poke around in my brain all day. Whoever you think I am, you're wrong. I'm just a harmless passerby."

He stands before her now, legs spread and arms crossed. His blaster is clipped on his hip, red and gleaming. His red-gloved fingers tap against it, another reminder. It's just the two of them and his droid. Anything could happen.

"You are Vi Moradi, code name Starling, known Resistance spy. And you have the very intel I need."

"And you're the Big Red Button. What happens if I poke you in the chest? Does a light turn on somewhere? Does something explode?"

"You don't deny it?"

She would shrug if she weren't manacled and strapped down. "You're the one running the torture, so you're the one who gets to decide what's true and what's not."

"You were on Parnassos."

Vi is too well trained to grin.

"Was I? And what's so important about Parnassos?"

Her captor considers her. "Nothing. That's the point. Now tell me what you know about Captain Phasma."

THREE

ON THE *ABSOLUTION*

VI MORADI IS GOOD AT HER JOB, SO SHE COCKS HER HEAD, HER BROW wrinkling.

"Who?"

Her captor says nothing to betray his annoyance, but he does move around behind her and adjust her bonds. Something slides over her head, brushing the tops of her ears. She's about to say something clever when the smallest electric shock zaps her, raising every hair on her body. Instead of dissipating, it runs down her spine, fizzing out through her nerves to burn in the tips of her fingers and toes. Her teeth clench together painfully, and for a long moment she's unable to pull them apart.

"That's not the highest setting," he says, coming back around to face her. "Not by a long shot. That's barely a taste." He has a remote in his big, gloved hands, and she can't see what sorts of controls it might feature, but she doesn't really want to know. Pain is easier when you don't know what's coming.

"It tickled a little." The words come out slurred, her jaw still clenched.

He cranks up the juice, and every muscle in Vi's body goes rigid. It feels like her bones are on fire, and her eyes roll back in her head, showing her a personal galaxy of exploding stars that in no way resembles the comfortable safety of hyperspace.

When the jolt is over, Vi lifts her head to look at him, her jaw shivering with the struggle of prying her teeth apart. The place where the metal band rested against her forehead feels like it's burned. The words come singly at first as sensation and control slowly return.

"I don't know anything. About anything."

Her captor says nothing, just gives her another jolt, turning the power up a little bit. She has no way of knowing how high it goes, of when it will start to do real, lasting damage to her body. When the electricity comes, it comes on strong, and it's all she can do to ride it out. Stars, pain, heat, shaking, an ache in her jaw and another behind her eyes. When her vision returns, she watches her captor through her eyelashes. Despite his calm, there's something desperate about him. He doesn't seem like the interrogating type, like he does this sort of thing frequently. Perhaps he's never done it before. He hasn't tried to use the brain probe, after all, and if his droid were programmed for interrogation, there's no way they'd pass up that hack.

Back in the Empire days, Vi knows, the Imperial Security Bureau could get anything out of anyone who wasn't trained in the Force. But this guy? He doesn't know what he's doing. And that means he could kill her before he even knew she was dying.

"Tell me about Captain Phasma," he barks again. "I know you've been to Parnassos, and I know that's where she's from. I know you were sent to gather intel on her. And now I want to know everything you know about her. So start talking!"

Yeah, like just yelling at her will force her to spill. Interrogation goes both ways.

Especially now that she knows he's onto her. She has to tell him something or he's going to break her, and soon.

Two more jolts, and he pulls up her hanging head by her hair. She spits blood on his boots from her bitten tongue and stares at the splotch on the flawless plastoid. The blood and the boot are not the same red, much as Brendol Hux might've liked them to be.

"Phasma," he warns. "Tell me about her, or it's going to get a lot worse."

Vi looks up at him through a haze of red. Her brain feels scrambled, like she's beyond drunk. Maybe that brain-stem jack is working, after all. Or maybe pain this intense really does loosen things up, with or without the fancy tech.

"You wanna know about Phasma? I can tell you about Phasma. Oh, the stories I've heard."

Her captor sits back on one of the chairs, arms crossed.

"So tell me one, and we'll work from there."

Vi smiles, just a little.

"Fine. One story. I'll tell it to you exactly as it was told to me by a woman named Siv. My brain isn't working so good right now, but I have a very good memory. That's why I'm such a good spy."

He places the remote on the table.

And Vi starts talking.

FOUR

ON PARNASSOS, 12 YEARS AGO

THE STORY BEGINS WITH A TEEN GIRL NAMED SIV. SHE WAS PART OF A BAND of about fifty loosely related people who lived in a territory on Parnassos they called the Scyre. Although the Scyre folk knew that their planet had once been rich with life and flourishing with technology, they also knew that some great cataclysm had befallen it, leaving them with an increasingly uninhabitable environment. The Scyre was ruled by the swiftly encroaching sea on one side and an unknown wasteland of jagged stone spires on the other. For Siv and her people, the only ground was rock, and food and water were always scarce. They ate mostly dried sea vegetables and meat, salty creatures from tide pools or dead things washed up against the rocks or, sometimes, the screeching birds that cleverly hid their roosts and eggs. Every now and then, some remnant of civilization would wash up against the pitted black cliffs, an old datapad or a bit of recyclamesh that they hoarded. But they had lost written language, and so all they could do was save what they could and hope that they would one day find the peace and comfort their ancestors had known.

Siv said their greatest boon was an ancient cave. The Nautilus, which had once been dry and safe but was now flooded by the sea most of the time. Once every few days, the tide would go out, and the Scyre folk could find succor in their cavern, resting and holding rituals and tending to their accumulated collection of broken tech, weapons, and human remains carefully stowed in hidden tunnels. The Nautilus was the reason the Scyre folk so fiercely defended their territory, for all that the cruel sea and neighboring bands encroached on their home. In a dangerous world, the Nautilus felt safe. And then one night, something terrible happened.

It started with a cry, and Siv jerked awake, ready to fight. She was young then, around sixteen, and already considered a deadly warrior. Leaping to her feet with a blade in her hand, eyes adjusting to the darkness, she scanned the cave for threats. Their entire band had been sleeping peacefully on pallets around a fire in the center of the cave, just under the hole in the ceiling that led back out to the cliffs. As a young, healthy person, Siv's sleeping place was far from the fire's warmth and light, but she easily found the source of the scream.

Their leader, Egil, lay closest to the fire, gasping for breath. A younger man, Porr, loomed over the graying warrior. Porr's blade dripped blood, and his well-armed friends stood by him, grinning with menace.

"Egil is dead," Porr shouted, hefting his blade, a crude thing made from a rusty saw. "He was too old to rule and growing slower by the day. I will lead you now. Siv, bring the detraxors and extract his essence so that even in death, he will protect our people."

Siv looked down at the bag she carried with her always before glancing around the room to see how the rest of her band felt about the power shift. She immediately understood the situation, saw that her friends were moving into position, and knew she had to buy time.

"Egil is not dead. I will only use the detraxors when there is no more hope. You know that."

"He will be dead shortly. Come here and prepare them. Or, better yet, teach me to use them. As the new leader, I will take over the ritual."

At that, Siv picked up her second blade and went into a crouch. She wasn't a large woman, but she was known for being a good, quick fighter with her two curved scythes made from old, sharpened agricultural implements. The well-kept silver flashed in the low light of the fire, and she bared her teeth.

"Detraxing is a holy ritual passed down through my mother, as I will one day pass it down to my daughter," she told Porr. "You can't simply use the machines on a body and move on. You must care for them, oil them, and offer the proper prayers as you withdraw the essence and craft the oracle salve. Without the detraxors, without the salve to protect our skin and heal our wounds, our entire band will die. A good leader understands such things."

Porr sneered and took a step toward her. He'd always been a bully, and Siv would die before giving up the detraxors to him. Fortunately, she wouldn't have to choose. The plan she'd seen beginning was coming to fruition, and a young man named Keldo spoke out from the crowd.

"Porr, this is not our way. Killing the leader is forbidden unless both parties agree to combat."

Everyone turned to look down at the speaker. Most of the band stood now, but Keldo remained on the ground. He'd lost the lower part of one of his legs as a child, and although he was tough enough to survive in the Scyre, he was now known for his wise counsel and clever ideas.

Porr laughed mockingly. "Oh, and you're going to stop me?"

In the silence that followed, a strong voice filled the Nautilus. But it wasn't Keldo.

"I will stop you."

A tall figure in full battle regalia stepped before the murdering usurper.

It was Keldo's sister, Phasma.

Over two meters tall, Phasma drew every eye. She wore her war mask, a rust-red terror of hardened pinniped-skin painted with black slashes and surrounded by scavenged feathers and fur. The eyeholes were covered in fine mesh salvaged from a wreck, making Phasma seem less like a human and more like a nightmare monster. Climbing claws tipped her gloves and boots to help her navigate the rocks and spires outside or fight any rival war bands. And now she faced Porr in her heavily wrapped leathers, mask, and spikes while he wore only sleeping clothes. He had planned his raid for the time when Phasma was outside on guard duty, but he had made a fatal miscalculation. Beside her, Porr looked small and weak.

"Stay out of this, Phasma. Your brother is worth nothing to the group, and you know it. Now that I rule, you will be my deputy, but you must submit to me first."

Phasma shook her head. "You will never rule me."

As if in agreement, a circle of warriors stepped forward to join her. Even in their sleeping clothes, they had a lethal edge. These young fighters were loyal to Phasma and ready to mete out justice as she commanded.

Siv was among them, and she first nudged her detraxor bag toward Keldo with a grateful smile, knowing he would keep the vital equipment safe. As she moved into position, the light of the fire flashed off her dark skin, and she was glad she'd tied back her long dreadlocks with a piece of leather so that she could fight more nimbly.

Nearest Siv was Torben, a big man with a bushy brown mane and beard, tan skin, and light-green eyes. He was good-natured and smiling even with his spiked club and huge ax in hand, the tallest and broadest man among the Scyre and always ready for a fight. His best friend, Carr, stood beside him, a lanky, quick-witted man with golden skin, sunbleached hair, and freckles. Carr had the best aim when throwing blades and was always ready with a joke, but for now he was serious and held two knives by their tips, his eyes scanning the room for anyone who might stand against Phasma. On Siv's other side was Gosta, an agile, quick girl who could dart in to disembowel an enemy and dance out of range before her victim began to fall. Stocky but all muscle, with medium-brown skin and curly black hair, she was just a few years younger than Phasma and looked up to her like she was a goddess reborn.

"I can't wait to sink a knife into Porr's toadies," Gosta murmured.

She was the only girl her age, just past becoming a woman, and Siv had noticed Porr and his friends watching Gosta in a way that Egil should've addressed. For all that Siv hated Porr, she knew that one thing was true: Egil was too old and weak to lead. Not that he deserved his current end, bleeding out on the floor of the Nautilus, staining the worn floor with yet more blood. Few people lived past thirty-five in the Scyre, and Egil had to be over forty. He was getting slow, and everyone knew it.

The helpless among the Scyre folk melted back to stand against the walls of the cave. That was part of life in the Scyre: If you couldn't fight, you quickly found a way to contribute to the group by scavenging food, water, or clothing, and you got out of the way of the fighting or died where you stood. Porr and Phasma circled each other, their warriors fanning out, weapons at the ready. Porr struck first, hacking at Phasma with his long blade, a dagger in his other hand. She was taller and dressed to fight, but Porr was older, more muscular, and more desperate.

Phasma parried the slash with her spear, a rough thing made entirely of metal with a bladed tip. Siv had one eye on the fight and one eye on Porr's minions, who weren't as tough or well trained as their leader. Phasma taught her warriors personally, sparring with them daily and challenging them to learn every weapon and remain constantly vigilant. They followed her not because she asked them to but because she had her own gravity, a greatness and courage that spoke to their hearts. But Porr demanded only attention and flattery from his followers, and so they hung back, waiting for a sign from Porr instead of wading in to fight and turn the tide in his favor.

Porr was quick with his blades, following up a slash from the right with a backhand from the left. But Phasma knew his moves, having trained with him for years under Egil. Every eye in the Nautilus watched Porr and Phasma hacking and slashing and parrying and grunting. Life was hard on Parnassos, and most fights were raids from rival bands, when even those who couldn't fight had to take up arms and defend the land. It was rare to watch two warriors battle, especially when it wasn't life and death for the band. It was beautiful, Siv recalled, watching how easily Phasma fought off Porr's attacks. Siv quickly realized that although Phasma could've destroyed him easily, the warrior was holding back. And then she saw why.

Porr screamed and fell to the ground, but it wasn't Phasma's blade that had struck him. It was Keldo's. While everyone had watched Porr's face, Phasma's mask, and the flashing weapons in their hands, Keldo had crawled across the floor with his own knife and sliced the tendons of Porr's ankles, permanently hobbling him.

By the time Porr understood what had happened, Keldo had backed out of reach and Phasma had her spear pointed at Porr's throat.

"You have broken our greatest law," Keldo said. "We do not raise weapons against our own people, and now you must be punished. You may serve the Scyre with your hands and mind, as I do, or you can serve by contributing the protection of your essence to the people. What is your choice?"

Porr was panting now, his eyes wide and round as he tried to stand and failed. "Fight for me!" he screamed at his warriors. "Don't let them win!"

But Porr's toadies found themselves trapped by the blades of Phasma's warriors, and they did nothing to help their once friend.

"You heard Keldo," Phasma said. "Choose."

"You can't make me," Porr bleated, and Phasma's warriors laughed, a harsh sound echoing off the walls of the cave.

"Oh, she can make you, mate," Carr said. "Either way, you're not gonna like it."

"I'll help," Porr said. "Just . . . please. Don't kill me. Bring the healer. It can be fixed."

Keldo shook his head sadly. He was the only one on the ground with Porr, but his strength, confidence, and dignity radiated, while

Porr shivered and bled and blubbered. Keldo was only a year older than Phasma, but Siv had long known that he would make a great leader.

"We accept your surrender, but you know such wounds never heal," Keldo said. "Phasma and I will rule now. You must find your own way to contribute. Anyone else who wishes to challenge us may come forward and be treated the same as Porr. That is: fairly, and according to the law."

Porr's threat neutralized, Phasma turned to face the people of the Scyre as they crowded against the cave walls. Even through her mask, it was as if she met every person's eyes, her spear held aggressively forward.

"Then we are the Scyre now," Keldo said.

"Scyre, Scyre, Scyre!" the people chanted, starting with a whisper and building to thunder.

Phasma's attention landed on her warriors, and she gave them the nod that meant she was pleased with their performance.

"Siv, the detraxors," she murmured.

Siv fetched her bag from where Keldo had stashed it and hurried to Egil's body. Even dead, every person contributed.

"Thank you for serving us, Egil," she said. "Your today protects my people's tomorrow. Body to body, dust to dust."

The prayer said, she removed the machine from her bag. The bulb, tubes, and needlelike siphon were already fitted with a fresh leather skin, ready to collect the nutrients from Egil's body, without which the Scyre folk would become diseased and weak. Siv used this essence to create an oily substance called oracle salve, which served many uses. Most important, when applied to the skin, it served as protection from the rain, sun, and many diseases. A different formulation created a liniment that helped wounds heal. For Siv, this process wasn't harsh or cruel or strange; it was the closest thing she had to a religion, and one day it would be her own turn to contribute. Egil was gone now; the graying leader she'd once looked up to had faded away sometime during the fight.

When the detraxor had done its work, she stood carefully and carried the full leather skin to where Phasma stood, holding her brother up with one arm. Siv gave the skin to Keldo with a slight bow, and he hefted it.

"For the Scyre!" he shouted, and the people cheered.

The Scyre had new leaders, and though they were young, they were strong.

But they still didn't truly understand Phasma. Not yet.

FIVE

ON THE *ABSOLUTION*

VI LICKS HER DRY LIPS AND LOOKS AT HER CAPTOR, WISHING SHE COULD see his face. Of course, she can already tell he's annoyed. He's tapping one heel and sitting forward, focused on her like he might explode.

"Not what you wanted to hear, huh?"

He shakes his head. "I need pertinent intel. No one cares about what happens to children on backwater planets, or this ship would be empty."

She takes a moment to tuck that bit of information away. "Pertinent intel. So I was right. This isn't just business for you, is it, Emergency Brake? This is personal. Really personal. You got a thing for Phasma?"

He snorts and cocks his head, considering, before picking up the remote and cranking the power up higher than he has yet, so high she's bowed back, up on her toes, fingernails digging bloody moons into her own palms. When it subsides, she collapses, and if not for the tight restraints she would slither to the floor and cry. The scent of cooked flesh fills the small room, turning her stomach. It takes her longer to come back this time, and her captor simply sits in the chair, watching her.

"Okay, the opposite, then," she finally says. She clears her scorched throat. "Look. You want something, and I want something, and we're all alone, so let's work out a deal."

It takes everything she has to raise her head and look him in . . . well, where his eyes should be. The black chasms of his helmet lenses show only her pleading face, drowned in red. He gives an almost imperceptible nod, so she continues.

"I know everything you want to know about Phasma." She pauses meaningfully, spits out another wad of blood with worrisome black specks in it. "*Everything.* Let's say I tell you. And let's say that after I do, you let me go. How about it, Emergency Brake?"

He crosses his arms and considers it, taking long enough that she's able to get her breathing back down and stop panting.

"My name is Cardinal," he finally says, and she has to stop herself from grinning. She knew this, of course, but getting one's torturer to disclose something personal is like the first crack in a dam. If she can just stay alive and keep talking long enough, maybe she can find some weak spot in his armor. Find a way to escape. Or, better yet, turn him. She knows Cardinal is a by-the-books soldier, but she also knows he's dedicated to working with children, running the program that turns orphans into killers. Maybe telling him what he wants to know about Phasma can expose him to some ugly truths about the First Order in general. She's got to keep building this small rapport.

"How come you get a name, Cardinal?" she asks. "The rest of the bucketheads are just numbers."

He ignores the question. "You wanted a deal, so here it is. You will tell me everything you know about Captain Phasma. Every detail. If you give me enough intel to destroy her reputation among the First Order and get her court-martialed, I'll consider letting you go. But understand that you have no hope of leaving if I'm not satisfied." The floating droid beeps a few urgent trills, and he adds, "And do it quickly. I'm on a timetable here."

"A timetable, huh?"

Cardinal swipes a hand through the air. "That's not your concern. Your concern is telling me what I want to know."

She's been slumped in the interrogation chair, held up by the straps and bands, but now Vi finds her feet and stands. She's much smaller than Cardinal, but she's strong, and she needs him to know it.

"If you promise you'll let me go, I'll tell you everything you need to take Phasma down."

Cardinal nods and holds out his hand like he wants to shake on it, but, well, he's got her strapped into a torture chair. Maybe, at some point, she can convince him that she's harmless enough to let her out. The hand drops.

"It's a deal," he says. "But only if I get what I need. So go on. Tell me everything."

She nods and chuckles. So he thinks he's in charge? Well, time to take back equal ground.

"Oh, you'll get everything." She cocks her head to look up at him. "But it would help if I could see your face. How about you take off your helmet, now that we're friends? You afraid I won't think you're cute?"

Her harmless smile must win him over—or maybe it's the fact that he plans on killing her once he gets what he needs. Vi knows a few more things about him, too, but those are cards she'll keep up her sleeve for later.

After considering the request, he checks that the door is locked, rechecks all the cams, and turns his back to Vi. The first thing she notices as he places the red helmet on the table is sweaty blue-black hair, clipped short. When he turns to face her, she sees a much younger-looking man than she was expecting. He's maybe forty, although the lines on his face and the distance in his dark-brown eyes suggest he's already lived a lifetime. His skin is golden tan with freckles and darker patches that speak to years of sunburn. Smile lines crinkle at the corners of his eyes and lips, but he's not smiling now.

"The face you're making suggests you're already thinking about your remote control again," Vi says. "But don't worry. I'll behave. Too much of that juice and I won't be able to talk. It makes me feel dumb, you know?"

He says nothing, just considers her, his mouth a grim line. Something in his eyes suggests . . . is it sorrow? Or guilt? Whatever it is, she's ready to dig for more of it.

"I knew you were from Jakku, but it looks like you had a rough time there," she says.

That closes him up. He wipes a gloved hand through the air as if smearing a trail in sand. "Where I'm from isn't important. Get back to Phasma. Unless you'd like to tell me where the Resistance base is located?"

She shakes her head at him like he's a naughty boy. "You think they just hand out that kind of information to people like me?"

"Yes."

"Well, maybe they do, and maybe they don't, but that wasn't part of the deal. So shock me all you want, and I just might forget how Phasma showed up one day and stole your job."

Cardinal can't hide his surprise at her knowledge, but he can point a threatening finger at her face. "Watch yourself, scum. Insulting me isn't going to help your case."

"Oh, honey. If it weren't true, you wouldn't be so angry about it. I bet it really burns you, how you both came from nothing and she still ended up ahead."

Vi has been trained in reading microexpressions, and in this kind of situation, carefully monitoring his emotions might be the only thing that keeps her alive. The feelings that cross his face are swift and impossible for him to hide. He doesn't have training in resisting interrogation or controlling his features, and she tucks this new bit of information away with her other intel. Now the lines of his face sag into resentment, anxiety, anger. His fingers rove over the remote button, but he seems to have been programmed with excellent self-control. He's fighting it, though. The droid burbles over his shoulder, and he shakes his head, evens out his features, and tries a new tack.

"You shouldn't provoke me. I've been hunting you for a while now, Moradi. I see that you've got intel on me, too. And that means you know I've been in combat, and you know I have no problem with killing my enemies."

No wonder they keep this guy behind a helmet. He's easy to read, easy to anger, easy to wound. She could take everything he owns at the right sabacc table.

"Speaking of which, what do you know about me?" he asks, voice aggressively clipped, as if the question is merely a formality.

Vi considers the request and gives him the barest sliver of what she knows. "You were born on Jakku, and General Hux—Brendol Hux, the original General Hux—took you offplanet and brought you into his training program after the final battle between the New Republic and the Empire. Now you run the younger half of the stormtrooper training program while Phasma fine-tunes your graduates for battle. You report to General Hux—Armitage, that is. Brendol's son." When he opens his mouth to ask for more, she shakes her head. "That's all I've got, Cardinal. Don't even know your real name, if you ever had one."

He stands and turns to the door, and she knows well enough what he's thinking and has to stop him.

"Wait. I know one more thing. You're an ideal recruit. A perfect soldier. Not a single mark against you in all these years. So you're probably thinking about going to tell on me right now, let your superiors know that you've got a captive Resistance spy. But if you do that, Cardinal, I won't tell you about Phasma. You leave this room, and I'll be dead before you return. I promise you that."

He snorts, but he does turn away from the door. "And why would you do that?"

Despite the chill in the room, sweat trickles down her forehead, and she shakes her head to flick it away before it can burn her eyes.

"You're willing to die for your ideals. Is it so inconceivable I might be willing to die for mine?"

He steps closer to her, but not in menace. With a sort of religious fervor.

"For the Resistance? Yes. That's foolish. They don't care about you. They don't care about anyone. They thrive on chaos."

Vi snorts. "Hate to break it to you, big guy, but most people just want to live their small lives, not get caught up and die in someone else's battle for ultimate power. The Resistance is about freedom. About doing what's right and stopping the bullies and tyrants." She can't help smiling as she thinks about Baako, studying to be a diplomat and excited by the prospect of doing good on Pantora. "And the Resistance rewards good people willing to help with that. If you don't like the way you're being treated here, if you've been, say, overlooked for a promotion, or if you get tired of sending children planetside to oppress innocent populations with blasters and flamethrowers, the Resistance would give you a full pardon."

"Defect? To the Resistance?" He barks a laugh and leans back against the wall, arms crossed. "And why would I want to do something that stupid?"

"Because people who try to take Phasma down usually meet ugly ends. At least, they did on Parnassos. I assume they do on this ship, too."

"Speaking of which, our records indicate Parnassos was destroyed."

"How was it destroyed if your men pulled it off my ship's log?"

He rolls his eyes. "The planet is still there, but the water level rose. Phasma's people are gone."

Vi smiles slyly. "They're not all gone. Someone just wants you to think that. I'm surprised you believed it. And that she hasn't wiped it from your maps completely."

"And why would Phasma do that?"

"Because she doesn't want anyone to know what happened the day Brendol Hux fell from the sky—and the day he made a deal with her."

Now Cardinal scoffs, sure he's caught her out. "That's a lie. Brendol Hux did nothing without my knowing it. I was his personal guard."

"Then you failed, because he was there, on Parnassos. I've seen evidence with my own eyes."

Cardinal leans forward, betraying his new interest. "When? How? What happened?"

With a sigh, Vi leans her head back. Her feet are killing her, and there's a dull throb behind her eyes. Every part of her hurts. She can't escape the smell of her own burnt flesh. But she must continue. She has to give him what he wants, but she needs to take her time doing so, and, hopefully, maybe, win him over to her cause. Or at least keep him from killing her.

"I'll get to Brendol when it's time. First, you need to know Phasma's story."

Cardinal shakes his head. "I don't have a lot of time. Get to the part about General Hux. If she caused him harm or actively worked against him, I just need evidence. Something to pin her with." The droid beeps in warning, and his mouth twists as he looks at it. "No. Iris is right. Tell me everything. I have no way of knowing what might ultimately be important."

Which is excellent, as that's what Vi was going to do anyway. She wouldn't be good at her job if she gave up the best information that easily.

"I agree with your droid. You need to hear the whole story. To truly understand who you're trying to take down."

His thumb plays over the remote. "And why do I need to understand her when I just want to destroy her?"

"Because every great hunter knows it's paramount to understand your prey, especially when they're a predator hunting you in return. For all the stories Siv told me, she made certain that I understood one thing very well."

"And what's that?"

Vi looks into Cardinal's eyes, hard, to make him understand.

"Phasma will do anything to survive."

SIX

ON PARNASSOS, 10 YEARS AGO

AT THE TIME THIS STORY HAPPENED, ACCORDING TO SIV, THERE WAS A CHILD among the Scyre, which was a big deal. The people of Parnassos valued children above all else, for they knew that without children their band would die out completely within a few generations. In the last ten years, however, babies had become rare and pregnancy most often ended in tragedy. Whether it was something in the air or the acidic rain, or maybe a lack of vital nutrients, most children were lost before their mothers' bellies even began to swell. But a healthy baby had been born to a Scyre woman named Ylva, and the clan was committed to keeping mother and child safe.

By the time she was five, Ylva's child was old enough to hunt frogs and urchins and contribute to the clan, so she was given the name Frey. It was a rare thing that a child lived long enough to be given a name, and Frey brought hope to the Scyre clan and was loved and indulged by everyone. Thanks to her small size and nimble fingers, she was able to venture into caves the rest of the clan couldn't explore and to snatch birds' eggs from the narrow shelves of rock on which they nested. She was the first child to reach the age of five in years, the only one, thus far, of her generation, and everyone loved her and doted on her.

Keldo and Phasma had been firmly in charge for about two years, and the group was flourishing. Although she still kept her warriors close, Phasma considered it her responsibility to keep everyone in the Scyre group in good physical condition and well trained with weapons, including those who had no talent for it or those too old or infirm to actively defend the group. Even little Frey begged Phasma to teach her to fight, and Phasma made her a child-sized ax out of stone and driftwood. Together, they would playfully practice on the floor of the Nautilus cave whenever it was dry.

One day, Siv and Phasma were sparring on the cliffs, leaping from rock spire to rock spire as they parried and sliced with their blades near the edge of their territory. It took agility and strength, maneuvering over sharp rocks with the crashing ocean far below. Suddenly Phasma put up a hand to stop the fight and used her ancient pair of quadnocs to scan the horizon.

"Balder," she said.

"Are the Claws attacking?" Siv asked, glad she had her scythes in hand.

The Claws were a local war band led by a particularly vicious Dug named Balder. All of the Scyre folk were human, but they had stories passed down from their ancestors suggesting that there had once been Dugs, plus Chadra-Fan and Rodians, among their numbers. Balder, as far as they knew, was the last of his kind. The Claws had more people and more fighters in particular, but what Balder didn't have was the brainpower of the siblings who led the Scyre.

"It's not an attack. It's just Balder. But he's watching us. Has been for a while now."

Siv's hands tightened on the hilts of her blades. "Do you think he wants the land? The Nautilus?"

Phasma turned her 'nocs in the other direction, toward the bulk of the stone cliffs where their band lived their communal life. The people were relaxed and working. Keldo sat on a soft skin, apportioning out water, and Torben was teaching Frey how to swing her ax.

"I think he wants Frey."

"Why?"

"Because she's the most precious thing we have."

Siv considered it and asked, "Then why now?"

"Because now she's useful. The Claws didn't have to spend the time and resources to keep her alive when she was an infant, but now they'd be happy to use her."

The thought made Siv's blood boil. "We can't let that happen."

Phasma looked again in the direction of the Claw territory. "No, we can't."

From then on, Phasma posted two guards at the edge of their territory, and every shift reported Balder's spies keeping watch.

So Phasma watched the Claws watching her people, and she hatched a plan. This was notable because until now she'd always worked in tandem with her brother, Keldo, as if they were two arms on the same body, but this time she told only her warriors. She didn't mention to Keldo that they would be raided soon. And she didn't tell him that she'd scouted into the Claw territory to spy on Balder in turn—but Siv knew.

Finally, on a moonless night, it happened. Phasma and her people were sleeping in their net hammocks, strung between the tallest rock spires, when the ululating cries of the Claws sounded, echoing off the stone. But Phasma was ready. She swung from her hammock, fully awake and brandishing her spear, leaping from rock to rock toward the most secure hammock where Ylva always slept with Frey strapped to her chest. Her warriors likewise burst out of their hammocks, armed and awake, ready to fight. The rest of the Scyre folk had no idea the raid was coming, but they rallied and readied their weapons. The first of the Scyre's night lookouts screamed and fell, cut down by Balder himself, her body splashing into the ocean below and quickly being dragged down into the dark water by gleaming white teeth at least a meter long.

Phasma watched it happen, too far away to save the guard, and screamed her rage. The Scyre had not lost a member in many moons, and a dirty way it was to die.

"The mother is there!" Balder shouted, hanging from an outcropping and pointing to where Ylva cowered in a rock cleft, arms wrapped around the bundle strapped to her chest.

"But I am here!" Phasma taunted.

The people of the Scyre moved to circle and protect Ylva, and Phasma moved between Balder and her people.

"You don't scare me, girl child," Balder growled.

Although he was much smaller than Phasma, the Dug had the natural agility and aggression of his species on his side, as well as a unique fighting style, thanks to the fact that he walked on his hands and used his nimble lower legs to manipulate his weapons. Phasma had never personally fought him before, but she wasn't going to give him any advantage.

As he circled, Phasma leapt for him. In one hand, she held her spear, topped with its slender blade, and in the other hand she had an ax of rusty metal. Of the many remnants of the old mines that her people scavenged, nothing was as useful as the old saw blades and machinery strong enough to hew through rock itself. She drew first blood on Balder and laughed, taking a fierce joy in the fight. Before now, the raids had been mostly tests, but this battle was for real.

It was hard to keep track of who died and who lived as the members of the Scyre fought for their lives. Although they kept a tight circle around Ylva, some Claw members managed to leap or fight through the protective ring. Torben stood closest to Ylva, the last line of defense with his mighty clubs bristling with spikes. For all that she had her bundle strapped to her chest, Ylva fought as ferociously as anyone, taking down two Claw fighters with the rusty saw blades Phasma had taught her to wield. Even Keldo took down a Claw for all that he could fight only in place, tethered to his stone spire by lines and forced to fight on one foot.

But Phasma was the warrior who did the most damage. Clad in

her mask and climbing spikes, she was strong, tall, quick, and the master of every weapon she carried. For all that Balder had the physical advantage, Phasma fought like she craved death at the enemy's hand, like she longed to fall on Balder's b'hedda, a famed Dug weapon he'd painstakingly crafted from an old mining blade. But the b'hedda was a weapon for distance, and Phasma quickly closed with Balder, fighting past his own circle of defense and forcing him to turn away from Ylva and use more intimate tools to best her. It was like a dance, Siv told me: a teen girl dressed like a monster, weapons spinning in her hands as she fought an adult male Dug.

Phasma parried every hit and struck back until Balder dripped blood from his stone-gray skin. One of the reasons he ruled was because he didn't fall ill from his wounds as easily as the humans so often did, but he was soon panting and slowing down. His knife fell from his cut foot as if the appendage was numb, but still he continued fighting. When Phasma lopped off one of his ear fins dripping with ceremonial baubles, Balder finally bellowed in rage, spun, and swung away, calling a retreat. The Claws followed him gladly, for they had lost a dozen members and sustained their own damage without obtaining the child they sought.

Phasma stood tall on her stone spire by a Scyre flag, hefted her ax in the air, and screamed her war cry. Her people gathered around, including Ylva, who was exhausted, having been the focus of the attack.

"How is the child?" Keldo called.

But when Ylva unbuckled her burden, there was no sign of Frey. Her bundle was full of ragged blankets. The Scyre people gasped, shocked that despite being routed, Balder's people had managed to steal the child they'd all been willing to die to protect.

And that's when Phasma untied her bulky coat to show that she'd carried Frey herself, the child strapped to her chest and unharmed.

"You took a great risk, sister," Keldo said, looking very grim.

"And it paid off. We won't be seeing Balder for a while. If ever."

That got everyone's attention. As Phasma unbuckled Frey and

transferred the child back to her mother, Keldo pressed her. "And why is that? After tonight, I would think him twice as likely to attack, now that we've denied him his prize."

"Did you see how Balder couldn't fight any longer? How his weapons fell from his feet, and he looked at his toes in horror? I tried another gambit, and it was successful."

"And you didn't tell me?"

"I wasn't sure if it would work. We've always assumed that wounds fester because of the air, but I realized that it's from the lichen on the rocks. Even touching it makes your fingertips go numb. So I pounded the lichen to make a paste and smeared it on my blades. That is why Balder weakened. Even Dug blood is no match for poison."

She held up her ax, and it was clear to see that a light-green substance was on the metal, mixed in with blood and bits of gray flesh.

"Why did you not share this with the tribe?" Keldo asked, his rage barely contained. "When we all could have benefited from this knowledge?"

"I had to test it first. I had to be sure. And I'm telling you now."

"Sister, I am ashamed of you."

Phasma hooked her weapons on her belt and made her way to the spire on which he sat, his good leg and his half leg dangling down over the churning ocean far below.

"Are you ashamed that I bested our enemy, saved a mother and child, and protected the Scyre's territory? Or are you ashamed that I chose not to include you in my plans?"

Keldo carefully considered her, as good leaders do. He knew that to lose his temper would be to lose face.

"We rule together, Phasma. We always have."

Phasma didn't flinch, didn't blink.

"And we still do. But fighting is my province, brother, and today we fought. And we won!" She gave a war cry, and the people of the Scyre echoed it, hefting their weapons at the night sky so full of faraway stars. "While Balder is crippled and his people recover, we should return the favor. Raid their settlement. Take their territory. They have a plateau big enough for their entire band to sleep on. They light a fire at night and cook their food and warm their flesh. Every night! The people of the Scyre deserve to feel that fire's warmth, and to watch our Frey walk on soft ground!"

At that, however, the people did not shout their agreement. They quieted and looked to Keldo.

Keldo's face was grim. "That, sister, I cannot allow. It is one thing to kill to defend our home and our sacred cave, but it is another thing to trespass against a neighbor, no matter how tyrannical. We are good and strong, but we are not murderers. I'd rather sleep free with a clean conscience than warm myself over an innocent person's bones. We should use this period of fragility to forge a peace with Balder's people. Surely they, like us, understand that if we spent more time surviving and producing children and less time fighting, all our people would be strengthened. If we continue to squabble over nothing, we'll all be gone. One, maybe two more generations, and there will be no one left to fight, nothing left to fight over."

The people of the Scyre nodded along to these wise words, but Phasma breathed out a hum of disapproval, the steam curling from her mask, which she hadn't yet removed.

"You are too fond of peace," she said simply.

"I am a leader, and a leader does what is best for the people."

Phasma shook her head and turned away. "I am a fighter. I do what I must to survive. And making peace with Balder will not save us."

After Phasma had left to sit alone on a far promontory where the night guard had fallen, the Scyre voted. It was decided to let Keldo pursue peace with Balder, although Phasma's warriors voted against it. Keldo's closest confidants helped him make the journey to Claw territory the next day; he did not request his sister's presence or aid. Phasma and her warriors watched, silent, as the procession passed them by. A vote was a vote, after all.

As the Dug was unconscious and still healing from the wounds Phasma had inflicted, Balder's people had no choice but to agree to Keldo's terms. A fragile peace was negotiated between Scyre and

Claw, without Phasma and without Balder. There would be no more raids. They would work together for a shared future, trading goods and encouraging new friendships that might lead to healthy children. Everyone cheered, and Keldo's chosen Scyre folk stood on actual ground for the first time in many years, enjoying the brief safety of Claw land.

Phasma and her warriors had remained behind, standing vigil on their rock spires, guarding the Nautilus and the most helpless members of the clan, as they always had. But they heard the cheers as Keldo's procession returned. Phasma wore her mask, but her hands were in fists. She turned her back on the celebration and stared out at the ocean.

For their very different roles in this new peace, Phasma and Keldo were celebrated as heroes.

But for Phasma, it wasn't a peace. It was a betrayal.

Maybe she'd withheld her plans from Keldo, but he'd directly opposed her, then scorned her.

She would not forget it.

SEVEN

ON THE *ABSOLUTION*

VI LOOKS UP. CARDINAL IS MESMERIZED BY THE STORY, LEANING AVIDLY forward.

"So you're saying she was a hero on her home planet?" he asks with a sad chuckle. "That she saved mothers and children and invented new weapons against her enemies? That she deserves her reputation as the perfect soldier?" He scoffs. "Unfortunately, that information doesn't exactly help me. There's a meeting tomorrow. General Hux will be there, and I need something that can take down Captain Phasma for good."

"Little Armitage is coming over to play? What's the occasion?"

"That's not mine to know. I'm a soldier, remember? Now tell me something I can use."

Vi clears her dry throat and shakes her head, feeling like a school-teacher with a particularly stubborn student. "That's just one story, just a taste of her life on Parnassos. Her origin story, say. It's easy to be a hero when your own survival is aligned with someone else's, when your victory is a victory for your entire clan. On Parnassos, you contribute to the group or you don't last long. There was nothing to lose in her fight with Balder. Her group needed that kid to keep their clan going. Saving Frey was saving herself, even if it looked a little sappy on the surface. The real information you need to take away from this idyllic scene is that Phasma betrayed her brother—and held a grudge. Sure, she saved the kid. And sure, she invented a new weapon. But she didn't let anyone else take a bit of her fanfare, and she didn't want peace. If it had been up to her, she would've killed every Claw."

Cardinal says nothing, just rubs his hands through his hair and stares into nowhere. Vi can almost see him doing the math in his head, see that the Phasma he knows now is the same Phasma who once stood on Parnassos, weapons in hand. But this story alone won't be enough to convince him of what Phasma really is. He'll need more.

And he wants it by tomorrow so he can, what, tattle on Phasma? Get her kicked out of the First Order? Their rivalry must be more serious than the Resistance had led her to believe. They told her Cardinal and Phasma were equals, each with their own domain, but that's definitely not how Cardinal feels. This is no little workplace tiff or friendly contest. And if Vi learned anything on Parnassos, it's that Phasma has her own plans for Cardinal, that she wouldn't let a brown-nosing rival stick around for long, especially if he became a threat.

Vi can see how the story is beginning to crack him. How the more he thinks about Phasma, the less formal First Order soldier he is and the more angry little boy he might become. She's got to encourage that, keep Cardinal's emotions hot and push him to break his careful programming. That's the key to getting him on her side.

But she's also got to avoid making him so angry that he kills her.

The remote is never far from Vi's mind. She can't take many more of those uncontrolled jolts of electricity. It's imperative that Cardinal doesn't lose his temper again. A fine balance to walk, and she's definitely not at her best just now.

She swallows audibly, chapped lips parting. "Hey, how about a little water, maybe? I get parched, laying the groundwork for the really juicy stories."

Cardinal wags a finger. "We don't have much time. Just tell me."

"That's not how it works. If I die of dehydration or electrocution, Phasma's story dies with me."

"Do I look like I brought you a picnic lunch? This is an interrogation, not a party."

"It's going to be less of a party when I pass out."

The floating droid—Iris, he called it?—zips around Vi and beeps imperatively at Cardinal. Vi wants to tease him for taking orders from a droid, but she knows well enough that when Gigi has new information to add, she always listens. She's going to miss that cheerful little astromech. She makes sure she's panting when Iris hovers right in front of her face.

Cardinal mutters, "I know, I know," at his droid and stands right in front of Vi, close enough for her to spit in his eye, if she had enough moisture, which she doesn't. He's from Jakku—he knows what dehydration looks like, and he'll have no choice but to agree with his droid that she's not looking so good. Something about the shocks this machine doles out did a number on her body. The droid's readouts must confirm that she's not playing him. Cardinal sighs and stands, putting on his helmet.

"I don't need to say it, but don't move. Don't try to escape. I'm taking the remote, I'm leaving Iris behind, and I'm locking the door. Can I trust you?"

She's not going to tell him that if he let her out of the chair right now, she'd just fall on the ground and twitch. Her muscles are burned out, her bones aching.

She also won't tell him that building trust is exactly what she's trying to do, and this is a great way to accomplish it.

"You can trust me because we made a deal. But when you come back and find me completely unmoved, I want you to remember it."

"Why?"

She gives him a small smile that cracks her lips. "Because I think we're going to make some more deals, down the road. A little food wouldn't go amiss. This machine is like one big, metallic hangover. It's terrible."

His voice through the helmet is impersonal and cold. "Of course it's terrible. It's supposed to be. It's a torture device."

With that, he taps on the control panel, and the door slides open. Vi closes her eyes to enjoy the small breeze and somewhat fresher air before the door shuts. Even though she's pretty sure she could get out if she gave it her all, she doesn't like her odds just yet. Plus, Iris is watching her, a red eye blinking like a warning. Vi is willing to bet this little communications droid has been rigged with some kind of defense mechanism, a laser or a shock arm. She's not going to find out.

She checks in on her body from toes to eyes, flexing every joint she can, tightening and then releasing the muscles. She's sore and drained, and her goal will be to somehow get stronger before he releases her from the machine or she finds a way to break free, either one. As is, she couldn't fight even one of his kid stormtroopers, and she knows it.

Without meaning to, Vi falls asleep. It's dark and warm inside her head, a pleasant cave where she can rest. She startles awake when the door slides open, filled with shiny red. Blinking to refocus her eyes, she does her best to perk back up so Cardinal won't know how very weak she is just now.

"Is that nerf steak I smell?" she mumbles.

"It's water and protein. Standard trooper diet."

"I was kidding. It smells like death."

Cardinal takes off his helmet and puts it back on the table. He's smiling, and Vi notes that he has a nice smile. Not that it matters. He's still the enemy.

"The protein is still sealed in its packet and therefore has no smell. The only thing in this room with an obvious odor is you. Guess you were in that cockpit for a while, eh?"

Vi can't even tip her head to sniff her underarms, but he's probably right. What with the mission and the shocking and the being trapped in this murderbox of a room, she's likely not a treat for any of the senses.

"I was in there awhile, yes," she agrees, and they can both hear the rasp in her throat. "And on Parnassos, which isn't known for the personal fragrance market."

The look Cardinal gives her—well, she already knew his job involved training the younger recruits, but she can see now why he's good at it. There's a kindness in his eyes, a genuine concern that she wouldn't expect to see in an enemy. He frowns and brings a water bottle to her, extending a straw to help her drink like her mother had when she was a little girl and feverish on Chaaktil. The water tastes fake and like it's been blitzed with vitamins and medicine, but that's not necessarily a bad thing. She swallows deeply and sputters, and he pulls the straw away.

"Not too much. You'll make yourself sick."

She smiles up at him, water still on her lips. "You just don't want to have to clean it up if I vomit."

"It's the only possible way you could smell worse."

That gets a real laugh, and she's glad to play along. Good cop is always better than bad cop, and her endgame has a better chance of fruition if they can build some camaraderie. It's a surprise, actually, to find that anyone working for the First Order can be pleasant; Vi expected an angry, indoctrinated, brainwashed bully. A jerk. But he came from Jakku, didn't he? Lived there into his teens, probably, and had a personality before the propaganda machine pulled him in. And his personality is, thus far, very different from what she knows of Phasma. He gives her a few spoonfuls of dreary gray paste, and she's so thankful to have something in her stomach that she doesn't complain about the taste.

Well, maybe she'll complain a little.

"You know, you get to eat real food in the Resistance," she says. "Made of actual animals and plants. With these crazy things called spices and salt. It'll blow your mind."

He sits down and waves that away tiredly. "I grew up on Jakku. A few sand rats, a stringy bird every now and then. Sometimes I found a nest of crickets, if I was lucky. I'm not concerned about my palate. But tell me: Why'd you join the Resistance?"

Vi shakes her head and takes a moment to think about the right answer. "I didn't join it. That would suggest I work for free, or that I went looking for them, or for a cause to throw myself at. I'm for hire, and they offered to pay me to do what I do best, and I had the time, so I accepted."

His look suggests he knows she's mostly lying. "Oh, so if the First Order offered you more credits, you'd flip sides right now?"

She can only shrug. "No. Never. You caught me. I won't work for the bad guys. I have the luxury of only working for organizations with both credits and morals."

Cardinal's smile disappears. "Morals? The Resistance? Are you joking? They advocate anarchy and destruction. Selfishness. Not morals."

"And the First Order is about morals? And not just the need to hold dominion over the galaxy?"

He shakes his head sadly, like she's a student who's disappointed him and needs a good lecture. "It's right there in the name. First Order. First, order. Fixing the mess left behind by the Republic and now the New Republic. Getting rid of bloated diplomats and lobbyists who don't represent real people with real problems. Bringing equality to all. The old system of government is ludicrous and doomed to fail. Sentient beings are incapable of making the choices that are in their best interests in the long run. The whole point of the First Order is stability."

"Easy to get the unstable to join up, then, isn't it?" Vi shoots back. "What about the individual? What about freedom? With so many people on so many worlds, don't our differences and our unique choices make us beautiful?"

Cardinal scoffs, leaning his back against the table, one hand on his blaster as if he can't stand the notion. "Our differences make us vulnerable. Vulnerable to misrule, to corruption, to getting mired in bureaucracy instead of effecting real change. Stability ensures progress for everyone. That's the whole point of government."

"Why, Cardinal. You sound like someone who doesn't even know he's just a tool for a tyrant."

"And you sound like someone who just wants to watch the galaxy burn."

Vi grins, her gold eyes sparkling. "Yes, well, some of us do see better by firelight."

Cardinal huffs in annoyance and feeds her some more protein. Vi swallows it down, hating everything about it. But he doesn't even know how horrible the grub is, does he? He doesn't know what he's missing. That's the problem with indoctrination—the whole point of the First Order's kind of education is to stop someone from thinking and instead kick their emotions into gear. Make them hate everything else so they'll cling to what you give them. It's hard to think for yourself when fear and anger are driving the shuttle.

But he can't see that, because he's inside of it. And he clearly thinks he's in the right.

"Look, I didn't know what it felt like to have a full stomach until Brendol Hux found me. I'd never slept off the sand, never gone a night without waking to rats or sand fleas or something worse nibbling at me. The other kids were cruel, the adults were worse. That's what your New Republic does. Ignores poor backwater planets and funnels money to the rich planets that can afford to have a voice in the Senate. Who spoke for Jakku? No one. Who spoke for the boy I was? No one."

"And what did the First Order do for Jakku, eh? Is it better, now that you've left it behind? Are the children well fed and getting proper medical care?"

Cardinal tosses down the paste and stands, his hands in fists. "They will be. It's not yet time. But that time is coming."

"Haven't you realized yet?" Vi asks. "It's never going to be fair. Even if you win, children will be forgotten. You were lucky. Your life got better. But that doesn't mean Brendol Hux was good."

"And what about Brendol Hux?" Cardinal is in her face now, and she wants to turn away but can't. He smells of sweat and metal and that low and simmering rage that Vi has smelled on men all across the galaxy. As if his anger seeps out of his pores because he's unable to focus it on its true target. This anger can destroy a man. Or it can be harnessed. Used. A tool for the greater good.

She just has to figure out how to get him in the harness and point him in the right direction.

He's still in her face. It makes it hard to focus. She clears her throat.

"Patience," Vi says. "Patience, and a little more water. I was just getting to the part about Phasma and Brendol."

Cardinal pushes away from the interrogation chair, rattling her bones within the metal cage. She knows he would love to hit her, but he can't. The electricity isn't personal enough. His anger at Phasma is a mad thing that hasn't yet found its target. Whether he refuses to hit her because he pities her or because he's been programmed, she doesn't know. Perhaps he could hit her if his superiors gave an order, but his superiors don't know he's down here. They don't know she's down here, either. And she needs to keep it that way. She says nothing, doesn't begin her story. Just licks her lips.

She needs that water. The droid beeps urgently as if reading her mind.

Cardinal fiddles with the screen on the wall, probably checking in to make sure he's not being missed. Vi is silent. He wouldn't turn on a comm, not with her down here, but she's still not going to take the risk of threatening their fragile peace. Finally, satisfied with whatever he finds, he brings her the water and waits for her to close her lips around the tube and drink.

"Not too much," he warns again, as only someone who's nearly died in a desert can.

"Wait," she says, suddenly realizing that the entire flavor of their discussion has changed. He's broken character with her, given away personal information. "Why are you being so nice to me?"

Cardinal sits back on his chair and smiles. "Because while I was in my quarters, I did a little more digging. You didn't tell me you had a brother."

Vi is immediately awake and alert, straining against her bonds. "I have no one. You know nothing."

"Something tells me that Baako doesn't know about your secret life. After all, spies aren't very good for the careers of diplomats, are they? Even diplomats shipped off to marshy moons?"

She's panting now, furious and terrified. She never even told the Resistance about Baako. She changed her name to keep him safe, paid very high-priced slicers to bury her path.

And yet Cardinal knows.

"Tell me what you want," she says, voice low and deadly.

Cardinal tosses the remote in the air and catches it. "Same thing I've wanted all along. Tell me about Phasma. And Brendol Hux."

Vi swallows, clears her throat, and starts talking.

EIGHT

ON PARNASSOS, 10 YEARS AGO

ONCE AN ONGOING PEACE HAD BEEN ESTABLISHED WITH BALDER'S TRIBE, things should've been good for Phasma and the Scyre. Or at least as good as they could be on a primitive world where every day was a fight just to eat while also not falling between rocks and getting eaten by giant sharks. But then came the day when Brendol Hux fell from the sky. Siv said he never told them what he was doing in the area. Conducting scans, looking for children to steal, who knows? The only thing that can be said for sure is that the old orbital defense system of Parnassos targeted him, hit his ship, and sent him plummeting toward the unforgiving topography of the now primitive planet.

Phasma and her warriors began making preparations the moment they saw the explosion high overhead. As the ship's remains streaked across the sky, Phasma tracked it with her quadnocs, taking careful note of the direction in which it fell. At the very least, ships like this could be pillaged; at most, there was always a hope that they could be salvaged and used to get offplanet. No one alive had seen such ships do anything but fall and crash, but they were evidence of the larger galaxy beyond Parnassos, of a future that had been denied them. It

was painful, living on such a treacherous planet with so many reminders of the ease and technology that had once been taken for
granted. At the very least, there would be metal, tech, clothes, medicines, food, and possibly working blasters scattered around what was
left of the ship. These were the greatest riches in Phasma's world.

But they had to hurry. Other groups in other territories would also
be watching and preparing for the journey. Falling stars, as they
called them, were rare, and this ship was the shiniest thing the Scyre
had ever seen—so bright that they had to shield their eyes as it ar-
rowed down toward the planet. Part of the ship popped off and
floated down separately, headed for the area where the Scyre territory bordered Balder's territory, which made it all the more important to hurry.

As Phasma and her warriors hefted their packs to depart, Keldo
called out to stop his sister.

"It looks like it will belong to the Claws," he said, sitting on the
stone spire Torben had hewn into a chair for him. "Our peace is more
important than any goods on that ship. I forbid you from attacking
Balder's people and breaking our hard-won truce."

Phasma did not cease her preparations. "But this ship is bigger
than most and appears to be undamaged. It could still be functioning. It could carry the riches and technology we need to save our
entire clan. I will not pass up the chance at a better life for us just
because you don't want to get into a shouting match with that tyrant."

"Sister, don't you see? If we all worked together instead of fighting,
we'd have a better chance at survival. Our bands are in the process of
joining. We will soon share the bounty of the ship."

"Brother, I think you're the one who's blind. Balder would never
share a ship with us. He may agree to your peace now, when he's weak
and wounded. But if he regains his strength, nothing will stop him
from destroying us. He will demand revenge, for all that we were
only defending our own. You dream of peace, but he dreams of
power. We must strike now, while he can't fight back. Part of the ship
is near Balder's territory, but the bigger part has fallen in the waste-

lands, and if we hurry it will be ours for the taking. No one owns the wastelands."

"But you must go through Balder's territory to get there. And we don't know what dangers wait beyond our borders."

"But we do know what dangers await us *here*. It's time to take a risk. We need that ship."

Keldo finally conceded to his sister. "I can't deny that the falling star might be our best hope of survival. Take your warriors and see where the ship has landed. If it's in Scyre territory, take what you can. If it's in Balder's territory, leave it be. And if it's in the wastelands, I will trust you to parley with our ally and find a compromise. The peace must be kept at all costs."

Phasma nodded at this, her face grim. "I will do my best to keep the peace," she said.

Siv noted at the time that Phasma's eyes simmered with rage, and that her voice was hard and unforgiving. But what could Keldo do? The most powerful warriors stood at Phasma's side, and thanks to his leg, Keldo himself couldn't even chase after her to rebuke her. He had no choice but to take her at her word. Although the Scyre had voted with Keldo for peace, they were of one mind when it came to the possibility of a better future. That ship was their greatest hope. Phasma took her closest four warriors and handpicked eight more, leaving the rest of the Scyre to defend Keldo, Ylva, Frey, and their beloved Nautilus.

The journey was not easy, for no journeys on Parnassos are. Well, unless you happen to be in a small, agile starhopper and are fast and clever enough to avoid those orbital cannons and pretty much everything else on the planet that wants to eat you.

The Scyre territory was mostly spires of black rock, jagged cliffs, ledges, caves, and occasional tide pools when the ocean was at its lowest. Within their accustomed living area, they maintained a series of ziplines, rope bridges, tethers, nets, and hammocks, and even the least nimble Scyre member could get from place to place without too much trouble. But beyond their nesting place, along their border with the Claws, the terrain grew even more dangerous. The bridges weren't sturdy, and one never knew when a support spike might be rusted through or a stone spire crumbling away to nothing. Phasma's warriors were lucky that the ship had crashed during a time of low tides, so they were able to traverse the terrain far more easily than if the tides had been high, not to mention that during high tide, the ship might've been swallowed by the sea—or a monster in it.

Although she'd lived her entire life near Claw territory, Phasma had little knowledge of what lay beyond the boundaries of Balder's home. What she'd seen during raids or when scouting suggested his land was far superior to the Scyre land, with flat, rocky plateaus, actual soil, and sparse green grasses. Many times, she'd argued with Keldo over the benefits of seizing Claw territory, raiding farther in and planting Scyre flags to claim some of the plateau land and finally give her people what felt like much-needed breathing room. But Keldo refused to even consider a land grab, and the majority of the Scyre voted along with him. Not all the Scyre folk were as skilled and tenacious as Phasma's warriors, and although their twenty middling fighters could defend the group as a whole, the older, weaker, and wounded members of the clan were happy enough to cling to the Nautilus and the rough but predictable life it provided. They were scared to take what they needed, which infuriated Phasma to no end.

Still, Phasma's knowledge of the world consisted of the sea on one side and Balder's plateaus on the other. What might lay in the wastelands beyond Claw territory was entirely conjecture. Keldo reasoned it could only be yet more rock and sea, but Phasma longed to know if there might be different places, different things worth fighting for on the other side. If the Claw were true allies, Phasma once reasoned while speaking privately with her warriors, then Balder's people should let them traverse the land, if not share it, rather than keeping the territorial lines so carefully drawn and tended.

They set off immediately, thirteen Scyre carrying the supplies that could mean the difference between life and death in a harsh land. Skins of water and dried foods that could travel well, strips of meat

jerky and salty sea vegetables shriveled in the sun. Net hammocks
and blankets and weapons galore. Climbing spikes and rappelling
gear. They traveled with long lines of woven rope strung between
each person, the only safety net should someone slip and plummet
toward the raging waves below. Considering the danger of cuts and
abrasions, they wore thick gloves and boots of leather, tipped with
claws to help dig into stone. And they wore their masks, always, both
to protect their faces from the elements and to strike fear in the hearts
of whoever or whatever saw them approach. Siv had apportioned out
her oracle salve beforehand, insuring that the warriors would have
their strength. Under their masks, each person wore thick stripes of
the dark green salve over their cheeks

The journey took time. Gosta was first in line, thanks to her agility
and lightness. She tested the footholds, planted the spikes that held
the lines, and moved ahead to make sure the path could support the
rest of the group. Phasma followed her and helped her plot the route;
Siv and Carr and the rest trailed after. Mighty Torben came last, both
the heaviest and the best defense against anything that might surprise the group from behind. It was their first scouting mission outside their territory in years, and Phasma made sure her people were
secure as they ventured forth.

When they reached the line of flags delineating the borderlands
between the Scyre's territory and Balder's, Phasma called a halt and
pulled out her quadnocs. The borderlands here seemed endless and
were characterized by their harshness and their uselessness as a home
base. Tall fingers of broken rock stuck up like spikes, and far below
them was not the ocean the Scyre were so accustomed to, but yet
more jagged stone littered with bones, trash, and brightly colored
fungi.

Scanning the area, Phasma caught sight of one of the Claw sentries
standing guard on a wider stone spire. Putting away her quadnocs,
she looked at each of her warriors in turn.

"Gosta, take him down," she said, pointing at the figure on the
horizon.

Gosta nodded, unclipped her harness from the group's rope lines, and took off, leaping athletically from spire to spire.

One of the Scyre who wasn't in Phasma's inner circle looked aghast. "But Keldo said we must maintain the alliance at all costs."

Phasma stepped over to share the spire he stood upon, glaring intently into his eyes through her ferocious mask. "Keldo isn't here, and he doesn't know how things work, outside of our territory. Balder won't allow us to cross the border, especially if he also wants the fallen ship. That guard stands between us and the thing that could save us."

The man looked as if he wanted to say more, but his boots sent pebbles tumbling down, the stone tower barely big enough to hold them both. Phasma seemed somehow to lean forward without having moved, and the man edged back, lost his footing, and began to fall. At the last moment, Phasma snatched his arm out of the air and caught him, their bodies balanced to keep them both from toppling over the edge.

"Are you with me or against me?" she whispered.

"I'm with the Scyre," he said quickly.

"When Keldo isn't here, I *am* the Scyre."

Her grip loosened, just enough to make him wobble.

"With you, Phasma. I'm with you."

She released him, righted him, and leapt to the next rock spire as if she hadn't nearly killed one of her own people. "Then everyone find a steady perch and ready your weapons. If Gosta does her job well enough, we shouldn't need them. Yet."

The twelve Scyre folk squatted in place and drew their clubs, knives, axes, and spears. It was a new situation, a group of them out in an unfamiliar place and aggressing for the first time. They were no longer on safe ground. Phasma held up her quadnocs, and when she laughed a short, brutal laugh, everyone tensed.

"The sentry is down. Gosta is signaling that the way is clear. Let's hurry."

No one spoke against her again as they moved silently and swiftly into the borderlands. When they reached Gosta, the girl pointed down to a man's body wedged far below at an odd angle, blood painting the rocks. Phasma nodded and picked up her quadnocs, scanning the path ahead for the next sentry, but they were either too far off or hidden.

"You." She pointed to one of the Scyre folk. "Stay here in the sentry's place."

"Why?" the woman asked, and it took some bravery.

"So that when the next sentry looks or returns, they'll find someone where they expect someone to be. If you meet anyone who isn't Scyre, kill them."

The woman looked like she wanted to argue, but the body down below convinced her otherwise. She merely nodded and knelt to tie her rope to the dead sentry's climbing spike. They left her and continued, following Gosta's slow progress across the rock formations as she found the best route.

Now, the thing about that part of Parnassos is that it was very hard to hide in. When the only way to move was to stand on top of a very tall rock, all without trees or bushes, it was impossible to remain concealed for very long. The upside of this problem was that the enemy was likewise limited. And so it came to be that Phasma and the Scyre folk realized they were approaching an unusual circumstance. Far away on Balder's plateau, all the Claw people were gathered, and luckily, they were all looking away from the borderlands and the approach of their supposed allies. Balder himself was shouting, and the main thing he kept repeating was, "Hurry up! Bring them! Bring them to me now!"

The Claw land Phasma had so coveted was bigger than she remembered it, or perhaps the Scyre had shrunken so small that Balder's territory simply seemed large by comparison. The plateau stood tall, with red dirt and greenery here and there. It was big enough for all of the Claw people to stand on, and a few even lounged or sat, especially the very old, who gathered near a fire. No children were in sight—which explained the desperation behind the Claws' attempt to capture Frey. The plateau ended in a stark cliff on one side, and on the other was a jagged bit of rock big enough to be called a mountain, for our purposes, but it was solid rock and not the sort of thing that a body could simply walk over or through. Some planets feature mountains that are pleasant things to traverse, carved with twisting paths and resplendent with beauty and beasts, but the mountains of Parnassos are more like the claws of some great and unforgiving animal, hungry for blood.

Without a word, Phasma urged her people forward, motioning for them to be quiet and quick. When they stood on the edge of the plateau, behind the crowd of Claw folk so mesmerized that they hadn't even noticed the interlopers, Phasma and her people finally saw the miracle occurring.

Five figures were being pulled up onto the plateau from the land below. Edging around the utterly riveted group, the Scyre folk were fascinated to see that on the other side of Balder's plateau lay not the heaving waters of the dark, churning ocean, but land. And not land made of rock, or not only of rock. It was sand. Sand as far as the eye could see, curving up in wavy dunes, the field of gray broken only by tumbled black rocks. Using her quadnocs, Phasma followed the footprints and drag marks back to where a metal machine waited, half submerged in the sand and beside a huge, crumpled piece of fabric. It was the part of the ship that had popped off and gently floated down. The Scyre had never seen so much fabric in one piece in all their lives, and it was clear why several Claw members were down there, busily cutting the long lines that held the fabric to the machine so that they might claim it for their own. The downed ship was nowhere in sight, but far, far away, across the sands and yet more rocks. Phasma tracked the thin line of white smoke that feathered up into the sky, marking the path to true riches.

A cheer went up as the first strange figure was dragged to standing on top of the plateau, his arm clutched in Balder's bandaged foot. It was a man, and for Parnassos, he wore very little, just finely woven clothes of a smooth, uniform black and tall, shiny boots speckled with sand. He was the oldest person the Scyre folk had ever seen, with pale-white skin and red hair going gray at the edges. Although his limbs were slender enough, his belly was big, and he had dark circles under his eyes. He smiled blandly at the whoops and whistles of the Claw folk but was clearly not celebrating, personally.

Balder pushed him gently aside and reached for the next figure, a warrior wearing white armor streaked with gray sand over a thin suit of black. A gasp went over the Claw folk, and the Scyre folk, too—such armor would've given anyone on Parnassos a huge advantage over the elements, and the solid helmet seemed an improvement over their light leather masks. Two more white-armored soldiers followed, and lastly came a droid. It was shaped vaguely like a human and made of matte-black metal, and it took the longest to haul up, due, most likely, to its weight and its inability to climb. The people of Parnassos had seen the component parts of hundreds of droids and even used droid metal for their weapons, but no one living had seen a droid stand of its own volition and hold up an indignant hand, as this black droid did when Balder attempted to touch it.

Now that all five figures stood on the plateau, Balder turned to his people and motioned them to be quiet. The Scyre folk hunkered down to avoid detection in the crowd. The Dug looked older and tired, the flaps of his skin and ears sagging and dirty bandages swathing his arms and legs. The place where Phasma had sliced off his ear flap looked jagged and ugly, the wound going black around the edges. Phasma elbowed Siv, pointing at her handiwork, and they both shook with silent laughter.

"My people, let us sit so that we may listen to the newcomers," Balder said.

The Scyre folk sat on the edges of the crowd, grateful to be lost among so many strangers avidly watching the show. There were perhaps fifty Scyre, but there were twice as many Claws, and they were so intent on the travelers that they didn't think to consider who might be lurking among them. The sun was punishing that day, and many of the Claw folk wore their masks, helping the Scyre warriors blend in.

Balder indicated that the leader of the new group should speak, and the man in black smoothed his red hair in annoyance before joining his hands behind his back, his legs spread as if he were more than accustomed to speaking to large groups and found the whole thing tiresome. The droid stood by his side, listening attentively, while the three soldiers flanked him, the slight twists of their helmets as they monitored the group suggesting they were more than ready for trouble. The soldiers held shiny white and black blasters in their hands and carried smaller blasters on their hips, and Phasma and the Scyre folks elbowed one another eagerly, anxious to find a way to claim some of the new bounty.

The droid spoke to the man in black, and everyone gasped at the mechanized voice. It was hard to hear on the plateau, surrounded by whispering and the sudden gusts of wind, but the language seemed both familiar and different. The man in black spoke back to the droid, and the droid spoke again, this time much louder, its voice projected by some sort of strange machinery.

"My name is Brendol Hux, and I'm afraid my starship was shot down by an automated defense system over your world. My language is a little different from yours, so this droid will translate to your more primitive dialect."

The crowd gasped and whispered. Hearing their language spoken through the machine, if strangely, was very surprising.

Balder stepped up, shaking his head to make the rings in his ear flaps jingle. "I am Balder, leader of the Claw people. We rule this land, and your ship has fallen within our territory."

The man in black, Brendol, put on a tight smile and spoke through the droid again. "I am glad for your aid, Balder and the mighty Claw people. My emergency pod has landed very far from my ship. I have lost several of my own people in this horrible tragedy. But if you are willing to help me, I can offer you the kind of technology and supplies that your world has lost. If we can reach my fallen ship, I will give you weapons, food, medicines, and water. I will be able to call down a larger ship to bring even further riches."

"Why are you here, Brendol Hux?" Balder asked, stroking his chin with his foot.

Phasma would've asked the same question. Nothing was free, and the riches Brendol Hux offered would not come cheaply.

The droid translated Balder's words for Brendol, and Brendol nodded as if this was a wise question and Balder was a great leader. Phasma nudged Siv in the side and said, "This Brendol Hux is a clever man."

"I'd be clever, too, with three warriors armed to the teeth at my side. With those blasters, they could kill everyone on this plateau in less than a minute, if they wished."

"Then we must make them wish otherwise."

Brendol spoke to the droid, and the droid said, "I come from a powerful band called the First Order that brings peace to the galaxy. I am tasked with scouring the stars for the greatest warriors, that they might join our cause. Our people are well cared for and well trained. Ask my soldiers, here. Troopers, is that not so?"

The three soldiers in white nodded and barked, "Yes, sir!"

"Each of these warriors was selected from a distant planet and trained to fight for the First Order. If your people help return us to our ship, I will take whoever wishes to join me back to our fleet. These soldiers will live in glory and wealth, never suffering for want again. Now, who will help me?"

The Claw people stood to cheer, but a new figure appeared beside Brendol Hux, a warrior wearing a fierce red mask.

"I am Phasma, and I am the greatest warrior of Parnassos." Removing her mask, Phasma faced Brendol and waited for the robot to translate. "I will help you find your ship."

In a heartbeat Balder had his toes wrapped in Phasma's jacket, and the warriors of the Scyre and the Claw were on their feet, jockeying for position around her.

"We are at peace, little Scyre," Balder hissed. "And yet you trespass."

"Would you have told us about your new wealth, Balder? Have you already sent messengers to the Scyre, urging us to join you in this quest? Would you include your allies in your journey to the fallen star?"

Torben, Siv, Carr, and Gosta had their weapons drawn, and the fighters among Balder's Claws were likewise ready. Brendol Hux looked from Phasma to Balder, but not as if he was worried. No, it was as if he was merely curious.

Balder growled. "I would have done so, little Scyre, but you have taken away that kindness with your lack of judgment. You have broken the treaty in coming here, and your lands will once again know our fury."

"So you will not allow the warriors of the Scyre to accompany the Claws on this journey to the fallen star, where we might all benefit?" Phasma asked, her voice even and her smile deceptively bland.

"I do not reward oathbreakers," Balder hissed.

"And if I apologize to you on behalf of the Scyre and promise to uphold the treaty?"

Balder considered her, his lips drawn back in a snarl. "Pledge us the Scyre's child as an apology for this trespass, and I will uphold the treaty."

Phasma's smile went thin and brittle, and although Torben put a hand on her shoulder in warning, she said, "Then I agree. Let us work together toward peace for all."

She took off her climbing glove and held out her hand, and Balder reached with his foot to shake it, as such deals were struck on Parnassos. But when they leaned in to complete the gesture of goodwill, Phasma pulled him in closer and slid a small stone dagger into his chest. Balder shuddered against her and fell. As soon as his body hit the ground, Torben picked him up and flung him off the plateau into the sand far below. Phasma and her warriors barely had time to spread apart and draw their own weapons before the Claw warriors attacked.

"Grab Brendol Hux and get him back to the Scyre!" Phasma shouted to Torben, and the big man picked up Brendol like he was a bag of sand and strapped him on his back, as easily as if the grown man were but a child like Frey.

Brendol's soldiers aimed their guns at Phasma, but she shouted, "Follow your leader. We'll get you to your ship. Balder would've killed you all and taken your riches, but I and my people will go with you."

As a fierce battle broke out, the stormtroopers must've done the math: Stay here and fight a bunch of strange primitives or follow the huge man bounding away with their superior. They might've shot at Torben, but with Brendol strapped to his back and screaming at them not to shoot, they had little choice. Blasters drawn, they followed Torben, picking their way across the rock spires with careful steps.

The battle raged in their wake. Phasma was truly in her element. Before, all the fights had been defensive, with a focus on repelling enemies from the land and saving the people who couldn't fight to save themselves. Now, with three of her chosen warriors by her side and eight more Scyre folk handpicked and hand-trained for their proficiency with weapons and willingness to follow her orders, she could experience a true melee for the first time. The plateau was crowded, bodies clinging to one another as the Claws panicked and sought safety, but they fled or fell before Phasma's ax and spear. Moving past the throng, Phasma aimed for the fighters, familiar masks and weapons she'd parried for years during raids and on whom she now could finally let loose her anger and fierce joy in destruction.

Phasma and her people fought around the perimeter of the great plateau, kicking the wounded and dead over the edge and into the sand to clear more room to fight. As Phasma had planned it, they fought their way back around the plateau until they were near the series of rock spires that would take them across the borderlands and back into Scyre territory.

"Now!" Phasma called, and her people retreated across the rocks as Carr covered them, ready to pick off any followers with his throwing knives dipped in Phasma's poison.

Soon the remaining Scyre warriors were moving fast, back toward home. They'd lost only two people, and those not even worth naming. The Claws had taken far more damage. Without Balder to lead them and more concerned with protecting their own property and their more fragile members, they'd taken greater casualties, and now several survivors stood at the edge, looking down to see who'd died and been tossed to the sands far below.

"You've broken the truce. This isn't over!" called one of Balder's lieutenants.

"Come find us when you want to die, then!" Phasma called back over her shoulder, laughing.

She and her people hurried to catch up with Torben and help Brendol's soldiers learn to traverse the dangerous rocks of Parnassos. In Phasma's eyes, the raid was an unqualified success. She and her warriors had not only ended Balder's reign and thrown the Claws into disarray, but they'd also acquired Brendol Hux and his soldiers. Her gambit had worked, and Keldo would have to see that her strategy would usher in a grand future for the people of the Scyre.

NINE

ON THE *ABSOLUTION*

"THAT'S NOT ENOUGH," CARDINAL SAYS, FROWNING.

"You asked how Brendol came to be on Parnassos, didn't you?"

"Yes, but this story isn't important. It's just more of the same." Cardinal frowns. "Phasma is great, Phasma is a liar, Phasma is dishonorable. Phasma might've lied a little, but it was for the greater good. The First Order doesn't care about any of it."

"But you should. She is the sum total of her stories, you know."

The droid beeps a question.

"Good point. How are you choosing the stories you tell? What's your angle?"

Vi gives a dry cough and waits for him to offer her a sip of water before she speaks again. "I'm telling you all this because like I said, I've been researching all the big names in the First Order, and you're on the list. I can't find a single black mark in your records. I have file after file of proof that you're not a bad guy. You have your principles and you stick to them. You're a great soldier. You practice what you preach. The kids who graduate from your training program all but worship you. I can't even find a way to hate you, and I can still smell the burnt flesh from when you shocked me. So I figure this whole thing can go two ways. Either you use what I give you to take down Captain Phasma, or you realize who you're really working for and defect. Either way, I win."

Cardinal sits back and barks a laugh, looking at her like she's gone mad. "You're a fool," he says, shaking his head. "All you've told me is what I already know: Captain Phasma is willing to do whatever it takes to bring her people glory. She did exactly what the First Order would've done in that situation, the thing no one else had the courage to do. The thing that would ensure prosperity for her people. Even I can't find fault with it. And I want to. No, you're going to have to give me something more if you want to get out of this alive. And if you want to keep your brother safe."

At the mention of Baako, Vi bares her teeth at him. "Ah, but that wasn't the end of the story," she hisses. "I haven't even gotten to the good part."

TEN

ON PARNASSOS, 10 YEARS AGO

PHASMA AND HER WARRIORS HAD THEIR WORK CUT OUT FOR THEM ON THE way back to the Scyre. It was slow going. The whole way there, Phasma focused on better understanding Brendol's strange accent and peculiar vocabulary. With the translator droid gone, lost somehow in the skirmish, she was determined to communicate on her own terms. He was polite and helpful, for the most part, but he did have to correct her frequently.

"Stop calling me Brendol Hux," he muttered. "So long as we're on this blasted planet, just call me Brendol."

"Your people have more than one name?" Phasma asked, fascinated.

Brendol shrugged. "Some do. Some go by numbers, like my soldiers."

"I don't think I'd want to be a number," Phasma said, turning to watch the three troopers.

"Depends on your priorities," Brendol snapped. "They consider it a worthwhile trade for a better life."

Phasma took it upon herself to help him traverse the terrain, and although he wasn't as nimble and strong as his warriors, between Torben's muscle and Phasma's patience, Brendol didn't slow them down too terribly. His soldiers, Siv reported, were well trained, quick to improvise, and tirelessly devoted to their superior. Although she'd already pledged to help them find their ship, Phasma continued to store away information on these strangers from the stars, trying to better understand their ways and speech.

The original journey had taken half a day, perhaps, to get to Balder's territory, but it took longer to return. The warriors were tired, several had sustained minor injuries, and Brendol himself was neither agile nor quick and had little muscle mass. His life in the stars must've been an easy one, the warriors whispered among themselves. As they stopped on one of the last of the plateaus to rest and eat, Phasma monopolized Brendol's time, asking him question after question as she struggled to master the intricacies of his language. She wanted to know about his life, about the ships, about why the First Order needed warriors. She was especially interested in their training programs, as she'd watched the troopers in white armor fight during the battle with Balder's Claws and had found much to admire in their calm, their aim, their nerves, and the way they reflexively followed orders.

Brendol seemed happy enough to talk though his watery eyes darted everywhere, scanning the sky constantly as if rescuers might arrive unrequested at any moment. He spoke slowly as Phasma sorted out their language differences, but it was obvious he had no interest in learning about the Scyre folk and their speech patterns. All his questions were about the planet as a whole.

"But what happened here?" he asked, waving an arm, his nose wrinkled up as if the air carried a bad smell. "There's a powerful defense system but nothing else. No cities. No signals."

"We don't know," Phasma told him. "Generations ago, we had technology. And perhaps your cities. But so much has been forgotten." She shrugged and chewed her dried meat. "All we can do is survive and hope something will change."

"So you've never seen active vehicles in the sky? There's no corporate or governmental presence here?"

Phasma shook her head. "There are only the Scyre and the Claws. And then the wastelands. No one who has gone there has returned in many years."

"Fascinating. None of this is recorded, you see. The planet is listed as uninhabited, but the rest of the files were wiped."

"What are files?"

Brendol ignored that. "Tell me, Phasma. Are there any other fighters in the area who share your prowess? Neighboring bands that might have worthy warriors like you?"

At that, Phasma gave a haughty chuckle.

"No, Brendol. My fighters are the best warriors here. Balder was mighty, but I killed him. Perhaps his clan still has fighters, but there are no other bands. There were, once, when I was young, but they either died out or joined stronger bands. We lose ground every year as the sea rises. That is why we're anxious to leave with you."

"It's funny that your land is being swallowed," Brendol said. "From the sky, we noted several other landmasses that appeared far more habitable. Grasslands and forests, perhaps, even a few large compounds that suggest some sort of civilization. But no one answered our distress call. What do you make of that?"

"I wish to see it myself from your ship. Are all the night stars planets like ours?"

"Some are. Most planets are significantly more advanced."

"But most planets don't have fighters as tough as we are." Phasma looked around at her war band proudly. "How will we become warriors for your clan, Brendol?"

Brendol went very stiff. "The First Order is not a clan, Phasma. It is a political and military organization."

"These words—*political* and *military*. What do they mean?" she asked, although she gave a one-shouldered shrug as if to imply that if they weren't part of the Scyre dialect, they couldn't possibly be important.

Brendol considered her as if assessing her intelligence. "It means, in short, that the First Order seeks to rule those who cannot rule themselves. To establish stability and promote progress for all."

Phasma held out an arm, gesturing at the horizon. "And what would the First Order think of this place?"

"This place." Brendol paused as he fought to chew a bit of dried meat. "Many parts of this planet could be useful, if we could disable the defense system. It could be colonized and used for training and support, possibly even farming or mining. It's unfortunate that your people have been trapped in such an unwelcoming area. But, as I've said, we can offer you something more than scratching away at the rock."

"What about those who aren't warriors?" Phasma asked. "Perhaps they could be transported to these better parts that you've seen."

"Perhaps," Brendol said, but he quickly changed the subject back to Phasma's fighting.

Siv made note that as Phasma spoke with Brendol, she matched her speech patterns to his. Her consonants became clipped, her vowels drew out longer, and in just a few hours she began to develop the stranger's accent. A natural mimic, although Siv had never heard the phrase. Most of the Scyre folk still had trouble understanding Brendol's accent and continued to focus on the most important aspect of Parnassian life: staying alive. Siv and her friends were constantly scanning the borderlands, waiting for the Claw folk to appear and reclaim their prize.

It wasn't long before they were on the move again, headed back into Scyre territory. Phasma went first with Torben and Brendol at her side and the rest of her warriors helping Brendol's troopers navigate the chasms in their armor. When the first sentry called out a greeting, Phasma and her warriors returned it with gusto, beating their weapons against their shoulders and howling their victory. The sentry did not reflect their triumph but shared solemn news: Keldo and the rest of the Scyre folk were waiting for them in the Nautilus. It was considered a great omen that the strangers from the stars had fallen to Parnassos when the cave was revealed, and Keldo held court within, sitting on the ancestral throne of stone.

A contingent of warriors guarded the cave's entrance. Phasma and Brendol passed them and entered side by side, trailed by the stormtroopers, who were allowed to keep their weapons and treated as valued guests. Torben, Carr, Siv, and Gosta followed. Despite the formality of the meeting, it was a time of great excitement and hope, for no living Scyre had met someone from beyond the stars, someone who had survived the orbital defense system that usually reduced every encroaching ship to a pile of component parts.

The great skylight shone down on Keldo's throne. He looked resplendent and solemn, wearing his full Scyre costume composed of bright fabrics and antique feathers carefully stored for great occasions of state. Across both his knees sat an antique staff made of golden metal, some ancient piece of mining equipment handed down from leader to leader among the Scyre and hidden in the Nautilus with other treasures while the sea level was high. There was room beside him for Phasma, but this time he sat in the center of the throne, denying his sister her rightful place.

"Brother, I bring gifts. First, for you."

Phasma's warriors knew not to pry, but they'd all been curious about the bundle in the pack on her back, which she hadn't possessed on the way to the Claw lands. Now she unwrapped it to reveal the unexpected: a leg. Siv recognized it as belonging to Brendol's missing translator droid.

"With a few adjustments, you could stand on your own again."

Keldo took the leg from her, careful not to betray how hard it was for him to hold such a heavy device. He considered it from all angles before leaning it against his throne, his face a war of hope and rage. Siv understood perfectly: Yes, it was a gift, but it was also an insult, perhaps even Phasma's way of saying *I told you so* in front of the entire Scyre. Keldo had forbidden her from leaving, but he'd been unable to stop her, to follow her. He was, in that respect, incapable. And it made him furious.

"And what else did you bring me?" he asked carefully.

"A visitor from beyond the sky," Phasma said. "This is Brendol Hux, and these are his soldiers. They call themselves stormtroopers, and their clan is the First Order. Brendol commands many great ships waiting in the sky."

But Keldo did not smile. His fingers went white where they curled on the stone and around the staff.

"Sister, what of our treaty? Surely our ally, Balder of the Claw clan, did not freely allow you to bring this Brendol Hux with you into the Scyre territories?"

Phasma held her temper. She stood tall, still wearing her mask, and did not bend to her brother in any way. "These people and their ships are more important than any treaty. If we can help him reach his fallen ship, Brendol Hux will contact his people, and they will give us food, water, supplies, medicines, and access to the many advancements our civilization has lost."

Keldo glared his dissatisfaction, his voice booming in the cave. "Were these people found in the borderlands, then?"

"They were beyond Claw territory, in the unclaimed wastelands."

"And did Balder allow you safe passage?"

Phasma breathed out, making steam pour from her mask. When she spoke, her voice was harsh and low, almost animalistic. "No. He did not. Balder demanded the child Frey for my insolence in crossing the border, so I took these people for the Scyre and killed Balder for his presumption. That foul Dug will trouble us no more."

The cave went silent, the Scyre folk caught between Phasma's fierce joy and Keldo's disappointment.

"And how many of our people died during this pointless skirmish?"

Phasma's voice was tight. "Two. And at least twelve Claws. But the loss will be more than paid back. Brendol Hux will help us. Our children will be born and raised in safety among the stars, and our warriors will join the glory of the First Order and bring honor to our people."

Keldo sighed. "These are a child's dreams, sister. Your actions have broken the peace between the bands, and your foolishness has lost precious lives."

"These are a warrior's dreams, brother, and they are real. Balder is dead, and the Claw band has been defeated. We killed a dozen of his finest warriors and claimed this prize fairly. Brendol Hux is our greatest hope for the future. With his help, we can become the most powerful band on the planet and keep our people from going extinct. There are better lands beyond the sea, Brendol tells me, lands where buildings still stand and the ground is solid and yields crops and fruits and beasts. He can take us there in his ship, relocate us and all our treasures to a safer place. This will be our reward for returning him to his people. He need only call them, and they will appear."

Siv noted here that, to her knowledge, Brendol had not promised any such thing, but she would never dare to correct Phasma, especially not in public.

Keldo held up a finger. "If his people are so great, why do they not simply find him on their own? If their technology is like that which we lost, their ships should already be able to immobilize the orbital defense system and search the planet's surface for his lost ship. I have read the old manuals, Brendol Hux. Does your ship not have a homing device?"

Siv couldn't see Phasma's face, but she watched her leader's hands tense into fists. Even Siv hadn't known that Keldo had taught himself to read, although she had noted he had an old datapad among his belongings. He'd been keeping secrets of his own.

Hearing Keldo's patronizing tone, Brendol spoke for himself, albeit slowly and as if talking to a child. "The orbital defense system may have destroyed my craft, as well as any beacons that could contact my people independently. Even if they should come looking for us, we're far from the ship's crash site and now even farther from our escape pod. It is of utmost urgency that I am returned to my fallen ship, so that my troops and I might repair the comm array and make direct contact with my superiors. Your sister is correct: An entire fleet of ships, millions of men strong, awaits my order."

Keldo sat still as stone on his throne, glaring at Phasma. He was livid, but he was hurt. Siv knew him well, and she had never known the siblings to fight. Everyone was on new ground—a rare thing in the Scyre. Phasma stepped forward, but he held out a hand as if commanding her to come no farther.

"Brother, listen. This is for the best. My warriors and I will take Brendol Hux and his people to find this ship. I have seen the unclaimed wastelands beyond Balder's territory, and it is like nothing we have seen before. Land as far as the eye can see, barren and covered with only sand. No rocks, no water. Without your leg, you will be unable to make this journey with the required speed, so I beg you, stay here where you will be more comfortable, and I will deliver glory to the Scyre when the goal has been achieved."

"But sister, you brought me a new leg."

"But brother, you must first learn to use it."

The inside of the Nautilus suddenly felt far too small, and the Scyre folk huddled together, confused by their leaders' hostility and by the presence of strangers from space. They looked to Keldo and Phasma for answers, but all they found was tension. Somewhere, softly, Frey began to cry.

When Keldo spoke again, his voice was unfriendly and cold, far from Phasma's warm, anxious pledge. "But sister, the ship is past Balder's territory. Do you know whose territory that is, or how they fight upon their ground? The Claws will have chosen a new leader by now, and they may even be planning a counterattack that would bring violence to our land. We have lost several of our own warriors, and I see wounds among our remaining people already beginning to fester. It's simply too risky for you and your fine warriors to leave us here, unguarded, when you've upset the balance of peace."

"But brother—"

"Phasma, hear me. People of the Scyre, hear me. Brendol Hux, hear me. I forbid any of my people from pursuing this quest. Brendol Hux and his people are welcome to stay here and join the Scyre, but the risk of leaving is simply too great. Our people have fought and died to protect this cave and this land. You may have destroyed our hard-won peace with our greatest enemy, Phasma, but I will not let you destroy the Scyre. A recovery mission is out of the question."

He slammed his staff on the ground, and the sound echoed throughout the now silent Nautilus, rippling down through all the hidden caves and out, somewhere, to the sea.

"The Scyre has spoken."

Phasma said nothing; when the Scyre had spoken, there were no further arguments. Tonight, her brother had chosen to take on the formal mantle of rulership, denying her the place she'd earned at his side, as his sword arm. As she well knew, there was no fighting among the people of the Scyre; here, in the Nautilus, the gathered people were his to command. She nodded her acquiescence, turned on her heel, and strode off into the darkness.

If only Keldo had understood his sister better.

That night, while the Scyre folk slept in their hammocks among the rock spires, Phasma crept into the swiftly filling Nautilus cave and loaded several packs with the tribe's collected food, tools, and water, the carefully scavenged and hoarded stores they kept for emergencies. Perhaps she reasoned that the First Order would be more than happy to replenish everything she took. Perhaps she cared only about forging an alliance with Brendol. Whatever reason she gave herself, Phasma headed out into the night with her four closest warriors, Brendol Hux, and his three troopers, leaving a crippled and defenseless tribe behind them.

ELEVEN

ON THE *ABSOLUTION*

"YOU SEE WHAT PHASMA WAS DOING, DON'T YOU?" VI ASKS.

Cardinal shrugs. "Aligning herself with the stronger party while getting rid of her weaker brother's influence. But all of that is well in line with the First Order's ways. She was loyal to her people first, and when she didn't agree with her brother's decision, she did what she thought best. If he'd been her true superior, I would object. But as you've described it, they were equals. Therefore, she broke no covenant."

"So you think she did the right thing?"

Vi appreciates the care Cardinal puts into his answer. It's clear he's frustrated, but he's also willing to debate. It's a rare thing to meet someone willing to challenge their own prejudices, especially on a topic as important as this one is to Cardinal.

"It doesn't matter if Phasma did the right thing. My loyalty is to the First Order and what happens within our ranks. Whatever happened before Phasma pledged her loyalty to us is not my business. I have no way of knowing the intricacies of their culture and leadership structure. What you've told me so far might be an interesting character study, but I need documented proof of Phasma's wrongdoing within the First Order. And you still haven't told me about how General Hux died."

"I'm getting to it," Vi says. "But I need a medpac. If I get much weaker, I won't be able to talk. And what about my personal needs? It's not easy to tell a tale when you're about to bust."

Cardinal leans in, shakes his head. "Time for all that later. Tell me about Brendol."

Vi steels herself. "Medpac first. I need to be fortified for this part." She drops her head and grins wryly. "You're not going to like it."

Cardinal stands to check the readout on the panel by her head, the one tracking her vitals. Whatever he sees must confirm what she's saying. The droid gives a reluctant beep, and Vi realizes she's begun to think of Iris as the friendlier of her interrogators.

"Your personal needs are your own problem. I will bring a medpac and more food and water. Try anything, and the deal is off. And remember: I know where your brother is. And Iris is watching you." He puts on his helmet and goes to the door.

Before it opens, Vi says one thing, carefully chosen to trouble him.

"Tell me, Cardinal. Do you remember when Phasma first came to the *Finalizer*?"

TWELVE

ON THE *ABSOLUTION*

CARDINAL STEPS INTO THE HALL, LOCKS THE DOOR, AND CHECKS IT AGAIN. This Resistance spy must remain his dirty little secret—at least until he gets the information he needs from her. He checks the time and mutters a curse, vulgar slang from Jakku that would be frowned upon if there were anyone nearby to hear it. Captain Phasma and Armitage Hux will be on the *Absolution* for a meeting tomorrow, which means Cardinal doesn't have long to wring Phasma's secrets out of his prisoner.

It feels good to think of her as Phasma, rather than Captain Phasma. A dirty, ignorant, desperate, traitorous villain from a dying colony, willing to do anything to get offplanet. Yes, that sounds like the Phasma he knows—or, at least, what he'd like to assume. He knows practically nothing about her, but everything Vi has said rings true. He's taken into consideration that the spy might be lying, but the stories are too specific, too easily matched with his rival. It's odd, that he could hate Phasma with such intensity. On the surface, they have so much in common. Young, scrappy fighters snatched up by

Brendol Hux and driven by the promise of a better life in a ship among the stars.

Ha. Cardinal was Brendol's first and finest project. Phasma was a later addition. An afterthought. And one given unfair attention.

As he marches toward the mess, Vi's final words ring in his head.

Does he remember the day Phasma came to the *Finalizer*?

Of course he does. How could he forget?

That was the day he lost half of everything he'd fought for.

With Brendol gone on a recruiting mission, Cardinal was left to steer the training program. It was a job he loved and one for which he was uniquely qualified. Who else could soothe and inspire new recruits as well as a man who had once stood in their heavy, ill-fitting boots? Ever since leaving Jakku with Brendol, Cardinal had either been in the program himself or helping shape young minds into perfect soldiers for the First Order. Brendol's officers handled the programming, but Cardinal handled the actual physical instruction. Hand-to-hand combat, blaster practice, running simulations, testing their mettle again and again, and subtly shaping their young minds—he was the ideal leader. No one believed in the First Order like Cardinal did, having been lifted from crushing poverty and given a purpose, and he prided himself on helping each young orphan find inner strengths and tap into that resilient core within that would one day live to serve the First Order.

He'd been training a battalion on the use of riot-control batons when the order came in from his comm.

"Cardinal, report to meeting room one-oh-seven immediately, on orders of General Hux."

When such orders came, much like for the meeting tomorrow, there was no questioning them, no asking if he was being called in for commendation or reprimand. There was also no delay. He left Iris and the next most senior officer in charge of training, gave clear orders, and hurried down the corridors toward the familiar meeting room, anxious to learn what his superior wanted. Although he was formally Brendol's personal guard and accompanied the man on all important errands of state, Cardinal was well aware that Brendol often made such recruitment trips, generally to scout a new planet for cadets with the right combination of disadvantage and strength. The galaxy was full of orphans who had grown up, as Cardinal had, alone and struggling on a hard planet. To such children, the First Order was the ideal savior. Even the unwilling cadets—those taken against their will but for their ultimate good— would learn to see it as such, eventually. So perhaps Brendol had brought a new cadre of students for Cardinal to gently introduce to the wonders of clean water and regular food. That was the best-case scenario.

But when Cardinal arrived in the meeting room, armor and helmet fully polished and posture straight, he found not the usual group of scruffy children or a datapad of new identification numbers, but a single, tall figure at Brendol's side. He—for at the time, Cardinal was sure it was a man—clearly wasn't a proper stormtrooper, but he wore white stormtrooper armor, ill fitting and utterly filthy. Blood, muck, and scorch marks were everywhere. Under the armor, he was blasphemously wrapped in red fabric instead of the requisite black body glove, standing taller than Cardinal or Brendol and giving off an air of quiet menace.

From the very beginning, Cardinal knew this new upstart would be trouble.

"Cardinal, this is Phasma," Brendol had said. "You will introduce her to the ship and to her duties. The training program has grown beyond our greatest hopes, and once her own training is complete, your current role will be split between the two of you. Cardinal will continue to handle the new and young recruits, while Phasma will eventually take over the teens and adults, especially in regard to combat and terrain simulations. Cardinal, I will be taking on a new personal guard. You have performed admirably, and I now wish you to focus on our expanding program and training Phasma in all our weapons. Be sure to get her up to speed on using datapads, tech, that sort of thing."

This introduction caught Cardinal entirely off-guard.

Not only was he not prepared for the tall intruder to be female, but he had also lost his highest honor as Brendol's guard—and half his training program. All that, and he was expected to train her, too.

If anyone else had required such a task from him . . .

But it was Brendol Hux.

"Has she been assigned a number, sir?" he asked, hating the squeak of desperation in his voice.

Brendol smiled that secret smile of his and chuckled. "Oh, no. Like you, she is a special case. She will also require an armor fitting. I've already had her assigned a separate suite. We've had a long journey, so we will rest today. You will begin her training tomorrow morning. And now I must go make sure our other new recruit starts out on the right foot. I have great expectations for these warriors of Parnassos."

Cardinal saluted, but Brendol was acting strangely. He'd been watching his mentor for years, ever since that first flight off Jakku, and he'd seen Brendol on good days and bad, under great stress and when gloating over a bureaucratic victory. Something was off with him today, something more than just his sun-reddened skin, but Cardinal couldn't say what. Perhaps the older man was simply exhausted from whatever had happened on Phasma's planet.

Brendol left, and Cardinal felt like he'd lost something valuable and was being given a pathetic replacement. He turned to Phasma, determined to make the best of it. Because that was what Brendol and the First Order required, and if nothing else Cardinal wanted to do his job and do it well.

"What planet did General Hux say you were from?" he asked, opening the door and waiting for her to pass through.

"Parnassos," she said, her accent as clipped and flawless as Brendol's but, Cardinal noted, nearly emotionless.

"I haven't heard of it." She still hadn't gone through the door, so he added, "After you."

Phasma shook her head. "You go first. I don't know my way."

Cardinal had shrugged it off at the time. She was tired, had clearly been fighting, and was obviously from some war-torn backwater planet. Of course she wouldn't want to speak of it. So he nodded and led her from the room.

Now, walking the halls of a different but identical Star Destroyer, his *Absolution* instead of what has become her *Finalizer,* Cardinal is forced to remember that Phasma never mentioned her home planet again, that she has always sidestepped any mention of her origins or previous training. Any digging, and she simply digs in harder with silence or doubles down on her onslaught in what should be a friendly training exercise.

No wonder Vi's past destinations struck a chord with him. Although he looked it up on the star charts and saw that it was labeled DESTROYED, he's never heard the name Parnassos again, has he? Until today.

As he enters the mess, Cardinal lets his concerns slough off his shoulders so he can stand tall. He moves among his soldiers, nods back to those who nod deferentially to him. Sure, he thinks of them as soldiers, but they're all under sixteen, aren't they? Ever since the division of training programs, Captain Cardinal's older recruits leave to complete their training on the *Finalizer* with Captain Phasma, while the younger cadets stay on the *Absolution* with him. Cardinal has no idea what happens to the older ones, over there. Judging by the military victories celebrated on both ships, he suspects Phasma's methods continue to be exemplary. He knows his own are flawless.

In line, he selects several water bottles and another protein pack, this one in a different flavor. Not that his prisoner will care for it, but he wants to keep her alive so she'll keep talking, which means she needs to eat. Iris confirmed that her stats weren't good, so Vi wasn't lying about that. Even though he's learned plenty from her stories so far, he feels certain that she's holding something back, drawing the story out for longer than is truly necessary. She knows something about Phasma—something that can help him. If he can just pry that intel out of the spy before Armitage and Phasma arrive, if he can obtain real, concrete proof, perhaps he can get rid of his rival once and for all.

Not because she's better than him, and not because he's worried about friendly competition. But because the more he learns about Phasma, the more he believes that she's not the perfect soldier she appears to be. That there's something dangerous about her, something potentially threatening to the First Order. She's like a ball of rot in an otherwise edible protein pack, something that shouldn't be allowed to exist and that is controlled for . . . but that has somehow passed inspection.

And it's all going to hinge on the story of Brendol Hux—Cardinal just knows it.

And that's personal, too. When Phasma showed up, Cardinal was relieved of duty as Brendol's personal guard, and that distance prevented Cardinal from protecting Brendol when he needed it the most. Brendol had been just fine before Parnassos, and he was fine for a while after he returned. But then he grew more and more sickly and just . . . died. Or so young Armitage Hux said in a particularly poignant speech before the entire crew of the *Absolution*. Brendol's true cause of death was never disclosed, and Cardinal's inquiries were ignored, as if he'd been just another nameless stormtrooper.

His recruits look so young in the mess, their helmets carefully placed on numbered shelves so they can eat. They wave to him cheerfully, and he waves back. Here, dining and drinking in groups of their own choosing, they are simply children. Collected from some of the loneliest of the unclaimed territories of the galaxy, they come together to become great soldiers under Cardinal's watchful eye. Their hair and skin cover every possible shade from pale to dark; their eyes range from ice blue to pitch black and every hue in between. Their buzzed scalps show sweat from training, and their laughter defies the misery of their origins and histories. They have risen from their own ashes.

Cardinal feels a swell of pride. This, *this* is what the First Order is all about. Giving everyone equal opportunity to succeed, no matter how lowly their beginning or how far-off their planet. There are no rich kids here, lording it over the orphans. No lobbyists or interest groups or bribes. No one is starving or thirsty or dying of exposure. As far as Cardinal is concerned, anyone who opposes the obvious benefits of the First Order is a fool.

And anyone who swears an oath to the First Order and betrays it will answer to Cardinal.

He looks over the mess one last time before heading back into the hall. Cardinal should be going to sleep for a four-hour shift now, but that's not going to happen. He is, however, required to attend his nightly morale session, which is mandatory and monitored by the officers upstairs. Slipping into his room, he takes his place before the screen and relaxes as he absorbs the message. When he was young, he found it a little terrifying, watching all the horrible things happening in the galaxy under New Republic rule, the chaos and tragedy caused by terrorists and rebels. But now it's relaxing, because he knows that the First Order will rise above to conquer all that oppose it. He's had a hand in training the troopers who will fight for stability, and he is confident in their prowess.

When the session is completed, he stops by the barracks medbay, tells the droids he's feeling under the weather and could use some vitamin packs and stims. And he's Captain Cardinal, so they give him what he requests with no question. He takes a circuitous route back to the lower-level room where the spy is waiting. And, if she's smart, not trying anything stupid. She has to see by now that it's foolish to resist—both him, and the power he represents. No one can fight the First Order and survive. And despite her obviously rebellious nature, there's something about her that he likes. It's a gamble, questioning her independently. This interrogation is his first instance of defiance within the First Order. Iris, at least, has covered his tracks. Anyone searching the logs will find an anomaly, as if the spy never existed or someone else botched the records. It's a bold play, and possibly a damning one. But for him, this is the last straw. He has one chance to remove the cancer that is Captain Phasma, and he's willing to bet his gambit will pay off. This spy—she knows how to end Phasma.

Could the spy be playing him just to stay alive? Maybe. But Iris's programming was written to pick up on lies, which helps with the younger recruits. So far, Vi believes the story she's telling. He needs to try to trip her up and see how she reacts. But he'll also get more out of her if she believes he's sympathetic or naïve, so he can't push her too far.

It almost feels like a betrayal, showing empathy to a Resistance spy, but what he's doing is in service to the First Order. If Phasma is a bad seed, it's up to him to help his superiors see, to excise her before something dangerous takes root. Somehow, they've missed what he's seen all along. Perhaps if Brendol were alive, he would have caught on. It's a shame about Armitage. He's never liked Cardinal, and the younger Hux and Phasma are close. But Cardinal's going to change that.

Or at least, that's what he tells himself.

The turbolift opens, and he steps into the dark hall, hating the loss of order and cleanliness that is omnipresent everywhere else on the *Absolution*. This lower level—well, they have their uses for it, clearly, but it doesn't represent the better parts of the First Order. Cardinal knows about this particular room only from witnessing several interrogations done by Brendol years ago, also in secret, and he doubts many others have ever seen it or know such places exist. Even the troopers assigned to cleaning duty don't have chores this deep in the gigantic Star Destroyer.

He stands outside the room, supplies in hand, getting a handle on his emotions. He has to maintain control but seem cheerful and sympathetic. He has to be threatening but keep her happy, keep her talking. He can't lose his control and hurt her—too much. And he has to get to the meat of the matter fast, before Armitage and Phasma arrive on the ship and start asking questions about where Cardinal has been. He needs evidence—actual physical evidence. No one would take a Resistance spy's word against a proven warrior and captain of the First Order Guard, especially not the vaunted Captain Phasma.

The irony does not escape him. Cardinal is breaking First Order rules to out Captain Phasma for breaking First Order rules. But he's not doing it for personal gain, not because he wants a promotion or a reward or power. He's doing it because she has the potential to destroy the thing he loves most, and she must be stopped.

He has to get the answers he needs. Or else.

Or else he's a traitor, too.

THIRTEEN

ON THE *ABSOLUTION*

"OH, GOOD," VI SAYS, GUMMY EYES BLINKING OPEN. "I'M NOT JUST dreaming."

"Don't call it a dream until you've tasted the food," Cardinal replies as he places his helmet on the table, but there's something about his forced jocularity that tells Vi he's not entirely genuine. "The vitamin packs are tough to swallow."

He helps her with the water, sticks her with the stims, forces the vitamins down, and squeezes yet more gray protein paste into her mouth as a chaser. "Almost tastes like chicken," she says, struggling to swallow, "if you deconstructed a chicken and forced it through a happabore. Now, when are you going to let me out of this fancy chair so I can eat with my own hands?"

"When you tell me what I need to know."

"You already know what you need to know. Phasma is bad news."

He shakes his head, exasperated. "Oh, of course. Let me just go to General Hux and pass that on. *Yes, sir, so it turns out that this Resistance spy I'm hiding in the bilge said Phasma is a no-good nerf herder huttnugget.*" For just a moment, what she thinks might be his original accent comes out, broad and rough. Then he returns to his best approximation of the clipped tones of the First Order. "They'd kick me out an air lock. This isn't a child's game of tattling. I need real, actual evidence of wrongdoing. And not the New Republic's specious idea of wrongdoing. It's got to be a clear violation of First Order law."

"Like murdering Brendol Hux?"

That gets his attention. He spins around to face her, and the droid zooms excitedly to his side. "Yes. Exactly like that. We're finally getting around to the important part. Do you have proof?"

Vi leans her head back, grinning. "I can tell you where to find proof, although it's nearly a suicide run. But you've got to let me get there. It's all part of the story." She chuckles. "All part of the legend. Doesn't that ever bother you?"

"What?"

"That it's like they chose her over you. Wanted to turn her into a myth. The little girl from nowhere who became the most lauded engine in the greatest war machine."

He turns away, and she knows she's got him on the hook.

"It bothers me if she's not what she seems."

"And didn't you ever wonder if it was all just a lie? If she's not really the shining, chrome-plated paragon on all your propaganda posters, that billowing cape flying behind her? Not the ideal soldier?" A pause. "That she might not actually believe in the First Order like you do?"

Cardinal goes very still. He's facing away from her, but she can see the pain in every line of his body. His fingers briefly tug on his own armorweave cape, identical to Phasma's, not that he's on any posters. All they see is her polished chrome. This barb of hers has hit him hard.

"Of course it bothers me. Every day."

"But you've done nothing about it."

He turns to face her, teeth bared. "And what could I do? No one knows anything about her. Brendol is gone. I searched the records and found nothing of Parnassos, nothing until you showed up today. I can't toss her suite looking for clues. She speaks to no one, has never confided in a single person. How can you fight a legend, especially one that continues to win favor and impress her superiors? How can you fight a myth that they built from nothing?"

"Maybe if your superiors learned the truth, they'd do the right thing. They'd realize that she's a mynock gnawing at the heart of their ideals. That she's a fiction. All smoke and mirrors. That the legend is indeed a lie. That she'll one day betray the First Order like she's betrayed everything else she's ever professed to love."

Cardinal is suddenly in front of her, fervor burning in his dark eyes.

"Then give me the evidence so I can end this. End her."

Vi grins. "All right, then. Let me tell you about the beginning of Brendol's end."

FOURTEEN

ON PARNASSOS, IO YEARS AGO

AFTER SHE LEFT THE SCYRE, PHASMA NEVER LOOKED BACK. HER WARRIORS had always considered her their true leader, and their real loyalties were no longer hidden. No one spoke of Keldo or the rest of the Scyre or the Claws; no one spoke of regret. They were silent as they traversed the rock spires that made the Scyre land so treacherous. While Gosta scouted ahead, Torben helped Brendol again, and Phasma, Carr, and Siv helped the troopers. Despite the inescapable noises made by anchoring their claws and leaping from rock to rock, no one from the tribe stirred as they left, not even the sentries.

When they reached the borderlands, the last Scyre sentry was asleep in his hammock. Later, secretly and out of earshot of Phasma, her warriors discussed this peculiarity, and it was mentioned that perhaps their leader had slipped something into that night's stew to aid the group's leave-taking. Phasma had served her people personally, and they had considered it an honor. Her warriors and the First Order folk had, of course, been served first. After leaving the snoring sentry behind, they couldn't help considering that perhaps Phasma's gesture of goodwill had been less an honor and more an insurance policy—not that they had a word for that in the Scyre. Still, they knew that something was up, and it was chilling, seeing this new side of Phasma.

Siv was undergoing her own personal crisis at the time. As the keeper of the detraxors, she had been raised to understand that her duty was to keep her people alive and healthy by withdrawing the essence of their dead members and crafting the oracle salve for those left behind. Leaving with Phasma and taking both detraxors meant that she was abandoning, betraying, and possibly dooming the majority of her band. She felt it keenly. But she had made her choice, and so she continued without complaint. Phasma was the key to a brighter future, she hoped, for all the Scyre. They would one day bring the riches of the First Order to their people, and then they would no longer need the salve.

Rather than going directly through the borderlands and into Balder's territory, where Claw sentries might raise an alarm, Phasma angled east. Her warriors followed without question, but it was considered a bold move. The Scyre knew little about this region, only that the rocks rose highest near the sea, and that there was very little to scavenge there. If the land had been ripe or welcoming, Balder would've worked to extend his territory, but there seemed to be a pall over the area, as if there was a reason no one wished to go there. The borderlands didn't end so much as the Scyre and the Claws independently came to the conclusion that the land wasn't worth fighting for.

Just before dawn, Phasma called her group close on an outcropping that afforded enough room for everyone to sit or perch relatively close. Very little was visible by starlight, and they had no fire; only the flashing bits of metal on Brendol's black uniform and the gleam of stormtrooper armor shone in the darkness.

"We can't go directly through Claw land," Phasma said, immediately addressing the question on everyone's mind. "We don't know how hungry his people are for blood. If they're smart, they'll send a contingent out into the sands toward Brendol's ship while leaving a defensive force to maintain their territory and harvest the bodies."

"Harvest the bodies?" Brendol asked, half disgusted and half curious.

"Siv, explain."

Siv reached into her pack and pulled out a detraxor. "As you know, our planet is sick. The sun is too harsh, the rain burns our skin, and we can't get all the nutrients we need from our food, which leads to disease, brittle bones, and loose teeth. When someone dies, we use the detraxors to reclaim what minerals and liquids we can, and I craft those nutrients into a balm we call oracle salve. Every member of the band receives an allotment. Spreading it on the skin insures we remain as healthy as we can be, protected from the elements. The Claw people use them as well."

"It's inelegant but necessary," Phasma said, her voice harsh and brooking no refusal.

"I see," Brendol said, always diplomatic. "And how did you come to possess this machine?"

"It's been passed down since the cities died. They once used them on food animals. My mother taught me how to care for them." Siv stroked the worn leather lovingly. "And I've made some improvements. My mother's oracle salve smelled like rancid fish, but mine, at least, smells—"

"Like fresher fish," Carr broke in, and Siv elbowed him with a grin.

"It's barbaric," Brendol noted.

Siv bristled. "No. It's holy. It's how to keep your people strong, even as you leave them. Body to body, dust to dust."

"Death is inevitable, but it means the rest of the tribe will be stronger," Phasma said. She looked around the circle, gazing into each person's eyes as the sun came up and giving a long look to each stormtrooper, their faces, as always, hidden behind their helmets. "Learn to respect both ends of this machine, if you wish to survive your time on Parnassos."

"Do you not have such problems among your people?" Gosta

asked. The girl was in awe of Brendol and his troopers, just as she was in awe of Phasma and her warriors.

Brendol's smile was kinder when he spoke to the girl. "No, child, we do not. We benefit from the greatest advances in technology and medicine. We simply add the vital nutrients to our food so that we stay strong."

"But where do you get them from, then?"

"We buy them from merchants."

"But where do the merchants get them?"

Brendol wasn't smiling now. "These foolish questions waste valuable time. The wonderful thing about civilization is that you buy what you need, thereby supporting merchants and artisans. Where the sellers source their goods is not my problem. But I assure you that they do not come from humans. Such things are generally frowned upon in more civilized parts of the galaxy."

Gosta looked crushed, but Phasma spoke next.

"I look forward to benefiting from such civilization, but until that time we will use all available resources to get us off this planet. There is no shame in using every advantage to staying alive."

Brendol seemed surprised when one of the stormtroopers spoke next, his voice strange and somewhat amplified by his helmet. "We had something similar on Otomok, but for beasts. It's similar to a moisture detraxor."

Phasma's warriors couldn't miss Brendol's sneer as he turned to look at the trooper and noticeably glance down at his number. "Perhaps you forget, PT-2445, that I have visited Otomok several times, as well as planets with even harsher conditions. And when on those planets, I still hold my rank."

"Yes, General Hux. Sorry, sir."

Brendol nodded, but there was a chill among the group now. On Parnassos, with everyone fighting to survive, such formalities were saved for rare instances of ritual or leadership, like Keldo's pronouncement from his throne in the Nautilus. During regular moments, everyone was considered equal. Apparently that was not how things were done in the First Order. The stormtrooper did not speak again.

As for Phasma, she was already looking beyond the group to the hard line of the horizon. Siv knew her leader had carefully noted where Brendol's ship had landed and where the smoke had risen, and although they didn't know the lay of the land between here and there, they all expected trouble.

"No matter which direction we go, we're headed into land we've never seen before. Eat and drink, apply your salve, and then prepare your rope lines. It's a long way down the other side of these mountains."

"How do you know?" Gosta asked.

Phasma gave her a long stare. "We know there's flat land beyond these rocks because we've seen what's on the other side of Balder's territory. It stands to reason that land would stretch to these rocks. Does anyone disagree?"

No one dared, not even Brendol.

"It will be, I think, several days to the fallen ship, even without major impediments. We may encounter animals and people, or we may simply face harsh conditions unlike those of our own land. General Hux, can you tell us what you saw of the terrain between your ship being shot down and your journey to Balder's plateau?"

Brendol considered. "We used the escape pods shortly after being hit. Each pod fits six people, and we had eleven bodies, so we had two pods. Two pilots in the cockpit were already dead, so our pod only held the four of us and the droid. We haven't seen the other pod, nor have we been able to communicate with the others through our comm system. There's no telling if the other five troopers made it. We were unable to see what happened to the ship, but when we exited the pod, the smoke was quite far away. At least the smoke suggests it didn't land in the ocean, which would make it irretrievable. The land we saw was all sand, just endless sand. We walked for the plateau because we could see smoke, which meant people. We did not expect to be greeted by a murderous Dug and claimed as . . . spoils." The look on his face suggested that he would've very much liked to have been the one who stabbed Balder.

"I've never walked on sand," Torben noted. "What's it like?"

Phasma's people looked to her, but she nodded to Brendol.

"It shifts under your feet. Coarse and rough. Irritating. Gets everywhere. Slips into your clothes and boots."

"But you passed no animals or people on your way to Balder's land?" Phasma pressed.

Brendol shook his head. "No one and nothing. We feared we were on an entirely uninhabited planet, although we did see several factory complexes and uninhabited cities from the sky."

"How far away?"

"In my ship, mere hours. By foot, several days, most likely. It's hard to make accurate navigational estimates while plummeting to one's death." He sighed and went a bit wistful. "It's a shame we landed here, where the terrain is so unforgiving. Across the ocean, there is a larger continent, lush and green. As you told your brother, if we are able to reach my ship, perhaps your people can be moved there to give them a better chance of reclaiming what once was. Perhaps there are survivors there, a civilization."

"Perhaps," Phasma said. "But we know for a fact there is a better life among your stars."

"May I speak with you privately?" Brendol asked.

Phasma's warriors had always understood that they lived under two rulers, with Phasma acting as the muscle and Keldo as the brains and spirit. It was easy enough to accept that Brendol would now be one of their leaders, and it made sense to them, at the time, that Brendol might wish to talk to Phasma alone. The pair disappeared around a cluster of larger stones, their whispers obscured.

Now, when people grow up in small bands in rough lands, they become accustomed to never having privacy and to giving those who seek seclusion what little space they can. The warriors turned their backs to Phasma and Brendol and began talking among themselves, gabbling about their hopes for a new home, whether it be on a nearby continent made of solid ground or up in the stars wearing white armor. The three troopers stood outside this circle, looking very out of place.

"Do you like it?" Gosta asked one of the stormtroopers, pointing at the starry sky. "Up there?"

The man considered her and seemed like he was about to answer, but PT-2445 interrupted them.

"We shouldn't be talking," he said. "Not without the general's permission. We are not at ease."

With his helmet on, it was impossible to guess what the silenced trooper might be feeling. Still, he must've agreed with his compatriot, as he did not answer the question and instead turned away, hand on his blaster. Phasma's warriors traded looks. Would a good leader prevent his soldiers from speaking their minds? Did these warriors give up their own power, their own personalities, so easily? It was a new way of doing things, and one that didn't sit well with the free folk of the Scyre.

The sun was coming up as Phasma and Brendol returned from their private conversation. Phasma must've used part of their time to prepare the other leader for the next step of their journey, as Brendol now wore Scyre gloves with climbing claws and had a pair of spikes tied tightly around his shining black boots. He was an awkward man, as you know, mostly belly and sneer, and he stumbled as he walked and grew accustomed to the new tools.

Phasma reached into one of her packs and tossed out three more pairs of gloves and boot spikes, all stolen from the Nautilus, which her warriors quickly helped the troopers strap on. They were almost ready to go, and Phasma looked to Siv, who held out the pot of oracle salve. It was a dense greenish-black, and Phasma dipped in two fingers and drew dark lines under her eyes. Siv held out the pot to each of the Scyre members, who did the same. When she held it out to Brendol, he shook his head in disgust.

"We can survive a few days before resorting to such indelicacies," he said.

"Suit yourself," Phasma said, pulling on her mask. "Let's go."

Again, her warriors traded glances. They were accustomed to knowing Phasma's secret plans, even when Keldo didn't. But this time, she revealed nothing. They, too, put on their masks. If they were to die on the mountain, they would die fierce.

The mountain itself represented a new kind of challenge. The Scyre folk had to use all their tools and tricks to navigate the perilous ledges of the jagged tower of rock. It was hundreds of meters to the sandy ground below, and they had to edge around the sheer cliff face using only their boot spikes and hand claws, all while roped to one another, the impossibly maladroit Brendol, and the clumsy troopers. With every slip of a foot or breaking bit of rock, the entire group clung to the mountain, bracing themselves to absorb the weight of a falling body. Phasma and Torben kept Brendol between them, showing him where to plant his spikes and keeping him close so he couldn't drag them down. Each step took them around the mountain and down, just the smallest bit. The wind whistled past, and curious seabirds rode the air, watching and hoping for the signs of an imminent feast of crushed human down below.

Now, anyone canny and strong enough to grow to adulthood in the Scyre knew that a smart climber never looked down, but everyone later admitted to looking down anyway. It wasn't often they had the chance to see something totally new for the first time. On the side of the mountain they'd come from, the dark and familiar ocean endlessly bit at the rock, but on the far side, the mountain began as a straight face, then gradually began to slope down to yet another dark sea: endless gray sand. When the morning sun struck the valley below, it sparkled in vibrant reds and oranges, a beautiful sight promising the rare chance to walk without fear of tumbling to one's death. Siv confessed that this sight was so unexpected and arresting she nearly let go of the mountain. If she had, I suspect we wouldn't be here talking right now. When everyone is distracted and one person falters, there tends to be a grand tragedy, does there not?

Step by step they edged around the mountain, ever closer to the sandy ground. The sun reached its zenith, and the air began to warm. The Scyre folk began to twitch and shake their heads, sweating underneath their masks; they'd never felt this kind of heat before. Although the sun was harsh back home, they were always cold, thanks to the ocean's chill, the cutting winds, and the shade from taller rocks. But now sweat began to trickle into their eyes and down their backs. Taking off their masks wasn't an option: The wind swept sand into every pore, while the sun beat down with more than its usual punishment. Poor Brendol was the only one without any face protection, and nothing could be done for him until they were on the ground and able to access their packs. Every finger and toe was lodged into a crevice in the rock. He was soon traversing the mountain with his eyes squeezed shut, gloves and boot tips probing blindly for cracks, his cheeks red and his lips already blistering.

The troopers were surprisingly tenacious, for all that their armor made them bulky. Siv noted that whatever training they'd had was well done. The three troopers were physically fit, strong, and able to quickly master the art of climbing. No one complained, not even Brendol, who was clearly having problems. Even Phasma's warriors suffered, as their usual terrain involved leaping and rappelling from spire to spire, not clinging to a rock face for hours on end. Their arms began to ache and burn, their curled toes going numb in their boots. Each time someone found a ledge, they took turns standing there for just a moment, swinging their arms and bending their knees, urging feeling back into their bones. If not for those small moments of mercy, someone would've made a misstep.

But by some miracle, no one did.

Phasma's boots were the first to hit sand sometime after noon. She gave a cry of triumph that drew every eye. For the first time in living history, a Scyre stood on the actual planet. Not high above on a rock, not in a cave, but on solid enough ground with nowhere to fall. Next Brendol hopped down, and Phasma had to help catch and steady him. When Torben jumped down, the sand puffed around him like gray smoke, and he laughed his booming laugh, making Siv smile.

One by one, the warriors and troopers landed on the sand. The Scyre folk couldn't help flipping back their masks to look down and marvel at the feel of actual land beneath their feet, and they undid their ropes and knelt or sat in the sand, amazed at the sensation. For all of their lives until that moment, they'd been aware that they were high above the land, and that falling from such great heights meant death. Here, there was nowhere to fall. Siv had never felt so safe, for all that they were in entirely new territory. She learned later that the sand was half mineral and half volcanic ash, which accounted for its feathery softness and tendency to billow up and irritate eyes and mucous membranes.

As for Carr, he removed a glove and ran sand through his fingers, laughing.

His laughter stopped abruptly.

"Ouch!"

Phasma leapt to his side. "What's wrong?"

Carr held up a hand to show a raised red bump. "Something bit me, I think. There it is!"

He pointed to a tiny, shiny creature burrowing swiftly back into the gray sand, and Phasma dug for it and pinned it between two fingers of her glove. It was a beetle with a gold carapace, horns, and a sharply pointed proboscis. Held in the sun, it glittered gold and green with an entire iridescent rainbow in between. Of course, I can describe it to you because I've been to Parnassos and studied one, but none of Phasma's people had ever seen anything like it before.

"It's pretty," Gosta said.

Phasma held it up to the light, and a single drop of blood fell from the insect's proboscis and plopped in the sand, where it was immediately soaked up. All around the drop of blood, more beetles exploded out of little hills of sand, furiously sweeping the area with their own proboscises and sucking up the blood-covered grains.

Crushing the beetle between her fingers, Phasma threw the wet

gold-and-black carcass into the mess of beetles fighting over the drop
of blood. The beetles fell upon their fellow, devouring every drop of
viscous fluid within until there was nothing left but sparkling shards
of exoskeleton. As soon as the moisture was gone, the beetles burrowed back underground, leaving the once smooth sand pebbled
with peculiar, cone-shaped mounds. Phasma stood.

"Gloves stay on, and don't remove them without my say-so. Does
it feel infected?"

Carr looked at the throbbing red wound and slipped his glove
back on with a wry grin. "It feels silly. And a bit embarrassing. To
think: I lost a fight with a bug."

Phasma sighed, but no one could be angry with Carr for long. "Be
serious, for once."

"It itches, but I don't feel the fever."

"Let me know if you do. General Hux, are you familiar with this
creature?"

Brendol shrugged. "Not this particular species. Every desert has
insects that hunger for moisture. Still, I agree—better to stay away
and avoid giving them what they want."

He was still squinting through the blowing sand, his eyes gone red
and puffy. Now that they were on the ground, Phasma was able to
pull a length of cloth from her pack and help him wind it around his
face, leaving only his watery blue eyes exposed. Gosta stepped forward to offer him a pair of ragged old goggles, which he accepted
matter-of-factly. When Siv again held out the pot of oracle salve, he
considered it more carefully but still did not accept the gift.

When Brendol was outfitted to withstand the sands, Phasma
looked to his troopers and said, "It would be best if we could further
stain your armor. The clean parts stand out in this gray desert."

They were already somewhat dingy from their earlier trek, but
the troopers must've concurred. One of the soldiers took up a handful of the sand and rubbed it into his armor, where it left a dark-
gray sheen. Soon all three troopers were staining their armor with
help from the Scyre folks, all of whom were careful to keep on their

gloves and check every handful of sand for more of the blood beetles. When the white armor and helmets had been more uniformly
stained a messy gray, Phasma nodded her approval and began walking. The Scyre folk had already wound up their climbing ropes and
removed their boot claws, and they followed their leader into the
great unknown.

FIFTEEN

ON PARNASSOS, 10 YEARS AGO

THE GRAY SAND STRETCHED IN EVERY DIRECTION BEYOND THE MOUNTAINS, as far as the eye could see. It rose up in great dunes patterned in windy waves, and plummeted into deep valleys. To the Scyre folk, it resembled the sea they'd so often watched from their stone perches, a dark, unforgiving, roiling thing—and yet uncomfortably, unnaturally still. There were no plants or animals anywhere to be seen. The farther they walked from the mountain and stone towers of the borderlands, the more agitated everyone became. They'd never spent a day of their lives without clinging to a tall spire, and it was disorienting to be mired in shifting sand, each step sinking and sliding. There were no landmarks, no clear goals, no place to hide.

Brendol and his troops somehow seemed more stolid, traversing the desert as if comfortable there, and it happened that Gosta grew brave or perhaps terrified enough to ask them about it.

"We've visited planets all over the galaxy," Brendol said, not slowing in his slog forward, although his lack of athletic conditioning kept him breathing heavily. "Desert planets, water planets, ice planets, and ruined planets like yours, with all sorts of topographies and environments. Every environment has its own unique mercies and horrors. Even in the harshest conditions, like these . . ." He looked around, and although no one could see him frown through his wrappings, it was clear he was uneasy. "You're never as alone as you think you are."

"But if we don't find water soon, we'll be in trouble, won't we?" the girl asked.

"We continue," Phasma said, her voice hard. "We move forward. We'll find what we need or we won't. But we'll get there."

Her words made the Scyre folk nervous. What did Phasma have planned, and why was she suddenly so very determined? They'd seen her fight against all odds and take great risks for her people, but the way she marched through the sand without pause struck them as almost suicidal.

Carr was the last one in line, and as the day wore on it became apparent that he was slowing down. Siv fell back with him to inquire about his health, but he just shook his head.

"I feel dizzy and feverish," he said. "And not in the good way."

"*The* fever?"

He gave a sad laugh, a pathetic echo of his usual good humor. "When your skin feels like it's on fire and your skull feels like it's going to burst, one fever is the same as the next, I suppose."

When she pulled up his mask and put a hand to his forehead, he was almost cold. There was a strange color mottling his usually tan face, a worrisome paleness. She could see a blue vein, just under the skin of his temple, beating rapidly with his heart.

"Phasma, come look at this," Siv called, and Phasma left Torben and Brendol to lead the pack as she hurried to the end of the line.

"What's wrong?"

"Carr feels light-headed and hot, but his skin is cold."

Phasma lifted her own mask for a better look and frowned at what she saw. "Show me your wound from earlier."

When Carr slipped off his glove, they were surprised to see that the beetle's wound was nearly gone. It had been swollen, red, and hard right after the bite, but it appeared to be healing nicely, leaving just a light pink rash around the pinprick puncture wound. Phasma put her hand to his forehead and checked the whites of his eyes, but in the end she only shook her head.

"We must keep walking. Let me know if anything changes. If this is an infection, it's different from the dangers we face in our territory. It's not the fever, at least. Stay vigilant. Apply more salve. And put your mask on. If you're contagious, we need to take precautions."

"I'll try not to kiss anyone," Carr murmured.

Still, he obeyed, drawing on a second set of stripes with Siv's salve and pulling down his mask, as Siv did hers. Phasma jogged to the head of the line, and everyone continued walking. The Scyre folk could hear Phasma consulting with Brendol in a hushed voice, and they thought they heard talk of his promised medicines. That was good, then—their leader was making plans to help their injured friend. They were a close-knit folk, and they would all pitch in to make sure Carr reached Brendol's ship, even if they had to take turns carrying him.

They walked all afternoon, stopping once in the shade at a dune to nibble jerky and take careful sips from their water skins. Phasma had distributed multiple skins to each person, taken from the stores of the Nautilus, but Siv ran the numbers and instantly knew it wasn't enough to get them to Brendol's ship. This far from their territory and without a living plant or creature in sight, water would be an increasing worry. At home, they had other ways of collecting enough to drink, and although there was rarely more than they needed, they'd never prepared for a spell as dry as this one. Collecting and filtering urine was a regular part of life, but they would eventually run out of that, too. The Scyre folk didn't speak their worries out loud, though. Phasma would take care of them—they had to believe that.

The desert heated up with the afternoon sun beating down, and although they were tempted to lift up their masks and tug off their wraps to let the wind cool their sweating skin, they knew better.

Keeping covered was always a better option: Any slice of exposed flesh would quickly burn and possibly blister without a thick coating of salve. The sun was not as kind as it had once been. When Siv looked back, she saw Carr lagging even farther behind, his mask up on his head. His cheeks were swollen and pale, his eyes bulging somewhat, his lips dry and puffy.

"I know," he said, catching her watching him. "I look terribly handsome."

"You need to rest."

"I can rest later. Help me up the hill."

Siv hurried to his side and helped drag him up the next dune, feeling him wobble against her as if he'd lost his once solid sense of balance. It would be days yet before they reached Brendol's ship, and Carr would slow down the entire group if he didn't shake off this new sickness.

When they crested the dune, they were dismayed to find it was the first in a series of high hills straining into the horizon like a sea of gigantic waves. The wind was high along the top, and they jogged down each hill into the cool of the valley before slogging up the next hill. Time stretched out strangely then, Siv told me, as they constantly struggled up and down but didn't seem to go anywhere, didn't make any visible progress. It was like battling the same enemy again and again, never gaining a foothold; all too much like their old life in the Scyre, truth be told. Any wonder at the new world was lost to dread and discomfort, plus worry for Carr. The muscles used for walking in sand proved very different from those used for climbing and leaping among rocks. Their arms still ached from clambering down the cliff face. It was, in many ways, an unexpected hell for a people forged in the crucible of struggle.

I've seen these dunes, and I can't imagine what kind of mindset it would take to tackle them without simply lying down to die in a valley. We grow so accustomed to our speeders, our ships, our hyperdrives. To be in a world where only your feet can move you, centimeter by centimeter through infinity . . . let's just say there's a reason Phasma wanted off that rock.

The sun was setting as they tumbled down a dune into the valley below, cold with shadow and whispering with eerie wind. Carr was the last one down, and he slid like deadweight, landing on his back at Siv's feet.

"We'll camp here tonight," Phasma said. "Keep covered. Recycle bodily fluids. Every drop counts. Be careful with your supplies. Sleeping close will conserve body heat." She sighed heavily and added, "It's going to be difficult, but I won't hear any complaints."

Her warriors nodded listlessly, and the troopers looked to Brendol, who added, "Phasma is correct. Conserve your resources."

They sat in smaller groups to eat, the Scyre warriors together and Phasma sitting beside Brendol with his troopers. The three armored soldiers took off their helmets for the first time, and Siv was oddly fascinated to see that they were just people like any others, their hair shorn close to their heads and their skin sweaty and red. One of them was a woman, although it was only perceptible through her facial structure and she had her hair cropped the same as the men. Her armor showed no difference in physiognomy, and Siv recalled being pleased that among the First Order, women were considered equals and warriors. Her mother had told her stories, you see, of a different world in which women were considered somehow weaker or lesser. Perhaps that prejudice had died off as it was determined that the women of the Scyre could climb better than the men and began to outnumber them among the warriors. At that time, however, sitting in the dune's shadow with these strange folk from beyond the stars, Siv considered what it would be like to wear the shining white armor herself, to be faceless and mighty and one of countless others fighting for a worthy cause.

Were her people bothered that their leader sat with the strangers instead of among her own folk? A little, but they also understood that Brendol Hux was a powerful commander in his own right, and that leaders often spent time together making plans for the betterment of the people. They still had trouble understanding Brendol, sometimes, thanks to his sharp accent and some odd changes to his vocabulary. If anything, Siv said they felt some pride that a woman of the Scyre would be considered the equal of a wealthy, powerful general who commanded starships.

As for Carr, he was growing listless, staring off into space and swaying a little as he sat. He refused the jerky Siv offered him and nibbled only at some dried sea vegetable, gulping down his allotted sips of water. He had no bodily waste to add to the recycling unit, though, which was the sort of thing that was noticed when water was scarcer than usual. He was the first one asleep, falling to the ground in a puff of gray sand and snoring gently through swollen lips. There was nothing they could do for him—this was a new ailment, and their only hope was that it would go away on its own or be easily fixed by the medical equipment Brendol promised was waiting on his ship.

The next morning, Carr was even worse. His flesh was swollen and pale, all the blue veins of his body visible and throbbing near the skin. He reminded Siv of the creatures that sometimes washed up from the deep sea, ghostly white and partially transparent, gasping for breath and crushed by the very air. His gloves were too tight on his swollen hands and nearly had to be cut off with a knife. When asked how he felt, he couldn't speak; his tongue and lips were too swollen. He could only shake his head. But the surprise and fear Siv expected to see in his eyes . . . wasn't there. He seemed sleepy and resigned. They pulled him to standing, and Torben helped her propel him up the next dune, Siv's every muscle burning as the injured man wobbled between them.

As Phasma crested the dune's ridge, she was lit by the rising sun, half molten gold and half indigo shadow. She put up her hand to shield her eyes and screamed, "Enemies! Scyre, fight!" as she clutched her spear and reached for the ax hanging on her belt.

Siv and Torben had no choice but to drop Carr in the sand and run to Phasma's side, drawing their own weapons. The troopers pulled their blasters and began firing down the dune, and as Siv hit the top with Torben on her heels, she saw the attack unfolding. Figures swathed in gray seemed to glide across the sand, pulled by huge lizards with pebbled gray skin. They skimmed over the ground far faster than the Scyre group could run, and they held long, shivering lances tipped with glassy blades.

Siv considered her blow darts, but she couldn't find skin on the attackers and didn't want to risk wasting the metal barbs. Instead, she pulled out her two curved scythes. The attackers were close now, six of them dragged by six lizards. A trooper's blaster sent one of the lizards flailing down the dune, his master tumbling behind him. The five remaining skimmers didn't swerve.

Phasma was closest, and she sidestepped the lizard's lunge and swiped her dagger across the folds of its neck, slicing deep into muscle and making the creature scream. The skimmer behind it was able to nimbly leap off a flat piece of metal and run at Phasma on overlarge feet, and their silent fight drew everyone's eye—until the next skimmer glided near. It got past the troopers, but Torben was running right for it. He slammed his club into the lizard's skull, darted around it, and hacked into the skimmer's chest with his ax. The figure fell down, and Torben put a huge boot on its gut, ripped out his ax, and yelled his battle cry, splattered in blood just as red as his own.

So these attackers were human, then. Probably. For all their strange costumes, they could die, and that emboldened the Scyre folk. Gold beetles erupted from the sand to lick up the blood, and Torben staggered back, hunting his next prey.

Siv let out her own ululating scream and ran down the dune toward one of the skimmers, ready to do her duty for her people. The lizard dodged sideways, great mouth open to show hundreds of serrated teeth. Siv skidded to her back and slid along the sand, slicing up the creature's belly as she zipped underneath it and rammed her feet into the legs of the enemy pulled behind it. The figure fell over with an all-too-human curse. Before Siv could stand and continue fighting, little Gosta leapt over her, brandishing her blade, and stabbed down in a vital spot while shouting her war cry. That skimmer didn't get up again.

Gosta held out a hand to help Siv stand, and when she looked around, she saw that the Scyre warriors and their trooper guests had utterly destroyed the attackers and their lizards. The fight had been unusually quick and brutal. No enemies were left breathing, which meant no answers would be had. Where had these attackers come from? What did they want? Had their people traced the path of Brendol's ship across the sky, and were they, too, racing there to claim the bounty?

It couldn't be helped. At least the Scyre folk had won.

"Well, that wasn't too bad," Siv said with a smile, but she didn't get to enjoy the victory for long.

"Quick. The detraxors," Phasma barked.

Siv hurried to the lizard she'd just gutted, pulling the first detraxor from her bag and jamming the spike deep into the creature's muscle. Considering the bloodthirsty beetles already scurrying into the bleeding cavity, she had to be quick. As soon as it was working, she went to the figure Gosta had just felled. Although she recognized that time was of the essence, she had to see who would be providing the life-giving essence for the salve that would protect the Scyre warriors on their journey. To Siv, this wasn't just a physical act; it was a ritual. Tugging at the wrappings on the figure's face, she didn't know what she would find—an alien species, a mutated human, something native to Parnassos that they'd never seen wash up on the rocks.

But it was a human like any other. A young woman, just like her. Medium-brown skin, hair long and plaited under her wrappings. Clean and healthy. No visible signs of trauma or disease. Even the woman's teeth were intact. Siv closed the woman's brown eyes and said the quick prayer the Scyre folk always said when they harvested minerals and liquids from a body.

"Thank you for giving me life. Your today protects my people's tomorrow. Body to body, dust to dust."

Before Phasma could bark at her again, she jammed the next detraxor into the meat of the woman's thigh and set it running.

The Scyre folk and the troopers had taken no damage, and it was deemed a great victory. The nutrients and water skins they'd claim from their assailants would save their lives and possibly help nourish

Carr back from whatever trauma he was suffering. Siv collected her first detraxor from the now desiccated lizard, traded the full skin for an empty one, and jammed the machine into the next lizard. As both machines did their work, she joined the others in hunting among the human bodies for spoils and bags of water. They were careful to scrape the beetles away, crushing the pernicious things when necessary and never letting them get anywhere close to their skin.

Each of their attackers carried pouches that hung over each hip, and although the Scyre folk didn't recognize everything within the pouches, they took them and grew determined to understand how to live in this arid place. The most valuable thing found in each pouch was a dried cake of densely packed minerals and salts that reminded Siv a little of the detraxors' rich essence. The sleds the skimmers had ridden would be a great boon, allowing them to drag their packs effortlessly over the sand instead of carrying the weight, now increased by several skins of water. The lizards were an especially rich resource, and Gosta was already slicing off strips of their dried meat for the road.

"Oh! We can pull Carr," Siv said, suddenly remembering that she and Torben had been forced to drop their fellow warrior to rush to their leader's side during the fight.

Torben nodded and followed her back down the other side of the dune, dragging a sled behind him on its rope. Carr was just a dark lump at the bottom of the valley, fallen on his side, his breath ragged and troubled and his heartbeat swiftly fluttering.

"Carr, are you worse?" Siv asked.

A low groan was the only answer.

"Flip him over."

Torben gently turned Carr over so that he was facing up and helped him to sit. Carr seemed twice the size he'd once been, his body swollen and his flesh thin and pale and stretched. Siv reached for his bare hand to hold it and found that his fingernails were gone. They'd popped off and fallen to the sand.

"Stay with us, old friend," Torben said, so gentle despite his size and might. "We'll drag you behind us, we'll be your own personal sled lizards, and then Brendol Hux will fix you and take you up into the stars."

Carr moaned again and tried to close his eyes, but the lids wouldn't slide down over his bulging orbs.

"Hurry," Phasma called from the top of the dune. "The detraxors are full and ready to be moved, and we need to leave before someone comes looking for these people."

Torben nodded to Siv, who pulled the sled closer. Carr shuddered and groaned, and Siv stopped tugging on the sled to focus on him. He was quivering, shaking all over, his eyes wide open and his lips and swollen tongue struggling to speak.

"What is it?" Siv asked.

In response, Carr rolled his eyes toward her and shuddered. His skin trembled, too swollen to touch. He gave one last moan and exploded in a cloud of water. It was as if his skin had dissolved, and liquid splattered Siv and Torben and sank into the sand, coloring it a deep black. There wasn't much blood, and his organs appeared to be shriveled, dark things connected by pale-blue tubes and nearly translucent bones. As Siv stood and stepped back, watching in horror, the ground around Carr's clothes erupted in beetles bursting out of their cones of sand and licking at the water with their long proboscises.

"Up! Get away!" she shouted at Torben, who was frozen in shock and grief.

The big man stood and stumbled back as yet more of the bright beetles, hundreds upon thousands of them, ripped out of the sand to gorge upon the water that had been their friend and fellow warrior. Beetles sucked on his shrunken organs and tried to scuttle up Siv's legs to lap at the liquid soaking her pants, but she knocked them off and ran a few steps farther back.

"Both of you, come away."

Siv and Torben looked up to find Phasma at the top of the dune, haloed in morning light as she watched them, ax and spear still in hand. Brendol stood by her side, his head canted curiously as he watched the horror unfold.

"But Carr," Siv said.

"He's gone now. He can't be reclaimed. He can't nourish his people. Now it's up to us. We must prepare what we can and go."

"At least he's in no more pain," Brendol added, but his words sounded hollow and cloying. He hadn't lost any of his people, and Siv suspected that if he had, he wouldn't have mourned them.

Never had Scyre folk died without in turn nourishing their people. Even those who fell into the ocean were thought to feed the creatures there, and those creatures eventually died and washed up on the rocks where the Scyre would use them for clothes, food, and moisture. But Carr was simply gone. There was no prayer to say over him that worked.

"Thank you . . . for being you," Siv said, standing over bones wrapped in wet clothes and covered in frantic, vicious beetles.

"Yes, thank you," Torben added before putting a hand on her shoulder and gently urging her up the dune. "Carr was a good friend and a fine warrior."

For all the hills they'd climbed in the desert, that one was the hardest. When they finally struggled to the top, Siv saw that Phasma had moved some steps farther away and was squatting with Brendol in hushed conversation.

"This one's done," Gosta said, gesturing to the second lizard, which was now no more than a loose skeleton wrapped in leathery hide and dry as the air itself. The detraxor was full and purring, and Siv knelt to switch out the skin and place the siphon in the next lizard. As she worked, she described every step for Gosta, showing her how the pieces of the detraxor fit together and how they had to be cleaned. No one else among them knew how to work the machines or concoct the salve, and she had to pass this knowledge on. It was dangerous, here among the dark sands, and Siv might be the next to fall to some unknown terror. With no child yet to pass on her knowledge as her mother had passed it on to her, she would teach Gosta all that she knew. That was all they had, in the Scyre: one another, and hope.

SIXTEEN

ON PARNASSOS, 10 YEARS AGO

WHILE SIV AND GOSTA WORKED ON CLAIMING AS MANY NUTRIENTS FROM the fallen as possible, Phasma directed the rest of the crew in harvesting the meat of the lizards and adding the light layers of clothing the attackers had worn to their own costumes.

"If we look more like them, perhaps they won't attack so quickly next time," she explained, slipping her arms through wispy gray robes the color of the sand.

Their next focus was on the troopers, covering their armor with cloth so they didn't stand out against the stark landscape. Brendol Hux was an odd figure, his sharp black clothes hidden under long robes and tied with a sash around his paunchy belly, a feature none of the Scyre warriors had ever seen on another human. In the Scyre, ribs were countable and stomachs were convex.

As they stripped the bodies down to skin, they found a carved wooden box hanging around the neck of each of their attackers. Phasma opened one, and everyone was amazed to see yet another beetle like the one that had bitten Carr.

"What is it?" Gosta asked.

"A weapon," Phasma guessed, snapping the box shut. "The beetle bites someone, and whatever they inject into the body silently destroys the flesh and organs. An easy and elegant way to kill unsuspecting enemies."

"Clever," Brendol mused.

"Dangerous."

Phasma tossed the closed box down the dune, where it tumbled into obscurity. Since Torben had nothing to contribute to the harvesting, he stomped on beetles while he kept watch for more raiders. Every time a drop of blood from a kill hit the sand, one or more beetles burrowed up to gorge on it, and Torben pulverized them with his club or stomped them with his great boots, leaving shiny gold husks covered in thick, black goop that attracted yet more beetles. As time went on and the detraxors did their brutal work, the beetles seemed to be crawling in from far away, making long streaks of gold across the sand, and the troopers joined him in crushing them. As they cut strips of desiccated meat from the last of the lizards, there were so many beetles that stomping them wasn't enough.

After Brendol smacked one off his robe, he grimly announced, "It is time to go." Phasma nodded and did not argue, Siv noted.

There was no question regarding whether they should follow the sled tracks that were being swiftly obscured by wind. They had no time to find out where their attackers had come from. This was a rescue mission with the sole purpose of getting Brendol Hux to his ship, not a raid or even a scouting errand. The warriors, so inquisitive about this new part of the world, didn't have the luxury of curiosity and would have to hope the attack had been pure coincidence. Phasma scanned the desert with her quadnocs, following the sled tracks over a dune, off to the right. Siv knew her well enough to know she was marking the spot in her mind, adding it to her flawless mental map of the planet's topography.

Loading Carr's pack and the bags of the raiders onto two of the sleds, the group took off down the other side of the dune and headed onward toward the fallen ship. The curl of white smoke had long since disappeared, but Phasma and Brendol both agreed they were headed in the direction where his ship had crashed. Torben pulled both sleds as Siv and Gosta shouldered the packs containing the cleaned and ready detraxors and their skins. For all that no one would ever welcome an attack, their quick defense and fighting skills had earned the water and nutrients they had so sorely needed for their journey. Overall, it was considered a good omen, and everyone felt confident, if wary, that should more of the skimmers appear, they would be prepared to meet the challenge.

Siv looked back over her shoulder to the bodies on the dune, sand already shifting to cover what was left of their skin and bones. Lizard and human alike, they would soon be lumps and then merely smooth sand. She was glad she couldn't see down into the valley to the remains of her friend. And she couldn't help wondering how many dead things slumbered under the glittering gray dunes.

Poor Carr. In all her twenty years, Siv had never seen a Scyre member die in such a strange and discomfiting manner. Even those lost to the sea fed the sea creatures, and it was considered a valiant and natural death. But here, in these strange and endless sands, Carr's bones wouldn't find their home in the hidden caves of the Nautilus. His remains would slowly be hidden by sand and forgotten forever, surrounded by enemies and emptiness. It was a lonely place, and his good nature and hearty laugh would be sorely missed around the campfire.

Still, life in the Scyre was rough and short, and Siv had seen many friends die. It was considered weakness to mourn too much, so she turned her face to the hot sun and followed Phasma onward to their destiny.

For the rest of that afternoon, they saw nothing but sand and dunes. Up each dune they trudged, pulling their sleds and carrying their packs and carefully sipping the smallest amount of liquid. At the crest of the dune, they couldn't help halting, scanning the area ahead for something, anything, that was not sand. Again and again, they were disappointed. All they saw were endless gray dunes rising in endless waves against an endless sky of molten blue. Gray clouds bunched, far off, darkening the horizon back the way they'd come. The Scyre seemed doomed to dwell under an oppressive pall and the threat of thunder. But here, just a few days away, not a single cloud dotted the sky; there was nothing to provide either shade or the hope of water. The air wavered over the sand, the dry heat bouncing up to burn Siv's eyes. The land itself drove them forward, spurring them toward the promise of Brendol's ship and the imagined peace and coolness of space.

That evening, Phasma stopped at the top of a dune and held out her hand in the universal signal to approach with caution. Siv turned to meet Torben's gaze, and he transferred both sled ropes to his left hand and hefted his club.

Up ahead, Phasma pulled out her quadnocs, looked through them briefly, and then passed them to Brendol, who also gazed for quite some time.

"What do you make of it?" he asked.

Phasma shook her head. "This is not our territory. We know nothing of this place. Have you not seen something like it before in your travels?"

The reprimand in her tone must've escaped him. He shook his head and frowned his pinched little frown. "I can't even tell what it is. Animal or mineral, we shall find out. It's directly in our path."

Phasma looked to her people. "Draw your weapons. Be ready."

"What is it?" Gosta asked, cresting the dune by Phasma's side.

"We don't know," was all Phasma said.

Phasma and Brendol led on, the troopers and Gosta behind them. Siv and Torben came last, their weapons drawn. As they topped the dune, Siv was itching with curiosity. What could possibly have both Phasma and Brendol at a loss? What she saw beyond gave her no answers.

The sand stretched out flat for a long time, with no dunes for what would be several hours of walking. Out in the middle of that infinite flatness was a large black mound. From this distance, and with the air wavering and hot and full of whipping gray sand, it was truly impossible to guess at what it might be, or even how large it was or if it was alive.

The shape was black with sparks of reflected sun, here and there, that suggested something about it was shifting or possibly metallic. It was lumpy and seemed big—bigger than a person, bigger than the Nautilus. The sand around it was the same gray that had become their entire world, and there was nothing to mark a difference of topography—no greenery, or rock, or metal. Just the slightly heaving, shifting, dark blob out in the middle of nowhere.

Now, one must remember that Siv and the other Scyre warriors had never seen anything living on land that was bigger than a human. They'd seen mouths in the ocean but not the giant bodies they had to be attached to. They'd seen bits and pieces of huge beasts washed up and battered against the rocks, but truly, not a one of them could've named or described the monsters whose skins had become their own cloaks and boots. There were no mammals in their world bigger than the few remaining tiny goats, and even the lizards that had pulled the sleds had been a revelation to them. They'd never seen a building or a machine that hadn't been relegated to parts and blades. So how could they possibly know what they were looking at? As for Brendol, perhaps he had some idea, but no one could ever tell what he was thinking, and he certainly offered no hints.

"We'll skirt around it. Keep your weapons ready," Phasma said.

Not that she had to tell them to do so. Her warriors were well trained. She'd made sure of it.

"You okay?" Torben asked, and Siv glared at him.

"Of course. Don't doubt me."

They crept down the dune and into the great, flat valley. Everyone was twitchy, weapons in hand, scanning for signs of life, for more lizards and attackers, or for the big, bulky thing to do anything but just sit there, throwing an equally big and bulky shadow onto the sand. It didn't act like an animal, though—didn't shake or snort or blink great, yellow eyes at the trespassers. There was something uncomfortably alien about it, about the way it didn't seem to care or even notice them there. They drew even with it, then moved around it, and Siv went pallid and white-eyed when she told me about it.

The words don't take long to say, but the actual journey went on for hours. Hours approaching the thing, hours moving around it, hours getting past it. All the time, it did nothing but shiver to itself, for no reason they could discern.

I remember this part of the story because for all the violence she described in our time together, Siv looked the most haunted when she said that bit.

After they were around the thing, Brendol stopped. Everyone else stopped and stared at him; no one felt safe. They were in the middle of the open, near something disconcerting they couldn't explain, and every nerve in their well-tuned bodies told them to get the hell away. But Brendol stopped, because that was his way, wasn't it? Brendol was curious, and Brendol needed answers.

"Give me your blaster," he said to his nearest trooper.

Once he had the blaster, he took aim and fired at the heaving black mound.

And it exploded.

The black skin they'd been watching shift and quiver was a huge flock of birds, or bats, or some mixture of the two. Whatever they were, they were black and small and fast and sharp, and they burst away and into a cloud that moved as one, screeching like death. The glimmers underneath the black proved to be more of the golden beetles, and when they, too, shifted aside, the true form of the lumpy thing was revealed. It was a monster, a dead thing being torn apart by the scavengers. Something like the lizards they'd seen earlier, but bigger and with great ridges and spines up and down its sides. There wasn't much left of it, just blankets of the skin hanging off stark bones and a brown hole flapping in the side.

"We don't need the water that bad," Phasma decided.

"Not with that many beetles," Brendol concurred.

"Wait, what's that?" Gosta asked.

The insides of the dead beast rippled, and two bright-red lights appeared in the hole in its skin. A growl went up, and a beast slunk out of the carcass, a wet-looking thing like a hairless boar-wolf, its skin the same color as the gray sand. It stalked out on long legs that bent backward and was covered with warts and bumps, all splashed with rusty red gore stains from its feasting. Its red eyes were pinned to the group, and it crouched briefly before leaping into a run right for them. Two more of the creatures appeared and followed it, loping in a V-formation to attack.

True to form, Phasma pulled her spear and her dagger and ran for the first beast, shouting her war cry. Gosta was on her heels, and Siv and Torben followed. Siv's leg muscles ached from so much struggling up and down through sand, but they loosened up on the flat run, and she veered slightly right as Gosta veered left, each of them swinging for one of the foul, glistening creatures. There was a clash of flesh and metal, but Siv's entire being now focused on the wolf-thing. Her job was to kill it before it could hurt anyone else. The Scyre folk knew that any wound could go toxic, but the lore said that animal bites and scratches were more likely than most to kill.

Unlike the lizard, the skinwolf, as they later named it, didn't go down on the first slice. Its skin was thick and rough, and her sword slash made a cut that seemed to stick itself back together, not even getting down into the meat of the thing. It went for her arm, and she yanked back and slashed at its slender ankles, hoping to hack through thin skin and into tendon or bone. Her scythe hit and skittered off, barely doing any damage, and the creature caught the hem of her robe and shook it, yanking Siv onto her back. She shoved up with her curved blade, but it didn't pierce the wolf's wrinkled neck, and she had to drop her scythes to hold its bulk away as it snapped for her face.

Pew!

A red-hot bolt zipped past her wrist and hit the beast, and it howled and backed away, pawing at what was left of its nose.

Pew!

Another bolt caught it in the ribs, and the creature limped once and dropped to its side, a hole steaming in its wet, gray chest.

"Need a hand?" The female trooper held out a glove to Siv, who gladly took it and stood.

The other troopers were taking care of the two remaining skin-wolves, which had both absorbed numerous cuts but refused to slow down or respond to their injuries. The blasters were brutally efficient, though, and the creatures didn't last long under the assault of laser bolts. Two shots each, and they died.

"Did anyone take damage?" Phasma asked.

Brendol held up his arm, showing a rent in the cloth that went down to his skin. It wasn't quite bleeding, more like a burn, just a red line against the pale belly of his arm.

Phasma exhaled in annoyance. "We should've put you in Carr's leathers. Siv, put liniment on it. General Hux, let me know if it gets any worse or the fever comes. If you're lucky, it won't."

"And if it does?" Brendol asked, faced pinched as he inspected the wound.

Phasma gave him a grim, determined stare.

"Then you lose your arm at the elbow."

Brendol glared at her like she was a fool. "But wouldn't that make an even worse wound? Attract even more infection?"

"No." Siv knelt before him with the ancient metal tin that held the oracle liniment her mother had taught her to make. The liniment formulation was different from the salve, crafted specifically for abrasions and wounds and including soothing herbs that still grew near the cliffs of the Scyre. When she held out her hand, Brendol paused a moment before offering up his arm. "The infection comes from the animal or lichen, not from the air. A clean blade makes a clean cut, fire cauterizes the wound, and the liniment prevents further contagion."

"Are you trained in medicine?" Brendol asked her, looking interested in someone besides Phasma for the first time.

Phasma stepped forward. "This knowledge keeps our people alive. Children learn it as soon as they can speak. Children who don't tell adults about their cuts die by nightfall. Tell him, Gosta."

In a singsong voice, Gosta chanted,

> *"If you get the smallest wound*
> *Better tell your Mama soon*
> *Edges red and skin gone white*
> *Gonna lose a toe tonight.*
> *Don't tell Mama and you'll see*
> *Wound goes putrid, dead you'll be."*

Brendol shook his head as if to rid his mind of the words. "How very macabre."

"We don't know that word. But you make it sound like something bad. Like we have a choice to be other than we are. This is our life. This is why my people are strong." Phasma put a hand on Gosta's shoulder, and the younger girl glowed with pride. "Even our children can fight for the clan. We grow up knowing exactly how hard life on Parnassos will be and what is expected of us. We don't mourn the weak."

"Are you saying that the man we lost today, a man you chose and trained, was weak?"

Brendol said it like it was a sort of test, and Phasma stepped toward him, just a little too close.

"Carr was strong and I trained him well, but he was unlucky, and now he's gone. Those who survive must move forward."

Brendol smiled as if these words pleased him, but Siv couldn't imagine why.

"If only I had a comm," he mused. "These slogans would do so well in our program."

"Your program?"

Siv had finished applying the liniment, and she pulled down Brendol's sleeve. Brendol inclined his head toward her in mute thanks, stood, and began walking, his hands behind his back. After jerking her head at her warriors, Phasma moved to walk by his side. Everyone else hurried in their wake. Siv was glad that she wasn't expected to use the detraxor on the foul dogs. For all that they were tough and strong, they looked diseased and wrong. She secretly worried that their essence might carry whatever pathogen had caused the hideous boils and warts to form on their skin. As Torben took up his sled ropes, he and Siv hurried ahead to hear what Phasma and Brendol were discussing.

"I have a special task in the First Order," Brendol said. "My rank is general, very similar to your rank here among your people. I'm a leader. My greatest responsibility is to design the program that will train up the young warriors, teach them how to fight while helping them understand *why* we fight. As you can imagine, this involves not only the physical aspects of instruction, which I leave to younger and fitter officers, but also education. We have sayings like the rhyme about wounds, songs and stories and parables that we use to instill our values and beliefs into our fighters from the earliest age. The end result is what you see here before you." Brendol gestured to his three troopers. "The finest warriors in the galaxy, trained to follow my orders precisely using a variety of weapons and equipment and while navigating a wide selection of environments. They must know how to think on their feet and act quickly no matter how hostile the situation. It seems like a task for which you, Phasma, might be particularly well qualified."

Phasma snorted, unmoved by his praise. "You say you raise the finest warriors in the galaxy, but I would test my fighters against yours any day. A life like ours adds a determination, a grit that can't be instilled with clever songs."

Brendol nodded, looking amused. "I look forward to hearing more of your strategies and how they might be applied in a more, say, controlled environment. Perhaps we will one day sit together and watch your warriors test mine, but under ideal conditions. You would be most impressed, I think, with our training barracks on the *Finalizer*."

Behind her mask, Phasma's face was inscrutable. "That would be most instructive," she said, her cool accent and cadence matching Brendol's perfectly. It sent a chill up Siv's spine.

They walked across the flat plain until the sun began to set and the air grew heavy and cold. The world was the same in every direction, endless sand with no place to hide. They would be exposed no matter where they camped for the night.

"We'll rest here," Phasma said, stopping in a place no different from any other place. "The warriors will keep watch in shifts, and we rise at dawn. I'll take first watch."

Her warriors nodded in response, and after glancing at Brendol, so did the troopers. Brendol was left out of the guard duties, and Siv wasn't sure if it was because he appeared to have few fighting skills or because Phasma considered him superior in rank and above such tasks. Back in the Scyre, Keldo had never held guard duties for this same combination of traits. But it wasn't Siv's job to think about the hierarchy. Her job was to heal wounds and distribute the water and salve. Normally, Gosta would've been collecting bits of kindling all day, and as they settled down, she would build a fine fire, but here, in the sand, there was nothing to collect, nothing to burn.

Although the Scyre was a lonely and forbidding place, Siv had never felt so miserable and exposed in the world. The hard winds caught at her robes, plucked at every edge of cloth, and blew so much sand about that the only way to eat was to slip chunks of jerky and dried sea vegetable underneath her mask. It was a wretched night, and everyone seemed to sleep very lightly, tossing and turning in the sand and waking, startled, half covered in gray, to dust the sand off and try to find a more comfortable position. There was none. The Scyre folk were accustomed to sleeping in their net hammocks, alone or with a trusted companion, but as the temperature dropped and dropped yet again, they moved close together, searching half asleep for some kind of warmth. Siv was glad enough when Torben woke her for her watch, as sleep had brought little comfort.

She spent her watch on high alert, scanning the pitch darkness for any new sensation. There was little light, the stars obscured by swirls of sand, and nothing could penetrate the blackness. The only sound was the high keening of the wind and the soft shuffling of the sand. Everything smelled of minerals and bodies, for the Scyre folk had sweated through their layers during the day and were now drenched with the sour tang of unwashed flesh, sticky with sand. Even through her mask, sand flecked Siv's lips, and when she grew frustrated enough to lick it off, it crunched unpleasantly between her teeth. The Scyre began to seem a friendly place by comparison. Whatever Phasma thought they would gain from Brendol Hux and his ship— Siv could only hope it was worth this suffering, worth losing Carr.

When her hour had passed, she went to wake one of the troopers, as the Scyre folk had all taken their turn at guarding the camp. Her eyes had adjusted to what little light there was, and she scanned the loose group of sleeping bodies and chose the one closest to her, reaching out to gently touch the sleeping soldier's armored shoulder.

"It's time," she said, quite low, and a glove landed on her hand and twisted it so that her wrist nearly popped.

She knew better than to cry out. "I'm on your side," she whispered.

The trooper jerked upright, his mouth going from a snarl to a frown as he released her hand. "Sorry," he said. "Training, you know." The man's voice was low and rough, not nearly as clipped and proper as Brendol's.

"It's fine," she said. "We're all jumpy."

"I'll take it from here, then."

"Be strong." When his eyebrows drew down in confusion, she explained, "That's what we say when switching watch."

"You do this every night?"

"Of course. Both in the home camp and when sitting as sentry."

He shook his head. "The *Finalizer*'s barracks seem more and more cozy the longer I'm here."

She nodded and moved closer to Torben, pillowing her head on the sandy sleeve of her robe. Torben was on his side, and she wiggled toward him until her back touched his arm. He reached out and drew her in close to the warm curl of his body, and they both sighed in relief. For all the horrors of the sands, this embrace was an entirely new experience, so different from bodies tumbling together in a hammock swinging precariously over the sea. Memories of Keldo and Carr flashed through Siv's mind, though it wasn't the way of the Scyre to mourn those who were lost or gone. Dwelling on the past risked everyone's life in the present. But it was lucky she took that moment to pause and put away her sorrow, for in the stillness, she was certain she heard a sound that should not have been there.

Siv froze, holding her breath and sending her senses out into the night. Before she could ask the trooper on watch if he'd heard it, too, she was blinded by the brightest light she'd ever seen.

"Attack!" Siv shouted, going for her scythes as she struggled out from under Torben's huge arm.

"General! Troopers!" the watchman shouted.

Everyone came awake at once, leaping to their feet with weapons at the ready. The troopers didn't shoot, though, and the Scyre warriors couldn't see what to attack. As they stood there, waiting, ready to fight, the fight never came. The camp was bathed in the harsh light, and as her eyes adjusted, Siv saw that they weren't facing more skimmers or skinwolves. Not even humans.

Her scythes dropped to her sides as she realized she was looking at a stark white droid. It wasn't like the one Brendol Hux had brought from his ship. This one was spindly and rough, a little shorter than Siv herself. It didn't appear to be carrying any weapons—just a box emitting the blinding light.

"Our prayers have been answered," it said in a monotone voice that still somehow managed to express excitement. "Praise to the creators! I do hope you'll come with me. We've been waiting for you for such a long time."

"General Hux, what do we do?" Phasma asked.

But when they looked to Brendol, he alone still lay on the sand. He was unconscious and unmoving, red with fever, and when Siv looked at his arm, it was too far gone. Even amputation wouldn't help.

Brendol Hux was dying.

SEVENTEEN

ON PARNASSOS, 10 YEARS AGO

"I CAN'T HELP HIM," SIV SAID. "THE FEVER'S SET IN. IT'S TOO LATE."

"Oh, my," the droid said. "That does look bad. Fortunately, our station's medbay is well equipped, and we would be pleased to administer the proper antibiotics."

Phasma approached the droid with her ax and spear ready. The stormtroopers flanked her with their blasters. "Who are you, and why are you here?" Phasma barked.

The droid cocked its head at her. "I am Teebeethree of the Con Star Mining Corporation. If your companion is currently dying, perhaps we should continue this discussion as we walk back to the station. It is not far."

Siv checked Brendol's pulse and found it uneven. "We need help," she said. "Torben?"

The big warrior quickly maneuvered Brendol onto the sled and hefted the packs himself. But Phasma still faced off with the droid.

"Do you mean us harm?"

"Ha ha ha!" The droid's laugh was monotone and strange. "It is against my protocols to harm sentient beings. Indeed, my only wish is to serve you. Praise to the creators. As you can see, I am not equipped with weapons of any sort, nor are my brethren."

"Your brethren?"

"There are forty-seven droids currently functional at Terpsichore Station. I am a protocol droid, programmed to aid the human work-force with languages, statistics, strategies, and basic necessities. Please do follow me."

No one agreed, and yet the droid turned and shuffled away from them, pointing his light out into the desert. Siv stood from helping arrange Brendol and noted that the droid was walking in its own footsteps, a trail that went over the next dune.

Phasma knelt beside Brendol, looked at his wound, and hissed through her teeth. "You're right. It's too far gone."

"He must be saved," one of the stormtroopers said. "No matter the cost."

"Do you trust this droid?" Phasma asked him.

He shrugged. "Looks like I don't have a choice."

Hefting his pack, he followed the droid. The other two storm-troopers fell in behind him. Siv and the Scyre warriors looked to Phasma.

"Brendol is our only hope. We don't have a choice, either."

Phasma took up her pack and hurried after the troopers, and Tor-ben doggedly followed her, towing Brendol behind him. The droid lit the way. Siv felt as if she were still half asleep, dragging her boots through the sand and gritting her teeth against the nighttime cold. No one spoke, and Siv kept close to Brendol even though his wound was beyond her meager skills as a healer.

Dawn was just beginning to light the sky when the droid stopped before an especially steep dune. His trail had long ago been covered by the shifting sands, but he seemed to know exactly where he was going. Although she didn't see any gender characteristics in his phys-icality, something about the droid's voice and gait struck her as mas-culine, and so she thought of TB-3 as a him.

"Oh, goodness. The winds are so brutal. One moment."

The Scyre warriors shared a look of suspicion as the droid dug around in the dune.

"Ah, here it is."

The wall of sand shuddered, and a layer of gray fell away to reveal an unnatural opening. I know what a door is, of course, but Siv had never seen anything like it. She described it as if the world as she knew it had opened up to reveal a strange mechanical heart. Inside, the gray sand met a smooth white floor with matching walls and a ceiling covered in lights.

"Welcome to Terpsichore Station, the prime mining facility of the Con Star Mining Corporation on Parnassos," TB-3 said proudly. "Please enter so I can shut the door and keep too much sand from blowing in. We can't have the mouse droids getting fussy." As if on cue, a tiny black droid rolled in from somewhere and started busily sucking up the sand that was beginning to swirl down the clean hallway.

Although Phasma usually took the first steps in any engagement, this time she looked to the troopers. Even Phasma was intimidated by entering a building for the first time, when the Nautilus had been the only enclosed space she'd ever known. The troopers walked inside and moved a little farther down the hallway as if everything was utterly normal, so Phasma followed them, but delicately, as if she expected the floor to collapse underneath her worn boots. Once she had crossed the threshold, she motioned for her people to join her, and Siv stepped onto the smooth floor, trailed by Gosta and Torben pulling Brendol behind him. As soon as they were all inside, the droid pressed a button, and the door slid closed.

In that moment, a great sense of terror washed over Siv. She was enclosed, utterly unable to see the sky. Even in the Nautilus, they had a skylight. But here, everything was unnatural and nothing familiar. She wanted to hunch down on the ground, and she felt as if the building might fall on her at any moment and crush her. Judging by Torben's unsmiling face and Gosta's shifting eyes, Siv wasn't alone.

"This way to the medbay," TB-3 said, leading them down the hall.

They followed, and Siv marveled at the things she saw in the station. There were windows in the walls covered with clear panes to show wonders of the past world that Siv had never witnessed in their entirety. She was a little familiar with antiquities, but she'd never seen an intact table and chairs, much less a computer bank or collection of factory machines. In some rooms, droids stopped to watch them go by, and Siv felt strange, to be stared at by machines with eyes. The hallway twisted and turned, and sometimes TB-3 would push another button to open a new door. Eventually, he led them into an open room filled with machinery.

Three droids waited beside a metal platform, all bulkier than TB-3.

"Please place the patient on the bed," one said, holding out an arm. "Praise to the creators."

Torben looked to the troopers, and one of them gave him a nod. The big warrior took Brendol in his arms like a baby and carefully laid him on the bed, arranging his arms and legs so that his body was contained. Stepping back beside Siv, Torben murmured, "I've never felt a fever so hot. He's as good as gone."

The droids immediately began performing actions that Siv didn't understand, scanning Brendol and injecting him with fluids.

"Now that your companion is being treated, please come with me to discuss payment options," TB-3 said. One of the stormtroopers groaned, but Siv didn't yet understand what was happening.

"I should stay with him," she said.

"One of *us* should," the female trooper shot back.

TB-3 held out his arms to herd them out of the room. "Please allow the med droids to perform their function. Your companion has a seventy-two percent chance of survival at the moment, but any stress or unfamiliar pathogens could lower his odds. We'll be just down the hall."

The droid led them into a room dominated by a long table with several chairs.

"Please have a seat, and I will return with the datawork. Perhaps you would like some refreshments?"

"This is confusing," Torben said. "Can I kill it?"

Before Phasma could answer, TB-3 hurried from the room, closing the door behind him.

"Droids," one of the troopers muttered. "They can get strange if they're not properly calibrated. This one seems a bit eccentric."

"And why haven't we seen any people?" another trooper said. "Something's wrong here."

The door slid open to reveal another droid, this one squat and rolling, carrying a tray loaded with drinks and food. Siv and the Scyre folk hesitated, but the troopers took off their helmets and began eating and drinking. Phasma took a tentative sip of a drink, and Siv was glad enough to follow her leader's example. The water was plentiful and cool, and the food was strange, smooth and sweet, and she wanted to go on eating it forever.

"Are we sure this is safe?" Phasma asked, holding up a piece of foodstuff.

"Look at it this way," a trooper said. "If these droids wanted us dead, they could've killed us in the desert. They could've gassed us in this compound. Maybe Teebeethree doesn't have weapons, but there are more of them here than there are of us. Whoever's running this place must want us alive or else we wouldn't be." And then he went back to eating.

When the food was gone, TB-3 reappeared carrying a working datapad. He stood at the head of the table and pointed out numbers that flashed on the lit screen. "Con Star Mining Corporation is pleased to report that your companion is alive, and his infection is under control. Our protocols suggest he remain here, resting and under care in the medbay, for at least two days. How would you care to reimburse the Con Star Mining Corporation for this medical care?"

"Reimburse?" Phasma asked.

"He wants creds," a trooper said. "Payment. Nothing is free."

"Correct. Here is the bill."

TB-3 slid the datapad to the trooper, and Phasma stood to look over his shoulder. From where she sat, Siv could only see endless lists of symbols that made no sense.

The trooper barked a laugh and carelessly tossed the datapad back. "We don't have creds. Maybe you could send a bill to the First Order, but we're just soldiers. Not accountants."

The droid's head drooped as if he were disappointed to hear this. "Unfortunately, we are temporarily unable to transmit data offplanet. If your companion wishes to leave, either the bill must be paid, or your group can accept positions with Con Star Mining Corporation as laborers. With a sixty-day plan, you can work off this debt while enjoying comfortable accommodations and employee benefits. Praise to the creators."

"What does this mean?" Phasma asked the trooper beside her.

"To be blunt, either we take jobs to pay them off, or Brendol dies."

"But we don't have sixty days. We must get to the ship."

The trooper looked up at TB-3. "Can we have a few moments?"

The droid inclined his head and said, "Of course. I will return shortly," before disappearing out the door and closing it behind him.

"Can we fight our way out?" Phasma asked, and the trooper motioned her close.

"Keep it down. They might have listening devices. As it is, we don't know who's running this place or where the main control room is, so chances are we wouldn't be able to get Brendol and escape before they took action against us."

Phasma considered it. "So we need Brendol whole, and we need to know more. We should accept these positions, gather the information we need, and escape."

The trooper shrugged. "It's our only option, really. But there are advantages. They might have vehicles we could use to get to the ship faster. And the general will know what to do, when he's awake again. He's a master tactician."

TB-3 had left the datapad on the table, and Phasma pulled it over and experimented with it, dragging her finger here and pressing there. Her eyes took on a gleam of fascination, and Siv realized she'd never seen Phasma this interested in anything. Phasma looked at everything as a tool, but she looked at the datapad almost as if it were holy.

"Show me how this works," she said, and the trooper took it and started pressing buttons.

The droid returned and fussily reclaimed the datapad. "Have you made your decision?" he asked.

"We'll accept your offer," Phasma said. The stormtroopers looked at one another, but no one spoke against her.

"Praise to the creators! We are all so very pleased. Let us begin immediately." The droid took their fingerprints and said many things that Siv didn't understand, and then he announced them to be Con Star Mining Corporation employees.

"And now it's time for a brief orientation disk," he said. The lights went down, but not so much that Siv panicked, and a brightly lit moving picture appeared on the smooth white wall, along with the patter of a cheerful woman's voice.

"Welcome to Con Star Mining Corporation. We're glad you've decided to join us on beautiful Parnassos, where you'll be part of a unique community of pioneers on this exclusive planet!" The image panned out from a large white box, making Siv dizzy, and the box grew tiny, surrounded by mountains and green and then oceans of crystal blue. "Parnassos is rich with metals and minerals, and we've specially designed your habitat to bring familiar comfort to your species." The image zoomed back in and moved inside the flat thing, the scene changing so quickly that Siv felt her stomach swoop. She recognized the hallway that had led into this very room.

"You'll be living in Terpsichore Station, situated in a rich valley replete with nature's bounty. It's just a short tram ride to the Siren Sea for a day at the beach." The image showed something shiny and silver zipping along two tracks, cutting through the green. Then a man, a woman, and two children stepped out and waved their arms. The image changed, and the family smiled by the ocean. But it wasn't the dark, forbidding, cold ocean that lapped at the rock walls of the Scyre

and teemed with hungry beasts. This water was light blue and welcoming with a sandy bottom, and the children ran willingly into it,
splashing around and laughing.

"This is insane," Siv muttered to Phasma.

"This is what Parnassos might have been, over a hundred years
ago." Phasma snorted, watching the always smiling people on the
green lawn throw a red ball for a four-legged animal with a floppy
tongue to chase. "Our ancestors were strange. Strange, and soft."

The images and booming voice went on and on. Siv learned that
the flat thing was a building and the zipping silver thing was a tram.
She saw labs, factories, mines, and endless rows of tidy homes with
every sort of peculiar comfort provided by machines that were now
just bundles of rust stowed in the Nautilus. She learned that there
had once been dozens of separate communities on Parnassos, each
with its own station and purpose. And she discovered that once, long
ago, this sandy desert had been a fertile green valley full of plants,
animals, and eerily happy human beings, all brought to the lush
planet to work for Con Star.

"And so we welcome you to Terpsichore Station, where your today
protects our tomorrow," the voice boomed. "We're certain you'll be
very happy here."

The screen went white, and the light blinked out, leaving them in
momentary darkness.

"Do you think," Gosta said, sounding awed, "that maybe the Scyre
was named for the Siren Sea?"

"And why do they keep saying 'praise to the creators.' Do they
really love whoever made them?" Torben asked.

A trooper shook his head. "I told you. Droids get strange when
they're not kept properly."

"It doesn't matter," Phasma said firmly. "The past is dead and the
droids aren't our business. Our only aim is to get out of here and finish the mission before someone else can."

The lights came back up, and a new droid strode into view. While
TB-3 looked harmless, meek, and subservient, this new droid reminded Siv of a tool, of something blunt made only to do work.

"Hello and welcome to Con Star Mining Corporation. Praise to the creators. I am Deefourseventhree, and I will assign your tasks. Normally, you would be given a barrage of tests to assign you to the correct position for your abilities, but time is of the essence and quotas are overdue, so you will all be working in the mine. I do hope you find this acceptable?"

"We're not miners," one of the troopers barked. "We demand to speak to a supervisor."

D473 clasped his metal hands, his head cocked in an apologetic sort of way. "I'm so sorry, worker, but we are very shorthanded right now. The supervisor is currently unavailable. It is hoped that reinforcements from the main office will be sent shortly, praise to the creators. Con Star Mining Corporation regrets this inconvenience. Now please enjoy this mining orientation disk. Praise to the creators."

The droid exited, the room went dark again, and a new image appeared on the screen. Instead of pretty pictures of the past, this disk informed Siv of how mining was performed and what tasks would be required of them. She learned about proper safety procedures, what to do in case of a cave-in, and to always wear a hard hat and carry her Con Star datapad, which would warn her of gas leaks and let her know when rest breaks were allowed. The people on the white wall smiled as they did their work in long tunnels that resembled the Nautilus but didn't contain the paintings done in blood, or the collections of carvings and ritual objects.

"They're going to use us to do this work?" Gosta asked.

"Only until Brendol is better," Phasma answered. "And then we shall see."

The door opened, but instead of a droid, they heard only a voice, the same calm female from the disk.

"Please follow the red line to the barracks for outfitting, praise to the creators."

On the wall, a red line appeared, snaking away and disappearing down a curve. Phasma went first, and Siv realized that with Brendol out of the picture, the troopers had calmly accepted her leadership. They walked at the pace Phasma set, slowing to look at each new opening in the wall. Siv knew Phasma well enough to know that she was gathering knowledge to inform her future choices, trying to learn everything she could about this new environment.

The red line terminated in an open door, the room within lit in that same cold light so different from the sun outside. Racks of hanging cloth stood along the walls. Another droid waited there, silent and still until they'd all entered the room.

"I am Deefoursevenseven," it said in a softer woman's voice. "I will fit you for your uniforms, praise to the creators. Please step up one at a time."

All eyes went to Phasma.

"Why?" she asked.

"All Con Star Mining Corporation employees are required to wear the appropriate uniform," the droid replied calmly.

"And if we refuse?" Phasma asked.

The droid's head canted toward her in a way that reminded Siv of a predatory insect known for biting the head off its mate after laying eggs. "You will show respect for the creators and follow orders, or your terms of servitude will lengthen accordingly."

Phasma stood firm. "I did not agree to this foolishness and will perform my duties as I am."

The droid's head sparked, and Siv drew back.

"*DOES NOT COMPUTE PRAISE TO THE CREATORS ALL EM-PLOYEES WILL FOLLOW ORDERS AND ALL DROIDS WILL FOL-LOW CREATOR PROTOCOL!*"

The group tensed until the droid stopped sparking and regained its calm. It straightened its head and reached into the rack, withdrawing a folded cloth hanging from a twisted bit of metal wire. "This should fit," it said, holding it out to Phasma. She took it but did nothing further. "Please do try it on," the droid said, polite again. "We want you to be comfortable, praise to the creators."

Phasma nodded at the droid, but as it began to turn back to the rack, she yanked the cloth off the wire and whipped it around the droid's head to cover its facial sensors. Planting a boot in its chest, she kicked it over backward. It fell to the ground with a heavy clank, and in a heartbeat Phasma was straddling its torso, jamming the metal wire into its eyehole.

One of the troopers fell to his knees by her side, scrabbling for a panel on the droid's chest and digging his fingers in, trying to pry it open. The droid's hands flailed and reached for its assailants, but it was clearly unaccustomed to combat. The other two troopers each sat on an arm and Torben restrained the droid's legs as the first trooper got the panel open and began yanking out wires by the fistful.

"REQUIRED REQUIRED PRAISE PRAISE DOES NOT . . ." the droid screamed.

The lights clicked off, a klaxon began to ring, and something wet fell from overhead. Siv turned her face up to the ceiling, amazed by the concept of falling liquid like the harmless rain she remembered from her childhood, but it wasn't water. She breathed in the foul, unnatural odor, and everything went black.

EIGHTEEN

ON PARNASSOS, 10 YEARS AGO

SIV WOKE UP ON HER BACK, STARING AT THE WHITE CEILING. WHEN SHE SAT up, she was dizzy, and her companions were likewise half asleep around her. Tiny black droids scooted among them, drying the floor, but Siv was still wet. TB-3 stood over them, fidgeting.

"I did warn you," he said. "You're employees now, and you cannot shirk your contractual obligations, praise to the creators."

Still muddled, Siv asked, "Why do you keep saying that, praise to the creators?"

TB-3 proudly tapped a badge on his shining white chest. He'd been polished since bringing them to the station, all evidence of the gray sand buffed away.

"The Con Star Mining Corporation landed here one hundred and eighty-six years ago. We were built and activated on Parnassos by our creators, who designed us to perfectly perform our duties. Once the facility was under proper management and the human personnel had arrived, the creators left. Time passed, and we experienced temporary signal interference. We can no longer communicate with the creators or the other stations. Our human contingent ... well, we have been waiting ever since. For the creators. We are very pleased you've arrived."

"But we're not—"

Phasma interrupted her. "We're happy to be here."

"Very good. I hope you will consider bathing and dressing in your uniforms now. Poor Deefoursevenseven was quite disturbed by your insubordination. You will need to eat before your shift, and punctuality is important."

Siv looked to Phasma, and Phasma just shook her head. "We're happy to comply."

TB-3 led them to a room filled with spraying water and requested they disrobe and bathe. Siv was loath to trust the droid with her weapons, and the troopers were likewise adamant about their armor, but TB-3 showed them lockers in which to store their belongings. When Phasma didn't argue and placed her ax and spear in the metal box, Siv had little choice but to follow. It was strange to be without her scythes, and she was dumbfounded by the feeling of bathing, nude, with Con Star soap. A warm wind machine dried them, and a new version of D477 gave her strange, light clothes with a Con Star badge on the chest, just like the one TB-3 wore with pride.

They were instructed to follow the yellow line to the cafeteria, where they were served identical foods on identical plastic trays. Following Phasma's lead, Siv ate the food, which all had the same texture but vastly different flavors and colors. The drink, served from a pouch, had the tang of minerals about it. Once the food was gone, she stood with her friends—now co-workers—to empty her tray and follow the blue line to the turbolift, which took them down into the mine.

When Siv told me this story, she was still astounded by how different the station was from the Scyre. Everything was clean and sharp and cool, with smooth walls and perfect corners and cold lights that sometimes flickered but never went out. She had to learn words she'd never heard before, understand how to perform the repetitive work demanded of her. After a few hours, it was as if her hands had been made to hold the handle and push the cart. She wore her hard hat and goggles and did everything she was asked to do, a team of helpful droids instructing and overseeing her.

At each new task, everyone looked to Phasma. Instead of a mask, claws, and weapons, Phasma wore her crisp uniform, and although she didn't smile, she watched everything that happened, her bright blue eyes darting to every control pad and console they passed. Secretive looks passed among them all; they were biding time, and they knew it.

Siv's hands were blistered by the time a blinking green light announced the end of their shift. She put down her jackhammer and pushed her cart to the turbolift, where she stood quietly between Phasma and Torben. They followed the green line to the barracks, where they changed into their sleeping clothes and slipped into their assigned bunks. It was the most comfortable place Siv had ever been, with plenty of room to stretch out completely and turn in any direction she desired without feeling the warning creak of a net or the grainy slither of sand. But she wasn't sleepy. None of them were. They were just waiting until the door closed, leaving them alone in darkness and silence.

"This is crazy," one of the troopers said. It was the one Brendol had shouted at, PT something. After that outburst, the troopers had kept their distance from the Scyre folk, but with Brendol gone, perhaps he felt it was safe to speak. Out of his helmet and armor, he seemed so much smaller and like any other man, not a stranger from beyond the stars.

"We need to play along until we can get Brendol," Phasma said, her voice low.

The trooper nodded. "Yeah, he'll understand more about the droids and their programming. We know how to take them down individually, but we can't fight forty-seven droids without our weapons, not to mention whoever runs the control room."

"And there could still be people."

"True."

"What's your name?" Siv asked, feeling bold. "Not the number Brendol called you, but your real name. It feels wrong that you know our names, but we don't know yours."

He gave a wry grin. "We don't have names. The First Order only gives us numbers. I'm PT-2445, and this is LE-2003." He nodded to the woman. "And HF-0518." He nodded to the man.

"Your names are hard to say," Gosta said. "Can I call you Petey?"

For a moment, PT-2445 looked kind and amused. "That's more of a child's name, but I suppose you can think of me as Pete when the general isn't around."

"And that would make me Elli," the female trooper said. "And you're . . . Huff."

The third trooper, now Huff, scowled. "That's not even a name."

"Ah, but we don't have names, do we?" Pete said, and the troopers shared a private chuckle.

"Enough about your names. I want to leave. These clothes are useless," Torben said. His uniform was too small for him and could barely stretch over his shoulders. "Can't fight in them. They can't stop a blade. No wonder they have trouble keeping people here."

Siv laughed, grateful for a moment of mercy in the strange place. But Phasma was having none of their jocularity.

"Then we all agree," she said sharply. "We do as the droids ask until Brendol is with us, and then . . ."

"And then?" Gosta asked.

"And then we turn the tables."

Time passed in a blur for several days, or at least what Siv assumed was days. They couldn't see the sky and had no concept of time. Sleep, then food, then work, then food, then work, then sleep. It was monotonous, being an employee of the Con Star Mining Corporation. The droids she encountered when walking down the halls or delivering her cart full of ore were cheerful and helpful, but she never saw another person, and she didn't entirely trust the droids or feel safe around them. She longed for life outside, even if it was harsh. At least it was honest.

Two sleep cycles later, Brendol Hux appeared at breakfast. His skin was paler than usual, blotchy with purple bags under his eyes, and his uniform, although clean and pressed, fit a little looser. As soon as he saw them, he hurried over with TB-3 shuffling anxiously in his wake.

"What the devil are you wearing?" he barked, staring at them each in turn.

"Our uniforms, sir," one of the troopers said, his eyes cutting to the hovering droid. "We've been indentured to the Con Star Mining Corporation to pay your medical debts."

Brendol turned a peculiar shade of red and began to splutter, but Phasma waved a hand.

"It's only sixty days each," she said with a smirk. "I feel certain our time here will be worthwhile. But we must remain calm. We angered one of the droids recently and were punished harshly."

"Good behavior is expected of Con Star employees, praise to the creators," TB-3 agreed.

"You should get a tray and join us," Phasma said. "Our work shifts are long, and you'll be hungry."

"Work shift? I nearly died. I barely survived in the medbay under those butchers. I can't work!" Brendol stormed.

"General—" one of the troopers began.

Phasma interrupted him. "If there's one thing we've learned here, it's that insubordination is punished, so we're happy to help you acclimate. I feel certain our time will pass swiftly under our watchful hosts."

The smile she aimed at TB-3 was cold enough to freeze water, but the droid didn't notice.

"You are a model employee, Phasma," he said.

Brendol's mouth twitched as he considered the situation, but in the end, he fetched his tray like everyone else. Once he was settled, TB-3 left. They knew well enough by now to follow the blue line to the turbolift for their shift when the bell rang.

As Brendol approached the table with his breakfast, Phasma slid over to make room. He sat, contemplating the tray as if it were filled with slime.

"This is madness," he said.

"We know," Phasma answered, leaning close to whisper. "But we can't escape without you. We can kill the droids one by one, but your troopers don't know how to shut down the system. There are too many of them, and they are always watching. And listening." She inclined her head to the cafeteria droid frozen in place by the trays.

"We need to find the control room." Brendol tried the food and nearly spit it out. "And quickly."

"Tonight. They're least attentive at night. I've made several forays and encountered no droids."

Siv was shocked to learn that Phasma had ventured out of the room at night without her, without any of the Scyre warriors. She gave Torben an inquisitive look, and he shrugged. Poor Gosta looked just as surprised as she was. They had always known Phasma's plans before.

"Good," Brendol said, and he continued eating with the arm that had nearly killed him—an arm that was still whole.

"How is your wound?" Siv asked, because she had never seen someone recover from the fever before.

Brendol rolled up his sleeve to show her. The skinwolf's gash was a neat pink line, and his arm was a normal color. All signs of infection were gone. No redness, no streaks, no foul pus. Siv nodded her approval, but inside she was filled to the brim with a new sense of hope. The medicines here truly were miracles. If Brendol's First Order had such curatives available, it was imperative that they claim his ship and get off the planet, no matter the cost.

Their two work shifts took forever, and then they were finally back in the barracks for the night. Phasma and Brendol held a whispered discussion, and soon they were ready to move.

Instead of following the red, yellow, green, or blue lines, they hurried to the showers, where they traded their Con Star nightclothes for their regular clothes and weapons and slathered on their oracle salve in preparation for their escape. Brendol was the only one who didn't need to change, and he spent his time identifying cams that might be watching them.

"They're recording," he mused. "And yet no one has come to stop us."

"An issue I discovered days ago, while you were still in the med bay. Instead of pondering that, let's take advantage of it," Phasma snapped, pulling down her mask.

Siv felt better the moment she was back in her leathers, and she grinned at Torben, grateful to see him looking like himself again and happy to feel the weight of her scythes on her hips. She caught Phasma studying the troopers as they put on their armor and checked their guns. She'd known Phasma since they'd been children, and yet she was seeing a new side of her leader. Phasma had always been dedicated to power, but now she was hungry for more than just stability in the Scyre. She coveted the armor, the blasters, the tech. Siv began to wonder if perhaps Phasma wanted it too much.

Back in the hall, they followed Brendol as he read the plaque beside each door. Siv had her scythes out, ready to face down any of the droids that might challenge them. Oddly, none appeared, not even the little mouse droids that always seemed to show up when the slightest bit of dirt marred the gleaming floor.

Finally, Brendol found what he was looking for. He tapped the plaque and said, "Control room. This is it. My soldiers will go first, since blasters will do more damage to metal and we've only seen droids thus far. Should there be any sentient beings within, feel free to subdue them."

Phasma nodded, and Brendol pressed something on the wall. The door slid open, and the troopers fanned inside, blasters up. But they didn't shoot. Seconds had passed before a trooper called, "All clear, sir," and Brendol led the rest of them inside. Without being asked,

Torben remained outside as a guard. In the Scyre, one never went into a tight space without a friend to stand watch. It was all too easy to get trapped.

The room inside was like all the other rooms: white and pristine. There was no one within to threaten. The troopers had their blasters up, and Siv realized that with their armor on there was no way to tell them apart. They were no longer Pete, Elli, and Huff. They were just faceless soldiers.

Brendol went directly to a bank of machines that beeped, blinked, and flashed strange symbols. Screens all around the room showed various images of the station, including all the rooms Siv had seen and many more. One room, to her horror, was filled with human bodies piled haphazardly. At least they weren't fresh, from what she could see. In another room, she was surprised to see all the droids standing in neat rows, holding perfectly still with TB-3 facing them at the front. But her attention was drawn back to Brendol.

His fingers flew over a keyboard, and Phasma stood nearby, watching his every move.

"Come on," Brendol grumbled at it, poking buttons and twisting dials.

He must've done something important, as all the lights clicked off, leaving them in complete darkness. The gentle hum of machines always in the background wound down to silence. The air, which was a constant and regular cool, went still and stale and carried the unmistakable tang of death.

"Just give it a moment," Brendol said, and he was right. A red glow softly filled the room.

"What's happening?" Phasma asked.

"I've turned off the main power and shut down the droids. I'll give it a few moments before rebooting. The droids, however, will remain deactivated."

"Meaning?"

"Meaning the lights and air circulators will be on while the insane droids will be off. There don't seem to be any other beings about—and if there were, they'd be running right here to stop us."

The lights came back up and the screens flickered back on, but nothing else happened. Siv watched the door, waiting for Torben to call out or for some new threat to appear, but neither happened. Brendol clicked away until he found what he was looking for.

"These records show that the only remaining supervisor is Dr. Kereg Ryon, but that's all I can find. Does anyone see him on a screen somewhere?"

"I think I found him," Gosta murmured.

She stood in front of one of the screens. On it, the remains of a man sat at a large desk, a blaster on the table before him. Brendol glanced quickly and nodded. "That's what his nameplate says. So now we know what happened. The only thing worse than unsupervised people without a leader and a purpose is a bunch of droids in the same situation. I don't think there's anyone else here to challenge us."

"But what are they doing?" Siv asked, pointing to the screen that showed the droids lined up perfectly in rows.

Brendol walked over to look more closely. "It's almost as if they're worshipping something. See how their heads are bowed and their hands folded. Strange behavior."

"Their creators," Siv said softly, pointed to the wall behind TB-3, where a huge Con Star Mining Corporation logo was painted. "They just want their creators to come back."

Brendol shook his head. "This is why droids need routine maintenance. Their programming goes strange, and they start to act . . ."

"Human?"

He gave her a sharp look. "Mad."

"But they were kind to us. They healed you. They were only doing their jobs. And they were so happy to see us. Can't you turn them back on after we've left?"

"No," Phasma said, moving to stand beside Siv. "We can't risk anything that could imperil the mission."

"They might disable the vehicles, lock the doors, or have access to weapons," Brendol agreed. "It's better this way. Droids were never meant to be people. They're only meant to serve the purpose of their masters."

Siv couldn't help glancing at the troopers to see their reaction to their superior's words, but their expressions were concealed by their armor. When she looked to Gosta, the younger girl merely shook her head, clearly out of her depth. With Torben still outside, Siv was the only person who felt for the droids. With the stroke of a few keys, Brendol had effectively destroyed their civilization and wiped out their personalities and purposes. Even if they weren't people with feelings, it still seemed cruel.

"When I am among your people, will I learn to operate these machines?" Phasma asked, pointing at the keyboard Brendol had used.

"If you wish."

"I look forward to it, General Hux," Phasma said. Although Siv couldn't see Phasma's face under her mask, she knew her leader was smiling.

With the droids disabled, it didn't take them long to find the hangar. Brendol walked inside, moving from object to object, considering. The hulking shapes made little sense to Siv, but Brendol knew what he was looking for. Finally, he stood in front of a row of pointy metal machines.

"These are speeder bikes," he said. "And those big, blocky ones with the turrets are ground assault vehicles, or GAVs. The speeders are made to fly over ground, and the GAVs were designed to move through sand or other rugged conditions. I would suggest my troopers take speeders, as they're already trained, and they can scout ahead and behind us. The rest of us can ride in a GAV, which will also have room to carry our packs."

"What powers them?" Phasma asked.

Brendol gave her a patronizing sort of smile. "That's very complicated, but the GAV is the only one we need to worry about. If the tank is full, it should get us as far as we need to go. We'll take another barrel of fuel with us, just in case. See here? It has a slot made for it. We only need to get to my ship, after all. Once we're there, the First Order will take care of everything else."

Always curious, Siv couldn't help exploring the enormous room while Brendol and his troopers prepared the vehicles. She found another set of lockers like the ones from the showers. They were unlocked, and some held folded clothes or polished boots, while others held weapons.

"We can take anything we want, can't we?" Siv asked, amazed.

"These old clothes are useless," Phasma said, dumping a pile of fabric on the floor and picking up a short, smooth boot that wouldn't last a day on the Scyre's rocks. "Whatever these people did to survive clearly didn't work. We know we can count on our boots. We made them ourselves of leather, stitched them by hand with sinew. Who knows how long this thing will last, or if it will rip at the first jab of knife or claw?"

"But if we're going to join Brendol's people, won't everything be like this?" Siv held up a shirt so soft and fine that it felt like a light breeze would blow it away.

Phasma shook her head. "I was born for that armor. We've seen how strong it is. Balder's people didn't even make a dent during the fight. Things like this"—she took the shirt from Siv and ripped it in half—"were never for me."

"So strange." Siv walked down the row of lockers, running callused fingers over the metal. "Our ancestors used these things. Lived here. Worked here. Who knows if they came to Parnassos on purpose or were brought here unwillingly. They tried to make a life here. And then everything just . . . fell apart."

Phasma pulled a blaster out of a bag and grinned. "They weren't strong enough. We are. This planet is dying. But we will make a new life in the stars." She handed another, smaller blaster to Siv.

Siv took the gun, noting the strange smoothness of the grip, how light and simple it seemed. This weapon could do more damage than both of Siv's blades, and from farther away. If not for the troopers' blasters, the skinwolves might've bested their entire group.

Siv smiled. "We just need a way to tie the blasters on. And we can find extra ones for Gosta and Torben."

Phasma opened all the lockers, tossing out their contents as if searching for something in particular. Siv sorted through them, collecting blasters and other items that seemed useful. Finally, Phasma held up her prize: a helmet. It wasn't much like the smooth, rounded stormtrooper helmets. Beat-up and painted in bright colors, it had a black line across the eyes, another black line from the nose to the chin, and a tiny antenna poking up from the top. Phasma took off her mask and put it on, then reached for the matching heavy-duty gloves and a chest plate. Siv told me it was like watching a droid being assembled, piece by piece. Phasma began to look less and less like an animal and more like a trooper. Under that helmet, she could be anyone or no one. She didn't even seem human.

"There will be no stopping us now," Phasma said.

NINETEEN

ON PARNASSOS, 10 YEARS AGO

NO MATTER HOW BRENDOL EXPLAINED THAT THEY WOULD RIDE INSIDE THE vehicle, Siv didn't understand how it could work . . . until she was inside it, and it was moving. Brendol sat in the front, working complicated levers and buttons with his hands and feet, while Phasma sat in the turret beside him, her blaster on her hip and her hand on the huge gun that swiveled around under a clear dome. Siv, Gosta, and Torben sat squashed together on a bench in back. The vehicle buzzed and thrummed up through her, making her teeth grind. She wrapped her fingers around the bench and hoped it would be over soon, or that they would at least be out under the sky instead of wedged between the smooth, unnatural walls of the building.

Siv had complicated feelings about Terpsichore Station and the droids who had effectively died there, rendered silent and still by a few swipes of Brendol's thick fingers. They'd wiped out a civilization about the size of the Scyre, and neither Brendol nor Phasma had given it a moment's thought. Siv glanced at the troopers hovering on the speeder bikes. Thus far, they hadn't shared their real names or shown any sort of personality. Did Brendol's First Order care so little about basic humanity that they wanted their people, or at least their soldiers, as pliant and uniform as droids? How could Phasma so quickly adhere to this frame of mind?

Recently, Siv had seen Phasma kill an ally, defy her brother, abandon the Scyre, and now this. Her leader wore a helmet and kept her plans to herself. Perhaps Phasma was changing, or perhaps she was merely showing her true nature for the first time.

The hangar led to a smaller hallway, much like the ones they'd traversed on foot but wide enough to accommodate their vehicle—or even three vehicles—abreast. Brendol's troopers zoomed alongside the GAV on their speeders, skimming over the ground without touching it. The hallway was very long and sloped up slightly, lit by the same cold, whitish-blue light that had plagued Siv ever since she'd entered the station. Up ahead, yet another smooth, white wall stood in their way. Brendol stopped the vehicle, got out, and tapped on the pad until a door slid open.

Siv didn't know what she was expecting. Day or night or yet more endless white. What she saw was a solid wall of gray sand that collapsed inward to reveal a bright point beyond.

The sun.

She shielded her eyes as Brendol climbed back into the vehicle and set it in motion. The wheels caught and dug in, spinning uphill until they caught purchase. Rumbling up out of the hole, they emerged in the middle of the gray desert, the GAV's wheels churning and spitting out a plume of sand. The troopers on their speeders burst out of the hole and flew over the sand as swiftly as diving seabirds. Once the GAV was free, it found some speed, but Phasma called out for Brendol to stop.

"We don't know which direction we're going," she said.

He obligingly halted the vehicle, and she climbed down from the turret and walked a few steps away, looking at the sun and the area around them. There was no telling where they'd been when TB-3 had found them, nor where Terpsichore Station was by comparison. Most of the compound was buried under sand, round humps of white shining through and disappearing again as the wind swirled around it. Siv shivered, knowing they'd been underground all along.

"We were headed north before," Brendol said.

Phasma slowly turned, the wind whipping the feathers and fur around her collar. It felt strange, Siv thought, to see her leader in a smooth helmet instead of her fierce, rust-red mask. Siv wondered if the others knew her own lichen-green mask better than her face, as she sometimes felt about them. Torben was Torben, but when he wore his white mask with its black slashes and stylized horns, he became a brutal monster. Gosta was Gosta, but her dark-gray mask disappeared in the night, making her seem almost a nimble shadow with huge, white eyes. It was funny how wearing their masks hid their faces and yet somehow made them more themselves.

The helmet only made Phasma seem more like a machine. As she wandered around outside, Gosta's fingers sought Siv's where they wrapped around the edge of the seat.

"We're so far from home," the girl said, her voice going high and reminding Siv of how very young she still was.

Siv smiled, although Gosta couldn't see it under her mask. "But we're closer to our new home in the sky."

"I feel like I liked it in there. Is that wrong?"

Torben leaned over, his terrifying mask at odds with his gentle voice. "It is normal for the bird to love captivity," he said. "At least, until it longs to fly again."

"What's that mean?"

"I don't know. But my mother used to say it quite a bit when I told her I wanted to stay in the Nautilus forever. It was open for a whole week at a time, still, when I was little."

Gosta looked down, pouting. "The Con Star food was nice."

"The food was easy. Doesn't mean it was good for you." Torben handed her a bit of jerky. "This stuff's better for your teeth and your gut. Soft food makes for soft people."

As Gosta took the food with thanks, Phasma got back in the vehicle and pointed.

"We need to go that way."

"Which direction is that?" Brendol asked.

"The right one."

"And how did you calculate that?"

"She just knows," Siv said.

"You don't know where we are, and you haven't seen the smoke in days. Are you sure?"

Phasma leaned down from the turret, her leathers creaking. She pulled off her helmet and pinned Brendol with her glare. "I would stake my life on it. I *am* staking my life on it. If you want to find your ship and your people, we go this way. If you want to die on Parnassos, choose your own direction."

Brendol considered it, chewing his lip for just a moment, unsure. He now wore a thick jacket with a furred hood Phasma had brought from the storage room, as well as Gosta's old pair of goggles. If another skinwolf went for him, at least he'd have some protection. For the first time, he wore a thick line of oracle salve over each cheek. Siv considered warning him to cover the rest of his skin before he got burned, but she didn't want Brendol Hux to give her that stare of his, the one that suggested he had just added someone's name to an enemies list.

"Well, then," he said. "We'll go your way."

But the way he said it suggested that he considered it a losing bet, and if things went wrong Phasma would suffer. In truth, if she was wrong they would all suffer—and die. Both hands on the wheel, Brendol turned the vehicle in the direction the Scyre warrior had indicated. Phasma put her helmet back on and climbed back into the turret, and the next leg of their journey began.

TWENTY

ON THE *ABSOLUTION*

"WHY DID YOU STOP?" CARDINAL ASKS. HE'S BEEN STARING AT HER SO intently that Vi knows she's doing a good job. However he feels about Phasma, he's just as fascinated by her story as Vi is.

"Because my throat is as dry as the gray sands of Parnassos." She licks her parched lips and, for just a moment, lets the pounding head-ache subsume her, lets Cardinal see what very bad shape she's in. The stims help, but they also make her muscles more tense, and she can't stop the trembling.

Frustration written in every line of his face, Cardinal holds out the drink, and she lips the straw and drinks deeply. She wonders, briefly, if the water might contain sedatives or some other First Order special addition—not that it would stop her from drinking. But considering the needs of an entire ship this big—hundreds of thousands of people—surely the water contains vitamins and nutrients, probably medicines. A little boost to morale, a little softening of the chemicals to keep alert brains from coming fully awake and rioting. Or worse— questioning. Vi knows more than a little about how the new breed of stormtroopers are trained, and not the part where Cardinal teaches them how to wield weapons, as friendly to the children as a favorite uncle.

No, the young recruits are plugged into their beds like datapads downloading new information. Gentle, droning voices at night fill their heads with sayings, propaganda, warnings, reminders that the First Order is the only answer, the only way to save the galaxy from itself, from destruction. Armitage Hux grew up at the Imperial Academy on Arkanis, watching his father deliver, manipulate, and program children to become killing machines. But Armitage has gone even further with his sharp theoretical knowledge of battle, crafting complex simulations that realistically replicate every aspect of combat. The children lose all sense of individuality, of self. They're never allowed to play, discouraged from laughter or frivolity or creativity, outside of how those emotions or urges can be used to win war games.

But Cardinal is fine with all that. He's a product of that system. She's not going to flip him by attacking the heart of who he is and what he stands for. No, she's got to keep drawing the story out, showing him who Phasma really is while buying herself enough time to escape in case he doesn't eventually see her point of view.

The droid beeps, reminding them both of the task at hand.

"Go on," he says. "We're running out of time."

"Don't you know a story can't be rushed?" she teases, but tiredly.

"I know the truth doesn't take nearly as long as a lie."

Vi laughs, or tries to. It ends up as a cough. He allows her another sip of water.

"Sometimes, the truth takes a while. Much like Parnassos, it doesn't care about you."

Cardinal picks up the remote, and Vi can't stop herself from flinching.

"Then care about this remote," he says. "Because Phasma will be on this ship soon, and I will have what I need before she gets here. Or else you and your brother, Baako, will have bigger problems than a little shock."

TWENTY-ONE

ON PARNASSOS, 10 YEARS AGO

THE VEHICLES EMERGED FROM THE COMPOUND IN THE AFTERNOON, WHICH gave them several hours of light to navigate by. Not that there was much to navigate. The sand was as gray and endless as ever, although there were some smaller dunes, almost like a giant body covered in a sheet, curving up here and there. As the sun set, a dark shape rose along the horizon, too far off for anyone to guess what it might be. Another compound, another dead beast, one of those destroyed cities Brendol had mentioned seeing as his ship went down—there was no telling.

Brendol stopped the vehicle on top of one of the small dunes. When Phasma's helmet turned to glare at him, he shrugged. "Riding the speeders at night isn't safe for my troops. We'll stop here and rest until dawn. Whatever that is, up ahead . . . I've a feeling we'd rather face it in the light of day."

"And if it decides to come for us first?"

Brendol gave her a level, weighing stare. "You're a warrior. You'll do what you need to do."

Phasma didn't reply, but her silence always spoke volumes. Siv knew well enough that Phasma would've kept going until the vehicle died, then walked the rest of the way. It was odd, seeing her proud leader bend to the will of another, especially one who would obviously lose should the two enter any sort of combat. It had to be like the arrangement Phasma had with her brother, Keldo, Siv reasoned: So long as it served her, Phasma recognized and yielded to a cannier mind, or at least one that fulfilled a purpose hers couldn't.

They'd brought supplies from the Terpsichore Station lockers, neatly packed tents and metallic blankets that held heat and protected the sleeper from sand—and, hopefully, beetles. As they arranged their pallets in a circle formed of the speeders and the hulking vehicle, Siv settled her blanket close to Torben. It always made her feel safer, being near his big, comfortable bulk.

"What if there are more droids?" Gosta asked. "Or what if the old ones wake back up?"

"Don't be ridiculous," Brendol said, although she hadn't directly asked him in particular. "Droids can't reactivate themselves any more than a dead person can get up and start walking around. Terpsichore Station is, for all conclusive purposes, lost."

"But there could be other stations," Siv said, and Gosta gave her a thankful smile.

Phasma regarded her warriors, her helmet close to her side on the ground. "We could spend all night talking about the things that we fear may come to pass, but I'd rather eat and sleep. If something is coming, we'll fight it, but there's no point in inviting trouble. Life here is no more dangerous than it was in the Scyre. It's simply a different kind of danger."

"It does take getting used to," Torben admitted. "All the sand. Endless nothing. Shifting, blowing, itching. At least on the rocks, you know where you stand. Nice, solid things, rocks."

No one could argue his point. For a man of more muscle than brain, he sometimes made much sense.

Siv pulled food and water out of her pack, settling in between Torben and Gosta as the troopers kept their own company in the other large tent. The structures were open on the sides, but they provided a little shelter from the constant howling of the wind. The metallic plastic flapped with each gust, but the stakes were planted deeply, thanks to yet another skill demonstrated by the troopers. Phasma and Brendol went to the vehicle, silent but secretive, and Siv wondered if perhaps they were finding comfort in each other. Phasma had not mated among the Scyre, at least not as far as Siv knew, and there was little chance for privacy among the rocks.

Thinking about better times, she leaned against Torben's shoulder as she chewed on her jerky.

That night, blessedly, nothing terrible happened. It was a rare enough thing anywhere on Parnassos.

The next morning, they woke up to a day that was already sizzling at dawn. The dark shape on the horizon had neither moved nor changed, and they all watched it as they sipped water and chewed their breakfast. They made good progress, thanks to the vehicles, and Siv had grown accustomed to rolling with the machine's movement. The monotony of the sand was a strange thing, and as they got closer and closer to the dark blot, it grew bigger and bigger. So big that it was clear it wasn't one beast or one building, but the thing Brendol called a city.

"On most habitable planets, beings gather in large groups to live together, build domiciles, and share resources," he explained. "Some planets are nothing but buildings and cities. Others have enclaves, capitals, towns, villages."

"What is this one?" Phasma asked, staring through her quadnocs.

Brendol stopped the vehicle, held out one hand, and wiggled his fingers, and Phasma put the quadnocs in his palm. He frowned as he looked back and forth, left to right.

"A city, but a primitive one. What worries me is that bit in the middle, standing high over everything else."

"What's so bad about that?" Gosta asked.

Brendol pulled down the quadnocs to stare at the girl disdainfully. "When everything is at one level except for one building, that generally means one of two things, neither one good. The first possibility is a church representing a religion that seeks to reach some silly god in the sky, and the second is a king or despot desperate to maintain his holdings. Either way, you've got someone with resources who thinks they're superior to the people they rule. There is no greater enemy to justice than a little king on a little hill."

Phasma wordlessly reached for the quadnocs and looked again as she chewed her jerky. "Does your First Order not seek to rule, then? Yet you seem to be opposed to ruling."

Brendol grunted. "There is a difference. The First Order wishes to bring equality to all and destroy the petty politics and rotten bureaucracy that plague the galaxy. I speak of an enlightened government of thousands of people, working on behalf of billions of unenlightened people. In a place like this, however, the decisions are being made by one person only, or perhaps a small handful of wealthy despots. And their first interest is in lining their own pockets and maintaining their golden lifestyles."

Siv watched him silently. Something told her that Brendol was either concealing some truth or directly lying, but she wasn't about to challenge him. His words were too pretty, his stated motives too pure. Even though Siv couldn't read Phasma's face through her helmet, she could tell her leader likewise was not convinced.

"And so what does the First Order do with such little kings?" Phasma asked.

Brendol stared over the sand as if he could see straight to the heart of the city.

"We destroy them," he answered.

Phasma put down her quadnocs. The way she looked from each member of her party, to their gear, then back to the city beyond told Siv that she was making plans. Her warriors were familiar with this look, as it generally signaled a new strategy.

"We need to go around it," she finally said. "Way around it. We have all the supplies we require. Whoever lives there will only keep us from our goals."

"May I see?" Siv held out her hand for the quadnocs.

Phasma gave her the 'nocs, along with a sharp nod that suggested any questions she had had better be intelligent. Siv often helped Phasma with her plans and only participated in the discussion when she was sure her ideas were good. This time, she looked, and what the quadnocs revealed was startling.

"What's all the green?" she asked. Because green was everywhere, and not the dusty green of lichen, but a vibrant and poisonous green. To the naked eye, the city appeared like a wavering black smudge, but the 'nocs showed green walls outside, green buildings inside, more green than Siv had ever seen in her entire life, which had heretofore included only the green lines in Terpsichore Station, a few people's eyes, and some ancient artifacts and gems hidden in the Nautilus. The greenest things in the Scyre were grayish mosses and sea veg on the verge of black.

"Green means plants." Brendol drank his water, more than a Scyre would, and wiped the excess from his mouth as if it were unimportant. "They call it an oasis. A green place in the middle of the desert. There's usually an underground spring, or perhaps the pool where a river ends. Sometimes, those who wander in the desert too long imagine such a place and stumble to their death chasing a shimmering dream that isn't really there."

"But it's there."

"It is, yes."

"They must be very rich," Gosta said. "With that much water."

Phasma scoffed. "Who cares about their riches? Everything we need is in Brendol's ship, and getting there before anyone else can is our first priority. What do we want with some green city? It's still on Parnassos. The planet is still dying. Nothing else good has lasted here. Within ten years, even that spring will dry up, and the plants will wither and die, the people along with them. That city is nothing but a corpse that doesn't know it's dead yet."

Torben put a hand up to his mask to shield his eyes from the sun. "Left or right, then?"

"Left," Brendol said.

Just as Phasma said, "Right."

The hot air grew tense. No one said anything. The troopers hovered nearby on their speeder bikes, gently drifting back and forth.

"Why do you think left?" Phasma asked.

"Because of our angle in relation to the city. It seems a slightly shorter route."

"I say right because we won't have to correct so far to reach your ship."

The troopers must've sensed the disturbance, as they rode their speeders closer, their hands on their blasters. Torben exhaled and adjusted the weapons at his hips. Gosta had hopped off the vehicle to stand, and her fingers danced over her new blaster, her eyes unwavering on Phasma.

"Splitting up is a bad idea," Siv ventured.

Phasma didn't move a muscle. Even with her mask, it was clear she was staring at the city, her sharp mind considering every gambit.

"Left, then," Phasma said.

The Scyre folk relaxed, but Siv was stunned. She and Torben locked eyes, and she shrugged. They'd never seen their leader give in so easily. Not even to Keldo. Still, they knew better than to question her. Once she'd made her proclamation in that voice, you went with her or you were left behind. And being left behind here meant certain death.

"Let's be off, then," Brendol said, and he did sound satisfied.

No one else had left the vehicle, but Gosta seemed reluctant to get back in. The girl seemed fascinated and charmed by the speeder bikes, or possibly by the troopers who rode them.

Phasma noticed Gosta skulking closer to the speeder and called to her.

"Gosta! Pull your weight."

"I was wondering if it would be possible for me to ride on the speeder with Elli," Gosta said, trying to sound brave and bold. "It would be good, if another one of us knew how to ride. In case we lose someone."

Phasma, again, looked to Brendol.

"I have no quarrel with the idea," he said. "Although the girl can't simply make up silly nicknames as if my troopers are pets. She's correct, though: We must plan on losing people. It's a long journey yet. LE-2003 can teach the girl. Let's take a break before we continue."

As Siv distributed sips of water and strips of meat, she surreptitiously watched the youngest Scyre warrior interact with Elli. Siv had taken little notice of the troopers: Except for the rare times they removed their helmets—and their brief stay in the Con Star mining facility—they seemed completely identical, other than very slight expressions of build or height. They mostly kept to themselves, and Brendol frowned on them showing too much personality or being too casual in their manners. Still, Elli didn't seem terrible, and she was pointing to parts of the speeder bike as Gosta, grinning like a fool, straddled the seat. Siv's mother had told her stories of her own childhood, and a big feature had been that children had once had freedom to play and time to do nothing. In the Scyre these days, everyone worked from the moment they were able, even if the only work was flapping a stick at birds to keep them away from drying meat or sea veg, a job Frey had done as a toddler strapped into a net harness securely hung from the rocks. Siv realized she'd never seen Gosta smile like this before—her expression open and unguarded and her eyes alight.

Putting a hand to her belly, Siv lifted up a prayer that they would get to Brendol's ship alive and intact. She'd told no one her own secret yet, as most children ended in blood before they began, but she had more reason than most to wish for miracle transport off the tomb Parnassos was swiftly becoming.

As they finished their meal, the Scyre folk paused to watch Gosta take her first short trip on the speeder bike, zooming over the dunes and laughing with joy. It was a lovely moment, and one Siv still treasures. Especially after what happened later.

"We haven't got all day," Brendol barked, and they peeled their

eyes away from the spectacle and climbed into the vehicle to continue their trip around the green city. They'd taken turns sitting in the
turret by the passenger seat, which was mounted with the heaviest
gun Siv had seen yet, something that Brendol called "disturbingly
destructive." So far, they hadn't used it, but he had tested it, briefly,
and the way it spit fire into the sand was impressive. When they'd
gone out to see the damage, it had been a good five minutes' walk to
the scorch marks, where they'd dug up twisted lightning bolts of
cloudy gray glass. Brendol explained that the laser was so hot that it
had melted the sand, and Phasma had taken more turns in the turret
than anyone else despite the heat caused by its protective overhead
dome.

She rode there now, her helmet on and her hand wrapped around
the massive gun's grip. When Siv looked to her leader, she felt reas-
sured that they would accomplish their goal. Hope was a new feeling
for her, and without Gosta in the backseat, she took the chance to
curl her fingers around Torben's and lean her head against the reassuring warmth of his shoulder. Feeling safe was also unusual, and she
wanted to enjoy it for as long as she could.

Brendol steered left to give the city a wide berth. Phasma made no
further comment, merely swung her gun around to face the nearing
green wall. Siv didn't like the look of the plants, which the quadnocs
showed to be long vines twisting with wide, green leaves and peppered with tiny pink flowers. Two of the speeder bikes zoomed ahead,
keeping point at the front left and right of the GAV but with plenty of
room between them. The last speeder stayed in back, protecting them
from the rear. As Siv watched Gosta's hair fly out behind her, the girl's
arms wrapped around Elli's middle as they caromed over the gray
sand, something caught her attention just ahead of the speeders. She
didn't know what it was, couldn't identify what made her call out.

"Stop! That thing—"

Brendol had just started to bark, "What?" when Elli's speeder
tipped, nose-first, and disappeared into the sand, throwing the
trooper and Gosta into the air.

"PT-2445, pull up!" Brendol shouted into the comm on his wrist as he braked the GAV hard, sending up a shower of sand when it slid to a halt.

The remaining speeder bike skidded sideways and spun to a stop, Pete's boots landing on the ground in a puff of gray. He immediately leapt off the speeder and ran for where Elli was sprawled in the sand. Before he could reach her, he disappeared completely.

"PT-2445, report!"

"There's a ditch, sir. Full of spikes. I fell between them, luckily. Didn't break anything. LE-2003's speeder is down here, along with . . . damn. Dozens of vehicles. And bodies. Old bones on the spikes."

"HF-0518, you heard him. Move ahead with caution. Get PT-2445 out of that ditch."

Phasma dropped down out of the turret.

"Siv, take the gun. I'm going to get Gosta."

Siv nodded and climbed up; a wave of heat swept over her from the plastic bubble, but she ignored it as she scrambled into the seat and scanned the area where Elli and Gosta had fallen. Gosta was sitting up now, her mask off, rubbing a bloody place in her hair and looking confused.

"I'm going with Phasma," Torben said.

Phasma bounded down from the GAV, a blaster in one hand and her ax in the other. Torben followed her, his club and ax ready, as if he'd completely forgotten the blaster in a holster at his belt. Brendol sat behind the wheel, Siv noted, and although he barked commands into his wrist comm, he didn't so much as put a hand on his door.

As she gripped the gun in trembling hands and tried to focus on her people through the haze of heat and sand, something flashed in the clear, shiny plastic overhead. By the time she'd spun around in the turret, it was too late.

"Brendol—we're being attacked from behind!"

She couldn't see what was happening with Phasma, but Torben told her about it, later. Phasma ran to the ditch and leapt over it, barely making it across and scrabbling out on the other side in the slippery sand. When Torben tried to follow her, he wasn't able to complete the jump; he was big and bulky, and Phasma was lighter and faster. He tumbled down into the sand, sliding between the spikes and landing among the bones and rusted metal hulks of ancient vehicles. When he spotted Pete reaching out of the pit toward Huff's outstretched glove, Torben ran and boosted Pete up so he could clamber out. But when Torben held up his own hand for help out of the trench, the stormtroopers had already left. He was alone in the pit, which was too deep for him to climb out of without aid.

"Phasma!" Torben called. "I'm trapped down here. Is Gosta safe?"

"Minor head wound," Phasma called back. "She'll live. Is there anything down there that you can use to get out?"

Torben shielded his eyes and scouted around.

"Their speeder bike. It's still a little . . . floaty."

"So ride it out."

"It's not *that* floaty."

"Lift it up to me, then."

Phasma appeared at the opposite side of the ditch, and Torben obligingly hefted the speeder until its pointy nose hovered within Phasma's reach.

"We need to make a bridge out of it," she explained.

Together they maneuvered the hobbled speeder so that it spanned the pit, the nose on one side and the rear on the other.

"Support it from the bottom while I take her across," Phasma said, for the ditch went so far in either direction that she couldn't just go around it. The trap was meant to catch everything that came near, but they learned more about that later.

Torben knew his role: He was the muscle. He'd been trained from birth to maximize his strengths to help his people. So he moved to the belly of the speeder and held it steady, supporting it from below.

"Ready?" Phasma asked.

"What, you want to wait awhile?"

As he held up the speeder bike, Phasma appeared at the edge with a now unconscious Gosta draped over her arms, the girl's head bleeding freely. Torben strained to hold the speeder steady as Phasma ran across it with what Siv called superhuman agility, carrying the younger girl. Once Phasma was across, she stopped.

"Now use the speeder bike to climb out on this side. I have to get her to safety." She looked toward the GAV and went stiff. "We're under attack. Hurry."

And then she was gone. Torben did as she'd commanded, heaving half of the speeder bike against the side of the pit like a ladder and climbing up it to get out. When he landed on the surface above, he heard the ongoing battle and pushed to his feet, racing back to where Siv was fighting.

As for Siv, she finally got to feel the destructive power of the GAV's gun. The attacking force comprised several GAVs just like theirs, each one branded with the same Con Star Mining Corporation logo. But the vehicles had been embellished with spikes and chains, turned from simple surveying machines into fighting monsters, much as the Scyre warriors transformed themselves into beasts with claws and feathers.

Siv managed to hit the first GAV in the approaching line, and it flew into the air, flipping several times before landing in a spectacular explosion. But before she could cheer, she felt the entire GAV around her rock from an enemy hit. Her hands slipped from the gun, and her head knocked against the plastic bubble, stunning her.

"Hold on."

That was Brendol. He put their GAV into gear, turned a sharp left, and floored it. Siv's turret spun around, and she struggled to stay focused and figure out where to point the gun. She soon realized that Brendol wasn't going to help any of their people; he was making a sharper left into the desert, speeding away from the city and the ditch. He didn't comm his people, didn't attempt to fight, didn't try to save anyone.

He just ran.

The other vehicles gave pursuit, and although Siv aimed her gun and pulled the trigger, she didn't see the same success as her first hit.

The turret jiggled her everywhere, and she was starting to feel sick to her stomach. She lost track of Torben and Phasma. One of the attacking vehicles ran over a speeder bike, breaking it like a child's toy.

"We have to go back!" she shouted. "They need us! We'll lose them all!"

"Wrong. We have to get away. To my ship. We can't help them now."

Siv roared her anger—this was not how life was lived in the Scyre. Every body was necessary, every person had a particular job. What a different place Brendol must have been from, if he was willing to abandon his people and run for his life. And what a conscience he must have possessed, to know he could live with such a decision and just go on with his days instead of being crushed by shame and regret.

Even in her condition, even knowing how badly they were overpowered, Siv almost scrambled down from the turret and leapt from the GAV to hurry back to Torben and Phasma and Gosta. But she didn't get a chance. The vehicle suddenly slammed to a stop in a huge burst of sand.

"What happened?"

"We hit something!"

At that, Siv did hurry down, and the moment she was in the passenger seat, she found a ragged spear point firmly held in front of her face. Brendol had his hands up, so she put her hands up, too. The attackers were strange, clad only in colorful, finely woven clothes like the ones the Scyre folk kept stored in the Nautilus as sacred relics. No armor, no masks. But every centimeter of skin was covered by cloth, down to thin gloves on their hands. Their heads were wrapped in long swaths of the vibrant fabrics, only their eyes showing.

"Get out. Don't try anything," the one she assumed was the leader said. His words had a strange accent, but it was closer to what she was used to than the way Brendol spoke. "We already have your other people, so don't bother trying to be heroes. Yet."

It was a baffling thing to say, but Siv didn't have time to consider it. Someone opened her door, and she slid down from the GAV, landing in a puff of sand. They slapped battered plastic binders on her wrists and searched her to remove all her weapons. On the other side of the vehicle, Brendol was undergoing the same treatment, his face red with growing fury. Two more groups of brightly dressed strangers joined them, bringing Pete and Huff in chains, seemingly unharmed, and dragging an unconscious Elli.

"And the others?" the leader asked one of his people.

"Still fighting."

"Are they winning?"

The woman chuckled. "They will. We always do."

"Arratu!" the leader shouted, shaking his spear and howling at the sky.

"Arratu!" the others answered, taking up the manic shriek.

Brendol looked beyond disgusted. "Madness," he muttered.

"Shall we watch, then?" the leader asked his people.

The only answer was another cheer. Siv was roughly turned with the others to face a wide spread of sand. Phasma and Torben were fighting back-to-back, Gosta's prone body on the sand between them. Phasma had her blaster in one hand and her ax in the other, and judging by the colorful, unmoving lumps in the sand, she'd already taken down two fighters on her side of the field. Torben twirled his ax and spiked club and had three bodies littering his side. As Siv watched, Phasma winged one of her attackers in the arm with a blaster bolt, then spun and caught him across the chest with her blade, kicking him in the stomach as he fell. The ring of attackers stepped back, uncertain.

Torben roared, and Siv knew what would come next and smiled to herself. With a fatal weapon in each hand, he ran into the circle of assailants and spun with an elegant grace no one would've expected from so big a man, hacking bodies across the gut and leaving a circle of blood. The sand bubbled up with a volcano of beetles, and Siv cried, "Torben! Back away!"

When Torben looked up at her, his face stricken—that's when they got him.

The attackers threw a net over him, pinning him to the ground. As he stood to toss it off, someone jerked it, and it narrowed around his ankles, tripping him.

The leader, standing between Siv and Brendol, laughed heartily.

"Even the mighty fall before the will of Arratu," he bellowed.

Phasma was the only one still up, and she hadn't slowed her assault. She'd wing one of the assailants with her blaster, then hit them somewhere mortal while they were still in shock. Looking around, Siv realized that these people weren't really fighting or using their blasters. They all carried guns, and they had the huge weapons mounted on the GAVs, but they seemed more interested in watching the show than protecting one another.

This, then, wasn't an attack or raid like one of Balder's, not a risky bid trading lives for resources. Whoever these people were, they wanted bodies. People. Even great Torben, who had killed so many of them, hadn't been harmed or punished. And yet they didn't seem to mind watching their own people die and thus far had lost at least a dozen, for all that they had fifty more just standing around, watching.

"What do you want with us?" Siv asked the leader.

"Wait and see, little sand flea," he said. "For now, let's watch the show."

Phasma's fight was valiant, extraordinary, and bloody. She used the blaster like she'd been born with one in her hand, showing unerring aim, even without the ability to stop and carefully focus her shots. She was adept at maiming an enemy and then perfectly timing the killing shot. One of the men went down in two pieces, bisected across the stomach, and much to Siv's surprise, the leader behind her just laughed his booming laugh.

"Justinian was always a bit tall, wasn't he?" he shouted.

The more Siv watched, the more disgusted she became. Whatever these people wanted, it wasn't as pure and true as what the Scyre wanted. They weren't fighting to live, to eat, to hold on to vital land. They weren't fighting to defend their elderly and young from attackers. They seemed to be fighting for entertainment only, a vile blasphemy to Siv's mind.

"I grow bored," the leader said. "Tell Seylon to end it."

The woman he'd spoken to nodded and darted off across the sand on huge, wide shoes that kicked up puffs of gray. Whatever she said when she reached the clot of people circling Phasma had the desired effect. A big man split off from the group and held up a long spear, which crackled with what looked like lightning. As three other assailants taunted Phasma from the other side, he casually poked her with the spear, and crackles of electricity wreathed her body and helmet. Phasma went stiff and fell over backward, flopping on the ground, her body rigid and slightly smoking.

"Package them up and let's hurry home before the next storm. The Arratu will be pleased."

The leader walked calmly to a GAV and took his seat while the rest of the group poked, prodded, and hurried along the captives. When Phasma stopped sparking, Seylon threw another net over her, dragged her away, and hefted her into a GAV, tossing her fallen helmet in behind her. Brendol and Siv were kept together, ushered into a spike-covered GAV that smelled of strange spices.

"See?" Brendol whispered to Siv as she watched Torben, now out of his net and forced to carry Gosta. The girl was still unconscious, and Torben draped her across the backseat of another GAV. "I told you. Whatever the Arratu is, it will live in the highest building, and whatever it wants will cost us more than we're willing to give. You can bet on that."

Siv didn't like Brendol Hux, and she didn't trust him, but she suspected that on this occasion, he was right.

She wasn't looking forward to finding out what the Arratu really was.

TWENTY-TWO

ON PARNASSOS, 10 YEARS AGO

RIDING IN THE ENEMY'S GAV, SIV QUICKLY BEGAN TO FEEL ILL. INSTEAD OF driving relatively straight, as Brendol had, the driver swerved this way and that and plunged up and down the small dunes like he had a death wish. Her stomach roiled, and she realized this was farther than she'd ever been from another Scyre member. The band was a family, and she was stuck here with Brendol Hux, who was hunched down as far from her on the seat as he could get, sulky and glaring.

At first Siv felt as if she were getting feverish, her skin alternating from hot to cold, but then she realized that the sky was growing dark. When a storm came to the Scyre, everyone quickly found a stable place to ride it out, making sure their lines were hitched to steady spikes, as the oil-slick rains and buffeting winds could easily knock a person off a rock spire. On the best days, they huddled in the Nautilus, in the corners away from the hole in the ceiling that gushed toxic rain, even when they put a woven cap over it. On the worst days, the Nautilus was full of raging water, and they hunkered down in the miserable, stinging, sputtering rain with no cover and no way to avoid random lightning strikes and cruel, cutting winds. Siv and Torben had a rock they liked, a bigger sort of spire that could almost hold them both comfortably as they huddled under a protective hide.

But this storm was strange. The air didn't feel heavy and wet and thick. It felt hot and sucking and sparking, and when the leader, now driving Brendol's old GAV, shouted something into the wind, Siv's driver accelerated even harder, making her put a hand over her mouth under the mask to keep the sick in and the sand out. It wasn't long before they were approaching the city head-on, and Siv had trouble grasping how very large it was. Bigger than the Scyre and Claw territories put together, bigger than Terpsichore Station. The wall had to be the height of ten people and was solidly covered in those dangerous-looking plants. Just when Siv was sure they were going to splatter against it, a door slid open, just wide enough to allow the GAVs entry. Although the wall had appeared entirely solid from the outside, apparently the vines hid their own secrets.

Once they were inside, the city was beyond overwhelming for a woman who had only ever known perhaps a hundred people by name in her entire life. It was so crowded with people hurrying to and fro that one of their brightly clad captors had to get out of Siv's GAV and shove people out of the way with a long, colorful stick covered in bells, calling, "Clear the streets! The Arratu's orders!"

The people were of all ages, some so old that Siv was fascinated by their stooped bodies, wrinkles, and gray hair. In the Scyre, few people lived past thirty-five. But like the Scyre, this place had few babies or small children; the majority of the population seemed to be in their older teens and twenties, the strongest and most robust ages.

The next thing she noticed was that the people seemed to be of two different sorts: gaunt and raggedly dressed or large and decked out in swaths of vibrant fabric and layers of gold jewelry. She'd never seen bodies carrying so much extra flesh, and it did not escape her that the larger and wealthier folk seemed far happier than their skinny neighbors. Everyone was running to shelter, glancing up worriedly at the darkening sky.

When Siv looked to Brendol, a question in her eyes, he shook his head disapprovingly. "I told you. The people who live up high have too much, and the people who scrape in the dirt are starving. Over-indulgence and suffering with no in-between, no thought for the city's welfare. This world needs the First Order."

"What can be done for them?" Siv asked.

Brendol raised a feathery red eyebrow. "They must be ruled by someone with a firmer hand."

But he didn't go into any further detail, and one of the captors poked him with a stick.

"Don't be talking like that where the Rats can hear you," she murmured. "You won't last long, making threats like that."

Brendol looked at the woman, whose face was baked a beautiful sandy brown that Siv had never seen before. She had pulled down the cloth that had previously covered her nose and mouth, and her light gray eyes were lined in deep black.

"What's to be done with us?" Brendol asked her.

She gave an elegant shrug. "Not mine to say."

"But we're not guests."

The woman smiled, showing dimples. "Oh, no. You'd have to earn that, first."

The driver grunted. "Hush. Don't give them ideas."

And then their captors went silent, which was disconcerting. Although Siv was accustomed to enemies, they'd always struck violently, never wasting time and resources on adult captives whose hearts couldn't be turned, as a child's could. Whatever these people wanted from them—well, Brendol was right. Siv didn't want to give it.

To take her mind off her concerns, she turned her attention to the wonders of the city. Since the Nautilus held so many artifacts, and since she'd spent time at Terpsichore Station, Siv knew a little more about the world that had once been. The structures in the city—those were buildings, where people would live and work. The structures, though—they were so close and tall and crowded together that there was barely enough room for the GAVs to pass between them. The paved ground they were on—that was a road. And up ahead, she recognized a building similar to the orientation disk's images of Terpsichore Station before the planet had gone strange. But this city had other structures built up around and atop the old station, making it the base of the highest building in the center of the city, the one that Brendol had so many thoughts about.

"Who lives up there?" he asked, arms crossed. "Your god or your king?"

In response, their captor pointed a blaster at him and growled, "Do not speak ill of the Arratu."

"Sounds like both," Brendol murmured, barely loud enough to be heard. The woman glared daggers at him but didn't shoot him, although she looked like she sorely wanted to.

Another curious thing Siv noticed as they slowly navigated the crowds was the proliferation of plants and greenery. They were atop every roof, hanging from every window, and lining every wall in colorful containers. Vines snaked across the roads, bare of leaves where they'd been ripped off by passersby but budding again as they dug into the sides of buildings and climbed closer to the sun. There were creatures in the plants that Siv didn't quite understand, things flying about that weren't anything like the seabirds and bugs in the Scyre. Small and delicate as gems, they buzzed here and there, dipping into the plants and smacking against one another with a pleasing thump before moving on.

"What are they?" she asked as they passed near a plant covered with blooms, each one surrounded by the jewel-bright creatures.

"Squeeps," the woman said with a brief smile before hardening her expression and returning to silence.

"Why do the starving people not eat them?" Brendol asked.

The woman aimed her blaster at Brendol again and shook her head. "Is everything you say blasphemous?"

Brendol's eyebrows rose, but he wisely looked away and didn't pursue the conversation further.

The sky was almost black now, the wind whipping sand into Siv's eyes under her mask. The air felt electric and uncontrollable, and the streets were empty. Finally, the GAVs reached the building that re-sembled a Con Star Mining Corporation station, although it looked nothing like the images Siv had seen on the screen at Terpsichore. This structure had been painted in bright pigments and was covered in vines. The sliding doors were open, showing a yawning white hall-way that made Siv's skin crawl. Naturally, they drove straight into it. Once within, the driver parked the GAV in a long row with other vehicles likewise decorated to look dangerous, and Siv recognized a room much like the one where they'd found the speeder bikes. A hangar. Each of the GAVs plugged into the wall, and there was a gen-tle hum of machinery. Brendol, for all his sullenness, had a sharp look about him as he took in the room, and Siv wished she had some idea of what he was thinking. She was pretty sure he was developing a plan. Among the Scyre, plans hadn't been something kept secret from the warriors. If even one person didn't know what to do in case of emergency, things tended to fall apart. But Brendol was crafty and strange, and once again she was reminded that something about him didn't sit well with her.

"Barely made it," the leader crowed, hitting the button that closed the hallway door. The howling of the windstorm stopped, and the room went unnaturally silent.

"Out," their captor said, blaster pointed at Brendol, as if she didn't even consider Siv a threat.

Brendol hopped down, followed first by their captor, then Siv. No matter which way she moved, blasters pointed in her face. After so much time spent on hot, shifting sand, it was strange to stand on the cold, hard floor, and she wobbled for a moment, trying to regain her footing.

"Walk," the woman said, nudging Siv in the back with the blaster. That, too, was a new experience. Having grown up with a cache of old, broken blasters in the Nautilus, Siv wasn't accustomed to think-ing of the small, blunt, harmless-looking machines as a real threat. But when the woman nudged her again, she moved in the direction indicated.

Brendol was already walking, his head turning this way and that, up and down. They were soon joined by the others, and Siv felt a profound sense of relief to be near Torben and Gosta and Phasma again. The stormtroopers fell in step behind Brendol, carrying poor Elli between them. Siv couldn't tell if the woman was breathing or not; she hung between her fellow troopers, limp and unconscious. Gosta was awake but still in Torben's arms, and Phasma, clearly dazed from being shocked, was having trouble walking in a straight line. When Torben's arm touched her own, Siv smiled slightly, but she knew where she was needed, so she bumped against him in a telling way and hurried to help Phasma.

Now, the Scyre were a people who enjoyed physical touch and comfort, considering that they faced a cold, unpredictable, cruel life. But Phasma had always held herself apart. Siv trusted Phasma with her life and knew she was the most talented strategist and the fiercest fighter on the planet, but that didn't mean Siv was just going to walk up and put an arm around the staggering fighter. Even then, there was an aura around Phasma, almost like an animal's unspoken warning to keep a distance.

"What do you need?" she asked, walking at Phasma's side and holding out one arm to show it was available to be grasped.

"My helmet and my eyesight," Phasma snapped. "My vision is blurry. And my fingertips are . . . burnt. Numb."

But she didn't take Siv's arm, so Siv let it fall back to her side and merely walked slightly closer to her leader than she normally would, ready to catch her if she fell.

"No talking," one of the captors said, waving one of the electric sticks. He looked like he had a temper, so Siv stopped talking.

As soon as they left the hangar and entered a hallway, the station became eerily similar to Terpsichore, with the same smooth white walls and floors and cold, bluish lighting. Siv saw no droids, though, and she did notice some changes in the layout. Wide windows opened on busily working machines, and although they were being marched quickly along, Siv saw that many of the machines appeared to be making or manipulating the bright fabrics everyone in the city wore.

She realized they were following a green line on the wall, so she wasn't surprised when the next door their captor opened led to barracks. The room was quite similar to the one at Terpsichore Station, but it held twice as many beds and was occupied by at least thirty people. Most of them were thin to the point of emaciation. That didn't bode well, Siv thought.

"Hands out," the leader said.

One by one, he unlocked their binders and shoved his prisoners into the room, all while the man with the sneer and the electric prod blocked the exit.

"What about Gosta and Elli?" Siv asked as soon as she was free. The leader shrugged at her, so she added, "The women who were hurt?"

He shrugged. "Not my problem. They'll get better or they won't, as the Arratu wills it."

"But what do we do?" Brendol asked as the leader turned to leave.

"You do the only thing you can do," the man said, his eyes twinkling. "You wait for the gods to shine on you and hope you don't die."

Their captors left, laughing, and the Scyre and First Order folk were left to deal with an entire room full of strangers, none of whom looked friendly.

"Fresh meat," someone murmured.

Despite her injury and the fact that she'd been stripped of her weapons and helmet, Phasma's posture changed, subtly shifting into a fighting stance.

"Not for you," she growled.

And then they charged her.

TWENTY-THREE

ON PARNASSOS, 10 YEARS AGO

LUCKILY, IT WAS THE GAUNT ONES WHO ATTACKED. TORBEN GENTLY PLACED Gosta on the ground and prepared for the onslaught, and Siv bared her teeth and screamed. The first person who reached Phasma was a man so thin they could see every bone pressing angrily through skin. Phasma didn't wait for him; she head-butted him and threw him aside. Taking her lead, Torben batted their attackers away like they were made of kindling, and they crumpled and rolled across the hard floor, moaning. Siv waded in, fists flying, and discovered the strange sensation of beating people who were too exhausted to fight.

"Stop this instantly!" Phasma called as one of the fallen men reached for her from the ground.

"D'you have any food?" he asked.

"They're still strong," another one added.

"Won't last long," someone else said, deeper into the room.

Brendol and his troopers stood behind the Scyre folk. The troopers had put Elli down beside Gosta, but Brendol hadn't given them the command to fight, and no one had yet threatened him, so they merely stood, waiting. Now that the other prisoners had stopped attacking, Brendol stepped forward, pushing past Torben to stand at Phasma's side.

"Someone explain this place to us."

A short, bearded man in a long-sleeved robe who still had some muscle about him hopped off a top bunk and strutted over as if he owned the place.

"This is Arratu Station," he said, his voice dramatically pitched to fill the room. "Once the leading supplier of fabrics, recyclamesh, and tarpaulins for the Con Star Mining Corporation's operations on Parnassos. You know what happened. It all went to hell. And we're what's left behind."

Brendol flicked his fingers at the man. "Get to the point."

"This is a prison."

"We know. But what do they want of us? To merely suffer? Because I suspect something more."

The short man crossed his arms and smirked. He wore a draped crimson robe like the soft people outside, the fabric wrinkled and worn but still vibrant in comparison with anything in the Scyre besides freshly spilled blood.

"There are too many people here," he said simply. "Not enough food, not enough room. So we serve the Arratu and hope for his favor."

"And what does the Arratu ask?" Brendol pressed.

The man walked to one of the skeletal prisoners on the floor, still creeping toward Phasma although she'd proven beyond a doubt that it was an idea doomed to fail.

"If you're troublesome, he wishes you to suffer in an amusing fashion. If you're interesting, he wishes to be entertained. So I ask you, my drab friend. Are you troublesome or entertaining?"

Brendol huffed a sigh and glanced around the room as if he'd expected something better.

"I am bored."

"So is the Arratu. So I'd suggest you find a way to be entertaining." The man kicked the crawling prisoner, who fell over with a listless grunt. "Because the suffering doesn't look so pleasant. Everyone has a chance to earn food and possibly freedom, but the Arratu is picky, and those who don't delight him don't eat. They clear these poor souls out once a week." He grinned through yellow teeth. "The soup's always extra good that day. I'm Vrod, by the way." He held up both hands, letting the sleeves of his robes fall down. His left hand was entirely whitish pink, while the rest of him was warm brown. "Vrod of the White Hand, they call me. I'm lucky. I always amuse the Arratu, which is why I'm in charge of this prison full of arena fodder. Your time will come soon. Let us hope you find your own gift quickly."

With that, Vrod turned and walked to the door. When he barked a command, it slid open, and he sauntered out. The moment he was gone, the room's original occupants focused once more on the newcomers.

"I am General Brendol Hux," Brendol shouted, loud enough for anyone to hear. "We have no food. It was all stolen by your oppressors. But I warn you now: We are trained warriors. Trouble us, and you will suffer even more than this." He nodded to one of his troopers, who stepped to the half-dead figure on the floor at Phasma's feet and pressed his boot down until a loud crunch echoed in the still air.

Around the room, heads nodded in understanding—and respect. Siv was horrified, both at the prison and that Brendol had encouraged one of his men to murder someone who was already half dead. Perhaps it was a mercy killing, but the dramatic snap of bone suggested a more sinister intent. Looking at the two troopers now, Siv couldn't even tell which one was responsible for the act. Gosta shouted, and Siv turned to find one of the gaunt men grabbing for the injured girl's hand as she lay on the floor, floundering.

"Torben!" Siv motioned for the big warrior to help their friend, and he lunged to kick the man away and swing Gosta back up into his arms.

"We need a bed," he noted.

Phasma was still somewhat dazed, and Siv almost spoke for her, but Brendol stepped in.

"There."

The bunk beds he pointed at held five prisoners, so thin that they could squeeze in two up top and three on the bottom, even though the cots were made to fit only one. Siv quickly realized that it would be easy enough to evict these weak prisoners, but particularly cruel. Still, she was a woman of the Scyre, and Gosta and Elli needed a safe, defendable place. Pete and Huff were already headed toward the bunk, everything about their posture and gait suggesting that the people in the bed should get out before they were forced out, which they did, slithering down to the ground as if they didn't have the energy or strength to stand. Siv felt bad, watching them crawl away, but at least Brendol let them live.

Torben carefully placed Gosta on the top bunk, and Siv crawled up to sit beside the younger girl. There was an animal comfort in feeling the warmth of a friend's flesh and smelling her familiar smell. Since they'd been in the city, Siv's nose had been tormented by the scent of too many bodies combined with cloying fragrances, both layered over the sharp bite of the growing vines.

"You okay?" Siv asked as Pete and Huff put Elli in the bottom bunk.

"My head hurts, and everything feels really bright and loud, but I think I'll do."

Siv grinned at the girl's plucky spirit and elbowed her gently. "Good. We don't really need your head anyway. And this place is bright enough, so you're not alone there."

"What's going to happen, Siv?" Gosta asked. "What do they want with us?"

Siv smoothed her hair back reassuringly. "We'll find out soon enough. Until then, rest. You'll need energy for whatever's coming."

Gosta agreeably snuggled down. Siv let herself relax just a little, enjoying the bed's padding after the bone-jarring ride in the GAV. Her nausea had stopped, for all that she was ravenously hungry. Nothing could be done about that. She settled down as well, preparing for a quick catnap. Torben was on her other side, standing guard by the bunk, his shoulder even with the bed. He brushed her cheek with huge knuckles before standing up tall and giving the room a withering dare of a glance. Phasma and Brendol stood at the foot of the bunk, whispering in hushed voices. The stormtroopers guarded either side, and Siv had to assume that they were as safe as they were going to get, and she might as well give in to the bone-weary heaviness in her limbs.

As Siv drifted off, she noticed the gaunt prisoners edging toward the body the stormtroopers had stepped on, their eyes hollow and glowing and desperate. She closed her eyes and turned away. Using the detraxors was one thing, when everyone grew up knowing their responsibility to the people, alive or dead. There was a dignity to the machine, even the way the needle left the smallest hole, nothing garish or noticeable, really. But here, it seemed, bodies were something more. Siv had been hungry, but never hungry like the people on the floor. She hoped she never had to learn what it felt like.

The next day, Vrod appeared in bright-blue robes, his long beard braided and dyed purple. When they'd met him yesterday, he'd appeared to be just another prisoner, but it must've been some peculiar game or ploy to test them. Now he seemed like a caricature of a person, with colorful paint around his eyes and stitching on his sleeve that emphasized his white hand. A whisper of worry went up around the room. He looked at his prisoners with a satisfied, anticipatory smile and clapped his hands.

"Yesterday's bounty, come along. It's time to meet the Arratu and see what you can do."

Brendol stepped forward. "All of us? One of my people is still injured."

Vrod shrugged. "That's not my problem. You only get once chance to meet the Arratu, so you'd best leave her behind."

They'd removed Elli's helmet sometime in the night, and when Siv jumped down she saw that the woman's color wasn't good. She was pale, with purple circles around her eyes and matching blue lips.

Phasma leaned in and confirmed what Siv suspected. "Her neck is broken. Even if she wakes, she won't be able to move her legs, maybe even her arms. Brendol thinks she might pull through, but in his world, one grows accustomed to medical miracles."

"One more reason to get back to his ship," Siv noted.

Phasma nodded. "But we won't get there if we have to drag dead-weight."

Standing, Phasma called out to Vrod, "Will you allow us to keep our clothing?"

Vrod chuckled. "If your appearance amuses the Arratu, yes."

Brendol and Phasma traded a glance. Whatever passed between them ended with Brendol inclining his head in a nod.

Without another word, Phasma began stripping Elli's body of the white armor.

Although Phasma was never clumsy, it was an awkward job. The other two troopers didn't know whether to help or repel her until Brendol sighed. "Fine. Help her."

"And now you have until *I'm* bored," Vrod said, turning his attention to a mess under a ragged blanket in the corner. "Who drew the short straw last night? Ah. He wasn't very interesting. No great loss. You'd all best hope the new blood is amusing, or you'll be licking bones for dinner."

Every eye settled on Siv and her group, and she felt as if she were being picked apart by knives. These people were beyond loyalty and kindness, reduced to only hunger and desperation. Perhaps Brendol's First Order was the answer he claimed for such folk, if they could take a city this wretched and overcrowded and bring peace.

With the stormtroopers' help, Phasma soon had the white armor attached over her regular clothes. The fit was inelegant, as Elli was a head shorter than Phasma and a bit stockier, but the end result was that their greatest warrior had the best armor ever seen in the Scyre. When Phasma put on the helmet, she gasped briefly.

"You get used to it," Brendol said as Phasma's helmet turned this way and that.

"What do you see?" Siv asked.

Phasma laughed, a rare thing. "More" was all she said, and Siv burned with curiosity to know what it was like to look out through those mysterious black lenses. Phasma had seemed ill at ease ever since she'd lost her old helmet, and now she visibly relaxed, for all that they were headed toward an uncertain fate.

But then Siv's eye was drawn to Elli, and a sad view it was. The woman was limp, one of her feet at an odd angle that had been invisible under the armor. Phasma was right. This was not a person up to the struggle of life in the Scyre, much less a perilous journey across the gray sands. Wearing only the formfitting black suit and with her bruised, twisted neck revealed by the helmet's removal, Elli was a small and pathetic sight, her hair roughly chopped and her cheeks marked with old scars.

"I don't have the detraxors," Siv said, suddenly overcome with loss.

There was a reverence to her job, a certain awe and appreciation the band owed her for what she did. Without the oracle salve and liniment, her people would quickly take burns, weaken, or succumb to minor infection. She'd watched her mother perform this holy ritual when she was a child, and the day her mother had died, having fallen from a rock spire and hit her head while dangling from her line, it had been Siv's responsibility to mount the effort to retrieve her mother's body and the detraxors in her pack. The moment the needle had slipped into her mother's arm, Siv had cried. Tears were infrequent things in a place bereft of water, but she'd caught them in a small vial and added them to her mother's essence, a final act of love. Since then, Phasma and the other warriors had become her family. Being in the presence of a body well on the way to death but missing her tools, Siv couldn't help feeling a knot of failure in her stomach. The dark green stripes had faded on everyone's cheeks, and she could do nothing to help protect her people here.

"Are you ready yet?" Vrod asked. "The Arratu is anxious to meet you."

Brendol and Phasma walked side by side, their warriors falling in behind them. Siv noted that Phasma walked a little prouder with the armor on—although she also admitted that Phasma had always walked proudly. Still, the armor suited her.

Torben helped Gosta down from the bunk, and the girl leaned on him, limping, in Phasma's wake. As the group walked out the door, Siv heard shuffling footsteps approaching their bunk. She did not look back. There was no helping Elli now, and the rules were different in this place.

And when she thought about it, was it not strange that they'd been in binders and chains yesterday, but now, walking out into the hallway, they had but one leader and no restraints? She understood immediately when she'd passed through the door. Vrod's people waited in the hall, and they had among them two of the gray-skinned dogs on ropes. Just like the skinwolves they'd fought in the desert, these beasts had strange knots and wrinkles and warts all over, and they also had bared teeth and deeply thrumming growls that suggested they'd love nothing more than to have something fun to chase.

"Running would be unwise," Vrod said, stating the obvious. "But if you do decide to run, at least put some panache in it. The dogs crave entertainment, too."

Vrod marched them down several familiar hallways and toward where the turbolift had been located in Terpsichore Station. Here, however, that hallway ended in tall, broad doors. When Siv wordlessly pointed to the slashes of paint over the doors, Brendol frowned and muttered, "It says *Welcome to Oblivion*. Well, that's cheery." Vrod planted a hand on each one and shoved hard, flinging them open dramatically. The room within was more cavernous even than the hangar, as big as the rest of the entire factory, it seemed. It was as tall as six men, the walls perfectly straight and solid and the ceiling so high that the colorful squeeps darted among the struts.

When Siv described what filled the room, I had to teach her the right word for it: arena. Rows and rows of benches surrounded a circular pit with high stone walls and a gray sand floor. Even if she didn't know what to call it, she understood immediately what it was for.

Fear trickled down her spine. The Scyre was an unwelcoming place, meaninglessly and randomly cruel, but humans had created this loathsome monstrosity on purpose.

Vrod led them through a gate and into the arena. Standing in the center of the ring, it was only natural to spin around, looking up and feeling small. The seats were empty save for a sort of box nestled among the benches and protected on all sides by elaborate fabric awnings. Within this box sat a throne that dwarfed the one Keldo and Phasma had once shared in the Nautilus. Several older men and women in violet robes sat on benches on either side of the grand chair, chattering excitedly and pointing with their fabric fans, but they were clearly not the focus.

On the throne sat a figure swathed in voluminous red robes and wearing a tall, ornate hat. It was a human man, pink and fat as a baby. His mouth was pursed in displeasure, but when he noticed them approaching, he grinned. The tiny, jewel-bright squeeps lined his shoulders and sat on his hat, flickering and resettling restlessly against the vibrant crimson. Now he sat forward avidly, steepling his fingers.

"What is this?" he asked.

Vrod bowed, giving a flourish with his white hand. "New bounty for your pleasure, my Arratu. Caught yesterday in the eastern trap."

"What are they?"

"I wouldn't want to spoil the fun for Your Majesty."

The Arratu cleared his throat and waved a hand at them. "Explain your exotic origins."

Brendol stepped forward, and Siv noticed that his manner had changed completely. His movements were bigger, his accent snapping, his voice cultured and deferential and smooth.

"Great Arratu, we are but noble pilgrims passing through your magnificent land."

The Arratu bounced in his seat. "Yes, but what can you *do*? The last group of strangers had an alien covered in fur!"

Brendol faltered briefly, then bowed. "I am an educator and strategist for the First Order, great Arratu, and my talent is for administration and shepherding the young toward strategic ends. If you require intelligent men in your employment, I can assume many roles. I could perhaps help parcel out the resources so that fewer people might starve."

"I don't like him," the Arratu said, pouting. He wiggled his fingers at Brendol as if trying to shoo him away and pivoted in his chair, making the tiny birds erupt and flutter around him. "Wait! Why does that one"—he pointed at Phasma—"look different from those ones?" He pointed at Pete and Huff. "Their armor fits, but the tall one is funny. Is it a clown?"

Brendol stepped up again and began, "O great Arratu—"

"No. I asked *that* one. The tall one. What is it?"

Phasma spoke from inside the helmet, her voice flat and half robotic. Siv wouldn't have recognized this voice, this accent, just a week ago. "I am Phasma of the Scyre, and I am a warrior. I have taken this armor from a dying soldier, so it was not made to fit me. And if you require skills, my skill is death."

The Arratu sat up, looking fascinated and excited.

"Death?"

"I will fight anyone or anything in return for my freedom."

Later, Siv realized that Phasma had spoken only for herself, not for her people.

The Arratu shook his head, his hat waggling. "That won't do. If you're pleasant to watch as you fight, I'll want you to stay. I shall require you to have some theatricality about the death you deliver."

"So if I do well, I stay, and if I do poorly, I stay?"

"Well, yes, but if you do well, you'll be fed. And given treats."

"But Vrod said we could earn our freedom if we pleased you."

The Arratu glared at Vrod, who took several steps back. "Yes, well, he was lying. Only I can make the rules."

Phasma nodded, and Siv knew her well enough to understand that she was running a variety of scenarios through her head, trying to select the best angle of attack. The Arratu scanned the rest of their group but did not bounce in place again.

"The rest of you are quite boring. Even your clothes are dull. Can anyone do anything other than fight?"

An uncomfortable silence followed. When the Arratu's mad eyes landed on her, Siv felt as if an insect's legs were picking apart her face, hunting for some crevice to cling to.

"I can tell stories," Siv said.

The Arratu cocked his head. "Oh? About what?"

"Life in the Scyre. Our past battles, and the stories from my mother's time, which she passed down to me."

His eyes narrowed. "So these are just . . . histories of people like you? That doesn't sound very thrilling."

"It's thrilling if you've lived it."

The Arratu snorted in disgust and flapped a beringed hand at them. The birds flapped and resettled as if they, too, were bored.

"Take them away, Vrod. Dress them in something exciting, and bring them back tonight."

Brendol had remained silent, but now he spoke again, and his voice held none of the respect or showmanship he'd used earlier.

"And what will we do tonight?" he asked.

The Arratu grinned like a child who relished pulling the wings off butterflies.

"The only thing you can do, apparently. The best thing. Fight."

Vrod led them to another room in the compound and made them undress completely, bathe in sharply scented waters, and put on new clothes he handed out from an endless rack of colorful garments. The style of dressing was entirely different from the Scyre, and Siv couldn't get used to the loose shirt that billowed around her as she walked and the wide pants that swished with every step. Her years of fighting on rocky, uneven terrain told her immediately that such clothes would only trip her up, catching on obstacles when she most needed agility. She missed her tightly fitted leathers and thick boots, a second skin that could withstand all but the sharpest blade.

Even Phasma was given new garments to wear under her storm-trooper armor. As she was prodded into the shower, she kept glancing back at her armor as if suspicious it would be stolen. The Arratu must've indicated that he preferred the costume, though, as it waited, unchanged, on the bench when they returned. The leathers she'd worn underneath, however, were gone.

As they waited for Phasma and the troopers to finish attaching their armor, Torben sidled up to Siv, bumping her shoulder gently. He'd been helping Gosta through the bathing process, as the Scyre folk were more shy about wasting water than about nudity, but the girl was doing fine on her own, arranging her long, curly hair into a thick braid. Turning to face Siv, Torben caressed her stomach with a wide, warm hand.

"I noticed in the showers," he said. "How do you feel?"

Siv smiled. She had been wondering when he would recognize the change in her shape. For a murderous beast of a man, he was tender in many ways, and she had been certain he'd catch on quicker than the others.

"Good so far."

"You should eat more."

"I'd like that, too."

He paused, hands on his hips, looking away shyly. "Mine?"

Siv chuckled. "I think you know the answer to that. Yours or Keldo's. Not much privacy in the Scyre."

Torben smiled and nodded. She knew he considered those good odds.

"Brendol's ship will have things to help you," he said. "His medicine."

Swallowing the lump in her throat, Siv looked down. She'd lost two children that she knew of, after she'd begun to show but before they were fully formed. Fewer and fewer children were kindled in the Scyre and even fewer than that were born. Ylva had nearly died birthing Frey, who had been a small and frail little thing. Frey was going on six now and still their band's only child under twelve. This baby would've been a great boon to the Scyre, but only if she'd been able to bring it to term and survive the bloody fight to bear and deliver it. Selfishly, perhaps, she'd decided that she'd rather have a live child in space than give the Scyre another scant handful of salve and another dry package tucked into the hidden chambers of the Nautilus.

"I hope so," she said.

Gosta appeared, smiling, still squeezing water from her braid. The girl had noticed nothing of Siv's altered form, but then again, as far as Siv knew, Gosta was only fourteen and hadn't yet chosen any partners to couple with—or established that she was interested in doing so. Since the girl's mother had been dead many years, perhaps no one had taught her the ways of life, although there was no way to avoid witnessing the act that kindled it. Siv flushed with shame, thinking that she'd been so worried about her own possible child that she'd perhaps neglected this younger girl, already alone in the world. That was another boon to finding Brendol's ship and joining his clan among the stars: not only fewer lost babies, but fewer lost mothers, as well.

Brendol appeared, and the tender moment was over. Although Siv desperately wanted access to the safety and resources of his ship and his people, she didn't like the man himself. She liked him even less when Phasma wasn't in the immediate area, as he could be a bully, especially when it came to the needs of his warriors as compared with those of the Scyre. Perhaps it would be different once the Scyre band formally joined his First Order, whatever it was. Perhaps they, too, would become his people. Siv would gladly pledge her loyalty to Brendol for the promise of medicine like that her ancestors had enjoyed. Magic injections that could cure disease and pain, knowledgeable droids that could easily guide a mother through her birth with the insurance of a positive outcome. His recovery from the fever at Terpsichore Station had fully convinced Siv that she'd made the right choice. Being around sour, crafty Brendol would be worth it when she held her first child.

But until then, she looked to Phasma whenever Brendol was near.

The warrior was having trouble adjusting her armor over the excess fabric of her billowing costume. Siv walked over.

"Horrible, isn't it?"

Phasma looked up, her eyes full of ill humor. "They want us to die and look like magnificent fools doing it."

Brightly striped fabric poofed out between the dusty armor segments, but Siv knew better than to try to help Phasma in any way. With Gosta, she wouldn't hesitate to reach out, tucking here and there and clucking, but Phasma didn't rely on touch like the rest of them. Even Keldo took his comfort, as Siv well knew. Even though he was very private and had rarely spoken of his troubles or feelings, still he had his tender moments, when he pressed his forehead to hers in the quiet darkness of the Nautilus or whispered secrets that she promised to keep. But not Phasma. She held herself aloof, always, and would be more likely to dart between one of her people and an arrow than to slap someone on the shoulder in a friendly fashion after a victory.

"They want us to die?" Siv said, flashing a grin. "Let's disappoint them, then."

At that, Phasma smiled, and a feral thing it was. Siv hoped never to be on the wrong end of it.

"Yes, let's."

Vrod appeared in the doorway. "The fine fabric of Arratu blesses your audience." He flicked the colorful tunic spanning Torben's chest, and Torben growled. "But a word to the wise: If you wish to fill your empty stomachs, entertain the crowd. Get them on your side. Especially the Arratu. Cheers will earn your meat and water."

Gosta shifted closer to Siv, who sensed her dread. The girl was a nimble fighter, swift and silent, an excellent scout and undetectable under cover of night or when crawling among the rocks. But whatever had happened to her leg during the fall would take time to heal. Her fighting would not be, as Vrod had requested, entertaining. Siv resolved to remain close to her and defend her, if need be, from anything that might sense her weakness and target her. She wrapped an arm around Gosta to help her walk. They still had no idea what they would be required to fight—soldiers, the other prisoners, the hideous dogs, or something even more dangerous. And they hadn't been given weapons, or even asked which weapons they favored.

"Put on your brightest smiles for the Arratu!"

With that, Vrod held out his arm to the door, urging them into the hall. As they walked toward the vast room containing the arena, herded by blasters and skinwolves, they could sense a certain change in the air. Before, all had been still and quiet but for the smooth hum of the air recirculation machines. Now they heard a growing noise, something like the rumble of thunder combined with the gabbling of seabirds and the harsh slap of the angry ocean.

"What is it?" Gosta asked.

"Arratu," Vrod cheerfully replied.

"The person?"

"The city. Arratu is the city. Arratu is the leader. Arratu is the heart of this place."

"What does that mean?"

Instead of answering, Vrod whistled an unsettling tune and skipped a little. When he threw open the double doors, the sound and heat hit Siv like a wall of stone. She'd never seen so many bodies packed so tightly together, and the Scyre folk halted in the open doorway, frozen in place. Brendol and his troopers kept walking; they must've been accustomed to large groups of people. But Siv's heart pounded at the energy in the air, the assault on her senses. Thousands of people packed the benches around the arena, hip-to-hip, a riot of color, sound, and movement as they whistled, yelled, stamped, clapped, and waved colorful flags. A heavy scent rolled over her like the sea, the usual musk of bodies plus heady perfumes and strange spices that reminded her of the greenery clinging to their walls. Even the heat—so many hearts beating, so much blood! It made her woozy.

"What's wrong?" Vrod said, urging them forward with his spread arms. "The Arratu welcomes you!"

"It's an awful lot of Arratu," Torben noted.

Phasma looked around in a full circle, her helmet scanning the room.

"So be it."

She strode firmly ahead, past Brendol and his men and into the arena. There were no weapons visible, no obstacles, no hiding places. Merely the floor of the arena, covered in gray sand. Head up, Phasma walked until she faced the Arratu again.

"Well?" she shouted.

The Arratu stood, his arms up and lined with preening, glittering birds, and the people went mostly silent, although their whispers still tickled Siv's ears, as if they just didn't have the sort of self-control even small children showed in the Scyre.

"My people, we have fighters tonight. Whom shall we have them fight?"

The Arratu spoke into a machine that amplified his voice, filling the giant room with his booming words. A murmur of discussion went up in the stands, slowly cohering into a strange word repeated again and again like the call of a raptor. As the chant built and the voices went from whispers to cries, Siv realized that whatever it was, it wasn't good.

"Wranderous. Wranderous. Wranderous!"

"What's a Wranderous?" Torben asked.

Siv turned around to ask Vrod, but he was closing the doors with a madman's grin as he backed into the hall. The metal slammed shut, and the bolt drove home. A quick scan showed Siv that there was no way out. The walls rose far higher than even Phasma's head and were made of smooth metal, nothing like the craggy rocks they'd grown up climbing and clinging to like barnacles.

With the doors closed, the Scyre folk stayed close together, quickly moving into a clot, backs touching as each person faced outward toward some unknown threat. The troopers recognized the strategic advantage of this grouping in the larger circle of the arena and joined in. Brendol slipped between his men to stand in the center. It was just as well. If there was fighting to be done, someone like Brendol should stay out of the way and let the real warriors handle it.

Phasma still stood alone near the Arratu, who was goading the crowd into ever-louder cries for Wranderous. As if of one mind, the circle of Scyre and First Order fighters moved together to the center of the arena and waited. Siv's heart pounded in time with the crowd's chants, and her hand drifted, unthinking, to her belly. She felt safe enough with weapons in her hands, confident that she was trained to fight and would die a good death if her time had come, but this situation was unnatural and unsettling in a way that life in the Scyre was not. There was an artificial flavor to the spectacle that she found distasteful.

"Just come kill us!" she shouted back at the crowd.

No one heard her. The faces she saw were lit by a mad fervor, spittle flying from lips and fists pounding the air. Her gaze landed on an old man with a mustache dyed blue, then on a plump woman dripping in necklaces, next on a cluster of small, starving children throwing rocks that fell far short as they screamed. Their faces made her feel like a cornered animal—but then, weren't the people in the stands the ones behaving like animals?

When it seemed the raised voices could get no louder, the bodies on the benches parted like waves around a shark's fin to reveal a huge man, even bigger than Torben, casually swaggering down to the arena. He was dressed in the usual colorful pants of the Arratu's people but wore no shirt, and his pale chest was a riot of scars and tattoos under his thick blond beard. He carried no weapons, but his hands were wrapped in stained white fabric. As he walked down the stairs through the stands, he slapped hands and punched the air and shouted his own name with the crowd. When he reached the railing at the edge of the arena wall, he leapt over it easily and landed on the soft sand in a dramatic crouch.

But Phasma was already running for him, and as he rose and bowed to the crowd with an exaggerated flourish, she landed a flying kick that should've shattered his leg. The crowd roared in disapproval, but Wranderous didn't fall down with a snapped bone. He turned, slowly, and gave Phasma a look that would've made a lesser fighter quake. Gosta, in fact, did quake; standing so close beside her, Siv could feel the tension in her body, the jerky shake in the girl's arms.

"So that's Wranderous," Torben murmured. "He looks like fun." Cracking his knuckles, he strode away from the circle and toward Phasma and the fight.

The troopers and Brendol stayed put, so Siv and Gosta closed the circle, waiting for more fighters to appear. Phasma, however, wasn't waiting. She continued her attack on Wranderous, barreling into a combination of punches and kicks that any Scyre warrior would recognize, as she'd taught it to each of them. It involved a sequence of shots to bewilder and shut down the victim, rendering a fair fight less fair. A jab to the throat, a cross to the face, a hook to the ear, a cross to the solar plexus. But instead of doubling over to catch his breath, Wranderous punched Phasma's helmet, and her head rocked back in an unsettling way. She shook the hit off and watched him, hunting for a new angle; the helmet must've been built to absorb some damage and protect the skull, or Phasma would've been on the ground already.

"Why are there no weapons?" Gosta asked, leaning heavily on Siv.

"Be quiet and learn," Siv said. "You know everything I know."

Phasma circled around Wranderous, fists up and protecting her head, as Torben came up from the other side.

"I see you, little man," Wranderous warned. "And I'll get to you next."

Before he was done talking, Phasma slammed her helmet into the big man's chin, catching him by surprise and making his head rock back in turn. Torben caught Wranderous's long hair and yanked him back so Phasma could punch him in the throat, but Wranderous caught her fist as easily as if she were a child. Pivoting, Wranderous slung Phasma into Torben, and they both went down. Phasma had never fought in the armor before, and although it should've helped absorb damage, it also made her less agile. Still, she recovered quickly, rolled off Torben, and stood, so perhaps it served its purpose.

The moment she was on her feet, Phasma went for a brutal flurry of kicks, but Wranderous blocked them all, laughing, then clipped her legs and fell on top of her in the sand. Before Torben could react, Wranderous had popped off Phasma's helmet and started to choke her.

"Won't you help them?" Siv muttered to the troopers.

"Not until I give the word," Brendol muttered in return.

Siv wanted to help, her deep-running Scyre loyalty wounded to see her leader laughed at by the crowd, but she was the only person standing between Wranderous and Gosta, should it come to that. It was clear that the troopers wouldn't help the girl, not if they still had Brendol to protect. And perhaps Siv would get beaten and choked as well, but at least it would be for the right reason.

Torben was up now and landed a blow to Wranderous's spine that made the Arratu man abandon Phasma's beating and leap to his feet with a howl. They circled each other, one big and pale and the other big and dark. The red drained out of Phasma's face, and she shook her head and stood, dazed and planning her next attack. When Torben went for a clinch, Phasma tripped Wranderous to help get him to the ground. Torben landed on top of him, straddling Wranderous's chest, and the men began to grapple while Phasma rained down blows from above and kicks from the side.

Watching the fight, it was clear to Siv that Wranderous had different skills than they'd learned in the Scyre. His grappling wasn't just rolling around, aiming for a better position. He was twisting his arms, looking for certain holds, and eventually he found a way to choke Torben unconscious in the crook of his elbow, his face buried in Torben's neck so Phasma's blows couldn't injure him. The moment Torben went limp, Wranderous stood and grinned at Phasma.

"You're next," he said. "If the Arratu wishes?"

He looked up at the Arratu, one foot on Torben's chest.

The Arratu stood and waddled to the railing, the birds fluttering in his wake. He held three pieces of fabric in his soft hands, one red, one green, and one black. Tapping his fingers on his chin, he considered the scarves, then selected one and tossed it out on the sand to the crowd's riotous elation. The cloth was red, and whatever that meant, Wranderous laughed.

Phasma later told Siv that what Wranderous whispered in her ear as the crowd went mad was this: *He wants to see you beaten but not killed. Take a few hits, and you'll eat well tonight. But make it look good.*

And Phasma also told Siv what she whispered back: *No.*

What occurred next was something Siv had never seen, never thought she'd see.

Wranderous pounded Phasma into the dirt.

He held her hair and punched her face. He picked her up from the sand and slammed his fist into her chin. With her armor intact, he couldn't beat her body to a pulp, so he took out his measured anger on her face. Phasma struggled and kicked and punched and clawed, but she couldn't defeat Wranderous, a man of twice her mass. If she'd had her ax and spear, or even a dagger—then, she would've had a chance. But starved, exhausted, unfamiliar with fighting in armor, and utterly without weapons or supporters, Phasma tasted her first defeat.

And the Arratu loved it. He laughed and clapped his hands with each fresh punch. When Phasma finally fell, dripping blood in the sand and unable to get up again, the Arratu jumped up and down in delight like he was less a leader and more an overgrown child, and a stupid, cruel one at that. The birds shrieked as they flew circles around his hat. Siv looked around the arena at the cheering, jeering people, and felt a surge of pure hatred. It must've been easy to be petty and mean and cruel when you had an excess of people. In the Scyre, lives were so few and so hard to create that death was no laughing matter. This type of barbarous inhumanity was a new thing, and Siv felt an answering fury burn in her own heart.

The Arratu and his people, she hoped, would one day pay for what they'd done.

At least Phasma wasn't dead. As the people cheered and shouted for Wranderous, a hidden door slid open in the wall of the arena, and Wranderous picked up the red scarf and walked out, arms up, shouting his own name. The door slid closed the moment he was within, and there was no visible outward mechanism to show how it was accomplished. Far away as it was, even if she'd been willing to leave Gosta behind, Siv couldn't have escaped that way. But at least now they knew there were doors.

"Go get her," Brendol said to his men, and the troopers jogged to Phasma and picked her up by her arms, dragging her back to the group and leaving a long, bloody trail in the sand. At the very least, there were no blood beetles.

When no further threat presented itself, Siv shoved Gosta at Brendol and muttered, "Help her," before running to Torben. She skidded to a stop in the sand on her knees and shook his shoulder, calling his name. When he didn't answer, she patted his face gently, then slapped it.

"Torben!" she shouted in his ear, desperate to wake him up before something else came at them.

Finally, his eyes flickered open and focused on her.

"I don't like the way he fights," he said.

Siv smiled. "Me neither. You should stand. We don't know what's coming next."

He nodded and sat up, and Siv helped him to his feet. Together, with the crowd's jeers pelting down, they hobbled to where the rest of the group waited. The circle re-formed with Phasma and Brendol at the center this time. Phasma lay on her side, curled up around her broken face. Noticing that the helmet still lay near the splatters of blood, Siv sprinted to it, picked it up, and returned to her people. Phasma would want it, when she woke up. It was hard, once someone had adopted a mask, to give it up, Siv well knew.

"Let's try one more thing," the Arratu shouted. "Shall we release the lupulcus!"

He pointed to the arena wall, and another door slid up. Two gray shapes burst out of it, loping easily into the arena as if they were well accustomed to it. It was the hairless gray skinwolves again, grotesquely moist and covered in warts and boils. These two seemed larger, thicker, and meaner than the wild ones. They quickly focused on the fighters and increased their speed, teeth bared as they ran across the gray sand.

If she'd had a weapon, Siv wouldn't have found the creatures threatening at all. Two against seven were good odds, even for creatures that were harder than most to kill. But without her blaster or blades and considering that Torben was still only half awake, she was not quite sure if she could stop these beasts unarmed. Wary but determined, she stepped in front of Gosta.

Phasma groaned and held out her hands. "My helmet," she muttered. Gosta kicked it to her, and Phasma shoved it over her head. The moment the helmet was in place, Phasma was on her feet at Siv's side, the stormtroopers joining them to make a wall of four people.

"You okay?" Siv asked Phasma.

In response, Phasma tensed into a fighting stance and shoved Siv backward. Siv landed in the sand and rolled back to standing in time to watch the first skindog leap at Phasma. The Scyre leader's whiteplated arm went up, the dog's teeth closing around it. With her free arm, Phasma chopped the back of the dog's neck, and it crumpled to the ground, where she put a boot on its neck and stomped. The other dog lunged at the stormtroopers, who did their best to fend it off.

"Stop playing," Phasma said, striding between them and holding out her arm to the beast. The moment it latched on to the armor, she slammed a gloved fist into its skull, and it, too, went down.

She stood, looked directly at the Arratu, put a foot on the beast's head, and waited.

Siv knew she should've felt pride and satisfaction to see her leader not only live through the beating she'd received but also take down the attacking dogs. But she couldn't help finding something blasphemous about the wanton killing. Even these ugly creatures could've provided water, nutrients, and meat. Instead, they were strewn across the sand, their value ignored, and by a people without enough resources to feed their poorest members.

The arena went silent but for the muted whispers of the people in the stands. Every eye went to the Arratu. He stood, his head cocked, considering—but he did look pleased. He raised his arms into the air, and the little birds swirled around him, chittering happily.

"That was wonderful," he said. "Take them away and bring me something new to watch. Bring them back tomorrow for more fun."

A cheer went up, and the words soon coalesced into the demand for "Something new! Something new!"

The door they'd entered through earlier reopened, and Vrod appeared, motioning them along, his warriors waiting with their blasters ready.

"Bring the wolves," Phasma said.

Siv was too busy helping Gosta and pulling Torben to follow the command, but the two stormtroopers immediately turned to pick up the limp bodies of the gray beasts. Siv noted that Brendol's face went through some fascinating contortions from indignation to anger to fascination to measured consideration, seeing his men follow Phasma's orders. Vrod didn't argue as they stepped through the door carrying the dead skinwolves and followed him down the hall.

"Was the Arratu not pleased?" Brendol asked, stepping ahead to pace their captor.

"That wasn't entirely terrible," Vrod said, his robes snapping in his wake. "You could've worked a little harder to give it some flair. Next time, it's likely you'll be given weapons to see what you can really do."

"But we won."

"Yes, well, *she* won. Sort of." Vrod fluttered a hand at Phasma. "You mostly watched. It's not so much about winning, you know. It's about showing the Arratu something they've never seen before. The crowd and the Arratu himself are connoisseurs of experience, you see. The arena has shown us beautiful things and terrible things, and we live for the excitement. Every now and then, something is so startling that the Arratu grants the performer freedom. But you're nowhere close. If you can't entertain, you'll wither away like the rest and die."

"Why is that? Does this grand city not hold enough charms?"

Vrod snorted. "We can't leave the walls. Nothing ever changes. There are too many people and not enough food. Entertainment is all that we have. And the strangers we capture are the best sort of entertainment."

"And does no one challenge the Arratu?"

At that, Vrod stopped walking and stared at Brendol like he'd grown an extra head. "Why would anyone challenge him? He has the best taste."

They were put in a different room this time, one that might've once served as a storage closet. It was barely big enough for them all to sit on the floor and eat the food left there, strange stuff that wasn't dried meat or sea veg. None of it tasted good, but taste wasn't currently their problem. There was plenty of water, and it was the best water Siv had ever tasted, with no tang of salt or nutrients or the sea. The two dead wolves lay near the door, untouched, as Vrod stood over the group, watching them eat.

"What do you plan to do with the lupulcus?" he asked, amused.

"Eat them," Phasma answered.

It was a wonder she could talk, much less eat, considering that when she removed her helmet, her face was purple and black and bleeding. Her lips were smashed, one eye swollen shut. Siv watched her tenderly touch several teeth and grimace at the results. At least the food was soft, mostly gelatinous cubes and soft bits of some kind of sweet fruit.

At that, Vrod laughed heartily. "Eat diseased beasts? Is our food not good enough for you, then? There are those in the outer rings of the city who would kill for such riches."

"It's fine enough," Phasma answered, "but who knows how long you'll keep feeding us?"

"A comedian, too! You should work on that act. It'll get you fed as handily, but without the bruising and black eye."

The food was soon gone; there hadn't been much of it. The Scyre folk were accustomed to taking only as much as they needed and to considering the needs of those around them. Torben was big, and keeping him big benefited everyone. Gosta was small, but she was still growing and would need proper food to heal her hurt leg. Phasma would also require nutrients to heal. Siv ate very little, knowing that she was well and also that she was not large. What she did eat, she ate for the child inside her.

Still, it bothered her to see Brendol Hux, who had done so little, take as much food as anyone else. In the Scyre, the elderly—that being anyone over forty—naturally took less food. They couldn't fight, they didn't need extra weight, and they depended on the strength of younger backs and fists to keep them fed. But Brendol took what he wanted, and even Phasma didn't speak against it, although Siv saw her eyes narrow as Brendol took the last bite.

"Back to the barracks, then," Vrod said. "With your dead dogs, since that little request amused the Arratu. I do think he'd come watch you figure out how to butcher the bodies without knives if his keepers would let him set foot from the safety of his hallowed tower."

Phasma jerked her chin at the dogs, and the troopers picked them up. The entire group followed Vrod down the hall, and he walked as if he didn't have a care in the world. And perhaps he didn't, considering his guards had their blasters pointed at the dangerous prisoners walking, uncuffed, down the hallway. Siv couldn't grasp the attitudes here, the blatant disregard for safety and vigilance.

"Did you know this was once nothing but a fabric factory?" Vrod knocked on a glass window, and Siv peeked in to see great machines moving, spitting out yet more of the billowing fabric. "Arratu Station. Made the uniforms for Con Star Mining Corporation. They built it here for the water. A huge spring and, once, a river that ran past. Now we have machines that can make fabric. Endless fabric. Just dump sand into one, and it'll make fabric all day long. But it can't make food, and it can't make the days go by any quicker, so you'd best find a way to entertain the Arratu without breaking all your bones. Because those machines don't make medicine, either."

He opened the door, and every eye in the prison barracks looked up. Phasma walked in first, wearing her helmet and showing no out-ward sign of having been beaten nearly to death. The troopers came in behind her, and she pointed to a bloody stain on the floor.

"Put one of them there."

The stormtroopers looked at each other, and one of them tossed down his skinwolf without questioning her. The other one continued to hold his bloody prize, the gray skin drooping and smearing his armor with slurry blood.

"Have a good night. Be ready for tomorrow."

Vrod waved at them with his white hand, and the door slid closed.

"One of these dogs is ours. You can have the other one," Phasma said to the room's other occupants.

"Why?" someone asked from the floor. "What do you want?"

"We want no trouble. And the meat will go bad, anyway."

Phasma turned away from the people slithering toward the carcass on the ground and went to the bed where Elli had lain that morning. The woman was gone, and two people lay in her bunk, their bellies round against their scrawny bones. One look from Phasma and they all but leapt out of the bed and crab-crawled out of her sight.

"Torben and Gosta."

"I can't fit in there," Torben complained.

"Try."

Gosta clambered up top, and Torben filled in the entire bottom bunk, the metal frame creaking under him. As Siv moved to check him for hidden injuries, not that she could do anything about the damage, she noticed something peculiar. Brendol and Phasma were conversing in the corner, their whispers too low for her to catch. But she watched Brendol reach into his jacket and produce something, a shiny tube, which he stabbed into Phasma's shoulder, right between the plates of her armor. She didn't budge, didn't grunt, and certainly didn't grab his hand and crush the bones with her glove as punish-ment. Siv didn't know what was in that tube, but whatever it was, Phasma had agreed to it. And when it was done, the empty tube dis-appeared back into Brendol's jacket.

"Get some rest," Phasma said to her people.

She took off her helmet and lay down on the floor beside Torben's bed. While Siv still fidgeted around him, checking his eyes and the dark bruises on his throat below the shadow of his beard, Phasma slipped into a deep sleep. Back home, Siv would've tended to Phasma's bruises first, offering her the strongest liniment and some herbs to chew that would help reduce swelling. Here, with no resources and no herbs, there was nothing she could do. Just like with the detraxors, she was helpless without her pack. She checked on Gosta again before Torben caught her around the hips and pulled her into the tiny bed, tucking her in against his warm side and holding her close with his arm.

"This place is so wrong," she murmured against him.

"Then we'll leave it behind."

"I think you're concussed."

"Probably."

She fell asleep against him, and when she woke up, she was starving. She looked at the dead dog on the ground, the one Phasma had saved for their people. Reluctantly, hating herself for it, she began prodding it to find a soft spot.

When she looked at Phasma's sleeping face, she found it mostly healed. The bruises were yellow, the swelling gone, the split skin drawn together by pink lines of scars. Whatever had been in that tube must've been more of Brendol's amazing medicine.

It was a miracle. But what other miracles had Brendol been withholding?

TWENTY-FOUR

ON PARNASSOS, 10 YEARS AGO

TIME IN THE PRISON BARRACKS DRAGGED ON FOREVER. NO WONDER THE people of Arratu craved entertainment. The taste of raw skinwolf clung to her lips, and Siv wished for anything to happen. Vrod appeared in the doorway several times, pulling people out and shoving new people in. The new prisoners all seemed to be from Arratu, as they wore bright clothes and were more anxious than terrified, as if they harbored hope that they might please the crowd and earn the Arratu's favor. Phasma was asleep, all that time, her back to the room as she curled on her side toward the wall, which was unusual. Phasma was generally alert and protective, popping awake at any possible threat; whatever Brendol had given her must've been strong medicine indeed.

Finally, Vrod appeared in the doorway and gestured to Phasma's back.

"Wake your fighter, if she can see out of those black eyes. It's time to entertain the Arratu."

Siv had been dozing, and she went to wake Phasma, but Brendol was already there. He had her helmet in his hands, and she snatched it from him and put it on before she stood. She said nothing as she led her people to the doorway. Torben, at least, was back to his old self, fully recovered. Gosta's limp was gone, although she wasn't in full fighting form and would've been useless on the uneven ground of the Scyre. They followed along behind Phasma, Brendol, and the other two troopers, and Siv felt a strange thing: fear. Going into a fight, she generally felt more alive and relished a challenge, but now, when she thought about going back into that arena without any weapons, she went cold and numb.

The door slid open, and the crowd inside stomped in their seats, whistling and calling for blood. Those vicious cheers had stunned her the first time, but now it was just noise. The Arratu waited on his throne, flanked by his purple-robed company, covered in colorful birds, and rubbing his hands in glee. He stood, and the crowd went silent, so quiet that Siv could hear the sand crunching beneath her feet.

"What shall we have today?" the Arratu called through his booming machine.

Siv shivered as the chant went up.

"Wranderous. Wranderous. Wranderous!"

It was like living the same moment over again as the big man plowed his path through the crowd, clapping hands and pumping his fist. He leapt down to the sand and bowed to the Arratu, who raised his hands for silence.

"And what kind of toys should we give him this time?"

The noise of the crowd built to a mad gabble, and the Arratu giggled.

"Did someone say swords?"

The door through which Wranderous had exited the day before slid open, and someone threw three swords out onto the sand. They were different enough that Siv assumed they'd been taken from previous prisoners. One was clunky and made of droid chunks and saw bits, one was fine and slender, and one looked more like the twisted glass they'd pulled from the blaster-struck sand. The weapons had barely landed before Phasma and Siv were running for them, the two fastest Scyre warriors determined to claim the weapons they so desperately needed.

Wranderous was closer, and he picked up the two heavier swords and turned to face them, grinning, a blade in each huge hand. With silent understanding born of years fighting side by side, Phasma and Siv split up, each approaching from a different angle, both vying to get the third sword still sitting on the ground behind Wranderous. Of course, that was exactly what Wranderous was trying to prevent, and he struck out at Phasma first, thinking her to be the more dangerous target.

Siv had known he would do that, and she slid to the sand on one hip, skidding past him and wrapping her fingers around the third sword's hilt as Wranderous sliced the air where Phasma had been standing. He was bigger, but he was slower, even with Phasma hindered by her armor. She rolled and came back up just out of reach, and his next swing seemed to slowly arc over her head as she stepped easily past it. While he recovered his balance, Siv focused on his left hand, holding the sword he hadn't yet used. His off hand. One quick slice of her blade and that sword fell to the ground in a gush of blood, along with one of his fingers.

Wranderous spun on Siv as she danced out of reach and handed her sword to Phasma. It was beautiful, how Phasma's posture changed the moment she had a weapon in hand. She rolled her shoulders back and got into fighting stance before darting forward to hack at Wranderous's arm. He stepped back, narrowly avoiding Phasma's sword, and Siv ducked and picked up the sword Wranderous had dropped. When he spun to slash at Siv, Phasma darted in and sliced the backs of his knees.

"Torben!" Phasma shouted.

She pointed with her sword, and the big man came running, planting himself where she'd indicated, directly in front of the Arratu, whose face was lit with bloodlust and excitement.

Wranderous turned on Siv now, his face racked with pain and fear as he sliced down right where she'd been standing, narrowly missing her. As soon as he turned away from Phasma, she jabbed the sword into his back, twice, fast, once on the right and once on the left, as if skewering meat. Which she had: his kidneys. When Wranderous turned back to deal with Phasma, Siv slashed at his ankles, bringing him to his knees, the sword still in his right hand as his left hand dripped blood.

The big man's face was red with rage, but he was losing a lot of blood, and his balance as well. Phasma hacked at his right hand, forcing him to drop the blade and leaving him weaponless. Siv moved to her side, ready to do whatever Phasma commanded. Although the attitude in the Scyre was that death should be quick and a matter of business when necessary, they were all aware now that theatricality would get them fed, and that if Wranderous had to die, it might as well be in a way that would benefit them the most. Siv kicked him over, and Phasma put a foot on Wranderous's spine.

They all looked up to the Arratu. His face was lit with excitement, as if he didn't even mind losing such a fine fighter. Taking his three colorful scarves in hand, he held them up, and the crowd screamed and cheered along with his coterie of birds. At last, he chose the green scarf and threw it down.

"Wranderous is free!" he said.

Little good it would do the man, Siv thought. If they truly had no medicine here, as Vrod had told them, Wranderous would be dead within hours. But the crowd didn't seem to care. Everyone stood in the bleachers, cheering and waving their flags. The door opened, and a hand within beckoned.

But Wranderous couldn't stand, and Phasma did not run for the door. She switched the sword to her left hand and stepped off Wranderous, moving around to where his face lay in the sand. Her fingers clenched into fists, and she pulled up his head by his hair, reared back, and punched Wranderous in the face, splattering his broad nose with a crunch. Blood gushed down his chin, and he made a

noise halfway between a shout and a blubber, scrabbling in the sand
for his lost sword. Phasma stepped forward and kicked it far away,
and Wranderous reached for her, his great clumsy paws closing on
thin air as she danced back. The crowd exploded, half excited and
half furious.

"Is this not what you really want?" Phasma shouted to the crowd,
her sword raised. "Death by a thousand cuts, a hundred punches?"

The crowd was becoming a mob now, screaming and shouting and
stomping. They were so loud that they drowned out whatever the Arratu was shouting into his amplification machine. Phasma held their
attention completely.

"Would you like to see a real show?"

They begged for it, and even the Arratu stopped his shouting to
watch.

Phasma looked around the arena, noting where all her people
waited. Gosta with Brendol, behind the two stormtroopers. Siv by
her side, sword in hand. Phasma jerked her chin at Torben, where he
awaited her command.

"Torben, kneel," she shouted. Then, quietly, "Siv, kill Wranderous.
But do it in an entertaining fashion. And a little slow."

Siv nodded and looked at Wranderous, considering for the first
time how to kill someone slowly and for someone else's sick amuse-
ment. Now that the big man had been bested, she felt no love for the
fight. He was on hands and knees, his multiple wounds gushing
blood to mix with the sand, his head down and his nose a mess. She
leapt onto his back, standing on him as if he were a rock, and the
crowd went mad. Raising her sword, she yelled back at them, feeling
their energy thrum through her. Still, no inspiration came, and her
heart couldn't turn to wanton murder. The moment faded away, her
sword unused in her hand. Luckily, the crowd's attention shifted,
heads swiveling to follow Phasma. Siv hopped off the broken man's
back and stepped out of range to watch the real show.

Phasma was running for Torben at full speed.

The big man had knelt, his back to Phasma, per her orders. Siv realized what was happening a second before it occurred. Phasma ran at Torben, leapt onto his back, and used him as a springboard to catapult herself directly into the Arratu's box, where she sliced her sword in a flawless arc that slashed the man's head from his shoulders in one clean stroke.

It happened so quickly that the Arratu was still grinning when his head flew through the air to land on the sand of the arena. His birds took to the air, screaming, as his body fell, and the violet-robed elders leapt out of the box and into the stands, melting into the crowd. The Arratu's four guards barely had their swords out of their sheaths before Phasma had dispatched them all.

What happened next was so strange that Siv thought she must be dreaming. The entire arena erupted in cheers. They weren't screaming and panicking. They weren't mustering to destroy their leader's attacker.

They were whistling, screaming, shouting, stomping.

They loved it.

Phasma stood there by the Arratu's throne, and Siv had to assume her leader was just as confused by the crowd's response, although her helmet hid her emotions. Brendol and his stormtroopers marched across the sand to stand, looking up, beside Siv and what was left of Wranderous. The once great Arratu warrior had fallen to the ground, his breathing shallow. Killing him didn't feel like a victory, so Siv left him lying there and hurried to help Gosta and join Torben. They watched as Brendol's stormtroopers helped him clamber up into the stands beside Phasma. He was not an athletic man, and it was not a smooth enterprise.

Picking up the Arratu's voice projector, Brendol raised Phasma's arm and said, "Behold your new Arratu! Phasma!"

The crowd went insane, their chant coalescing into the word *Arratu* screamed with a near-religious fervor alongside Phasma's name.

Phasma!

Phasma!

Phasma!

Torben leaned in toward Siv. "If they think Phasma is their Arratu, will they ever allow us to leave this cursed place?" he asked.

"I don't know," Siv said. "But I hope Brendol Hux has a plan."

Torben helped everyone up to join Phasma and Brendol in the Arratu's box. The stormtroopers pulled the big Scyre warrior up last. The crowd went on cheering and chanting, but no one seemed to know what to do. A few of the colorful squeeps tried to land on Phasma's shoulders, and she batted them away. Finally, Vrod of the White Hand appeared beside the throne. As if Brendol had been waiting just for him, he bowed his head the tiniest bit and said, "Ah. Vrod. Good. Please take the new Arratu to her tower."

Vrod grinned and bowed back. "An interesting tack, to be sure, but that's not how it works. The Arratu is chosen by—"

"No, she's not." Phasma stepped between them, the blood-slick sword still in her hand. "I have defeated your champion and your Arratu, and I claim the throne. Unless you wish to challenge me for this position, it is mine."

"The people will never stand for it."

Phasma chuckled. "Oh, they won't?" Stepping forward, she raised both her arms and began shouting, "Arratu! Phasma! Arratu! Phasma!" into the amplifier.

The people nearest the box reached for her, their faces alive with joy and excitement as they took up the chant along with her.

"Is she your Arratu?" Brendol shouted through the machine.

"Yes! Yes! Yes!" came the call.

Brendol turned back to Vrod, hands out, grinning. "Sounds like the people have spoken."

Vrod let the chant go on, and Siv could see him silently calculating. Finally, he exhaled and gestured to a door behind the throne. "Fine. We'll figure it out tomorrow. The crowd's too excited to get anything done just now. You have no idea what it means to be the Arratu."

"We know it means we'll get to sleep off the floor and with full bellies," Torben said. "For now, that's good enough."

"As you say."

Vrod led them out into a different hall and into a turbolift just like the one that had delivered them into the mines at Terpsichore Station. This one went up, and when it stopped, the doors opened onto a hall that was painted a garish red and hung with layers of colorful fabrics. Strange images and objects decorated every wall and surface, pictures and statues of people and beasts that Vrod dismissively called "art." Many of them were dressed in the same red drapery the Arratu had worn and appeared like gods, with halos and lightning and worshippers surrounding them.

"The Arratu is more than a leader," Vrod explained. "The Arratu is an idea. The heart of the city, the voice, the tenor, the sacrificial lamb."

"That part doesn't sound good," Siv said.

Vrod inclined his head to her. "You just watched it happen. When the Arratu is failing us or deemed unworthy, things tend to take care of themselves."

"How did the previous Arratu die?"

Vrod held open a door, motioning them into the room beyond. "The crowd tore him limb from limb."

The chamber they entered was designed for royalty and had every imaginable comfort. The bed was big enough to fit their entire group, tables were laden with fruits and bottles of colorful liquids, and soft rugs covered the floor. Several people dressed in matching purple outfits knelt around the edges of the room, their heads and eyes down. Across the back wall, words spelled out something that looked quite fancy, but of course Siv couldn't read. Later on, Brendol told her what it said: ARRATU STATION: CON STAR FABRIC DIVISION.

"You're dismissed," Vrod said to the servants, and they hurried out without looking up.

"Now that you're the Arratu, for better or for worse, there are some things you should know," Vrod said, availing himself of the dainty selection of fruits. "As I already mentioned, half the city is starving to death. Our machines can turn sand into any kind of fabric, but we can't make food. There are too many people and not enough land, plants, or beasts, and we've nowhere to go."

But Phasma ignored him and walked away to look out a wide window.

"So that's why loss of life doesn't matter to you," Brendol said. "How interesting."

Vrod nodded. "Sadly, yes. Anyone who dies means that much more food for those who remain. We've become quite selfish, I'm afraid, and far less picky. There are restrictions on childbearing, and those too old or sick to contribute must be euthanized. Perhaps you begin to see why entertainment is so crucial. It's the only thing that can take the people's minds off their empty bellies and dying friends."

"Has it always been this way?" Brendol asked. "Has there never been proper government?"

Vrod pointed to the words painted on the wall. "When Con Star came, this was a fertile valley surrounded by crops and trees and filled with plants and animals. And then—well, you know what happened everywhere. The weather changed. The sand crept in. Only the walls and our last remaining spring keep the desert from claiming us all. The spring has begun to slow, though, and it's clear our prosperity will never return. We've grown desperate. What happens in the arena . . . those are the death throes of our people."

"Very poetic," Brendol said, sneering, "but what does it mean to us?"

"Well, since you've gone to the trouble of getting rid of one perfectly good Arratu and replacing him with an outsider who doesn't know our ways, it's up to you to figure out how to keep the people from rioting in the streets. The problem with being the visible leader of a failing regime is that they tend to go for your head first."

"Is there a governing council? Elected officials? Religious leaders?"

"There is only the Arratu, his guards and court, and the Sentries, led by me. Every time we tried to have another kind of government, they all just stabbed one another in the back. It was easier this way. One fool in charge of a bunch of fools."

"And what do your Sentries do, besides attack travelers in the desert?"

At that, Vrod threw back his head and laughed. "That's one part of it. If you're hungry, it's easier to eat strangers than people you know. Meat's meat when everyone is starving. There's also the hope that we'll find some loot in their packs that might help us out of this mess. Seeds, technology. So many people are carrying artifacts around that one of them might eventually help us. Every Con Star station had a specialty, see? That means that somewhere out there is a facility like ours that can make food. We've sent out scouts, but no one has ever returned. Now we never go farther than the pit that trapped you. Fuel is running scarce, too." He swatted at a bright-yellow drapery. "But we have plenty of useless, pretty fabric. We'll be the best-dressed corpses on the planet, one day soon."

"You're optimistic," Torben said, stuffing a fruit into his mouth.

"So how can we help?" Siv asked, looking to Phasma, who continued to ignore the conversation and instead moved around the room, looking out every window with a pair of quadnocs she'd found somewhere among the Arratu's piled things.

"We don't need to help." Brendol poured himself a drink, sniffed it, and sipped. "It's not our business. We can't fix what's broken here."

"But people are dying."

"Then their leaders made grave mistakes, again and again. This place could've been a paradise."

"Look," Vrod said. "The problems plaguing us today were made by our parents and grandparents, most of whom are gone. If you have any experience in these matters and wish to truly act as Arratu, be my guest. You can't make it much worse. But the truth is that you're stuck here with us, and we're all going to die, so you might as well do what all the other Arratus have done. Come to the arena and encourage a lively evening so that people will stop killing one another. Or worse, realize that if they banded together, they could storm this tower and kill us all."

"No."

Everyone turned to Phasma.

"We will not stay here," she continued.

"You will. You're the Arratu. The people have chosen you, and it can't be helped. You might control the arena, but I control the gates."

"I can change that." Phasma stepped closer, and Vrod took a wary step back.

Phasma's sword slashed so quickly that it was barely a flash of silver. Siv had forgotten that her leader was still armed. When Phasma stood still again, her sword was wet with blood and a patch of red bloomed against Vrod's robes.

"But . . ." he started.

"That is what I think of your Arratu," Phasma said. "This is no way to rule."

Vrod fell, his eyes searching the ceiling. Siv squatted beside him and took his hand.

"Where are our things? The ones you took?" she asked.

Vrod pointed toward a corner, and Gosta hurried to it and opened the door. A pile of bags sat within, and Siv recognized her own. Without a word, Gosta brought them to her, and Siv pulled out a detraxor.

"Knew . . . that tech . . . might be useful . . ." Vrod sputtered.

Siv held his hand tightly, knowing his time was short.

"Medicine?" he asked.

"Shh." His hand was going cold, his lips blue. The rug underneath him was soaked in red.

"Fix me!"

"Some situations have no solution," Siv whispered as he drew his last breath.

Sending up the prayer, she set about recovering what she could from the fallen man. A great sense of well-being thrummed through her now that she was reunited with her detraxors and able to help her people.

As if reading Siv's mind, Phasma stepped forward and spoke.

"Gather your things. Eat and take what you need. Collect all the water and food you can carry. We must leave here and be on our way.

This place has been poisoned, and there is no saving it. I can see General Hux's ship from the window, and we've a long way to go still."

Even Brendol nodded agreement. Perhaps it was the borrowed veil of the Arratu, but there was a new power to Phasma, as if she'd become something more in this dying city. As if, in taking the Arratu's head, she'd also taken his authority.

"Go on. Now," Phasma snapped, and both the Scyre folk and the stormtroopers hurried to prepare themselves. As for Brendol, he merely continued enjoying the Arratu's food and drink and took up the quadnocs to look out the window for himself.

Their old clothes were gone, probably tossed out somewhere near the barracks. As Siv finished harvesting Vrod's essence with her detraxor, Torben found his weapons and Gosta put on her mask, sighing with relief. The stormtroopers strapped their blasters back on, and Brendol left the window and pawed through his own sack in his usual secretive way. Phasma methodically added her blaster, ax, and spear to her costume, although she kept the white helmet on and left her old helmet and her red mask in her pack. They split up the food on the table, wrapping it in whatever bits of cloth they found lying around. There was more than enough of that, after all.

Brendol searched the room until he found a screen like the ones at Terpsichore Station, this one hidden by draperies. After several attempts, he was able to enter the system and study the layout of the large factory. He pointed out the hangar where the GAVs would be waiting, and he and Phasma debated the best way to get there. They still hadn't seen another person besides Vrod and the servants he'd helpfully sent out.

"Anyone we encounter in the halls must be dispatched silently," Brendol said.

"Even the innocent ones?" Gosta asked.

Brendol rolled his eyes. "You've got to think of yourself as a soldier now. You're in a war, and no one is innocent. It's them against us, and they've proven that they'll gladly capture, beat, or kill whoever they want. You heard Vrod. Loss of life is an everyday occurrence here. We'll only get one chance to break out. After that, we'll be watched and probably imprisoned. If anyone gets in your way, destroy them."

"They are an attacking force," Phasma added. "And you know how we treat attacking forces."

Gosta nodded, but her lips twisted. The girl was conflicted, and Siv shared her doubts. For all that Vrod and his Sentries had been cruel, the majority of the population was pitiable. When she looked to Torben, she noticed the little furrow between his brows that suggested he wasn't happy. But she also saw the firm set to his jaw that promised he'd do what had to be done anyway.

Phasma didn't have to ask if her people were ready. All she had to do was move to the door and tilt her head. Siv still didn't know how Phasma was functioning after being beaten nearly to death by Wranderous yesterday, but she wasn't about to ask. Whatever medicine or magic Brendol had saved for that desperate moment had served its purpose. The helmet was becoming Phasma's new mask, and as long as she was wearing it, Siv wouldn't incur her wrath by trying to discover the other woman's feelings. She merely stood, collected the bags containing her things and the detraxors, and took her usual place between Torben and Gosta, her blade and blaster in her hands, ready to fight.

The door slid up smoothly. Outside the room, the servants waited in a row, their backs to the wall and their heads down. Siv wasn't sure if this was what Brendol meant about people getting in their way, but she understood the moment the troopers began shooting—well, executing—the servants with their blasters, and her heart sank.

"Hurry!"

At Brendol's call, they looked to Phasma and followed her, just as if they were back home in the Scyre. Phasma jogged ahead easily, blaster and sword in hand, leading the group down the twisting hallways she'd memorized from Brendol's map. At first, they didn't encounter anyone. But then Siv heard a soft, "Hey!" and watched a woman's body slide off Phasma's spear and crumple to the ground.

So that was how it was now. No questions asked. No one given the chance to sound the alarm.

When she heard footsteps in the hall behind them, Siv spun and sliced the interloper in one smooth motion. She'd long ago learned that the only way to survive was to do whatever Phasma told her to do. Perhaps she'd disobeyed in the arena with Wranderous, who was already dying, but now she would not dare to disappoint. They had to escape and find Brendol's ship. She had to keep her baby safe no matter what.

They found the hangar door, and Brendol tapped in the code. The door slid up, and all of Vrod's Sentries looked up from where they sat around a table, playing a game with colorful bits of fabric.

"Where's Vrod?" someone asked, and that someone took a blaster bolt to the chest.

Siv stepped forward and stood her ground between Torben and Phasma, waiting to see what steps her leader would take. Without a word, Phasma began shooting before Vrod's people even stood up from their game. The air filled with the sound of blasterfire, bolts of red lighting up clouds of smoke. Soon Siv could smell roasting meat, and there was no one left breathing around that table. The Arratu Sentries' untouched weapons lay strewn on the ground around them, bits of machines and clubs like those from the Scyre fallen beside ancient blasters on the smooth white floor.

"Get in the GAVs," Brendol urged as he tapped in a code to open the huge hangar door. "Those three."

The two stormtroopers unplugged the vehicles, and each of them took the wheel of a spike-covered GAV, with Brendol helming their old, undecorated vehicle. Siv jumped in with one of the stormtroopers, pulling Gosta with her. Torben was with the other trooper, while Phasma rode with Brendol. Gray sand danced in through the open door, swirling across the swept floor as the machines revved and spun out into the desert and the growing darkness. Siv held on tightly, one arm around Gosta and one on the vehicle's handle. The trooper was driving as if a mob of angry citizens was on their tail, following

Brendol at an impossible speed. The open door yawned black behind them as they accelerated into the desert.

It was clear from his path that Brendol was hoping that the farther they got from the city walls, the less likely they'd be to hit more traps like the one that had claimed both their speeder bikes and, later, Elli's life. Siv couldn't help looking back at the city, at that strange dark blot in the middle of the desert, now lit by colorful lanterns, feeling that she'd left some small piece of herself behind. She had not known Elli well, but they'd been soldiers in the same war, breathed the same air and fought the same fights, and she felt some regret that Elli's body had been left alone to a room full of desperate people instead of receiving the last rites of Siv's detraxors that would allow the woman to live on by protecting the health of her friends. Brendol and the troopers had not even acknowledged the woman's death. Siv had not had many regrets before then, but she suspected that the farther they got from the Scyre, the more she would collect. She put a hand on her belly and told herself that it would all be worth it, to successfully deliver a healthy child somewhere among the stars, where none of her ancestors had been for generations.

Siv couldn't relax, not as long as Arratu's walls were visible. She knew there were traps here, possibly worse ones than the pit they'd encountered, and the afternoon was winding down to a sinister darkness. She also knew that even with Vrod and his Sentries dead, there would be plenty of people in Arratu violently desperate for a way out of their current limbo. She glanced back nervously, scouring the gray horizon for more vehicles or a line of people with torches, screaming and cheering and stomping their feet, hungry for something that life had denied them. How strange, that this part of Parnassos suffered from too many people, whereas the greatest issue facing the people of the Scyre was too few people. There wasn't much food back home, and every drop of water was hard-earned, but at least everybody was welcome, useful, given meaning. Meaning beyond one's weight in meat.

Finally, the dunes hid the darkening walls and rising tower of Arratu. No further traps had sprung, and Siv was able to relax, just the smallest bit, and focus on the journey ahead. The sun set like a drop of red fire into a still, gray pool, a rioting rainbow with a foul end that left the world a cold nightmare. Night fell completely, and the desert became a quiet and monochrome place. The drivers slowed their speed and turned up their bright lights; ahead, the cool sands glittered like jewels before disappearing into indigo shadows. Gosta fell asleep against Siv's shoulder, and after watching the endlessly rolling sands awhile longer, Siv tipped her head over and found her own escape in dreams.

She woke to the last thing she wanted: a fight.

TWENTY-FIVE

ON PARNASSOS, 10 YEARS AGO

IT STARTED WITH WHISPERED QUARRELING, AND SIV TENSED, HER SENSES already on high alert. Her vehicle had stopped, and the stormtrooper who'd driven it was gone. She knew well enough not to jerk awake noticeably, but merely kept her breath even as she waited, curled up against Gosta, and listened.

"The ship is that way, General Hux. I saw it from the tower. As did you."

"And the last time we went that way, Phasma, we lost one of my soldiers and ended up in a ditch. We were captured by the enemy and lost precious time. You were nearly killed."

"But I lived, and we escaped. We've gone this far without finding another trap. As Vrod said, it's unlikely the Sentries would range such a distance from their city walls. They are cowards."

"How would you know what another people might do? You've only ever known one people, whereas I have visited and studied hundreds of societies."

"I only need to know the people of my planet to know what they would do. And you are not of this planet."

In the tense silence that followed, Siv could hear the troopers somewhere nearby, laughing, and Torben snoring. So they'd stopped to camp. She realized she was holding her breath, and she forced herself to breathe as if asleep so she could continue eavesdropping. For all that she had hopes for Brendol's ship, there was still so much she didn't know about what would happen once they reached it.

Finally, Brendol sighed, and she could imagine him rubbing the space between his eyes. "No, I'm not from this pathetic, limping, wounded, rotten rock. I'm a general in the First Order, and I'm the savior who will get you off this miserable planet and give you the chance to become something real, something more than just an animal squabbling among weaker animals for some pathetic bone. But if you are to join me, you must look to your pride, Phasma. You must learn to gracefully accede to a superior's will."

"Not if I know I'm right."

"Would you rather be right or would you rather be alive?"

A long silence suggested eloquently that they both knew who was more deadly and who would survive a one-on-one fight.

"Allow me to appeal to your intellect, then," Brendol said. "I value subordinates willing to trust my vast training, wisdom, and knowledge instead of challenging me in front of others. That's who I will need, once my ship comes. That's what the First Order needs."

"And I value experience and a firsthand understanding of an environment. I value a backbone and an unwillingness to yield in the face of foolishness and shouting. That might not be what makes the best soldier, but it does make the best leader of soldiers. And you, after all, already have plenty of soldiers."

Brendol made a humming exhalation, almost a concession but still a warning.

"Do not forget that once we're off this planet, I am the arbiter of life and death for you and your people."

"And do not forget that as long as we're on this planet, I will be the one playing that role."

Brendol sighed, and Siv could hear him scratching at his scrubby

beard. "Perhaps you are right. You would never make a proper soldier. But if you could begin that way, hide your hubris and play by the
rules for a while, I feel certain you would rise quickly through the
ranks to a position of leadership that would satisfy you. And then,
together, we could train the greatest soldiers ever seen. With my simulations and your experience, your dedication, we'd be unstoppable.
You are a sword, but even the strongest, sharpest sword requires hon-
ing."

A chuckle from Phasma. "And what would you know of swords?"

"How to obtain them, pay for them, give them to thousands of
soldiers, and let them loose on a world that needs subjugating. There's
as much power in controlling the distribution of swords as there is in
wielding one."

"There's more power in the crucible that forges the weapon."

"But someone has to pay for that crucible."

In the long pause that followed, Siv could hear the troopers talking, tearing dried meat with their teeth. It was a still night, and sounds
carried. She risked opening her eyes, and in the low light she could
barely make out Phasma and Brendol leaning against the hood of her
GAV, eating jerky and the small fruits from the Arratu's tower.

"Perhaps your point is valid," Phasma said at last. "All my weapons
were found things I learned to adapt, not pretty things given to me as
a favor. But I tire of politics. The fact remains that the ship is that way,
and if we waste any more time, we may find it stripped to nothing by
the time we reach it. We are not the only scavengers on Parnassos.
And I sense that we're being followed."

"By whom? The remaining fools of Arratu?"

Phasma was silent for a beat before saying, "Whoever they are,
they're definitely fools."

Then, a strange sound: Phasma and Brendol Hux, laughing. Although they were often together, Siv had wondered if their relationship might become more. Their stiff posture and the space between
them suggested it had not and never would. The chuckle fell off, and
Brendol took up the pair of quadnocs, and Phasma watched him, one

hand on her blaster as if she might still be trying to decide whether he was more useful alive or dead.

Brendol put down the quadnocs and tapped his fingers on the GAV's hood. "As time runs out, so do our options. We'll go your way. But we'll send one of the other vehicles out in front to spring any traps that might be lying in wait. The one with your two women and PT-2445. If we have to lose anyone, that's our best bet."

"No. Siv and Torben can ride together. We'll say that Gosta will need to lie down, so she'll be the only one of my warriors in that vehicle. Siv has the detraxors, and they may yet be what saves us. The liniment and salve are more powerful than you realize. A great deal of sand still separates us and your salvation."

Siv went cold to her toes as it sank in that the two leaders were deciding who among their company was expendable. Of only seven people, two had been chosen as an acceptable sacrifice. For all that she was horrified—and insulted that Brendol considered her disposable—Siv could see the wisdom in it. Gosta was young and still sore from the crash, and she had no extraordinary skills. Still, seeing reason didn't mean it was right. Siv loved Gosta like a sister, and she would try to find a way to keep the girl from being sent out ahead like bait for trouble.

"We'll ride at sunrise, then," Brendol said. "Best get sleep while you can."

Phasma didn't answer, but Siv could sense annoyance rolling off her leader like heat waves. Most likely, Phasma was practicing the skill he'd requested and not snapping at him for instructing her as if she were some foolish child. Siv began to see why Phasma, the strongest and most daring leader she'd ever met, would bend to such a lesser man. She was banking on getting offplanet, and he was the key to that goal—and any success that followed it.

Brendol walked away, toward the GAV he'd driven. Soon, Siv could hear him tossing and occasionally groaning or sighing as he shifted position. It was ultimately much more comfortable to lean on someone you trusted, she thought, her cheek still on Gosta's shoulder. But who would Brendol Hux ever trust? Who *could* he trust? No one. And so he deserved that hard, cold, cramped full seat to himself.

Phasma was pacing around Siv's vehicle, and finally she took off her helmet and set it down with a heavy sigh. Siv watched through her lowered lashes as Phasma put her hands on the GAV's hood, her shoulders shaking. With rage or sadness? It was impossible to tell. Knowing Phasma as she did, probably a combination of the two. For all that Parnassos had become a daily hell in which their people could barely scrape by and often went to bed freshly grieving and panting for water, it was still home. And leaving home for the stars that had always seemed so impossibly far away was an enormously daunting possibility. Phasma had not spoken of defying and abandoning Keldo, but her warriors had known they could never go back. Even if Brendol's ship had been reduced to ash, the Scyre was no longer a possibility. Phasma, Torben, Gosta—they had become Siv's only family.

Not that it stopped Siv from missing Keldo.

She wasn't sure if it was suicide or not, but Siv slipped out of the vehicle and walked around silently to where Phasma stood. The warrior had straightened and was looking through the quadnocs, back at the dunes they'd left behind.

"Are you okay?" Siv asked softly.

Phasma did not put down the quadnocs, which meant Siv couldn't see her eyes, or even much of her face. But she could see the tear tracks glimmering in the moonlight.

"I'm fine."

Phasma's tone was clipped, a perfect mimic of Brendol's.

"What are you looking for?"

Phasma didn't answer.

"I'm surprised you're looking behind us instead of forward," Siv ventured.

Phasma snorted and put the quadnocs back on the hood, careful to keep her back to Siv as she leaned against the vehicle and crossed one boot over the other. It occurred to Siv that she hadn't seen Phasma's face since she'd slept off her beating. Perhaps the proud warrior didn't want the others to see and pity her pain. Or perhaps, thanks to Brendol's medicine, she was perfectly healed and trying to hide it.

"In my experience," Phasma said, "it's the thing that sneaks up behind you that's the real threat, not the one that faces you."

Siv leaned against the opposite side of the hood, her back to Phasma's. "So you trust the strangers?"

"Of course not. But you know as well as I do that the Scyre is dying." Phasma chuckled sadly. "Only one child. Frey will be the only one of her generation. And she'll die alone."

"There might be more children," Siv ventured.

"Not if their mothers can't bring them forth. Perhaps it's the air here. Perhaps there's some vital ingredient that the planet no longer provides. Perhaps almost starving is not the ideal way to conceive new life. But you've lost too many children already. You may yet lose the one you carry."

That answered one question Siv had wondered about. Phasma had always been sharp. But did she know it might be Keldo's?

"The medicine on their ship will fix it," Siv said.

"That is the hope."

"Do you think—" Siv started. But she stopped herself, worried that she was probing too deeply.

"Do I think?" Phasma's rare gentle tone suggested, for once, that Siv might continue.

"Do you think the First Order will come back and help all our people? Bring them to the stars, too, or take them to richer lands, or at least drop some supplies? So rich a people should have more than enough to share. I hate to think of Keldo—"

"Do not speak his name again to me."

The night went especially still and quiet after Phasma's harsh bark, which seemed to tear unwillingly from her throat.

"They could help him, too," Siv finished in a far meeker voice. "His leg is only a problem because Parnassos is so cruel. Perhaps there are other functions he could perform, with their help. He is an intelligent man, resilient. He could be useful—"

Phasma's fist hit the hood of the vehicle with a clank. "That's not my problem anymore. He made his choice. And he made the wrong one. Let him suffer for it."

Pushing away from the GAV's hood, Phasma snatched up the quadnocs and a few of the remaining fruits, which released a sweet, syrupy fragrance into the night, as if they might begin rotting at any moment. She walked to the top of the nearest dune, retracing the swiftly disappearing tracks of their vehicle and leaving her own shifting boot prints like a small river in the vast gray. Sitting on the top of the dune, she put the quadnocs to her eyes and stared back in the direction they'd come from, back toward the Scyre. Siv didn't think of Phasma as someone who valued nostalgia or regret. Which meant, as Phasma had just told Brendol, that she suspected they were being followed.

Their conversation over, Siv ate most of the remaining fruits. They were the sweetest things she'd ever tasted, her entire mouth flooded with juice. Is this what the world was like when there was enough water? Is this what Brendol's people ate on their ships in the sky? Perhaps she should've left more for someone else, but her stomach cried out with hunger. Thinking of her child, she sucked down all but the last fruit and wiped the evidence from her chin. She was instantly overcome with regret. In the Scyre, she would've divided the fruit into portions for herself, Torben, and Gosta, carefully ensuring that each person received a share that matched their needs. But here she was, alone and hoarding food. She told herself it was the baby, but she knew she was partially lying. The farther she got from the Scyre, and the more she followed Phasma's orders, the less sure she felt about who she truly was.

That night was a longer one than most. The adrenaline from the arena fight still sang in her blood, and thanks to her earlier nap, she barely slept. She used the time to pull out her leather bag of herbs and craft a new pot of oracle salve, as the old tin was running low. The sun here was more punishing than it had been back home, and they were using three times as much of the balm, yet their skin continued to redden, even under their masks. The complicated process was challenging, especially in the low light of a lantern they'd brought from Arratu, and by the time she was done, she was exhausted.

The argument she'd overheard between Brendol and Phasma replayed in her head as she snuggled up with Gosta, reminding her that the world was, in many ways, turned upside down. There was hope now, but there was also a new sense of dread. Every time she looked up from Gosta's shoulder, she saw Phasma's silhouette, a lonely figure keeping watch on the sand. Whatever Phasma was waiting for didn't happen that night, and the next morning they divided up the remaining Arratu food and began the next leg of their journey.

Siv couldn't find a way to prevent the group from splitting up as Brendol and Phasma had arranged. The way Brendol suggested that Gosta ride alone sounded downright gallant, and the girl was pleased and relieved to have the space to herself.

"Wouldn't you like to stay with me, though?" Siv asked.

"I mean, it would be nice to have some room." Gosta looked down, blushing, unaccustomed to arguing with her elders. "My ankle is feeling better, but it can get cramped."

So the girl stretched out in the back of her own GAV, driven by a trooper, while Siv found herself pressed up against Torben. Part of her was grateful for his reassuring bulk and easy company, but she just couldn't relax as she watched Gosta's hair bounce in the front vehicle, knowing that any traps or attacks from the front would claim the girl first, as the hidden pit before Arratu had. But then she realized that she and Torben were in back, the very direction from which Phasma was expecting trouble. Phasma and Brendol's GAV was neatly placed in the center, and while this fact would've escaped Siv just a few days earlier, now she had seen a brief slice of the machinations that happened in secret between Phasma and Brendol. And she didn't like them.

Life in the Scyre had prepared Siv well for this sort of journey. Very little occurred, but she was always wary, waiting for an attack or natural disaster. The motion of the vehicle had once exacerbated her nausea, but now it lulled her into a strange, light sleep, and she could feel the sun pressing against her eyelids as her body jigged with every slip of sand. Torben was a pleasant companion, happy enough to be quiet or chat, his arm keeping Siv upright and feeling safe. The trooper in front, Huff, was a study in silence. Siv often forgot he was there, much less that somewhere under that helmet and armor was a human being with a history, thoughts, and dreams. When they stopped for a brief lunch and to relieve themselves, she found herself curious about the man.

"Where are you from, Huff?" she asked.

He had his helmet off and was picking at some dried meat taken from the lizard attack while sipping his water. He had pale skin that seemed as if it had never seen the sun before, and the longer he stood out under the burning rays, the pinker and sweatier he looked. Siv had offered him some oracle salve, but he made a disgusted face and waved it away. Although he appeared to be in his early twenties, judging by how folk aged in the Scyre, his buff hair was already going thin. His eyes were a light gray that verged on white, and he frowned as soon as she spoke to him.

"Where am I from? The First Order," he said, as if she were a fool.

Siv noticed that his accent was different from Brendol's, something closer to her own, maybe.

"Is it a planet?"

He shook his head. "Hard to say what it is. The government that should be. It's the right side to be on, I'll tell you that."

"But were you not born on a planet?"

Huff shrugged. "I was in an orphanage somewhere when I was little, don't even remember where. Doesn't matter. It wasn't good. The First Order is my real home now. A ship called the *Finalizer*. When I came on as a kid, I'd never seen a place so big. You could walk all day long and never see everything. There're thousands of people on there I've never even met." He looked around the empty desert. "Opposite of this, really. The food isn't much, but I miss it. This meat tastes rotten."

He threw a strip of jerky down on the ground, and without thinking about it, Siv knelt to snatch it up and dust off the sand. She gave him a reproachful look.

"Food is not to be wasted here. Can you not see how very rare it is?"

"The First Order will pick us up, and then it won't matter. Until General Hux orders me to be thrifty, I'll go on as I always have."

As she cleaned the jerky off with her fingers and stuffed it in her mouth, she tasted it: the rot. Nothing lasted long enough in the Scyre to begin to turn, but she instinctively wanted to spit it out. Still, food was food, and her teaching ran deeper than her distaste. She swallowed it down quickly and followed it with a tiny sip of water from one of the Arratu skins. When she stood to ask Huff if he liked the First Order, he was already walking away. Not that it mattered. They were closer to their destination than to their old home, and there was no going back.

They were soon loaded into their vehicles and plowing toward where Phasma swore Brendol's ship would be. For hours and hours, there was nothing. No lumps, no animals, no walls. Nothing but rippled gray dunes of sparkling sand and the sun beating down, making Siv sleepy and woozy and wishing she hadn't eaten that strip of rotten jerky. The taste plagued her, and no matter how much she swallowed water or nibbled on salty sea veg, it wouldn't go away. Torben dozed beside her, one huge paw always on his club. His long, wavy hair billowed prettily in the breeze in a way that he wouldn't have been able to appreciate if she'd taken the trouble to explain it. He was a practical man, and beauty didn't last on Parnassos.

Siv grew bored and restless, her glance lazily switching from the lead vehicle, in which Gosta slumbered, to the middle one that Brendol drove, hunched over the steering wheel, while Phasma sat up in the turret, her hand on the gun and her helmet constantly turned to watch the sand behind them.

Siv told me that she felt something strange in the air then. As if the desert were holding its breath, waiting. Everything wavered in the haze with the sun at its highest, white and punishing. Her eyes hurt from staring at the sparkling gray, and each time the sun caught on a bit of metal, it flashed hot enough to leave red spots dancing in her field of vision. The drive became endless, and for the first time Siv worried that they might not make it to Brendol's ship. How could these vehicles keep going? What fuel powered them? How long would their water, salve, and food last until they started eyeing the weakest of their companions?

Or, to be more honest, how long until Gosta suffered an unfortunate and unavoidable accident and Brendol Hux merely shrugged as he urged Siv to use her detraxors?

"There's something ahead!"

The shout woke Siv from her uncomfortable, half-asleep musing, and she went on alert, one hand on her blade. Even though she'd been carrying the blaster, it was the scythes she'd inherited from her mother that fit her hands best and sang of home.

Torben likewise tightened to alertness beside her, shaking his head and muttering, "Yes, but what kind of something? That's the bit that matters."

Scanning the sands before them, Siv saw two things. The first was a strange fence made of metal wire stretching forever in either direction. The second was a figure glittering so bright that it burned her eyes to look at it.

Without a word, the lead GAV changed its direction, aiming for the figure. Siv couldn't tell from so far back whether it was a structure, a droid, a machine, or something different. Another mystery seen only from far off involved white placards placed at equal distances along the fence, flapping against the metal and making an eerie, toneless song as they were buffeted by the wind. Any writing that had been there had long ago been scoured away. The fence went on and on, rising stark against the bright-blue sky, and they didn't slow as they approached.

When they were almost within blaster-rifle range of the bright thing, the first GAV skidded to a halt. Brendol and Phasma's vehicle drew even with it and stopped, as did Siv's. All in a row, engines growling, they stared at the puzzling figure. Phasma pulled out her quadnocs, considered the scene, and handed them down to Brendol. He, too, looked a long time, and when the 'nocs dropped, he was frowning, his whole face bright red and dripping with sweat.

"What is it?" he asked Phasma.

She shook her head. "Nothing I've ever seen before."

"The way the sun reflects off it," Torben said. "It burns my eyes."

The two leaders hopped down from their vehicle, and Phasma gestured to her warriors to join her while Brendol consulted with his troopers. Even with the quadnocs, Siv couldn't tell what the bright thing might be, and she had the sharpest sight among the Scyre folk.

Gosta sidled up to Siv and tried the quadnocs herself.

"Strange," she muttered. "It's too lumpy for a machine, but too shiny for a living thing."

Brendol put a hand on Gosta's shoulder. "You're still injured. You stay here and guard the GAVs. Everyone else, have your weapons ready." He pulled his own blaster and fiddled with the switches on the side. "This is not normal."

"Well, what is, these days?" Torben said, hefting his club and ax.

The troopers went first, blaster rifles up and ready, their boots slipping through the sand. Phasma came next, Siv and Torben flanking her. Brendol came last, his blaster shaking in his hand as sweat dripped down his forehead in a way that Siv found nearly blasphemous when she glanced back. Gosta clearly hated staying behind, but she held her blaster and took her place in the back of her vehicle as the others crept up the hill. Defying Brendol had somehow become as ridiculous a thought as defying Phasma.

The whole thing seemed silly to Siv. If the mysterious object was a machine, it either was deactivated or had been tracking them all along. If it was an animal, it was stupid or slow, as it hadn't budged. She couldn't think of anything else that could pose a real threat, and yet Brendol commanded them to sneak up on it? Still, her leader was following his orders, and so she would follow Phasma.

Closer and closer they crept in plain sight, every blaster aimed, every bit of metal reflecting in the sun, and still the glittering thing didn't make any move whatsoever. Soon Siv could make out the true shape of it, and it reminded her of a statue she'd seen in Arratu, a piece of claywork vaguely in human form, apparently representing some much-loved Arratu of time past. This shape was lumpy like that, and yet the material wasn't anything she'd seen before.

"It's not your ship?" Phasma whispered to Brendol. "You said it would shine."

"Not like this."

They were close enough to poke it with a spear when two silver eyes blinked open amid the mirrorlike gold, each one the size of Siv's fist and segmented like an insect's.

"Ah. Greetings, travelers. Churkk has been waiting for you."

"Let's kill it," Torben whispered. "I don't like it."

Brendol holstered his blaster, held up his hands in a calming sort of way, and stepped forward.

"You are a Gand, are you not?"

"Churkk is a Gand you speak with, yes. Churkk is the last guardian of the dead lands."

Torben gestured to the infinite sea of gray sand behind them. "You mean there are lands deader than that?"

Churkk buzzed a laugh, and as its head shifted, Siv finally understood the glittering metal appearance. The Gand, if that's what a Gand was, was completely covered with the same kind of golden beetle that had been responsible for killing Carr. As it laughed, beetles darted from around its eyes and down to where its chin would be, if a giant insect had a chin. The beard of beetles shifted and clicked, making Siv shudder in horror. The Gand's face revealed was no less horrifying, a chitinous bag with alien eyes and an apparatus that looked nothing like a mouth, even if that's where the buzzing, clacking voice was coming from.

"Those beetles," Siv said, pointing. "Why do they not kill you?"

"The beetles are the closest thing Churkk has to family. It is lonely in the wastelands, is it not? Pleasant to have beings with which to converse."

"They can talk?" Torben asked.

Another buzzing laugh. "There is little to discuss. It has been many years since sentient beings have approached the border of the dead lands. Churkk has been inactive for a long period of time. It is good for Churkk to have work again. If you are ready, Churkk will deliver a message."

Brendol had been in conversation with his troopers, but now he stepped forward. "You have a message for us? From whom?"

"The question would be from what. Now that the signs have been scoured away by sand and wind, Churkk is the only warning. Do not enter the dead lands. There was a great accident, and the radiation remains. Those who pass this border will die within the week. No one enters. No one leaves. It is an elegant arrangement, but lonely. Perhaps Churkk is being punished."

"Punished for what?" Siv asked. She had never spoken to an alien before. For all the times she'd fought against the Claws, she'd never conversed with Balder or learned anything of his story. Part of her was awed by her fearlessness now.

"The Gand should not leave Gand. It is not the way. But Churkk was young and the augury was clear. Churkk had to depart. Churkk has long expected the other findsmen to hunt Churkk down for leaving the sect, but every ship is shot down long before Churkk can be found." The Gand laughed again, and Siv felt certain she heard more than a little madness as the beetles hurriedly bustled around Churkk's face and resettled. "It is amusing, is it not, to want to be both found and forgotten at the same time?"

"You said radiation." Brendol stepped closer, throwing Siv a warning glance. "And an accident. When was it?"

"Churkk does not know. Time passes strangely here. Churkk watched the latest star fall into the wastes, and although there is no gaseous mist here to show the right signs, the beetles talk to Churkk. They said people would come and horrible things would happen. Churkk has been very anxious for this eventuality to occur."

"Horrible things?" Phasma repeated sharply.

Churkk laughed its unsettling laugh again. Siv couldn't tell if it was male or female—if it even had a gender. She couldn't tell if the Gand was old or young. All she knew was that it was sitting on something as tall as she was, making the Gand appear larger than it actually was. Up close, watching the beetles undulate, she saw that Churkk sat cross-legged, hands on its knees. It didn't seem to have any weapons, but it was covered with beetles, wasn't it? One flick of a finger, and a single insect could kill their entire party. And if the Gand could direct the insects, speak to them somehow . . . well, Siv resolved not to make Churkk angry.

"Horrible things will happen either way, if that makes you more comfortable with your fate. Churkk is here only to warn you. Beyond this fence, you have perhaps four days before the sickness will be in your bones. Churkk knows that there are medicines elsewhere that can easily cure such diseases, but Churkk doubts that such succor can be found beyond this fence."

Brendol leaned toward Phasma, and Siv was close enough to hear their whispered conversation.

"He's talking about radiation poisoning. That suggests there was either a nuclear weapon used here or an accident at a factory that made such weapons."

"Did the map not name the Con Star facilities, General Hux? Perhaps there is a weapon, but perhaps there is also a facility that will have the medicines to cure the disease it causes."

Brendol exhaled and scratched at his beard. "If we can get to my ship, the First Order will be here within hours. Our ships are equipped with medbays and cures for every known disease in the galaxy. It's merely a game of numbers and time. I say we thank this freak for his time and keep moving."

"You're not concerned about the sickness? Or the augury?"

A snort. "I don't believe in magic, Phasma. And even if I did, I wouldn't take my fortune from a mad Gand alone in the desert. They are a strange people to begin with. I am confident the First Order can halt the sickness, should his warning concern an actual radioactive event."

Phasma paused in that way of hers, when she was thinking through every strategy to its many possible ends. Siv well knew that Phasma's brain was like a spiderweb, and that she would not make a decision until she'd considered every thread and its every connection. Holding up the quadnocs, Phasma looked through the fence to the sands beyond, then turned to regard the path behind. It was clear that no matter what challenges lay ahead, going back was not an option.

"Then let's hurry," she finally said.

Brendol nodded and turned back to the Gand, who hadn't moved. Siv couldn't even see it breathing and wondered what Churkk was made of, if it even had the usual organs and fluids that her detraxors would make such quick work of.

"Thank you for your warning, Churkk. We understand that this area is dangerous, but we have no choice but to continue in pursuit of our goal. Do you have any knowledge of the terrain or creatures that lie beyond the fence?"

Churkk's great head wagged, sending the beetles scurrying. "You will go on, as the augury said you would. And what will find you will find you. Churkk knows what you will do, great General, and Churkk knows that you will reach your goal. The galaxy will take its toll, one day. Sometimes it is better to let a thing alone."

"But none have passed recently?"

"Not in years. Decades."

"And if anyone else tries, you will give them this same warning?"

"You do not control Churkk, and Churkk will say what the sands command. Churkk will tell whoever comes what they need to know. Churkk will tell them that only danger and death wait beyond this fence, the same thing that you now know, for all the good it did. Wisdom is wasted on zealots—that is one thing Churkk is sure of."

"So we may pass?"

Churkk held up a beetle-covered arm, gesturing with a brown, three-fingered hand. "You will find a hole in the fence if you walk that way."

Siv darted forward, leaving a bit of dried meat near Churkk's seat but not close enough for a beetle to touch her. "Thank you, Churkk," she murmured, bowing her head. Her mother had taught her, long ago, that there was some wisdom in madness, and that those who spoke with the beyond were to be respected and rewarded.

"When the time comes, keep walking," Churkk whispered, soft as an insect's buzz.

Siv nodded and turned back to her people, but her heart sank the moment she looked over her shoulder toward Gosta and their vehicles.

"Hurry!" she shouted. "They're here!"

TWENTY-SIX

ON PARNASSOS, IO YEARS AGO

A GROUP OF MASKED WARRIORS RAN TOWARD THEM, PULLING SOMETHING that resembled the sleds of the skimmers who had once attacked them. Siv couldn't pick out anyone else in the throng, but she knew the figure being pulled on the sled as well as she knew anything.

"It's Keldo."

Phasma had her quadnocs up, and she had an even better view.

"Keldo, all of the Scyre, and all of the Claws. This is madness."

"Looks more like revenge," Brendol muttered.

The group was coming on quickly, sliding down the dune toward their vehicles, where Gosta was just exiting her GAV and looking back for the source of the noise. She must've seen them, too, as she spun back around and ran as fast as she could toward the fence, hampered by her turned ankle. Siv took a few steps forward to help the girl, but Phasma caught her wrist, the hard glove of the trooper uniform digging into Siv's flesh.

"You can't save her," Phasma said. "We must keep going."

Behind them, Brendol shouted, "They can't be allowed to take the vehicles! Fire!"

The troopers put their blaster rifles to their shoulders, and they pelted the vehicles and the oncoming attackers with red-hot laserfire. The first GAV went up in a ball of flame that caught the second, and the third lost a wheel and listed sadly to the side.

"Phasma, help!" Gosta called, her arms outstretched toward the warrior she'd idolized.

But Phasma merely shook her head, her stormtrooper helmet a flat white mask. Siv tried to pull away, but Phasma's grip tightened.

"She's one of us," Siv begged.

"She's too weak to go on."

"Then we'll carry her!"

Keldo's warriors had almost reached Gosta, and the troopers focused their blasters on the crowd. Smoke filled the air, providing a hazy backdrop for exploding clouds of sand and blood-red lasers. Siv yanked and pulled, but Phasma wouldn't release her. She couldn't watch as the laserfire rocked into the mob of people she'd known all her life, as bodies cried out and screamed and fell, so she put her head down against the armor on Phasma's shoulder, a strangely personal gesture that Phasma allowed.

When Phasma pushed her away, Siv turned around. Behind what was left of the mob, Gosta lay on the ground among a dozen other bodies. The girl wasn't moving, her eyes open to the sky.

Little Gosta, the sweetest and most idealistic of the Scyre warriors, was dead.

"No!"

Phasma still had Siv's wrist, as if correctly guessing that Siv would be compelled to run toward the younger girl. Not only because there might be some hope of saving her, but also because to die alone without helping her people would leave Gosta's spirit uneasy and Siv's responsibility undone. Siv's fingers itched for the detraxors in her pack, for the calm she felt when she completed her holy rite, and her arms ached to hold the girl close and tell her she had been a good and brave companion, a worthy warrior of the Scyre. But Phasma was tugging Siv away, toward the rent in the fence, and soon Torben joined in, pulling Siv unwillingly along, murmuring apologies and kindnesses that did nothing to soften the blow of her loss.

All those bodies—or at least many of them—had received the gift of the detraxors, proudly wearing green stripes of the oracle salve, and now they would never contribute their own proper shares. When she'd chosen to side with Phasma and leave the Scyre on this quest, Siv had known she was abandoning her people, denying them the protective balm they needed to survive and stay healthy. She'd planned to return before they began to suffer, to help them build a new life in the stars with better medicines than anything she could provide. Now her people were dying. Guilt rested heavy on her shoulders, and it felt like a thirst that could never be slaked.

Siv's feet moved in the sand as if it were quicksand. She ventured a last look back at Churkk, where the Gand lay dead, toppled on the ground and leaking a fluid that wasn't blood. The beetles that had bedecked him ignored his moisture, leaving his face and body to feast instead upon the destruction rendered by the blasterfire. Underneath the beetles, the insectoid alien had worn the blood-red robes of the Arratu, his segmented feet bare and his three-fingered hands open to the sky. Siv looked to Brendol, his blaster still in his hand, but there was no way to know if the strange guardian's death had been collateral damage or a purposeful execution.

Torben and Phasma dragged Siv away for real now, each grasping the top of one of her arms. Her detraxors weighed heavy on her back, to see so many nutrients lost. When the shimmering gold beetles boiled up out of the sand to cover Gosta, Siv finally turned away, shaking her arms loose, and found her legs again. The last thing she saw was the crowd of Scyre and Claws, those who hadn't been hit by blasterfire and claimed by beetles, running across the sand, war cries erupting from their masks as they pulled Keldo's sled behind them. She had shared his bed but never seen his mask before, and from this distance she couldn't tell what might've inspired it. Harsh slashes of black, white, and red were surrounded by a mane of black feathers. The sight was enough to get her running.

They jogged parallel to the high fence, passing sign after wind-scoured sign, until they came to a rip in the metal wires. One of the troopers held it back while everyone crawled through, and Torben was nearly too big to fit. Siv was worried the loose wires would cut him and call forth the beetles, but Phasma silently shoved him aside and dug a deep furrow in the sand to make more room. Once they were all through, Brendol held the two pieces of fence together and slapped some sort of binder around the wire, holding it tight.

"It won't last long," he said, echoing Siv's thoughts, "but it will slow them down."

Once inside the fence, nothing seemed different from the other side. The sand was still gray, the sun still beat down, and the air didn't feel any more dangerous than it had before they'd crossed the border, as Churkk had called it. But Siv shivered anyway, sure to her bones that something was desperately wrong here. The words the Gand and Brendol Hux had exchanged—*weapon, radioactive, nuclear*—were on repeat in her mind as she probed the environment for some new sensation that would inform her of what to fear. Phasma guided them in the direction of Brendol's ship, and as Siv had never doubted her leader's unerring navigation, she didn't doubt it now. She took her place, after Phasma and before Torben, running easily and deeply feeling the empty spots in their formation that should've been taken by eager Gosta and cheerful Carr. They had left their land as five warriors, and even if the dead lands didn't live up to their threat, they would only ever be three. Four, maybe, if Brendol's medicine was as good as he promised it was and the child could survive whatever poison had destroyed this place.

They went down a long dune, and the land flattened out a little, as it had here and there throughout their travels. Judging by the disks she'd seen at Terpsichore Station, Siv thought this meant that long ago these areas had been naturally lower, true valleys and craters that had once held water and plants. At first, there was no sign of any such topography, but as they went on, strange shapes and shadows began to appear in the monochrome gray. They began to pass tall posts, each leaning sideways like a broken finger reaching from the ground.

Farther on, a peculiar skeleton of metal rose proudly from the sand, looping and whirling like the spine of the giant eels that washed up on the rocks sometimes at home.

"Were they animals?" she asked.

Brendol had fallen behind, slowing them all with this lack of physical conditioning, and he held his side and wheezed as he spoke. "Amusements," he said. "They once guided vehicles that people rode for fun. An archaic form of entertainment on planets without enough technology to stimulate the populace from inside their own homes. This planet had much land and little sense."

As they went on, forced by Brendol's reduced speed to slow from a jog to a fast walk, Phasma moved to the rear. She couldn't walk more than a few moments without spinning to scan the horizon behind them. Keldo and his people hadn't shown themselves yet, but they'd be following. In such an empty, deserted place and with the beetles and who knew what other horrors hiding under the sand, there was nowhere to hide.

Dusk fell, and they hurried toward a series of bleached white structures poking up from the sand like shattered teeth. Although their walls seemed sound, there were no roofs to the buildings, and sand filled them inside, dusted high into the corners.

"Homes," Brendol said before Siv could ask. "And we'd best shelter in one tonight. We can't go much farther without rest. If the other group has been on foot this whole time, they'll be no better off."

Siv knew well enough that Brendol's *we* actually referred only to himself. The Scyre warriors were more than capable of walking for several more hours, and the troopers were in excellent physical condition. But Brendol wasn't made for Parnassos. When he pulled down his goggles and fabric wraps to rub sweat from his forehead, his reddened face was bleached white around the edges; there were deep-purple hollows under his eyes, and his muscles quivered. His hand hadn't left the stitch in his side, and he stumbled every few steps, although there was nothing to impede his footwork. He must've recognized how dire his situation was, as he allowed Siv to swipe thick lines of salve across his cheeks.

"There." Phasma pointed to the last structure in the grouping, which sat a little higher and had part of what had once been a roof.

"PT-2445 will take first watch," Brendol said. "We'll switch every two hours. After the third watch, we'll keep going."

Casting nervous looks at the sand behind them, they walked through the empty doorway and spread out around the building, which was divided into many rooms, all filled with sand. Although it was clear the rooms had once been tall enough even for someone of Phasma's stature, the sand had filled the structure so that its walls were just tall enough to provide a decent backrest for Torben, with perhaps a meter of space until jagged metal support beams poked out of the uniform white. Siv went to a corner, sitting down hard and pawing through her bags for the reassuring touch of her detraxors. It was her duty to make sure everyone had a last application of oracle's salve before sleep claimed them, and the ritual of the task calmed her.

Torben sat down beside her, and she gently drew lines of salve on his cheeks and forehead. They were near Brendol's ship, and whatever hidden dangers lurked in the dead lands, she longed to protect him.

"Thank you," he murmured.

"Body to body, dust to dust," she replied.

Her mother had explained that it was part of a far older ritual, but the ceremonial words always made her feel tied to the planet and to her own lineage, for all that her mother was the only relation she remembered. When she offered the tin of salve to Brendol and his troopers, she received brief thanks from Pete and Huff, both out of their helmets, but Brendol only nodded, which would've been a rudeness worth fighting over back home in the Scyre. As she approached Phasma, Siv realized that she would never again smear the lines on Gosta's cheeks, fussing over the girl and reminding her to drink enough water.

Phasma was the only one sitting outside the building, her back to what would've been the outer wall. She still wore her helmet, and Siv's curiosity about the impact of Wranderous's beating continued unabated.

When she held the tin out to Phasma, Phasma took off her gloves, scooped out her portion, and paused for a moment, as if she'd forgotten what to say. When her words came, they were clipped and atonal, the very mimic of Brendol, if he'd been polite enough to say them.

"Thank you."

Siv bowed her head slightly. "Body to body, dust to dust."

She stayed standing, though, hoping Phasma would say something or take off her helmet or do anything that would provide comfort or understanding. Back in the Scyre, Keldo had been the voice and heart of their leadership, the one who always knew what to say, whether it involved offering kindness, support, company, or admonishment. Back then, Phasma's quiet had seemed like one half of a whole, as if her part of their sibling bond was the realm of the physical, of protection and defense and valor. Now, without Keldo's tenderness and empathy to ground her, Phasma seemed cold and inhuman. The helmet only served to heighten her resemblance to a droid like the ones back in Terpsichore Station, which had never changed their expression even as they did horrible things.

And yet the way Phasma focused on the sand—it was clear she felt something.

"You can take extra," Siv said, almost without thinking, as she weighed the tin in her hand. It was Gosta's portion for the day, and years of carefully monitoring her people's needs had trained Siv to mete out exactly what was required and hold back enough for all. Now it only served to remind her that Gosta had been little more than a child, for all that she'd sought to belong among the warriors and acquitted herself well in battle.

"Save it. Perhaps it will keep us going tomorrow." Phasma's voice was flat and clipped, and Siv could tell, even with the helmet, that Phasma wasn't watching her.

"The sickness that Churkk mentioned. Do you feel it?"

Phasma's helmet shook once. "No."

"I wonder if we'll even know. If it will come on like the fever, hot and itching, or if it will sneak up in the night like the old barking cough once did. Or perhaps he was merely mad."

"Perhaps."

Siv waited several long minutes, hoping Phasma would say something, anything, to reassure her that her leader had not, in fact, begun to head in the direction of madness herself. The longer Phasma sat there, scanning the horizon, holding her portion of salve while not removing her helmet to apply it, doing and saying nothing, her hand on her blaster, the further she felt from the girl Siv had grown up with and learned to trust with her life.

Siv tried one last gambit. "Do you think we'll make it?"

At that, finally, the helmet turned toward her and canted up. She felt Phasma's keen gaze crawling over her and wondered what her leader saw in her lieutenant.

"Perhaps."

Siv turned to leave, but she couldn't go until she'd had her say. Even if it was like prying sea creatures from their shells, she would know something of Phasma's mind as they entered a place that truly terrified her.

"Brendol Hux says we can make it. He says his ship will be there, and his people will come. He says they'll take us into the stars and give us medicine. That they can fix whatever is harmed here. Do you think it's true?"

Phasma's helmet clicked as her gaze left Siv and returned to the gray horizon, the setting sun casting long, black shadows from the metal bones of long-dead civilizations.

"We can only act as if it's true," Phasma said. "We can only keep going."

Siv nodded and walked away, considering. Phasma was right. At this point, there was nothing else to be done. They could only press forward, believing that Brendol Hux would be their savior.

If he was lying, they would be dead soon enough, anyway.

Siv woke covered by Torben's huge arm and a dusting of sand. Every crevice of her body itched, tortured by the feathery gray stuff, and she flung it off and stood, trying to find her balance. The grit stung her

eyes, and she brushed it from her eyelashes as she faced the direction
from which they were being pursued. She didn't see Keldo and his
band, but she had no doubt there was little time to waste. Phasma
was already awake, in conversation with Brendol. Siv's brow wrinkled, and she put on her own mask again. It irked her that she had to
work so hard to get a few meaningless words out of her leader, while
Phasma seemed more than happy to converse with Brendol in secret.
In her opinion, Phasma should've been loyal to her people first, and
her allies second. Phasma apparently did not see it the same way anymore.

"Get up, you big brute." Siv rubbed Torben's shoulder, smiling as
he twitched awake and frowned at the sand covering him as if he
were a great mountain.

"I'm buried," he said in surprise. "Another hour, and you'd have
lost me."

"Hardly. You're the biggest lump in view."

It made her feel good, tending to Torben, giving him bits of food
and his morning share of water and spreading him with extra salve.
With Gosta gone, she ached to take care of someone, to make some
kind of nurturing connection. As for Torben, he put up with her
clucking and pulled her into a hug, and it felt so good to be held that
she felt her eyes prick with tears as she slipped off her mask and buried her face in his chest, a stolen moment of comfort that felt all the
more precious in such a precarious situation.

If the Gand had told the truth, they were headed toward the
deadliest place on Parnassos, and that was saying a lot. Every other
enemy Siv had faced was something that could be fought head-on—
opposing groups, sea beasts, even a monster like Wranderous. But
whatever creeping death awaited them was some sort of disease with
unknown symptoms that could already be taking over her body,
somewhere deep inside. When the child wiggled within her, barely a
burble of bubbles, she put a hand to her belly and offered up thanks.
At least what she held most precious was still untouched. So far.

They set out before the sun had truly breached the sky, and Brendol grumbled that they should be walking at night, when the air was cool and clear, rather than saving their work for the heat of the day. Siv expected Phasma to share her own thoughts on the matter, but she remained silent. In the Scyre, Phasma would've had a sharp reprimand for any warrior in her company who complained or questioned her judgment, and there would've been punishment for anyone who slowed the entire party down with their lack of vigor and energy. Yet Phasma matched their pace to Brendol's without a word, subtly resetting their path every time they started to veer off. Siv was too well trained by now to question this strange and silent battle of wills. Her sole task was to get to Brendol's ship alive, preserving her child and Torben as well as she could. Even if she had her doubts, Phasma was her leader, and Siv was duty-bound to follow her orders, even when she felt conflicted by Brendol's interference.

They left the long-empty buildings, and new shapes rose up against the morning sky. These weren't small homes like those filling the last area. They were huge stations, as big as Terpsichore or Arratu but . . . ravaged. The first one was missing part of its metal roof, with black shadows ghosting up its white walls. The farther they walked, the more damaged the buildings appeared. Their roofs were gone, their walls burned and cracked and missing great chunks. Siv felt woozy as she looked around and tried to imagine what could do so much damage to such a large area. Even the mighty ocean took years to chip away at the stone cliffs of the Scyre. After they stopped to take care of personal needs behind a particularly mangled structure, Siv noticed several black shadows shaped like people painted on the wall.

"What is that? More art?" she asked Brendol, who was waiting nearby in the shade of a wall, his goggles and wraps undone as he scratched at his eyes.

He turned to follow her glance.

"Residue from a nuclear blast," he said, brow furrowed and mouth pursed. "We must be near the epicenter."

"Residue?"

"Oh, look. People were standing in front of the wall when the bomb hit. Everything exploded, and the power of the blast disintegrated them where they stood. Their remains were sort of pressed into the wall by the power of the explosion. Do you see?"

"No. I don't know what an explosion is."

Everyone except Torben had gathered around now to listen, and Brendol put his hands on his hips and considered them. He'd put his black outfit back on sometime after Arratu, and the color was being leached out by the sun, the careful pleats and folds and puffs dusted with gray sand and wrinkled. The once shiny black boots were dull and cracked. His beard had grown out to a patchy red-and-white scruff, and his face was flushed an unhealthy red with a few developing spots like the ones Siv had suffered during her teen years.

"Look, it's very complicated," Brendol said. "But you know what lightning is?"

Siv nodded. "Of course."

"Imagine a huge bolt of lightning. So big and with so much power that it destroys everything as far as the eye can see. Every person, every animal, every plant, every building. Only the very strongest surfaces made of the most resilient minerals might survive it. Organic matter is disintegrated, utterly destroyed and leaving nothing behind. The entire sky goes black with smoke, blocking the sun and turning the rain to poison. Literally nothing survives."

"I can't imagine that," Siv said, but her voice was hollow.

She couldn't imagine it, but she *could* understand it. Brendol's description explained so much about Parnassos, about why there was nothing left. She'd always been told that the planet itself had been the cause of her people's destruction, but this made more sense. Of course it was people. People had destroyed this place. And people had left behind the few survivors to piece together a violent life filled with pain and toil. Torben had rejoined them and heard the last bit, his face flushed red with fury as if he would gladly drag the person responsible out of whatever hole they were hiding in and beat them to death. He put his arm around Siv as if wishing he could protect her and the child from all the sorrows Parnassos had inflicted.

"Who did this?" Phasma asked.

Brendol chuckled. "Isn't it obvious? The Con Star Mining Corporation. Whether they were responsible for the bombing, whether a rival corporation accomplished it, or whether their faulty technology triggered a nuclear meltdown, it was clearly them. And instead of fixing their mess, they abandoned the entire planet."

"Do they still do business in your world?" Phasma asked.

"They are a large and profitable business in the galaxy, yes."

"Something should be done."

Brendol nodded, looking crafty. "Perhaps that can be arranged. They own many valuable assets, and the First Order always needs more assets."

Siv felt that Phasma and Brendol had just reached an unspoken arrangement, that they had some prior understanding of how their paths would . . . well, not intersect. Probably not intertwine, either, as Phasma didn't seem to particularly like him. *Align* was probably the better word. Brendol had something in mind for Phasma to do, some special place among his people that would benefit him.

Brendol was the first to walk on, turning from the imprinted shadows as if he'd finished looking at a particularly boring rock. The troopers followed him, as did Phasma, who quickly outpaced him to lead. Siv and Torben lingered a moment, and he pulled her more tightly to his side. The black shadows appeared to be two different sizes, and Siv imagined she saw adults and children there, an entire family group reduced to nothing but a hazy image on a wall.

"The faster we walk, the faster we'll find safety," Torben reminded her.

She turned in his arms to look up into his unmasked face and immediately put the back of her hand to his forehead. "Do you feel feverish?" she asked.

For though his anger had fled, his color remained high. A few tiny spots lurked under his scruffy brown beard, and his eyes were bright green against pink whites. His skin was cool against hers, though, and when she put her fingertips to his pulse, his heart was beating steady and strong.

"I feel fine," he said, eyebrows drawing down in confusion. "And you?"

She put her hand to her own cheek. Her skin, too, felt cool, but her fingers danced over a few bumps at her temples, where her hair pulled back from her scalp.

"Churkk said there would be a sickness," she said. "I wonder if this is how it starts."

Torben gently pulled her mask into place and urged her to walk as the others disappeared around the next building.

"We'll ask Brendol later," he said, giving her a squeeze. "Nothing to be done for it now. I feel strong as ever."

He thumped his chest and grinned at her, and she returned the smile, for all that it felt false. She'd learned much of bodies, tending the detraxors and, before that, caring for the elderly and infected in the Nautilus. When several people all showed similar signs of some new malady, it was never a good omen.

But Torben was right. There was nothing to be done but keep walking. Whatever this illness was, she'd never heard of it and had no curatives in her pack or in her memory. All she could do was make sure everyone took extra salve and liniment, and that it would continue to provide some sort of protection. Siv and Torben jogged to catch up with the others, climbing up the slight hill of a dune. Every time they clambered up out of a low spot, she grew excited for the sight of whatever lay over the ridge. Even if what she saw generally brought only trouble, from the skinwolves to Arratu to the fence and the dead lands beyond, she still felt a swell of optimism. This time, finally, her hopes were answered.

They topped the dune when the sun was high and looked down on two things: utter devastation . . . and the remains of a ship.

TWENTY-SEVEN

ON PARNASSOS, 10 YEARS AGO

"THERE IT IS," BRENDOL SAID, SOUNDING CHEERFUL FOR THE FIRST TIME IN Siv's memory.

"It appears untouched," Phasma added, looking through her quad-nocs. "If someone else had reached it first, it would be stripped to nothing."

From what Siv could see of the ship, it was the size of a building and covered in the shiniest metal she'd ever seen, bright enough to rival the beetles that had covered Churkk. But the ship was silver rather than gold, and the sun gleamed off it so fiercely that she had to shield her eyes with her hands. Hope swelled in her heart, and she could barely contain her excitement. For all that she'd let herself believe in Brendol's promised future, she had never fully trusted the man, or his story of the First Order's might and generosity.

The wrecked ship was just in front of a structure she recognized all too well: another Con Star Mining Corporation station. It had been utterly destroyed, as had all the outbuildings around it. Twisted chunks of metal and broken poles poked up through the sand, and two great cylinders the size of the station itself towered behind it, dead gray against the flat blue sky.

"That's what happened," Brendol said, almost to himself. Then, louder, "It was a nuclear accident. Someone must've cut corners on building materials or made another stupid error. The galaxy should be beyond this sort of tragedy. Under the First Order, a company could not simply devastate a planet and abandon it. Who knows how many lives were lost here." He shook his head and spit into the sand, and for once Siv didn't blame him. If wasting a tiny glob of moisture was blasphemy, then killing millions of people was even more so.

"So the sickness . . ." Siv began.

Brendol looked at her, his earlier cheer gone. "Yes. We'll feel it soon. Radiation poisoning. The redness, the boils. Then weakness. It will get worse. The faster we get to my ship and call the First Order, the faster they'll get us off this dead rock and pumped full of the antidote."

"Which is?"

He waved his hand dismissively. "Chelation, antioxidants, drugs. Not my field. This is why we have med droids. The point is that the more time we spend standing here talking about it, the lower our chances of surviving long enough to be cured."

Phasma took off running, and even Brendol found his speed in her wake. They surged down the other side of the dune and into the crater below, slipping and sliding in the sand, falling and getting back up to run again. A throbbing ache began behind Siv's eyes, and for just a moment she saw double and almost swooned. But then Torben had her arm, and she was up and running again. Even the Scyre warriors were winded by the time they reached the ship, close enough to see the angles of the smooth craft and the cracked plates of metal strewn around it and damaged by the impact.

Brendol was breathing so hard that he couldn't speak. He waved his arm at his troopers, and they attempted to climb up onto the metal, their boots sliding on the chrome. Siv didn't know that word—chrome—but I do. I'm sure you recall that craft, having ridden in it yourself a few times in your day. It was once Palpatine's favorite yacht on Naboo, and I don't know how Brendol got his hands on it, but he loved it. And then it disappeared from the records. Perhaps you remember when you stopped seeing it. Maybe Brendol told you he'd sold it, or that it had been retired. He probably didn't want to admit that he'd crashed it and abandoned it.

It was no easy task breaking into a damaged ship of that size without the right equipment, and the troopers were making a poor job of it.

"Leave this to us," Phasma said, and she nodded at Siv and Torben.

Pleased to have real work to do, they pulled their Scyre gear out of their bags, claw boots and gloves and rappelling lines and grappling hooks crafted from detritus and rusty mining equipment. In the Scyre, such things were necessary every day, but the climbing rigs had been useless ever since they'd rappelled down the mountain and landed in endless sand. For just a moment, having ascended her line to stand high on the silver wing of the ship, Siv was flooded with pure joy and accomplishment, forgetting all that had befallen her family in the last week. When she looked through the broken transparisteel of the cockpit, however, her happiness fled. Two dead humans sat within, strapped into their chairs in black helmets, beetles fighting to lap up the dried blood discoloring their black clothes.

As Phasma turned to drop a rappelling line to the troopers to help haul Brendol up into the cockpit, she froze. Siv followed her gaze and felt her heart stutter. It was Keldo. And all the Scyre and all the Claws, already over the dune and rushing forward, weapons ready.

"Pull me up!" Brendol shouted. "Hurry!"

Whatever he said next was lost in a volley of blaster bolts from the troopers and the mad cacophony of war cries.

At least fifty people were headed directly for the wreck, and Siv and Torben ducked as more blasterfire flickered off the ship around them. Keldo's people must've found Gosta's blasters and the spare blasters left behind in the GAVs.

Siv had never been on the receiving end of blasterfire, and it was disorienting. The shiny metal deflected the bolts, but that just meant there were two ways to get shot, from the initial fire and from the ricochets bouncing back in random directions. Phasma struggled to singlehandedly pull Brendol up onto the ship, but then the line flapped in her gloved fingers, shot by a lucky blast. Brendol fell more than a meter and landed badly, crying out and flailing on his back as his troopers knelt in front of him, returning fire at the approaching attackers.

"We must get to the ground and defend Brendol," Phasma said.

"He's not one of us!" Torben shouted, neatly conveying what Siv had struggled so long to communicate.

"But he's the only one capable of bringing the First Order to help. If we don't save him and get him up here to make the call, we die here."

Siv saw and hated the truth of it, and she knew her only chance was to follow Phasma's orders. When Phasma jumped backward off the ship to rappel to the ground, Siv followed, and Torben was right behind them. They landed in a cloud of sand, Siv's hands stinging from the rope's friction, even through her gloves.

"Protect Brendol at all costs," Phasma said, speaking to them and to the troopers, who were already doing so.

Phasma pried a rectangle of metal out of the sand and flipped the broken ship plating up as a shield to face the attackers, and Torben followed suit. Siv gladly joined him behind the makeshift barricade as the troopers did the same, sheltering Brendol between them behind their panel. With each blaster hit, the metal rang and shook, and Siv used both arms to push sand behind it and help Torben hold it up. Whenever she sensed a break in the shooting, Siv peeked around her edge and shot back. The sudden rush of triumph she felt each time one of her blaster bolts found home was immediately swallowed down by sadness as her brain registered who she'd just felled. These people had been there all her life, helping her toddle about the Nautilus and teaching her how to make strong boots and pushing her to be fearless as she learned to leap between rock spires. Now she was ending them with the single pull of a trigger, not even in a valiant and worthy fight. Most of them were armed with only axes and knives, the rough weapons of the Scyre, and still they kept running toward her, screaming as if they had a chance. One by one, she picked them off and watched them fall.

Despite their diminishing numbers and the ongoing blasterfire tearing them apart, Keldo and his people continued their attack. Someone had attached a piece of metal to the front of Keldo's sled, and he was ducked down behind it, avoiding the fire just as Siv's side was, which made Siv feel both frustrated and glad. She didn't want to hurt him. But she didn't want to die, either. The Scyre and Claws were coming fast, and Siv suspected that, soon, they'd be close enough to call one another by name and see the light leave the eyes of friends as they died far from their home territory, swarmed by beetles and crusted with gray sand.

The first warrior crashed into Phasma's metal shield, a Claw swinging a big ax, aiming for Phasma's body behind the metal plate. Phasma put a foot against the metal and kicked him over, dispatching him with an impersonal blaster bolt to the chest. If not for her imposing height and the flash of Arratu cloth between the joints of her armor, she could have easily been one of Brendol's faceless, nameless troopers.

Siv didn't have long to ponder her leader's transformation. The wave of warriors struck, and she was too busy hacking with her scythe and shooting with her blaster to consider philosophy. The blaster wasn't as strong or trustworthy as the ones Phasma and the troopers wielded, but Siv was grateful for the ability to fight at two ranges and to end a foe without having to pull a blade out of sticky flesh. She took down two Claws with the blaster, but it clicked and failed to shoot the third body in the line. Screaming her own war cry, taken over fully by the bloodlust of war, Siv rose from behind the shield and lashed out with one of her blades, a weapon that never failed. It bit into a woman's neck, half cleaving it from her shoulder.

The woman's surprised eyes met Siv's, and Siv realized it was Ylva, the mother of Frey. She pulled out the blade, horrified, and looked around for the treasured little girl, but all she saw were yet more warriors out for her blood. Ylva sputtered on the ground and began screaming as the golden beetles surged up from the sand, swarming over her and feasting on the blood. There was nothing for it; such wounds would not heal. Siv's only gift was mercy. She slashed Ylva across the throat and moved on to the next attacker, no time to use the detraxors or say the prayer for Ylva, no time even to clean the blood from her scythe.

She caught glimpses, between attacks, of her fellow fighters, her former family. Torben wrestled with his own brother, born much smaller and less inclined to brutality, and it was clear that Torben didn't want to be the one responsible for his older brother's death. They wrestled with bare hands, their weapons long ago fallen to the sand, and although Torben could've ended the fight in ten different ways, snapping his brother's neck or spine or bashing his nose up into his brain, he just kept growling at the man, holding him in something that might've been a hug if they hadn't been muttering ferociously at each other about loyalty, surrounded by the dead and dying.

Between assaults, Siv watched her side struggle, what few of them there were. One of the troopers was dead, and Brendol was industriously hunched behind the shield, putting on the man's armor. The other trooper had a blaster in each hand and was methodically shooting everyone in his path. A trail of bodies slid down the dune, full of blaster holes and gently smoking, some still crawling or moaning. This was not how fights went in the Scyre, not how Balder's band had faced off with Phasma's warriors. There had been an element of courage and respect in their skirmishes, the bands testing each other, whetting their skills against their opposition like a blade to a stone. But this? It was slaughter, and it turned Siv's stomach. There was no honor in this fight.

As for Phasma, she had abandoned her shield and entered her pure element: war. She danced from attacker to attacker, evading every sword stroke and ax hit. There was an elemental elegance to her every move, to the cold precision with which she dispatched every warrior who approached her with malice. Watching her, Siv could see the path she forged, and it led straight to Keldo. Unable to fight, thanks to his missing leg, he waited behind his shield, his mask hiding his true face and two discarded blasters on the sand by his sled. Tiny fingers curled around his shield suggested that the child, Frey, hid behind it with him.

That was the moment when Siv realized that even if Phasma was wrong, Keldo wasn't right, either. A good leader would've accepted the loss of his greatest warriors and worked to shore up his territory. He would've armed the next line of defense, secured food and shelter for those who remained, and focused on maintaining his relationship with the nearest band, likewise recently weakened. Instead, Keldo had abandoned his generational home, the territory for which they had fought so long and given up so much, and brought all his people here, across the wastelands, to die on a hopeless journey of revenge.

A soft cry drew Siv's attention, and she watched Torben fall. The big man landed on his knees, then gently slumped sideways onto the sand, blood gushing from a gash in his side and his mask slipping from his face. His brother stood over him, staring down at the blade in his hand in mute horror. It was, to Siv's knowledge, his first kill. Siv wanted to run to Torben, to comfort him, to hold him, to give him the proper prayers, but she knew well enough when a wound was fatal. Nothing she could do would save him. His eyes were already open to the blue sky, empty, the beetles swarming up in a golden river to suck on the gaping wound.

Torben's brother looked up at her, his eyes pleading for something. Forgiveness, maybe, or understanding, or that he might somehow wake from this nightmare. He was not a warrior and had never earned his mask, which meant that his tears were there for all to see. Siv could not give him what he sought. She picked up the dead stormtrooper's blaster rifle and shot Torben's brother, Torben's murderer, one lone bolt carefully placed to guarantee its lethality. A small smile lit his face before he fell, and she thought she saw his lips form the words *thank you.*

Siv looked around for her next fight and found that there was no one left. Torben was gone, and both of Brendol's troopers were on the ground, one half stripped of his armor. The only people still standing were Brendol Hux, cowering behind his shield, partially stuffed into armor that didn't fit, and Phasma, standing in a circle of bodies that were swirled in red blood and gold beetles. And, far off, Keldo on his sled. Bodies lay everywhere. Considering most of them were old or had never been warriors, it felt less like a victory and more like a slaughter of fools.

Dropping the shield, Siv gave Keldo a hard look, picked her way across the battlefield, and knelt by Torben's body on the opposite side of the beetle flood. Taking her detraxor from her bag, she attached a new skin and slipped the spike into place. As the machine hummed to life and did its work, depriving the beetles of their goal, she gently pulled the mask from Torben's head and snapped it in half over one knee. His skin was redder now, starting to peel, and his lips were so dry that they were shredded. His unseeing eyes glared up at the sun, asking a question that would never be answered.

"Thank you for serving us, Torben," she said, tears threatening. "Your today protects my people's tomorrow. Body to body, dust to dust."

His brother lay nearby, and she put the other detraxor to work, reciting the same prayer. Even if Brendol's people managed to save them in time, before the sickness truly took hold, and even if such unsophisticated medicines had no use in ships among the stars, this was Siv's task. This was how she helped her family. This was who she was. This was how she would do honor to her people.

But the fight wasn't actually over.

Phasma had her own responsibilities.

She and Keldo stared at each other over the field of battle. He'd taken off his fierce mask as if he could simply set violence aside. Although Phasma wore a helmet and her brother's burned, red face was bare, Siv knew well that neither one blinked. It seemed to be a battle of wills, at first, but it was clear that Keldo couldn't move. He had a sled with no one to pull it and only one leg, although he wore the prosthetic made from the droid and sat tall with tiny Frey in his lap.

An orphaned child and a field of sand and corpses formed an impossible divide between Keldo and his sister. When Phasma lowered her blaster and strode across the bloody field to him, it was in no way an act of subservience. It was a statement: *I walk because you will not. Because you cannot.*

And Keldo knew it. His face went even redder as she took powerful, deliberate strides toward him. Still she didn't remove her helmet, but she didn't have to. She was the tallest woman Siv had ever seen, and even if that didn't make Phasma's presence clear, her fighting prowess did. It felt like an eternity, the proud warrior in singed and dirty armor approaching the helpless man trapped alone in the desert. Brendol finally stood and straightened, quietly disentangling himself from the poorly fitting armor and brushing down his black uniform as if to acknowledge that something of import was occurring. He followed in Phasma's path, blaster in hand. But where she strode like a colossus, he picked and hopped over the bodies as if disgusted by the very real carnage of the war his presence had wrought.

Siv heard the telltale sound of a detraxor with no more work to do and looked to Torben. His huge body, once her shelter and her comfort, had been reduced to a sad and sunken husk. The beetles had fled, no more sustenance to draw them near. Recognizing her calling, she switched out skins and looked for the next body, but they were all swarming with beetles. She could only sit back on her heels and watch Phasma as she crossed an uncrossable gulf with Brendol, an almost comical figure, trailing in her wake.

"Phasma?" Keldo asked. "Take off the helmet and speak to me."

Phasma shook her head. "While you sit behind two shields? No. Warriors earn their masks, and I have obtained a superior one."

Keldo frowned in distaste. "What have you become, Phasma?

That's not your voice. Those aren't your words. That's not your mask. You've destroyed everything we worked for."

The next step Phasma took carried a new threat, and Keldo sensed it and flinched.

"Wrong, Keldo. *You* destroyed it. We had one chance. One chance to leave this dying shell of a life for something better. And instead of grasping for that greatness, you doomed your people."

"I didn't kill these people, Phasma. You did that."

"You delivered them to their doom."

Brendol took a step closer, his hands behind his back and his posture erect and formal.

"Phasma, we must call the First Order. Time is wasting. The sickness will soon take hold." His clipped, brutal words carried on the still air. "You know what has to happen now."

Kneeling in the sand, every breath tearing from her dry throat, her eyes burning and her skin peeling, Siv watched the scene unfold as if it were a dream.

Keldo put his hands up, pleading. "Phasma, don't do this. Don't *be* this."

"I know what I am, Keldo. I always have. That's the difference between us. I am willing to finish what I've begun."

Phasma took a step toward Keldo, pulled out her blaster, and shot him in the chest.

Keldo's eyes jerked wide, and his body went limp, slumping sideways out of the sled. A tiny, ragged cry ripped out of Frey, still hiding behind the shield. Phasma aimed her blaster.

"No!" Siv screamed.

Phasma's head whipped around as if she'd forgotten that Siv existed, much less that she'd survived the battle. But Phasma's blaster didn't waver. Her helmet turned to look at Brendol as if in question.

"The First Order can always use strong children," he said. "If she can survive the sickness."

Phasma nodded once.

"Siv," she called.

That's all it took to break the spell. Siv forgot the detraxors, her feet pounding across the sand to pluck the child from the sled and hold her tightly, the last remaining member of her family.

"Siv? What happened?" Frey asked. "Where's Mama?"

"Hush, love," Siv whispered into the child's wild brown hair. "We're going to take a ride to the stars."

TWENTY-EIGHT

ON PARNASSOS, 10 YEARS AGO

TIME WENT STRANGE AFTER THAT. AS THE MADNESS OF BATTLE EBBED, THE sickness took hold. Siv had been feverish once as a child, alternating hot and cold as her bones seemed to burn and her head throbbed in time with the ocean. This sickness was like that, plus peeling red skin, boils, and a feeling like her body was swelling, her skin stretching beyond capacity. Frey had it, too, and Siv covered her face in salve and gave her a waterskin to suck on, hoping the extra liquid and nutrients would help the girl fight it off.

Back at the crash site, Phasma easily rappelled up to the cockpit. Although it took some time, she was able to haul Brendol up onto the nose of the ship. Together, they bashed in the remaining glass, shoved out the dead pilots, and set to work on whatever sort of technological magic Brendol used to send his call for help out into space.

"What happened?" Frey kept asking.

Siv wasn't sure herself. A simple disagreement had resulted in an insane journey and an even more unbelievable genocide. How could she tell the child that everyone she'd ever known was dead because

Phasma and Keldo had failed as leaders? She couldn't. Especially not within hearing distance of the only two people who could save her life.

All she could do was what her mother had done: teach the child how to carry on. She explained the detraxors, showed Frey how to change the waterskins, and had her repeat the prayer with each new body, for all that the beetles had already claimed most of their liquids. Frey didn't seem particularly interested, but then again, the little girl had to be in shock and growing sicker by the minute. Siv's movements were becoming slow, her sight blurry. She looked up to the sky, hoping to see a ship appear there and wondering what it would look like. Would it shine with all the might of the sun? Or would it block out the sun, as big as one of the Con Star stations?

When it did finally appear, it was nothing like what she'd expected.

Brendol's ship resembled the falling star they'd seen, bright and silver and glowing. But the First Order ship that came to save them was black and sharp, cutting through the sky like one of the sharks they'd feared in the wild, cold waves of the Scyre. It hung there in the blue for a few long, dreamy moments before disgorging a smaller, blocky ship, which sped directly toward them and landed on a blank stretch of gray sand. A hatch opened in a hiss of steam, and two lines of stormtroopers marched out in step, their armor perfectly fitting and painfully shiny.

"What is that?" Frey asked.

"Our salvation," Siv said, smiling.

Phasma and Brendol rappelled down from his ship and walked toward the troopers. Brendol was in front, Phasma taking her position behind him, her blaster rifle held in both hands to mimic the other troopers. Between the two lines of white soldiers marched a young man about the same age as Siv and Phasma, a younger and thinner version of Brendol. The man's black uniform was spotless and crisp, his red hair carefully combed.

"The First Order is pleased that you survived, Father," he said with Brendol's clipped accent.

"I owe my good fortune to Phasma. Phasma, this is my son, Armitage."

Phasma inclined her head but said nothing. Armitage looked her up and down, barely concealing his skepticism.

"The First Order thanks you, Phasma," the young man said, clearly trying to impress his father.

"She will be joining us on the *Finalizer*. As will this child. Come now." Brendol turned and held out his hand, and Siv clutched Frey close to her, realizing that no one had yet spoken of Siv's own contribution, or her fate.

"Release her," Phasma said, and Siv's hands unclenched from Frey's shoulders. "Come, Frey."

Frey looked to Siv, her eyes fever bright and full of fear.

"It's just Phasma," Siv said weakly. "Go to her."

Phasma held her blaster in one hand and offered her glove to Frey, who gave Siv a last, troubled glance before running to take the outstretched hand. Siv stood, dizzy, and took a few faltering steps toward the others, careful to step around the bodies.

"And what of that one?" Armitage said, looking at Siv with distaste.

"She's too far gone," Brendol said. "And too soft for our needs."

Siv's heart dropped. "Phasma?" she implored.

Phasma's helmet turned to her, giving no hint as to what Phasma might be feeling. "When I ordered you to kill Wranderous, what did you do?"

Siv blinked against the sun, her world gone blurry. "I did what I thought was right. I showed him mercy."

"You defied a direct order, and that will not be tolerated."

Brendol smiled and nodded. "You'll do well in the First Order, Phasma."

Armitage inclined his head. "Shall we, then? The Supreme Leader has much to discuss with you, Father."

All this time, the troopers had remained as still as stone. At Brendol's signal, they turned and filed back up the ramp and onto their ship, Brendol and Armitage walking side by side between their neat columns. After a brief pause, Phasma followed, holding Frey's hand.

"Phasma?" Siv asked again, pleading this time, her world shattering as the last living person of her band turned to walk away.

Phasma stopped and looked over her shoulder. "There's another station just over the next dune. It has mostly escaped destruction. Brendol says it may be stocked with medical supplies." She continued walking. The last thing she said was, "He's right. You're too soft."

Without another word, without an apology, Phasma and Frey walked up the ramp and into the ship. Once everyone was on board, the ramp went back up, spilling gray sand. The ship took off in a gust of steam and noise, sending the sand swirling into great clouds that made Siv choke and squint. When she was able to see again, the only evidence that the First Order had visited Parnassos were tracks in the sand, an abandoned shipwreck, and the bodies of everyone she'd ever loved.

As the bigger ship devoured the smaller one and disappeared, Siv's legs gave out, and she fell to the sand. It felt soft, at first, warm and calmly accepting. But then it began to burn, to itch. Siv was feverish; her lips blistered and her eyes full of grit, though she couldn't tell if it was real sand or part of the sickness. But whether it was a dream or not, Phasma had given her a sliver of hope even as she broke her heart, and Siv was going to take it.

She crawled from body to body, collecting everything she could find. Water, food, weapons, cloaks. She put on Pete's helmet and looked around in awe at a whole new world. It seemed to help block the sickness, or at least the blinding harshness of the sun, and she knelt to say one last goodbye to Torben. As she slumped there, sand burying her knees, she almost gave up. But then that persistent flip in her belly urged her to wobble to her feet and shuffle through the sand, dragging her collected bags over the next dune and toward the structure on the other side of the giant cylinders that Brendol had called a nuclear reactor. The white walls of the building showed marks of a blast but were otherwise whole. The door slid open as easily as the doors on the other Con Star Mining Corporation stations; for all its faults, Con Star could build a hell of a door.

The sand cascaded into the hallway sideways and Siv tumbled in with it. She knew enough to press the button to close the door behind her, and moments later, the building rocked, knocking her to the ground. When the world went still again, she pulled herself to standing, confused but determined to keep on.

She was familiar by now with the smooth white floors, with the orientation room, with the cafeteria full of food she was too nauseated to eat. She dropped her bags and put a hand to the wall, following the violet line to the medbay, a trick she vaguely recalled from Brendol's recovery at Terpsichore Station. Once there, she realized that she couldn't read any of the words or symbols on anything. But she did understand pictures, and a very handy drawing of a person putting their arm into a machine suggested that putting her arm into that machine might be useful. As if it had not been abandoned for over a century, the machine chirped to life and bleated repeatedly as a red light flashed. Soon droids poured out of all the doors in the room, and Siv's first reaction was to panic. If these droids were as mad as the last batch, she was doomed.

The first droid that reached her told her quite calmly that she had radiation sickness and would require several rounds of treatment. It led her to a bed and urged her to lie down, and she was grateful it said nothing about praise to the creators. The last thing she saw was a cheerful silver face promising her that the Con Star Mining Corporation valued her health, and then she felt a needle prick her skin.

She fell asleep and was in and out of dreams for an indeterminate amount of time. Sometimes her gummy eyes would blink open on a smooth white ceiling; other times she would see a droid standing over her with various instruments that would've been terrifying if she hadn't been, as she later learned, heavily sedated and strapped down. Siv didn't remember everything that happened to her in the following week, but the droids took excellent care of her. Fluids and nutrients and the very medicines that Brendol had promised dripped right into her sleeping body, and for a while she was able to forget the horrors of her last days with Phasma and Brendol.

When she finally woke up, the droids were anxious to provide her with whatever she needed, and there was no mention of employment or remuneration. She was able to clean herself and slowly regain her strength and appetite. One day, they took her to a special room and showed her an image of her child moving on a big black screen, the baby's tiny frog fingers seeming to wave as Siv broke out into long unshed tears of sadness mingled with newfound joy.

The baby was healthy, the droids said. There would be no damage from the radiation. She would be born five months later.

Siv named her Torbi.

When I visited them last week, Torbi was a strong child, and Siv had found her peace, living at Calliope Station. I told her I would send someone back for them.

I hope I can keep that promise.

TWENTY-NINE

ON THE *ABSOLUTION*

VI LOOKS UP, HEAVES A SIGH, AND SMILES AS IF SHE'S FINALLY FREE OF A heavy weight. Cardinal has never wanted to shock her as much as he does right now, but he wants her to remain relaxed. Perhaps now that she's told this story and thinks she's safe, he can dig deeper or trip her up somehow. Still, he's angry. Because there's nothing in the story he can use, and she promised there would be.

"And that's it?" he says. "That's the end?"

"Well, to be fair, the story isn't over yet. You and I are still here, and Siv and Torbi are waiting on Parnassos. We could change that, you know."

He glances up at Iris, glad he had her disable the cams. Interrogation is one thing, but discussing defection is another, even if he's only tolerating the spy's screed to keep her talking.

"But you promised me intel that could take down Phasma and information surrounding Brendol's death. This was Siv's story. And I don't care about Siv. She has no idea what happened to Phasma after they left the planet. Anything else is conjecture."

Vi jerks her chin at the water, and he helps her drink.

"Thanks," she says. "Thing is, a good spy doesn't need conjecture because there are other ways to follow a story. If, for example, someone on my side was able to hack into a stolen troop transporter and access the cam feed from the day Phasma left Parnassos."

At that, he perks up and leans in. "That wouldn't tell you everything."

"Not everything, but plenty. Audio, visual, and body language can tell a good story."

Cardinal is concerned that the Resistance can steal and hack First Order ships so easily; do his superiors know about that? If so, they've kept such mistakes hidden from Cardinal even though he's a captain and should know when his transporters disappear.

But for now, he's more interested in taking down Phasma.

"Then tell it," he says.

THIRTY

ON A FIRST ORDER SHUTTLE, 10 YEARS AGO

AS THE SHIP SHIFTED UNDER PHASMA'S BOOTS, THERE WAS NO WAY TO TELL what went through her mind. But the video showed Frey squealing and pulling her hand away from Phasma's glove, so chances are she felt some anxiety as she began her first trip into the stars.

"Ow! Why are you squeezing so hard? What's happening?" the child asked.

Phasma looked down at Frey for a long time. I imagine her seeing glimmers of Ylva, or perhaps of Keldo's eyes, which the child shared. Perhaps she didn't know how to answer, or perhaps she was still lost in the tragedy she had just witnessed. In any case, she didn't answer, and Armitage stepped in.

"We're going up into space," he said. "To become good soldiers for the First Order. I was once very little and took a ride on a ship like this, and now look how big I am."

He smiled at the child, then shot a measuring look at Phasma, as if trying to guess whether she might be friend or foe. She looked strange, to be sure, with poorly fitting armor over ripped, bulky cloth, not very First Order at all. But even then, one imagines Armitage was always looking for ways to impress or destroy his own father. The look he shot at Brendol was pure loathing.

"Phasma, I wish for you to see this," Brendol said from where he stood by a great glass window looking out into the sky. He murmured instructions to the pilot, who dutifully turned the transport ship around to face Parnassos.

When I was floating over Parnassos, I was struck by its beauty. The ocean was a surging swirl of dark green and deep blue, the land a sea of gray interrupted only by the black of rocks and the smudges that represented stations. That green one was Arratu; the white one marked their final battle. Somewhere, hidden under sand, was Terpsichore. I've been to many planets, and even I found it quite a view. I imagine, for Phasma, it was the most enchanting, fascinating thing she'd ever seen. She looked out the window for a long time, anyway.

If she looked to the far left, across the ocean, she might've seen another landmass, this one brown and bright green and healthy looking, as compared with the place Phasma had come from. Her home, the Scyre and the Claw lands and everything around them except for that bright spot of Arratu, looked like a boil of rot, like dead bones waiting to be buried. Gray and black, all of it. And as she looked down on it, perhaps she realized it was possible to both love and hate a thing in equal measure.

"It's beautiful from up here," she said, in any case.

Brendol stepped closer to the bank of instruments. "That's not what I want you to see. Now watch carefully."

Whatever his fingers did, the movements meant nothing to Phasma. At least not until bright lights bloomed from under the ship, shooting out with a heavy boom and zooming right toward her planet. Her hand jumped from where it lay by her side to Frey's shoulder, but she didn't call out, or even give voice to a moan of pain as she realized what Brendol was forcing her to witness.

She didn't have names for what these weapons were, blaster bolts so big they could rain down from space, but she must've known instantly what they would do.

The first bolt slammed into the Scyre, and she watched the colors change, the black cliffs disappearing into the sea and great white plumes shooting up. The next bolt hit Arratu, leaving a black smudge across the gray sand where vibrant green had once been.

Before he initiated the next volley, Brendol looked back to Phasma. "Do you see now the power of the First Order? What we do to those who oppose us? Even those who inconvenience us?"

In response, Phasma only nodded. I wonder if her helmet hid tears. She silently stepped in front of Frey, blocking the child's view as the final bolt arced down to where they'd just been, to where their entire family had fallen. She was too far away to tell if it had hit the buildings or Brendol's crashed ship, but it was clear Brendol was sending her a message that couldn't be misunderstood.

Do what he wanted, or find herself destroyed.

"Powerful indeed," she said, when she was able.

THIRTY-ONE

ON THE *ABSOLUTION*

VI WATCHES CARDINAL TO GAUGE HIS REACTION. SHE'S MAYBE EMBROI-
dered what Siv told her, just a little, but that's the storyteller's gift, isn't
it? To take a seed and spin it into a flower of untold beauty, glistening
with dew? Cardinal did say he wanted to know everything, and she
gave him everything. She needed to buy herself some time, and she's
done that. And she never lied. Everything she said was true. Mostly.
And since she has an eidetic memory, she knows exactly which parts
she embellished.

It's worked, though. Time has passed. She's gotten a little stronger.
And as for Cardinal, he's trying to hide that the story has affected
him.

"I know this is a lot to take in," Vi says, her voice even and calm
and low.

"Do you really think she's still capable of tears?" he asks.

"I'd like to think she's still human under that armor. Or that at least
she was, then. The holo shows her shaking as she watched Brendol
ravage her planet."

Cardinal looks off into space and smiles. "I remember the child. Showed up in the youth barracks a few days later, still pink from the radiation, although the medbay cleared her. She did well. UV-8855. They called her Warcry because she couldn't stop herself from shouting during every fight. The little ones and their nicknames. When she was old enough, I graduated her. A year ago, just about. I passed her directly into Phasma's hands. I wonder if they recognized each other?"

He's so still that Vi knows he's working through some deep feelings. She doesn't want to lose him, though. She needs to keep steering him, steering the story. The less he thinks about the remote and about Baako, the better.

"Her name is still Phasma, and she's the tallest person around. Kind of hard to miss. But you can't feel bad about it. Frey was just another kid who would've died on a crap planet anyway."

For the first time, Cardinal's head falls forward into his hands, his hair sweaty and mussed. He's been running his fingers through it again and again, making it stand up in whorls. He looks . . . well, more broken than stormtroopers are supposed to be.

"Why would Brendol order such a senseless massacre? The First Order's purpose is to bring stability and peace to the galaxy. I've been on missions, and I've followed orders, but the people of Parnassos weren't in rebellion. They weren't even given a chance to cooperate."

Vi shakes her head sadly. "Sorry, but you're the only one here who's not playing dirty. The First Order goes to planets, and they steal children, and they subsume resources. I guess that way up here, you can't see what's going on down below. Do you ever leave this bucket? Take an R and R on some quiet moon with umbrellas in the drinks?"

"Of course not. Not since Brendol died. My duty is here. I train the children."

"And now you know who you're training them for."

Cardinal stands and paces. "General Hux was my mentor. My superior."

"Yeah, well, much like everyone else in this story, Brendol Hux was a liar."

Without being asked, Cardinal brings her water, helps her drink it. His hands are shaking, she notes. He can't quite meet her eyes, just now. Whether he can't handle her truth or he's planning his next move, she doesn't know. She still hasn't given him what he needs. For a strong and steady man, a man who's nearly had the emotions programmed out of him, he carries himself gently. As a spy, Vi has delivered a lot of intel to a lot of people, and it just takes them this way, sometimes. As if they wish they could curl into themselves and deny something they always suspected, deep down. Something they now know is true but they aren't quite ready to face.

"How do you know all this?" he asks, voice rough. "How do you know Brendol is dead? That's one of the most closely guarded secrets in the First Order. Outside of this ship, official word is that he's on a long-term mission."

"But you know he's dead, and not just because Armitage told you and ten thousand of your friends."

Cardinal snorts, like she's a fool. "I was his personal guard. He handpicked me on Jakku, trained me himself. I was infinitely loyal. From the time I first put on this armor, he trusted me to keep him safe." He holds up his arm, displaying the flawless red. "He designed it himself because he said red was a color of power. Every moment he spent in my company, he knew he was safe."

"But what about when he left your company?" Vi presses. "Did he say nothing about his time on Parnassos?" Vi is genuinely curious, and the interrogation is starting to feel more like two people of like minds colluding.

"Almost nothing. When they arrived, Brendol looked half dead and Phasma ridiculous, in poorly fitting armor, badly stained and blasted and hung all over with primitive weapons. It was just the two of them—and the child, but she needed longer in the medbay, so I didn't meet her until later. None of Brendol's troopers survived. They were my friends, trained alongside me. At the time, we were told they'd perished in the crash, shot down by enemy craft. I felt terrible that I hadn't been with Brendol, and the fact that Phasma was there with him instead . . . well, I felt like I had failed him somehow. I was terrified that I was being replaced. I guess I don't have anything to lose now, telling you that, do I?"

Vi shakes her head and does her best to look empathetic, to draw the truth out of him with her silence. From what she's learned of the First Order, they aren't big on sharing weaknesses and talking about feelings. This is a tricky role, but one she is accustomed to playing.

"With Brendol as her champion, she was welcomed into the First Order," he continues, looking off into the dead air of the small space. "I trained her, as he asked, and then they gave her a captain's cape of her own, and suddenly my own cape didn't mean as much. Brendol gave me this armor, and a year later, she was wearing her chrome armor. I still don't know how or where she got it. Brendol claimed he didn't know, but he had that smile about him. She became their darling, their poster child, their legend. And even though I resented her, I believed it. That she was as great as they proclaimed her to be. But she was always so quiet, so enigmatic. And then I began doubting. And now here you come, with this story. Is Siv really alive after that?"

Vi smiles gently, the band across her forehead creaking as she inadvertently leans forward as if to, what? Conspire? Comfort?

"Siv lives, as does her child. The rest of them are gone."

"But how?"

"Calliope Station was made to withstand anything, and it had already survived one radioactive event. She felt the hallway shake, but the Gand had told her to keep walking, so she got up and kept walking, right into the medbay. The Scyre breeds tough people. Even on her own, Siv was determined to live and to raise her child." Vi grins, a real smile this time. "Beautiful kid, has Siv's skin and Torben's eyes. Can scream loud enough to stun a Wookiee. Anyway, Siv was smart enough to close the blast door, and the station got some new scars on its white walls. She's been through a lot, still has lots of scars of her own. Not that there's anyone around to see them."

Vi tries to lift her arm to scratch her nose, but it's just as pinned down as ever. She had forgotten, with the informality of their conversation, that she's still in the interrogation chair, the remote for which sits on the table like a forgotten pazaak deck, and one stacked against her.

"But you saw her," Cardinal muses.

"I scared the hell out of her. She hasn't been outside in ten years. She's worried the radiation might harm Torbi. Whatever caused the explosion, it turns out the rest of the station was running just fine, and the droids are more than happy to help her. Siv has a full complement of helpful servants and enough food to feed an army for a century. They've been there for ten years without seeing a single soul. She was so glad to see me, her story practically fell out of her."

"Then why do you look troubled on her behalf? It sounds as if you got what you went there for."

Now it's her turn to look away. "I told Siv I'd come back. My starhopper—well, I'm sure your troops have turned it into component parts by now. I couldn't fit two passengers on that thing, much less three. So I promised Siv that I would come back and help her and her daughter rejoin civilization. I didn't tell—"

Cardinal perks up. "Tell whom?"

Vi sighs. "I didn't tell my superiors about that part. That poor woman will be listening for engines every day, waiting for a better life for her child than biding her time on a dead planet. I don't mind telling people they're screwed, but I hate giving anyone false hope."

He's suddenly in her face, balling his fist in her shirt. "Stop that. Your guilt is not my problem. We're running out of time. You said you had intel to help me take Phasma down, and you're still holding it back."

Iris beeps a warning, and Vi looks down at his hand and back up at his face. "You can let go of me, first."

He releases her shirt and backs away sheepishly. Maybe he's not used to losing control like that. Iris floats back to bob between them, as if reminding Cardinal that he must keep his distance. This is the first interrogation where Vi hasn't taken a single punch, which says something else about her enemy. He might've shocked her a few times, but he's still ashamed for grabbing her like that, droid reprimand or no. That kind of touch, that kind of rage, is simply too personal.

He's right, though. This thing she knows about Phasma ... it's a doozy. She's been holding it back, but she feels it's finally time for the big reveal. He's as open as he's ever going to be, and if she continues to defy him, she'll lose him completely.

She takes a deep breath and meets his eyes, commanding his full attention.

"What did they tell you about Brendol's death? What's the official word?"

He sits again, leans forward avidly like it's his favorite part of the story, but his eyes suggest it's going to be the worst part. "Unknown malady. I saw him that morning. He didn't look good. Like maybe he was coming down with something. He was too pale. I suggested he hit the medbay, have the droids check him out."

"And what did Brendol say to that?"

Cardinal's smile suggests he might've once been a mischievous boy. "He told me to mind my own business and respect my superiors. But he went. He was like that—followed good advice, but put you down so you didn't think it was your idea. And then ..."

"You never saw him again."

Cardinal doesn't answer, just stares at the floor.

Vi licks her lips. They're dry again.

"Tell me, then, Cardinal. That last morning, did he look ... a bit swollen?"

Cardinal shrugs. "Sure, but he always looked a bit puffy after a night at the officers' mess. Wasn't the healthiest of men, and he was getting into his sixties then. I didn't expect him to look the picture of health."

"But you never looked up his records?"

Cardinal is up and pacing again, and Vi realizes that when it comes to Brendol Hux, he's a raw nerve, utterly unschooled in concealing his moods or his tells. This is what he does when he's truly upset: He can't stop from moving, can't contain his nervous energy.

"That's not how things are done in the First Order. I can't just go to Records and ask for details. Or to the medbay and have a private chat with the droids. You can politely inquire of your superiors once, but ask a second time and they get suspicious. They called an assembly, and I was standing at the head of ten thousand troops in perfect formation when Armitage Hux put his hat under his arm and told us all that his father had passed on."

"Didn't even tell you privately. Huh." Vi tries not to look too smug. "And you didn't ask for details. They really do have you trained well."

Cardinal grabs the manacles around her upper arms and shakes the whole contraption, rattling Vi's skull and turning her legs into jelly.

"Of course I asked for details! An unknown malady, that's all they would say." He pulls away and clears his throat. "Must've been something he picked up on one of his planetary visits. The med droids had never seen anything like it, had no records of similar symptoms in their data drives. A complete mystery. Just be glad I hadn't gotten it, too, they said."

"Well, I guess our slicers are better at solving mysteries than yours are, because they managed to get ahold of an old medical droid and unscramble its data. Let me tell you the symptoms that led to Brendol Hux's demise. First he complained of a tiny bump on his neck, just under his collar, the skin red and hot and hard. Thought it might be a cyst, or possibly a bite from some strange and unfamiliar creature. The med droids couldn't find anything unusual. Then Brendol started to puff up. His skin became swollen. His eyes began to bulge, and his hair fell out, and his fingernails popped off. He complained that he felt disoriented and weak. His skin became pale and thin and translucent. And then, floating in a bacta tank in the medbay . . ."

"No!"

"He just sort of . . . dissolved into the liquid. Leaving behind only a few shrunken organs, bare bones, and a patch of graying red hair."

"So you're saying that Phasma brought one of those beetles from Parnassos. That she, what? Planted it on Brendol?"

Vi raises an eyebrow and desperately wishes she could cock her head at him; she hates when smart people play dumb. "Unless you know another way that people casually turn into big bags full of water and explode."

"But this is Captain Phasma we're talking about. Why would she kill General Hux? He was her savior, her superior. He made her what she was."

Vi shakes and slams within her restraints, wishing she could get out and rough this idiot up a little for being so naïve. "Why? Because as far as she knew, Siv was dead, and Brendol was the last person who knew about her humble beginnings. The last one who knew her history. Brendol watched her betray her leader, fight her people, murder her own brother in cold blood. Brendol was the only witness to her crimes, the only witness in the entire galaxy who knew that she wasn't the perfect soldier poster child for this lockstep hellscape you call the First Order. She needed him, though, for a while. Needed him to bring her back here to your floating paradise and tell everyone of her bravery, her strength, her resilience, her prowess. Needed him to think that he was her vaunted patron and mentor, and that she was his simple weapon. Needed to use him like a whetstone as she rose through the ranks, just as he'd foretold. And then, one day, when he'd forgotten she wasn't merely a leashed wolf, she flicked that beetle into his jacket and walked away. The perfect crime."

He's somewhere behind her now. Maybe he's leaning against the wall; maybe he's in a ball on the floor. She doesn't know. She wishes she could see his face, see how he's taking it. See if he's thinking about picking up the remote again. For all that he's shown some rudimentary kindness, giving her water and food, and for all that the vitamin packs and stims helped, a little, she can feel damage in her body, nerves burnt and muscles unable to loosen up. When he lets her out—if he lives up to their bargain and lets her out—she may very well fall flat on her face, unable even to crawl away.

And that's the best-case scenario.

For all she knows, he could still just shock her to death and be done with it.

Because the truth of it is this: There is no physical evidence. That beetle is long gone. Phasma made sure of that. "But what about Frey? She was a witness, too."

She died six months ago in a training exercise, weapon malfunction. Or at least that's how Phasma recorded it. Phasma is very good at getting rid of witnesses."

For several long moments, he was silent.

"Does Armitage know? About Brendol?" It comes out in a flat voice from somewhere behind her.

"I don't know what Armitage knows. I just know what was stricken from the original medbay records, which is a list of symptoms leading up to his death in the bacta tank. As you know, the official cause of death was recorded as Malady, Unknown."

"And you're sure?"

"I'm strapped into an interrogation chair with an angry man. This is as sure as I get."

"I'm sorry about this."

Vi tries to whip her head around but can't. "Sorry about what? You don't need to do anything you'll be sorry for."

The next thing she knows, electricity is coursing through her body, slamming her teeth together and making bright-red starbursts behind her eyelids. Vi Moradi goes unconscious.

THIRTY-TWO

ON THE *ABSOLUTION*

AS SOON AS THE SPY GOES LIMP IN HER BONDS, CARDINAL RELEASES THE switch. He knows what he has to do now, and ironic as it is, he'd rather not have a witness for this next step. He's worn ruts in this room, pacing and sitting and glaring at the walls as Vi has told her story. He demanded she tell him everything, and she certainly did. And it almost seemed like she enjoyed it. It's strange, how obsessed a man can get with listening to dark truths about his enemies. Before, he knew nothing about Phasma. Now he knows everything. Or, at least, enough.

Although Iris beeps at him in irritation for doubting her surveillance, he checks Vi's vitals to make sure he didn't hurt her too much and tests that her bonds are still tight before putting his helmet back on. It's become a part of him, an extension of his body like his blaster. The way it dulls some senses while expanding others soothes him. When Cardinal wears this helmet, he knows exactly who he is and what he was meant to do—so that's at least one thing he has in common with Phasma. And right now, he has to find Armitage Hux. There are still several hours before the meeting, which means the general is most likely commandeering his father's old quarters on the *Absolution*, brushing up on his intel and studying the agenda.

"Stay here and watch her," he tells Iris, and the red light blinks as if to say, *I know.*

Locking the door as he leaves, Cardinal storms through the hallways, his captain's cloak flying behind him. The turbolift takes forever, even though he stabs the button repeatedly. General Hux's old quarters are high up among the senior staff, and the journey has always felt long even on the best of days, when Brendol lived here and Cardinal felt welcome. When the lift door slides open on the officers' floor, Cardinal's heart is hammering so hard that he can feel it in his temples. He's slightly dizzy, as jacked up as he used to get as a kid recruit in a sim fight, when every nerve in his body was firing and his teeth refused to unclench.

For all that he's accustomed to sparring one-on-one, it's been years since he did his required tours planetside, helping to pacify rebellious worlds and leading his troops on missions. Those first few years after Brendol delivered him from Jakku were tough, as his body and mind hardened to focus on combat, but this will be a new kind of fight. Cardinal has never before been a man to question his superiors, and he's never been the bearer of bad news. Then again, he's never illegally detained a suspect and tortured them for hours in a hidden room in the bilge to gain secret intel on a colleague, either.

When he reaches Brendol's old suite, a protocol droid answers the door, placid and refined. This model once belonged to Brendol, and Cardinal wonders if its memory was wiped after the older man died. Or perhaps it contains all sorts of secrets, including the ones Cardinal has recently learned. The way the First Order uses and wipes and reuses droids—and, sometimes, loses them—there's a good chance this very model stood on that shuttle with Phasma, silently recording. Perhaps it was there the day Phasma released a golden beetle, unleashing her long-kept secret weapon on a high-ranking superior officer who had made the foolish decision to trust her.

"Can I help you, Captain Cardinal?" the droid asks.

"I need to see General Hux, please." The helmet keeps his voice from trembling like a boy's, and he puts his hands behind his back like he's at parade rest to hide their shaking.

"I'm afraid the general is resting before the assembly."

"It's an emergency."

"Oh. I see. How very unusual."

"I'm afraid it is. Very unusual. But of utmost importance."

The droid is still standing there looking befuddled when Armitage himself appears behind it. He's not in his crisp uniform but instead wears a robe, black and composed of sharp lines and pleats. For all that the entire point of a robe is to appear casual and comfortable, Armitage Hux has a way of turning anything into a uniform, any interaction into a judgment.

"How very unusual indeed," he says. "What is this emergency, Captain?"

In the lines of Armitage's face, Cardinal sees what Brendol once was, before he grew old and soft. Confidence, vitality, sureness. And yet there's something cruel and savage in the man, something forged by Brendol himself. Cardinal remembers hating Armitage when he first met him on Jakku. Spoiled, sullen, small, ratlike, soft while the orphan children were hard and sharp. But over the years, Cardinal was . . . well, not programmed. Taught. Sculpted. He learned that Armitage was untouchable, above him. Armitage is clever and wise and farsighted. Armitage will help the First Order eclipse the might of the old Empire and annihilate the New Republic. Cardinal was loyal to Brendol, and now he is loyal to Armitage. And Armitage appreciates that.

Of course, Armitage has always favored Phasma. They both reside on the *Finalizer,* and Cardinal has often seen them colluding. Together, they manage and control thousands of stormtroopers, planning invasions and attacks with Kylo Ren to lead the First Order to victory. In times of doubt, Cardinal wonders if Armitage supports Phasma out of spite for the Jakku orphan Brendol once took under his wing. Even if Armitage doesn't like Cardinal, he has long acknowledged the superiority of Cardinal's training methods and lauded his success with young recruits. Perhaps the sneer Armitage wears every time he speaks to Cardinal is the same expression he shows everyone.

Such petty concerns don't matter now. This is not an issue of personal politics. Since Armitage cares about the First Order as much as Cardinal does, he'll appreciate learning what Cardinal knows. Loyalty to the cause is more important than interpersonal rapport. Together, they can oust Phasma and rebuild the training program to the younger Hux's exact specifications. Once Armitage understands how his father died, there's no way he'll let Brendol's murderer stay on those posters, much less remain alive.

"Well?" Armitage prods.

"I have new information, sir."

"Spit it out. I haven't got all day, as you well know."

Cardinal draws a deep breath and holds himself up tall. "Sir, I've gained some intel you'll want to hear. About your father. About his death."

Armitage almost looks surprised, but he's too well bred for that. Instead, he leans out the door to look up and down the hall before stepping back into his rooms. "Come in then. Hurry. And you're excused, Kayfour. Please return in time for the assembly."

"Yes, sir."

The droid disappears down the hall, and Cardinal steps into Armitage Hux's rooms. He was here constantly when the suite belonged to Brendol, but the décor has changed under Armitage's rule. Brendol had liked classical, traditional styles, elegant rugs and fine artifacts and rich foods. But Armitage, just like Kylo Ren, seems to appreciate a certain starkness in his person and in his quarters. Everything is beautiful and comfortable and refined, sure. But each element is edged in silver that seems sharp enough to slice skin. Armitage drapes himself across a low, ice-blue sofa but doesn't invite Cardinal to sit. Cardinal, ever the good soldier, remains standing and considers it his duty to do so.

"Where's your droid, Captain? I don't know that I've ever seen you without your floating orb."

Cardinal almost stumbles but finds something close enough to truth. "On duty, sir. Can't leave my responsibilities behind."

Armitage smiles, a slinky thing that suggests he smells a lie. "True enough. Now, this emergency?"

"Sir, I've recently learned some troubling news about Captain Phasma."

"I thought you said this was about my father."

"It is. And also Phasma."

Armitage sits forward, one eyebrow cocked. "What about Phasma?"

Cardinal clears his throat. "She's not what she seems. Not a loyal soldier. Her past includes betrayal, murder, genocide. She is not worthy of her captain's cape, nor of your faith in her. She's performed atrocities that go against everything we stand for."

"And did she do this on the *Finalizer*?"

"No, sir. On her home planet, Parnassos."

Armitage smirks and leans into the cushions, one long arm draped over the back of the sofa. "Then how, pray tell, is this my problem? Many of our recruits, yourself included, lived violent lives before they swore their allegiance to the First Order. We are very forgiving of those who choose to serve us."

Cardinal stands tall, considering how to make Armitage understand without overstepping himself. "It goes deeper than that, sir. We entrust our recruits to her, and she's already betrayed the First Order's laws. She would move against us in a heartbeat if what we wanted didn't serve her needs. She's a risk."

Armitage shakes his head in a sad sort of way. "Cardinal, you're speaking in hypotheticals. I can't admonish someone for something they haven't done or might yet do. Captain Phasma's service record is exemplary, and she turns out stormtroopers that meet my own father's rigorous requirements. She has been commended, again and again, for her fine work. If you don't have some sort of direct evidence against her, against actual deeds she's performed since taking her vows and joining us, then I might as well go shout at the stars."

Cardinal's hands clench into fists at his side, but he's careful, so careful, not to make any sort of move that could appear threatening to a superior officer. "Sir, if I may say so, if Admiral Sloane were here—"

"Well she's not," Armitage snaps. "Any other threats you'd like to hold over my head?"

"Phasma killed your father," Cardinal says, going right to the heart of the matter.

Armitage jumps to his feet. "Did she? And you have proof? Show me. Tell me. And do not disappoint me."

"I . . . I can get proof. It was a beetle. From her own planet. From Parnassos. Its bite causes the victim to liquefy. That's why the med droids couldn't identify it. They never saw the beetle, just its bite and the effects of its venom."

"But where's the proof?"

"Let me go to Parnassos, and I can find a beetle and bring it back. The med droids will match the chemical signature to your father's records."

"But you don't actually have one with you? Or proof that one bit my father at Phasma's behest?"

"No, sir."

Armitage sits back down, a smug smile on his face. "Good."

"Good?"

"Cardinal, you're an idiot. My father knew it, and so do I. I know Phasma killed him, and I'm glad the old bastard is dead. We agreed on the right time for it to happen. I told her it had to be untraceable, and it shall remain so."

For a long moment, Cardinal can only stare.

"You . . . knew?"

"Of course I knew. I always know. I know everything. Now the question is this: What else do you know, and what do you think you're going to do with that information?"

Cardinal takes a step backward and feels as if he might be floating in space, on his way to his last breath and utterly lost.

"Nothing, sir. I know nothing, and I have no proof."

"Good. Because if you attempt to speak to anyone else about this matter, I can make you disappear, too. The thing is, you're a good man. A good soldier who does his duty, who follows orders. We need men like you in the First Order. I need men like you on my side. So the next question would be . . . are you on my side?"

Cardinal is nodding before he finds his voice.

"Yes, sir. My loyalty remains with the First Order and with you."

"Good fellow. I'll see you at the assembly today, then? And you will remain, as always, silent and steady?"

"Yes, sir."

"Excellent. Because for all that Phasma does an excellent job with our older recruits, and for all that she's always arguing against my harsher indoctrination, I just don't think she could be trusted with your little ones. Do you?"

Cardinal shudders at the thought. "No, sir."

Armitage sits back into his couch and smiles beatifically. "Then you're dismissed. And thank you so much for bringing this information to my attention."

THIRTY-THREE

ON THE *ABSOLUTION*

ARMITAGE HUX LEANS FORWARD, STUDYING CARDINAL AS HE EXITS. EVEN under the bold red armor, it's clear that something about the captain has been broken, which is a shame. Cardinal is an ideal officer, and his mixture of patience and sternness has turned out flawless recruits that even old Brendol couldn't complain about. No, Armitage doesn't have a single argument with Cardinal.

At least he didn't until today.

The chuff of the man, coming to tattle on Phasma like that. It's two strikes against Cardinal. One for the tattling, and one for being foolish enough to mess with Phasma. Three, actually. Cardinal thought Armitage himself was too dull to know what was occurring right under his nose.

Leaning back into his couch, Armitage flicks his comm.

"Officer Bolander?"

Her voice is crisp. "Yes, sir?"

"Please send over the guest list for today's assembly. I have some changes to make."

Like a good officer, she doesn't question him or his command. "Yes, sir."

Perhaps Armitage should worry about Cardinal. The man has clearly become unstable, and he has a grudge. He has also inexplicably gotten his hands on some highly confidential information that should be destroyed or buried so deep that a hungry wampa couldn't find it if it were soaked in blood. That dig about Brendol? Hilarious. Cardinal saw how the man treated his son. If he knew anything about the human heart, he should've understood that the stronger Hux would rise to supplant the weaker, older Hux eventually. Armitage has apparently done an excellent job of hiding his lesser traits from his inferiors. The ends justify the means, and the First Order cannot be held back by outdated ideals.

Armitage considers his comm and flirts with the idea of letting Phasma know her erstwhile rival has some unwelcome intel, but Cardinal himself admitted he has no evidence. Armitage is the highest authority on ship; who else could Cardinal possibly tell?

Better to let this little conflict play itself out. If Armitage understands anything about Captain Cardinal, having known him for well over a decade now, he knows this: Cardinal will do what he considers to be the right thing. And that means he'll continue to fulfill his duties promptly and to the best of his significant abilities. He will probably wrestle with his own conscience, fighting his First Order conditioning, until he has no choice but to confront Phasma himself.

Which is just fine.

Phasma is good at making problems disappear.

For now, Armitage has to get ready.

Kylo Ren doesn't like to wait.

THIRTY-FOUR

ON THE *ABSOLUTION*

THE DOOR TO THE HUX SUITE SLIDES SHUT BEHIND HIM, AND CARDINAL feels truly adrift for the first time since his mother died on Jakku, leaving him entirely alone. Ever since Brendol found him and gave him a purpose, something to aspire to and something to believe in, he's known that he was right where he was meant to be. The stars felt more like home than the hovel of salvaged metal where he grew up. But now the halls of the *Absolution* seem cold and impersonal, and he can feel the eyes of every security officer watching him through the cams that blink at regular intervals. Up here, among the officers and the elite, his every move is monitored. The dark room in the bilge where Vi waits now feels less like a prison and more like a haven.

Still, he has his duties, and they won't wait. The spy will. She has no choice. And if she tries anything, Iris will take care of her. The droid is beginning to feel like the only member of the First Order that Cardinal can actually trust. All this time, he thought Armitage was an ally, or at least a bastion of shared loyalty to the First Order. But as he's recently learned, the younger Hux is just as dangerous as Phasma.

Cardinal's training kicks in, and his posture straightens. How did the rhyme go? *Chin up, shoulders back, stand up tall, don't be slack.* Even the tiniest of his recruits can sing along, and the slogan is printed on one of the many posters plastered around their barracks and the youth cafeteria, along with an image of Captain Phasma at attention, her chrome armor shining and her cape rippling behind her. The little ones look up to her, want to be her. They think of Captain Cardinal as their teacher, but it's Phasma who has become their idol.

They'll be waking up shortly, the klaxon calling them out of their bunks, where Brendol's carefully designed program feeds them subliminal messages all night long. Recognizing the value of the system in molding young minds, Armitage has changed nothing about the program since Brendol's death. Cardinal finds it comforting, when he checks on the children at night, to hear the soft murmur of the First Order's doctrine droning on, the same as when he was a child. He used to lie in bed and pretend it was his mother's kind, loving voice, even if it spoke of loyalty, courage, and the rule of law, all things his mother never mentioned as she struggled to keep them alive.

In his own quarters, Cardinal shucks his armor and hangs it neatly, noting a few smudges from his time with Vi. There, on the glove, where he spilled some caf. There, on the shin guard, a stain. He didn't even look in the mirror before confronting General Hux. He's slipping.

He goes through the standard ablutions taught to him when he first came to this ship. The right way to shower, the correct way to clean his teeth and shave. His new bodysuit waits in the closet fresh and sharp, but he won't put his armor back on until it's clean. As he polishes the shining red, his thoughts drift to the day he received his first armor, the standard white trooper suit given to every recruit. Back then, he was just a boy learning to fight, and his number was CD-0922. He was so proud as he accepted the helmet and learned the subtleties of keeping a tidy kit. Standing there with his first platoon, chin up and shoulders back, a training blaster hooked on his hip, he'd never felt prouder. Brendol's hand had landed on his shoulder, and at the time it felt like the highest he could ever rise.

He'd aced every sim, mastered every weapon. Won accolade after accolade and left his platoon behind to help a less accomplished platoon find their feet. Brendol had called him a natural leader and lauded his patience and composure when teaching even the clumsiest or most nervous recruits how to shoot a blaster or wield a riot baton. He never lost his temper or had an unkind word. He took each new challenge in stride and enjoyed the process of finding ways to reach the unreachable, soothe the unsoothable, and boost the confidence of the insecure. In the early days of the First Order, there had been more of these negative traits, back when the recruits were all teens who arrived damaged in heart or mind. Once Brendol had perfected his methods and found younger children to indoctrinate, there were fewer such duties for Cardinal. He was able to focus on weapons and running the elaborate sims programmed by both Huxes.

There were many fine recruits, but in the end Brendol chose Cardinal above all others for this responsibility. Out of thousands upon thousands of troopers, it was CD-0922 who was called to lead and given the high honor of acting as the personal honor guard of Brendol Hux as they refined the training program together. The first time Cardinal saw the red armor was when Brendol Hux presented it to him in a ceremony in front of thousands of his fellow troopers. Although CD-0922's helmet had shown only the smooth, white face, inside, he'd been incandescent, joy beaming out of his eyes and stretching his smile to unseemly proportions.

"Thank you, sir," he'd said.

Brendol had looked at him, then . . . well, like perhaps a father would.

Which was a way Brendol had never looked at his own son, Armitage.

Cardinal recalled one conversation in particular, once he was considered a trusted part of Brendol's life and long before Phasma came along. Brendol has been preparing for a big meeting with Grand Admiral Rae Sloane and the other leaders of the First Order—well, the first set of leaders. Cardinal was waiting in Brendol's suite—the very one where Armitage was now staying—and Brendol had poured his customary glass of port from a crystal decanter and offered a glass to Cardinal.

"Thank you, sir, but it's against regulations," Cardinal said.

Brendol had smiled that smug but indulgent smile he used only when he was in the best of moods. "Ah, CD-0922. So upright in your red uniform. That's why you're first among my men. Cardinal, even." He laughed at his own joke. "How would you like to have a name other than a number? *Captain Cardinal* has quite a ring to it, does it not?"

It was an unusual honor, and Cardinal's heart had swelled. "As you wish, sir."

"That's what you always say. I wonder what you would do if I, as your superior officer, insisted you share a drink with me. Would you honor your First Order teachings or follow my direct command?"

Cardinal had flushed under his red helmet, panicking a bit. It was as if two thoughts were running through his head, separate but opposed, and neither was stronger than the other. Brendol poured a glass and held it out, but Cardinal didn't reach for it.

"I'm sure it is against your orders to invite me to go against regulations, sir," he finally said.

At that, Brendol had thrown back his head and laughed.

"Good answer, Cardinal. More for me, then."

The older Hux had swallowed both glasses happily and gone to his meeting in good spirits, Cardinal walking before him, blaster at the ready and captain's cape flowing behind him. When he'd served as Brendol's guard, he'd always felt larger than life, untouchable and grand. The red armor, Brendol often reminded him, invoked power. Out of all the identical troopers, one had risen above. One had flown higher. Cardinal was to be more than just a stormtrooper—the highest of the stormtroopers. Hence the color, hence the unique name.

Cardinal for the red bird, Cardinal for his standing as the first of his kind, the first trooper with a name and with red armor.

And then Phasma showed up.

She never had to give up her name for a number, as Cardinal had. She didn't get red armor, thank goodness, but it was obvious that Brendol considered her special, too. Given a captain's cape early in her career, the only one other than Cardinal. Offered the chance to mold the training program to her specifications, to program the sims and find new ways to challenge the teens who'd graduated from Cardinal's own curriculum. It had seemed . . . well, he felt guilty for even thinking it. But it had felt as if he did the heavy lifting, primed the pumps, and then she took his perfect troopers and twisted them to suit herself.

The more he thinks about it, the angrier he becomes.

It's unclear whose work is more important. They are two halves of the same whole. When the troopers perform ideally and are triumphant, it's considered a joint victory. When Brendol had stood before the assembled troopers to report a job well done, Cardinal and Phasma had flanked him to share in victory, and now they do the same under the new General Hux. But for all that their lives are intertwined, Cardinal has never known Phasma personally. At all. He has his academy on the *Absolution,* and when he deems a platoon ready, they get shipped off to Phasma's academy on the *Finalizer.* Even though he's the one that trained her, teaching her the intricacies of the First Order and even how to read, he still knows virtually nothing about her as a person. She has always shunned small talk.

One thing he does know is that Phasma memorizes her troopers' numbers. He once considered this a sign in her favor, an attention to detail that shows how much she cares about her responsibility. But now he sees everything she does in a more sinister light. Cardinal learns the troopers' numbers because he is proud of them and enjoys seeing them succeed. Perhaps Phasma keeps track of the numbers in case she needs to make someone disappear. Like Frey. Her own niece.

As these thoughts stream through his head, he polishes his red armor to a high shine and goes through the once comforting ritual of getting dressed. The klaxon blares, and he hears the sounds of footsteps and shouting. Brendol offered him quarters among the officers, up high where Armitage now stays, but Cardinal chose to be here, near his charges, acting as a living example of his service and modesty within the First Order. At first, being so near the chaos of thousands of children irked him, but now it feels like home. Listening to them now, even filtered through his helmet, he smiles.

These children will one day be the greatest fighters the galaxy has ever known, but just now they're jostling for showers and toilets and measuring their hair to make sure it's trimmed to regulation length. He gives them time to dress and get their breakfast before checking his reflection in the mirror. The outside shell doesn't show the cracks within. Perhaps this is a crisis of faith, but he will perform his duties. If nothing else, they give him time to decide what to do with the Resistance spy. It's too late to tell his superiors about her, to admit that he's been secretly tracking her and has her locked up on ship, all records of her presence cannily erased by Iris. But it's never too late to kill her and kick her body out of an air lock, distasteful as that seems. She is an enemy of the First Order, after all. A member of the Resistance. Her intel on Phasma, while elucidating, isn't enough.

When the time is right, Cardinal stands to go. But before he leaves, he turns back. His quarters are spare, nothing like the glowing elegance of the Hux suite. Growing up on Jakku and then sleeping in the barracks, he couldn't get comfortable on the soft mattress Brendol had originally supplied with his captain's commission. Now his bed is a spare thing, matching his equally austere furnishings. There are no rugs, no art, no cut-crystal decanters. No softness or color here. Just a few hard, basic chairs and a small table—strangely similar to the room where Vi waits. He kneels before the table and pulls out the single drawer. The box inside seems so childish in his gloved hands, the wood simple and rough, cradled in the shining red. He slides back the lid to reveal the only remnant of his life before the First Order.

It's a small and inelegant carving of a happabore.

Long ago, Brendol told his child army to bring nothing with them, that the First Order would supply everything they needed, become father and mother and employer. But a young boy named Archex smuggled this lone object in the pocket of his fatigue pants. His father had carved it, his mother said, when she was pregnant. A gift for the son he never met. At the time, the boy had thought himself very brave and reckless. For the first few years, he'd taken great pains to hide this artifact, feeling guilty and worrying that he would be discovered. But now, looking down, twisting the happabore between his gloves, he just feels very old and very conflicted.

He realizes, suddenly and with great emotion, that he has never killed anyone unless directly ordered to do so, while Phasma has killed many. Every time his platoon was sent planetside, he did his duty and followed orders, so he's never considered it a problem. His superiors have never questioned his performance. And yet . . . does he have what it takes to be that ruthless? Is this why he holds back with Vi?

Is he the one who's really the rot in the heart of the First Order? A knot of weakness amid strength?

No.

No, that's foolish.

Taking lives unnecessarily doesn't make Phasma strong.

He drops the happabore into the box, gently places the box back in the drawer. Here is evidence that he, too, has been imperfect from the start. His first response to the First Order's kindness was rebellion. Their main difference, it would seem, is that Phasma is willing to do anything and kill anyone to get what she wants, and he's happy to do as he's told and be satisfied with what he's been given.

Or, at least, he was.

All this time, he's been pressing Vi to give him the intel in time for the assembly. It's so rare that General Hux, Phasma, and the other leaders are all on the same ship. More and more these days, it seems as if everything of import happens on the *Finalizer,* while the *Absolu-*

tion fades from consequence. Although he was invited to attend, Cardinal wasn't even informed of the meeting's purpose. It could've been to discuss something sweeping like planetary occupation strategies, but deep in his heart he's always worried that he'll lose yet more responsibilities, whether to Phasma or another trooper. Everyone in the First Order has a job . . . until they don't. Cardinal was looking forward to presenting his case and watching Phasma as the truth was revealed, but now he dreads attending at all. Without Armitage on his side, he needs more than just stories.

He hurries from his room and walks down the hall to the cafeteria, glad that the children within won't be able to see him sweating, thanks to his helmet. The door opens, and every face turns to stare. As one, they rise to their feet and salute, their small faces earnest and their black uniforms spotless. Cardinal faces them, forces his chin up, and returns the salute. When his arm goes down, they stare for one moment more before returning to their food. Their chatter is much quieter now: No one would dare utter a harsh word or do anything remotely raucous while Cardinal is watching.

He knows every face here. Knows every number and every childish nickname. He's tucked them back into their bunks when they had night terrors, calling out for parents they'll never see again. He's placed their fingers on triggers, taught them how to squeeze just right. He's given them stern looks of disappointment and doled out their punishments. For fifteen years, he's stood here, looking out at a sea of faces, every one reflecting the boy he once was. Boy or girl, tall or short, light or dark, brave or clever, these children are him, and they are his. For the first time, he doubts why he would ever hand them over to a monster like Phasma for safekeeping. His children— she turns them into monsters like her, doesn't she? Killers without conscience. It makes him sick.

But he can't let that show. Not when there are thousands of eyes watching.

Following his usual pattern, Cardinal walks up and down the tables, calling out to this child or that to ask about their training, compliment their scores, or point out a belt buckled backward. When he reaches the food line, he's the only one there.

"Good morning, Captain Cardinal," the droid says. "Will you be having the standard breakfast?"

"Yes. And a prote snack and extra caf, please."

His tray is different from those sitting in neat rows before the children. Their meals are perfectly designed for their ages, genders, weights, and nutritional needs. He suspects that other chemicals are included to keep them healthy and boost any vitamin deficiencies they might've had, growing up on rough planets. Their food doesn't taste good, but hunger works wonders for the appetite, and the children are worked hard. His food tastes no better, but it's all he really remembers. The caf, at least, will help him stay alert—he had been on his way to sleep when Iris informed him of the capture of Vi's ship, and being awake this long isn't helping his mental state or his jitters.

Cardinal takes his tray to a table set perpendicular to those of his recruits. His place is always left empty, whether he's there or not, and surrounding him are the up-and-coming leaders in his program. He sits and looks around the room. There's no choice but to see the posters of Phasma watching over the children like some great silver goddess in a cape. They don't see a monster, though. They see a hero. A tall soldier, looking toward the future, her cloak dramatically outlining her shining chrome armor. The black eyes of her helmet reflect the stormtroopers they will one day become. They see what they're meant to be, what they might be if they work hard enough, if they fight well enough. They long to be molded in her image. He never noticed before how very many of the damn posters line the walls. It's like he can't escape her.

"Good morning, sir," FE-1211 says. She's his brown-noser, but she always scores highest on intelligence testing and has a mean eye with a blaster.

"Did you sleep well, sir?" This from FB-0007, a serious child who'd love nothing more than to supplant FE-1211 but can't quite outfox her.

"Yes, thank you," Cardinal says. As he stares down at his plate, he realizes he'll have to take off his helmet to eat, and then the children might be able to see the mental war he's fighting writ in the lines on his face.

The third child, FM-0676, just stares at him, her dark eyes as hard as a mask. She's the one to watch, he thinks. Because she's the one who's always watching.

"I've a meeting today. Do your best. I'll check your scores tonight. As you were."

He stands, picks up his tray, and forces himself to walk slowly and with gravitas back to his room, where he rips off his helmet and wipes the sweat off his face with a cloth before eating. The food sits in his throat, and he forces it down with the caf. It does no better in his stomach, where it roils like a stone ball and threatens to come back up. He can't cram down any more protein, so he pockets the extra packet and chugs the caf, wishing it were easier to get his hands on the real battle stims handed out to troopers when they're training in sims and later fighting on the ground. He could use an extra boost just now. The stuff he gave to Vi is child's play by comparison.

When he stands, his legs tremble.

The ship, once so solid, feels like it's shuddering all around him.

He should be overseeing the children's training, but he can't stop worrying about his little project downstairs. If some random trooper assigned garbage duty for the first time becomes lost and stumbles onto the spy, Cardinal's entire life will be destroyed. The odds are impossible, but paranoia doesn't care about odds. Clever as Iris is, she's not programmed to deal with that. He flicks his comm to contact his closest colleague on the ship. If Cardinal has a friend, it's SC-4044.

"SC-4044. I'm feeling a bit off today. Run the program as usual. Let me know if there are any issues. Put FE-1211 in the rear flank and see what FB-0007 can do with his own platoon."

"Going to medbay, sir?"

He pauses. "It's not that bad."

"Did you finally hit the cantina?"

Another pause. "Something like that."

He mops off his face again before putting on his helmet and heading out. He's never felt claustrophobic before, not about ships and not about his helmet. But now his helmet feels like it's made of lead, like it's pressing down, making him shorter and smaller and stupid. He can hear his heartbeat in his ears, smell his own sour breath laced with caf. When he checks his image in the mirror by the door, he can't help staring.

This is him.

This is Captain Cardinal.

This is the leader of the youth training program, once Brendol Hux's right-hand man.

He is polished perfection, upright strength and courage. He is the second most important trooper in the entire First Order, and he now knows that the number one trooper isn't what everyone thinks she is. He has done the right thing, reported malfeasance to his superior officer as outlined in the First Order laws, and in return he has learned that a murderer walks free among his people, given the highest honors above him, her actions supported by those who should be punishing her. And the only thing he can do is go back to a Resistance spy to see what other orts she will throw him in a bid for her freedom.

He's out the door and storming down the hall, his steps echoing, when he nearly bumps into a figure coming around the corner.

It's Captain Phasma.

"Pardon me, Captain," she says, her voice as cold and clipped as ever.

For a moment, Cardinal can do nothing but stand there and stare. Her chrome armor is as well polished as his, her armorweave cape equally long and impressive. She's taller than him, but he's more muscular, and although he's never seen her face, he imagines a twisted and feral visage torn by scars, something more akin to her Parnassian mask fringed in feathers and fur.

His hands ball into fists. His right one uncurls, and his fingers dance over the blaster on his hip. How he'd love to kill her, right here. Kill her and tell the truth, not just to Armitage, but to the entire First Order, to Ren and Snoke and anyone else who will listen. He could produce Vi Moradi, could go back to Parnassos and bring back Siv as a witness to Phasma's character. He'd bring them dozens of beetles. He could get rid of this monster once and for all.

He wants so, so badly to kill her.

His entire body trembles. He's so close to doing it.

One shot, and all his problems would disappear.

But he doesn't pull his blaster. In the end, he's utterly incapable of going against his strictest order. Just like with Phasma's old Scyre folk, there is to be no infighting among troopers. It's one of the first things they learn here.

"Captain?" Phasma says when he doesn't move or respond.

"Pardon me," he says, glad for the helmet's voice modulation.

He steps around her and hurries away without looking back.

THIRTY-FIVE

ON THE *ABSOLUTION*

VI DOESN'T KNOW HOW LONG SHE'S BEEN OUT, BUT IT'S BEEN LONG ENOUGH. Going unconscious isn't quite like sleeping, she thinks. Sleeping is like settling into a warm bath, whereas being knocked out is more like being held underwater. You lose time, and you have no control over when you can come up again. And when you do begin to surface, the world comes back in bits and pieces.

She feels the metal band across her forehead first, hot and hard and pressing, as if it had spikes driven deep into her skull. She pulls back the tiniest bit—all she can manage—and her skin clings to the metal and peels up with a light sucking sound. She's fallen forward, and the manacles have jabbed into her arms, digging rivets in her flesh. The bastard could've at least tilted the interrogation chair back instead of leaving her standing on legs that can't support her, held in place by restraints that dig into her arm muscles. It's obvious he's never interrogated anyone before. He probably doesn't even know the chair can tilt back to take some of the weight off the numb feet of the unbalanced subject within so they can be tortured for that much longer before going unconscious.

Vi's feet scrabble to find purchase, and she stands under her own power, an ache thrumming up her back. She's getting too old for this sort of thing. If she gets out of here, she swears that the next time General Organa—or anyone—asks her to just have a little look-see, she's going to run in the opposite direction and find a nice cantina to disappear into. She'd rather hang out on Pantora with Baako, up to her knees in bog, than be here. Dodging the planetary defense system of Parnassos was a simple affair, considering she looked up the right codes, but now she knows that it's impossible to dodge the First Order's Star Destroyers. Once they see you and get their tractor beam hooks into you, you're out of luck. The Resistance needs that information, but Vi's not sure if she'll be able to provide it.

Still, she hasn't lost faith. She's escaped worse situations. True, she generally had at least one crew member and some weapons with her when she did so—and even more often, she had a fast little ship—but there's hope.

"How about you, Iris? You got any hidden interest in defecting to the Resistance?"

In response, the floating orb beeps something that sounds like a laugh, and a shockprod pokes out, snapping with electricity.

"Can't blame me for asking."

There's plenty of time for her to consider the odds while she waits for Cardinal to return. Hell, maybe he won't return. He seemed pretty upset by her story. Not that he was surprised at all; he knew there was something dark lurking under the surface of Phasma in the same way most good-hearted people can smell a rat. No, what's really destroyed him is the knowledge that Phasma killed Brendol and not only lived to tell the tale, but also continued to rise in rank and reputation. That's the problem with following all the rules—somebody else is eventually going to get ahead by breaking them, and then where will you be? Vi's always made sure to break at least one rule, even something as paltry as putting her boots up on the dash or getting crumbs in the seat cushions. Just to keep herself from erring on the side of perfection and obedience.

The door opens, and her eyes cut sideways. When she sees that it's Cardinal, she sighs in relief and relaxes against her bonds. Not like she could actually do anything if someone else showed up, but she can't help being tense. Cardinal, she's guessing, is the biggest softy on the ship.

"Welcome back, Emergency Brake. Think maybe you could tilt me back a bit? I can't feel my feet."

Cardinal hasn't given her more than the briefest glance. He's tapping into the datapad and fiddling with the cams yet again. But is he turning them on, or—? No. He's ripped out a bunch of wires in one of them. If he was earnest earlier, he's deadly serious now.

After moving around the room, he appears in front of her, a solid wall of shining, flawless red, his cape swinging behind him.

"Iris, did she attempt to escape?"

The droid beeps a negative.

Now he focuses on Vi. "Good. Can I trust you?" he asks urgently, and this time it's different from the first time he asked her, hours or maybe days ago.

Vi licks her dry lips. "That's still a complicated question. Let's say you can trust me not to attack you or try to fight my way out of here. I haven't lied to you so far, and I don't plan on doing so, unless I think you're going to kill me if I tell the truth."

He snorts. "That's an honest answer for a spy."

She gives the barest vestige of a shrug, all that her bonds allow. "I'm a pretty honest spy."

Taking off his helmet, he places it on the table and hunkers down in front of her. Ha. As if looking in her eyes is going to show him any new truths just because the red face of his helmet doesn't stand between them.

And yet . . . he does look. Right into her eyes. As if he's trying to reach down into her soul, a drowning man searching dark waters for the salvation of a rope. Beads of sweat stand out on his forehead, under the dark circles beneath his eyes, above the freshly shaved skin over his lip, marked with one tiny, imperfect nick.

"I'm going to let you out of the chair. You won't be bound. You can eat and drink." He puts a bottle of caf and a silver foil packet on the table. "But you're going to tell me more. All of it. Everything you have. I told Armitage that Phasma killed Brendol, and it wasn't enough."

"What do you mean, it wasn't enough?"

"He already knew. And he seemed pleased about it."

This is just another tidbit of information for Vi to tuck into her memory. Armitage Hux hasn't left as much of a data trail as the other First Order leaders because he's had no life outside of this war machine. He was Brendol's hated son at the Imperial Academy on Arkanis, and then he was Brendol's hated son on the *Finalizer,* and then he rose through the ranks to become what he is now: the true heir to Brendol's command and a powerful leader of the First Order. But now they know he's got his own secrets, and that's useful.

"Well, what do you know? The greasy ginger weasel birthed a greasy ginger weasel."

Cardinal's arm flies back like he's about to slap her, but he stops himself before his droid can beep a warning. His arm drops and settles by his side again. "Say what you will about Armitage Hux, but watch your tongue about Brendol. That man was my savior, and he did more for me than my own father."

She narrows her eyes, unable to let that one go.

"Then your family stank." He gives her a stern look, so she chuckles sadly. "But speaking of terrible families, I can give you what you need to know. Just let me out first. That was a good idea. One of your best, actually."

"Do you swear that you won't try anything?"

"I won't try anything physical, but I'll try like hell to convince you to let me go for real."

He's already reaching for the band around her head as he sighs. "If that's the best you can do, I suppose it's all I can really expect."

The metal creaks open, and Vi's head wobbles forward as if her neck were made of rubber. The relieved groan she makes is almost intimate in nature, and then he's working on the straps around her wrists and arms. Each new increment of freedom, she's sure, is the best feeling she's ever known. When the strap around her chest is undone, she's surprised to find her body pitching forward, and Cardinal is forced to catch her or watch her fall. The impact makes her cry out, and then she's crushed by hard, smooth plastoid as he tries to help her move a body that's lost all feeling and strength over the last day. All she can see is red.

"This is awkward," she says as he tries to help her stand. She has all the elegance of a broken doll.

"I'm a bit new to this," he admits, sounding all too human for the man who shocked her unconscious earlier. "Didn't anticipate this part."

Working together, they manage to get her folded into a real chair, her arms and head on the table. It takes everything she has not to slither down onto the floor. If Cardinal were someone on her team, she'd beg for him to help massage feeling back into her shoulders in a purely platonic sort of way, but the thought is simply too absurd. It's hard to reconcile the Cardinal she's researched for weeks with the decidedly not monstrous man gingerly pushing the bottle of caf toward her. Which begs the question: Who is he, in his heart? The orphan from Jakku, yearning to belong, or the brainwashed soldier, programmed to kill?

"The caf is cold, and I drank half of it, but I didn't think you'd complain," he says.

Vi figures out how to hold up her head, just enough for him to see her smile. Maybe he's both of those things, after all. And maybe he's also the red-armored white knight who rages against injustice and betrayal and treachery and wants to see the monster that is Phasma cut out of the First Order that he loves.

That's another thing Vi has learned. No one is ever just one thing. The trick is finding out who they are in the moment and convincing that person to do what you want them to do. And in this case, that means she wants Cardinal to listen to her story and take the next logical step.

When she can get her arms to work, she slides the bottle of caf closer and nibbles at the straw until she gets it between her lips. She's not about to try lifting the bottle just yet, but she can sip. The thought of Cardinal on hands and knees, mopping up spilled caf with a hankie, just about sends her into a fit of giggles, but she covers it up with a laugh.

"I couldn't attack you anyway, you know. I think my whole body went to sleep," she says between careful sips. "First Order works a girl hard."

Cardinal snorts and his mouth twists into something like an amused grin. "So you're saying the Resistance is lazy."

At that, she really does laugh. "I'm glad you asked. But I'll be honest: It's a tough job. Not a lot of money, no official government support, brainwashed bucketheads and bounty hunters looking for you in every cantina, hoping to get whatever prize they've set on your head this week. It's downright restful in here right now by comparison, I tell you."

He seems quite surprised when a chuckle comes out of his mouth, but he quickly smothers it. "What keeps you going, then?"

Vi has managed to slide the food packet over, but she's struggling with the perforated corner, so Cardinal takes it from her, rips it open in a professionally violent sort of way, and slides it back. She sucks on a few squeezes of dingy paste as she considers her answer.

"Hope," she says. "Knowing that, one by one, we can beat something unstoppable. A giant that thinks we're merely wrong-minded ants to be crushed. But do you know the power of ten thousand ants? Of ten million?" She takes another mouthful, her stomach crunching with hunger. "Hope, and better food than this. What is it, all protein? No flavor, no spoonful of sweetener. No wonder you guys are so angry all the time. Although I bet your teeth are just perfect."

In response, Cardinal smiles, and he does indeed have perfect rows of white teeth. It's a nice smile, Vi thinks, and she smiles back without really giving it much thought. Something about her gesture unsettles him, and Cardinal reschools his face into the more usual troubled frown.

"You're free. You've eaten. You've had something to drink. Now tell me the rest." He puts his hands on the table and settles down as if the weight of the world is on his shoulders. "Because what I have so far . . . is not enough. And you might be out of the chair, but you're not safe, and neither is your brother."

She frowns. "Are we still doing that? The threats?"

"We're doing that until you give me whatever intel you're holding back. I'm not going to that assembly until I have what I need, and if I don't have what I need, our deal is off."

Vi looks up at him, and the room suddenly feels cold, as if she can taste the night air of Parnassos, feel the sand whipping across her face.

"Just one more story, then," she says. "And an older one. But it's a doozy."

THIRTY-SIX

ON PARNASSOS, 15 YEARS AGO

NOW, THIS STORY SIV TOLD ME TAKES PLACE A FEW YEARS BEFORE ALL THE others, when Phasma and Keldo were both children. Keldo still had both his legs and was the warrior in the family, and Phasma was not yet the fighter and leader we know today, although Keldo was training her. They weren't even part of the Scyre group yet. They lived with a much smaller, weaker family group, and their only territory was directly around the Nautilus, which was considered a great prize.

Keldo told Siv that his mother and father were getting older and weaker, along with his aunts and uncles. A younger cousin was too small yet to contribute. As you saw in the earlier stories of Parnassos, it was becoming a land hostile to anyone who wasn't in top shape and ready to fight at a moment's notice. In their family, Keldo and Phasma were forced to rise to the occasion.

Around this time, life went from unbearable to nearly impossible. The small goats died out, and the already stinging rain turned to acid that burned uncovered skin, and everyone's ribs began to show through their clothes. Their diet shrank to mollusks and sea vegetables. Teeth began to loosen. Wounds started to fester, and they learned that if they didn't amputate and cauterize, even the smallest scratch from the rocks would induce the dreaded fever. They were exhausted, their skin pallid and their hair falling out. They'd never heard of detraxors. The family group had lost half their members in the last year alone, and despite being children, Phasma and Keldo were their only hope.

It was all they could do to defend the Nautilus from the Scyre and Claw raids, and even then much of their strength came from weapons passed down through the generations, sharp bits of metal and one blaster that only occasionally worked.

As the raiding intensified, it became clear that the Scyre were losing their patience and wanted the Nautilus. Phasma and Keldo had to sleep in shifts so that one of them was always awake and ready to fight off any forays from older, battle-hardened Scyre folk. Balder stole their small cousin for the Claw folk, and the raids took on a new terror. They lost ground every day until there was practically nothing, and Scyre scouts could be seen always watching from the edges of their territory like vultures circling a limping eopie.

Keldo argued with their parents over how to handle the encroaching raiders. It was obvious their group couldn't last, but the older generation refused to give up their ancestral home, much less share it with vindictive invaders who wouldn't honor it.

"You'd rather die than share?" Keldo asked his father one night as they sat around the fire that burned in the center of the Nautilus.

"At least then I wouldn't be here to bear witness to the desecration," his father said. "Better to leave our dying world than see some other man sitting on this throne."

"You're no king," Keldo said. "You can't even fight anymore."

For that, his father slapped him. Although the man wasn't as fit as he'd once been, it left a mark.

"I understand," the boy said, and he climbed up out of the Nautilus to take his watch and relieve Phasma.

But when he crawled out onto the stone above, he didn't see his sister anywhere.

"Phasma?" he called, scanning the area.

Back then, stone tiers marked the border between their territory and the Scyre, but Phasma was nowhere to be found. He walked to the edge of the cliffs and looked down, but all he saw was the dark and roiling sea, the progenitor of all his troubles. Perhaps his sister had flung herself out into that great beyond, eager to be done with the cruel world, as Keldo sometimes longed to do. But no. Phasma, most likely, had never considered such a thing.

"What are you doing, brother?" she asked, appearing behind him like smoke with the blaster in hand.

"Looking for you. Where were you?"

She ignored the question. They didn't wear masks yet, and the moon was full, so he was able to see into her eyes. And she was able to see the handprint on his cheek, which only made her face go harder.

"What has he done," she said, and it wasn't much of a question.

"Father won't compromise," he said. "Not with the Scyre, and not with anyone. He'd rather die than lose the Nautilus."

"And what do you think?"

"I think I'd rather stay alive than die for something that's already halfway dead."

She put her hand on his shoulder, clamping down.

"Are you sure?" she asked.

"Sure about what?"

She didn't answer, just nodded decisively. Before he could question her further, she whipped out her small stone knife and buried it in the muscle of his calf, deep enough to hit bone.

Keldo screamed and went down, and Phasma guided him to the rough stone with a strange gentleness, lest he slip off the cliff into the sea.

"You'll understand later," she told him as she yanked out the blade. "But know that it had to happen this way, and I'm sorry."

Keldo was going into shock, and he could only mumble, "Why, Phasma? Why?"

She stood and dragged him toward the hole that led down into the Nautilus. When he was close enough to look down into the cave, she pushed him into it with no warning.

"Help!" she screamed. "We're under attack!"

Keldo landed hard and looked up from the ground of the cave, far below. Several masked faces appeared around Phasma, but they weren't fighting her, and she wasn't attacking them. They were waiting for something.

"Don't go," Keldo mumbled to the rest of his family, on the verge of blacking out. "She's . . ."

The last thing he saw was his small, tired, feeble family taking up their weapons, their blades and axes and clubs, and clambering up out of the Nautilus to fight the Scyre.

When Keldo woke up, he was still in the Nautilus, but he was laid out at the foot of the throne, nestled in his father's blankets. Phasma sat beside him dressed in leathers as the Scyre did, holding out soup. The sound of talking, laughing, and footsteps echoed around him, and as his vision came back into focus, he saw dozens of people, more people than he'd ever seen in one place in his life, happily lounging and cooking and eating around the Nautilus.

"What happened?" he asked. Because for all that he remembered plenty, none of it made sense.

"We were attacked," Phasma said. "By the Scyre. Mother and Father and all the rest . . . are gone."

She watched him strangely, like a hawk hunting for some small and telling movement.

"But you stabbed me. My leg."

He scrambled to sit up and look down, but his father's blanket was spread out over him. He realized that he couldn't quite feel his foot, and when he whipped back the blanket, he found he'd lost most of his leg. The stump was coated in a thick green salve that smelled of the sea.

"No, Keldo. The Scyre did that. They caught you on watch, and I threw you into the Nautilus. I saved your life. We are lucky that they've invited us to stay here, to live among them. All we must do is agree to join them in good faith. To fight for them and contribute. And then we can stay here, in the Nautilus. It will still be ours. What say you?"

Keldo knew she was lying. He remembered her apology on the cliff and the bite of her knife. And he understood in that moment that she had, in one fell swoop, rendered him alive but incapable of fighting her while securing the Nautilus for them both. All along, Keldo had argued that they should join the Scyre, but his father had disagreed. Now Keldo realized that Phasma saw things the same way he did, but her method of saving both their lives and keeping their cave had been decisive, dastardly, and unyielding. And he knew that he now had only two choices: join the Scyre with her . . . or die.

A brawny fighter came to stand behind Phasma, a tall man Keldo had never met but who looked like a leader forged in battle.

"Brother, this is Egil, and he is the leader of the Scyre. He is a good and fair man, and he will use the Nautilus for the benefit of his people. For the benefit of *our* people."

"Now tell me, Keldo," Egil asked, a hand on his blade. "Will you join us? Or will you join them?"

"Join whom?"

Egil stood back and pointed to six bodies laid out neatly along the wall, each wrapped in the fine fabrics they'd carefully hoarded in the Nautilus, filmy gray and too silky to ever use for clothes. Blooms of red shone through the gray, and Keldo didn't have to see their faces to know who they were or how they'd died. Two of them had machines stuck into their thighs like strange, unwanted growths, and a dark-skinned Scyre woman squatted beside one, her teen daughter by her side with a basket full of waterskins and dried plants.

Keldo went cold, and he later told Siv that he could feel the chill spread down to the toes that were no longer part of his body. He looked up at Phasma, his jaw dropped and his eyes pleading with her to tell him that he wasn't seeing what he was seeing.

"What are they doing? To Mother and Father? To our family?"

"Those are detraxors," Egil explained gently. "They recover vital nutrients from the fallen. Vala and her daughter, Siv, use this essence to make a salve that prevents disease and another that heals wounds. The liniment on your leg has saved your life, and this is where it comes from." He turned away and shouted, "Siv! Bring a tin of salve. The fresh one."

The teen girl picked up an ancient tin that had been sitting beside the largest wrapped shape, which Keldo recognized as his father. She stood gracefully and walked across the Nautilus as if she'd always lived there. Her eyes flicked curiously over Keldo, and she smiled shyly as she held the open tin out to Egil.

"Will you fight for the Scyre?" Egil asked Phasma.

"Proudly," she answered.

The leader drew his broad thumb through the dark green salve and swiped a wet slash under each of Phasma's eyes. Everyone in the Scyre had always worn such stripes, and Keldo's family had assumed it was to make them look more ferocious during battle. Now Keldo understood its true function: It made them strong enough to fight.

"Welcome to the Scyre, Phasma," Egil said with great solemnity. "Body to body, dust to dust."

Phasma bowed her head. "Body to body, dust to dust," she repeated.

But before Egil could repeat the ritual with Keldo, Phasma took the tin from the girl called Siv and dipped her fingers in. Without asking Keldo the question, she drew the slashes on his face.

"Body to body, dust to dust," she said.

But Keldo didn't repeat the phrase at first. And, of course, he couldn't have answered the same question; without his leg, he couldn't fight for the Scyre, could he? Phasma had seen to that. Egil's hand landed on the dagger on his belt, and the Nautilus went quiet as they waited for Keldo's oath.

"You have to say it," Siv whispered, her eyes wide and worried.

The salve was cold and thick on Keldo's cheeks, a dark line hovering at the edge of his vision. It smelled of the sea, of death, of darkness. At least it didn't carry the scent of his father, for all that it was drawn over the same cheek the man had slapped what felt like years ago, when Keldo had been whole and his family had still been intact.

He looked into Phasma's hard blue eyes and tried to remember what she'd looked like without the green paint, before he had seen her true face.

He couldn't remember.

"Say it," she demanded.

He had no choice. Egil and Phasma had made that plain.

"Body to body, dust to dust," he murmured.

Egil clapped him on the back and smiled.

"Welcome to the Scyre."

THIRTY-SEVEN

ON THE *ABSOLUTION*

VI WATCHES CARDINAL'S FACE AS SHE FINISHES THE TALE. THE TROOPER
has his chin on his fist as he stares off into nowhere, his mouth set in
a frown.

"So you're telling me they painted him with salve made from his
own—"

"They both did. That was how they came to join the Scyre. She
sacrificed her parents and family to survive."

Cardinal shakes his head and stands. "But he loved her brother.
She avenged his death by killing Brendol. It makes . . . a kind of
sense."

Vi sits back, finally able to hold up her head and laugh at him
properly. "Oh, is that what she was doing when she murdered Brendol? Avenging her brother? Funny, I thought she was getting rid of
the only witness who knew her true past back on Parnassos. Who
knew how far she would go to survive and succeed. Did she protest
when Brendol slaughtered her people? Did she beg for peace, or
speak up for her warriors? Or did she consider it a tidy way to begin

her new life with the First Order? It's the same way she joined the Scyre. She made a sacrifice, cut all ties, and pledged her allegiance to the stronger clan."

He slashes a hand between them as if to erase what he's heard. "This doesn't help me. Just because I'm convinced she's a traitor doesn't mean my superiors will care. They obviously don't."

Vi puts her hands on the table and tries to stand, but her legs aren't ready to hold her weight yet. She sits back down with a *whump* and drinks some more caf, hoping to invigorate her body before mobility truly becomes an issue. She's out of stories, and they both know it.

"Then they're fools. People don't change. Phasma will always be that little girl with the knife, the usurping Arratu with the sword, the stone-faced assassin casually flicking a beetle at the man who saved her."

"Again: According to this story, Phasma did nothing to betray the First Order. So why did you save it for last?"

"It's important," she says carefully, "because out of all the stories I heard on Parnassos—and I didn't tell you all of them, only the ones I thought would be personally resonant—this one chills me the most. Because it makes it clear that you can't win against Phasma. Not you. Not anyone. No one will go as far as she will to survive."

Although it won't convince his superiors, Cardinal knows Vi is right. Even as an orphan, he never took such bold, cruel means to survive. To think: As a teen girl, she purposefully disabled her brother with a knife and watched her parents die, then . . . painted her body with what was left of them to cement her next loyalty. When she accepted that salve, she became Scyre. And he already knows what happened to the Scyre. Armitage thinks he's got a Kath hound on a leash, but what he's got is a rancor just waiting for the gate to open. No one will see the real Phasma until the moment when what the First Order wants is no longer what she wants. One day—and it's coming—

Phasma will betray them all. Just like she did her family, and just like she did the Scyre.

Her loyalty? Means nothing.

Nothing, except that Armitage himself hasn't yet received a knife in the back.

Cardinal is the only one who knows.

And he's only one who can stop her.

The tiny interrogation chamber, or whatever closet it was built to be, suddenly feels very small and very close, and Cardinal can smell the spy's worsening body odors and the lingering stench of whatever part of her got fried by the shock.

He won't let her know, but he no longer doubts her. At all. He knows that Vi is right, that everything she's told him is true. It all fits together too well to be some story she's spun just to save her skin.

Iris beeps, and he checks his comm. It's almost time.

"Last chance. Is there any real proof?" he asks. "Your time is up, and the assembly won't wait."

Vi drums her fingers on the table briefly and nods. "There is something else, actually. But I need you to stay calm. I'm going to reach into a hidden pocket of my jacket and pull out what looks like a pretty scary knife."

"What is it?"

"It's a pretty scary knife. But I'm not going to use it. I'm going to put it on the table, real gentle, and then put my hands behind my head. If I can. And what you're going to do is you're not going to lose your cool, and you're definitely not going to touch the blade in any way that might get either of us cut. Because remember: It's poisoned."

Cardinal exhales in a disappointed sort of way, partially because he and his men searched her and missed a knife and partially because he held her to a higher standard and somehow expected her to be honest about hidden weapons while he was torturing her on an enemy ship. She just shrugs.

"I'm part of the Resistance. Of course I was going to resist. Do you want it or not?"

He pulls his blaster and holds it low, aimed for her belly. She rolls her eyes as if to say, *Aren't we past this?*

In response, he also rolls his eyes and says, "Just because we're on the same side of this argument doesn't mean we're on the same side of this fight. Now give me the knife. And hurry. My time is short."

She grins at him and slowly, slowly reaches into an interior pocket of her jacket.

"I'm going to use two hands, now," she warns.

And if he's honest with himself, he's not worried. She can't stand, she can barely lift her arms. Whatever she's got in there—well, she could've used it against him anytime since he'd untied her, and she hasn't. Hasn't so much as caressed that pocket. So he nods and waits, his blaster ready.

It takes some tugging, but Vi pulls a piece of shaped armor out of her jacket, puts it on the table, and pries it open. As soon as the sides fall apart, she scoots back from the table with her hands on her head, just as she promised. And there, lying on the table, is exactly what she described: a pretty scary knife.

It's about the length of his hand and made of hewn stone. The blade is coated in a flaking, rusty powder peppered with grayish-green, and the hilt is wrapped in leather stained a deep, rich chestnut with sweat and blood. It's a vicious, rough, inelegant thing meant for making holes that can't properly close.

"This is one of Phasma's knives. The one she put in her brother's leg and Balder's chest, so the story goes. Siv saved it during the Claw battle; she was quick like that."

"May I?" Cardinal asks, and Vi tips her head.

"You're the one running the show. Take it. Please. But promise me you'll tell me what Phasma's face looks like after she sees it. Like she's seen a particularly vengeful ghost, I'd guess."

Cardinal replaces his blaster and lifts the knife carefully by the hilt. He remembers the part of the story about Phasma using poisons based on the lichens of Parnassos. He's pretty sure that the med droids could identify and negate the poison, but he's not about to bet on it.

"No one ever sees her face," he says softly. "I never have. No one I know has. She has her own quarters, as I do, and never eats with her troops."

"Doesn't anyone ever wonder what she's hiding?"

Cardinal looks up, meets her eyes. "I always have. I suppose I know now."

Vi looks to the door longingly. "So how about it. You going to make good on our deal?"

He shakes his head. "It's still not enough. You know that."

"So you're going to kill me?"

His face wrinkles up in distaste. "I don't want to."

And he honestly doesn't. But . . .

Vi is grinning.

"You seem pretty happy about dying," he observes.

"I have one more thing. Promise me again you'll let me go if I give it to you."

Feeling just as exasperated as he gets with his newest and youngest recruits, Cardinal sighs. "The terms have not changed. You give me evidence, I let you go. Absolutely last chance."

"I'm reaching into my jacket again."

As she works another piece of armor out of the thick leather, Cardinal notes that he needs to train his men to search for non-metallic objects and to remove all outer garments from prisoners. When Vi snaps open the piece of armor, Cardinal can't stop himself from grinning.

It's a clear plastoid specimen case, and inside is a glittering gold beetle, still alive.

"You don't want to crack this open," Vi warns. "I've seen these guys get to business, and it's not pretty. Tossed a little water on the sand, and suddenly there were a thousand of them."

Cardinal holds up the beetle and feels his heart lift. Finally, finally, he has concrete evidence. If he can get this beetle to the meeting, all they need to do is give it to the med droids, who will confirm that the beetle contains the same chemical signature that killed Brendol.

"So what are you going to do?" Vi sips the caf and watches him. She's looking a little better, not quite as dehydrated. Perhaps her time unconscious actually gave her some rest. Cardinal feels a little bad about that; he shocked her harder than he meant to. But her eyes, golden and hard, don't blink as much as they should. How strange is it that he feels judged, and that he doesn't want to disappoint this piece of space trash spying for his enemy?

Doesn't matter. It's time now. She's given him what he needs. He can't leave General Hux, Captain Phasma, and the other high-ranking officers waiting. Cardinal stands and puts on his helmet. It's easier when Vi can't see his face.

Vi sits up with a grunt and frowns at him.

"I'm going to confront Phasma," he finally says. "Show her the knife and the beetle. In front of General Hux and the other officers."

At that, Vi's lips quirk up in a smile.

"Good luck. On a personal level, I hope you just absolutely destroy her."

That earns a chuckle. "Thanks." Carefully, he picks up the knife and slides it into his holster, behind the blaster. The beetle's specimen case goes into one of the ammo boxes on his belt.

At the door, he turns back and makes the first of many decisions that could unravel everything he's worked so hard to build. All those years, scraping by on Jakku. And then the years as he struggled to conform to the First Order's ideals, undergoing constant tests and programming under Brendol's training. Years rising through the ranks, fighting in the sims, besting his mates and challenging himself to succeed. Everything he's worked for and toward . . . well, it all changes here, doesn't it?

"I'll leave the door unlocked. I'm taking Iris with me. Count to a thousand and then . . . do what you will."

Vi raises one eyebrow. "Do as I will?"

"Escape if you can, sleep if you have no other choice, die in here if that seems easier. If anyone catches you, I'll tell them I met you on my rounds and you overpowered me and escaped. Hell, maybe I'll tell them you had Force powers. They'll hunt you down with extreme prejudice, but it won't be my fault. Or my problem."

"There's another option," she says.

That gets his attention. He was just about to punch in the code to open the door, but instead he turns to consider her.

"Defect. Escape with me. Come join the Resistance, or at least take their cash for some intel and run. They'll give you a full pardon. If you can't do that, I can still help you get off ship and onto any Outer Rim planet you like. Start a new life. You don't have to be on the losing side here."

For just a moment, he considers it, but then the last words hit him like a slap.

"I'm not on the losing side. You are. Good luck getting off the ship."

Without another word, Cardinal punches in the code and steps into the hall with Iris floating in his wake. He doesn't watch Vi as the door slides shut. She's no longer his concern. He has everything he needed from her. The truth, the understanding, the beetle. And this knife.

She might be on the wrong side, but he agrees with Resistance spy Vi Moradi on one thing.

Cardinal is on his way to show Phasma the knife, and he only wishes he could see her face.

THIRTY-EIGHT

ON THE *ABSOLUTION*

THE *ABSOLUTION* IS A VERY LARGE SHIP, AND IT'S A LONG WALK FROM VI TO the assembly room. With every step, Cardinal feels more desolate. Phasma is an empty fiction, a legend built of lies. And the First Order—and even Brendol Hux himself—chose Phasma over Cardinal. Brendol, knowing Phasma was out for herself, knowing she would sell out her own family to get what she wanted. Brendol had looked at Phasma and seen a great leader, someone to put on propaganda posters and raise up on a pedestal.

And Brendol paid for that mistake.

It's hard for Cardinal to think of what it must've been like for Brendol, dying of a mysterious disease, a deadly riddle that even the most state-of-the-art med droids couldn't solve. Did Brendol recognize the symptoms, try to tell the droids what was happening to him? Did Brendol know that Phasma was behind it? Did he look through his closet for some remnant of Parnassos that might hide a glittering gold carapace? Did he call in Armitage as he floated in the bacta, becoming more and more liquid himself, and speak to the boy about the future of the First Order, the only thing the two Hux men could wholeheartedly agree on? Did Brendol suggest then that Phasma be lifted toward greatness, hailed as the perfect trooper?

Or did he whisper to Armitage that Phasma had killed him and urge the boy to give her whatever she wanted, so long as it benefited the First Order and kept at least one Hux alive? Did he perhaps tell Armitage to drop Phasma out the airlock, and did he then watch his son slowly smile and shake his head no?

This is what it must be like, Cardinal thinks, to lose one's faith.

He knows everything, and now he knows that Armitage knows everything—or, at the very least, Armitage knows the most dangerous, damning parts. The First Order would rather have Phasma as she is, a bloodthirsty, disloyal murderer, than an honorable, faithful, true-believing, by-the-books soldier like Cardinal. Cardinal, who has done everything they've ever asked. Cardinal, who teaches and comforts and encourages the children. Cardinal, who has given everything he has for the First Order.

Thoughts and doubts and rage run on repeat in his head as the lift goes up and up and up. His fingers clench and unclench, and sweat drips down the back of his neck. But he's a captain in the First Order, and he will show no outward signs of weakness. Before, such meetings were always exciting. Cardinal's troops were praised, and he was congratulated for his ongoing excellent service to the First Order. But since Phasma became a captain, Cardinal has lost more and more of his program to her, his recruits taken to the *Finalizer* earlier and earlier. Now is his chance to stop losing face and start regaining control. Today, whatever they think their meeting will be about, it will become about revealing and stopping Phasma before she betrays the First Order.

As Cardinal stalks the long corridors to the assembly room, he prepares his speech in his head. What he'll say, how he'll say it. How to condense hours and hours of Vi's storytelling details into the simple facts that will condemn Phasma completely. Even if Armitage already dismissed his concerns, the younger Hux is not the only authority in the First Order. The others, perhaps even Kylo Ren, will want to know about the monster hiding in plain sight, her disloyalty merely a matter of time and opportunity. Perhaps they, too, will wish to see the face she wears behind her mask. Considering what Cardinal now knows about Armitage, he understands that this meeting is his only chance to make his case; a man willing to let Phasma kill his own father would have no problem ending Cardinal himself. Cardinal is willing to take that risk.

He's given himself plenty of time to get there, as he always likes to be early for such events. As he turns the corner where he last passed Captain Phasma, the air seems somehow colder. A few officers are chatting in front of the assembly room, their black uniforms spotless and their pointy caps perfectly straight. Armitage Hux appears behind them with Phasma in his wake, and the officers go silent and duck into the room. Armitage sees Cardinal, stops, nods, and goes in. Phasma pauses. She makes no move whatsoever, no nod or shrug or anything to suggest there's a human being under her shiny chrome armor. Without a word or even her usual nod to Cardinal, she follows Armitage into the room, and Cardinal picks up his pace, his cape snapping as he hurries, but not enough to make him appear worried.

The door is closed, and he taps in the code, but it doesn't budge. A sense of panic settles around his shoulders as he looks up and down the hall. He checks the time, but he's still thirty minutes early. No one else appears to be coming. He tries the code again, and still it fails. When he looks to Iris, her beeping suggests that she, too, is baffled. And Iris is never baffled.

"General Hux, has the code been changed?" he says into his comm.

He hears a sigh, and Armitage says, "It has. Your presence is no longer necessary. Please continue in your regular duties."

"But sir."

"A good trooper does not challenge his superior officer, CD-0922."

"Yes, sir."

"Dismissed."

The comm goes silent. The hall is empty. It's over.

THIRTY-NINE

ON THE *ABSOLUTION*

CARDINAL HAS NO CHOICE BUT TO DO WHAT HE'S BEEN TOLD. FOR ALL HIS recent rebelliousness, he was programmed by the best to be the best, and he has a job to do. It's kind of terrifying, how easily his training takes over, sending him on autopilot. He puts Vi Moradi out of his mind and returns to his duties in the barracks. The children are at dinner now; he's missed their training sessions, something that's never happened before when he wasn't directly under orders. As he moves among them in the cafeteria, he asks how they did and checks the scores posted on the wall. He was right about FB-0007; the boy did well, once FE-1211 was out of the picture. He makes a note to shuffle their groups around again soon, to find better fits for the bur-geoning leaders in ways that will maximize their performance. He can't let conniving FE-1211 have all the glory.

The irony is not lost on him.

Taking his tray to go, he makes a new request of the cafeteria droid: liquor. The droid isn't programmed to look surprised or care about such things, and it merely hands over a bottle as if this is an everyday occurrence; Cardinal is a captain, after all, and Brendol afforded him many privileges that he's never yet taken advantage of. The bottle is nothing special, nothing that would deserve the old General Hux's fine crystal decanter, but Cardinal wouldn't know a good vintage if he tasted it, anyway. He simply needs, for a while, to forget.

Back in his quarters, he takes off his helmet and throws it across the room before ripping off his armor and tossing it on the floor without polishing it. Iris beeps in alarm, and he orders her into a closet so she can't witness his aberrant behavior. He can't stand the stink of his own body, the stench of fear and sadness, so he strips off his bodysuit and takes the hottest shower he can. If only the heat could burn off the parts of him that are wrong, boil off his skin and leave him as new and innocent as he was before he ever met Vi Moradi. Sure, he'd detested Phasma, back then. But at least he'd been able to stand her. At least he'd believed that she wanted the same things he wanted, held the same ideals and fought for the same allegiance.

But he can't go back. Can't forget what he knows.

Still, he can drink, and he has heard that liquor makes a man forget like nothing else. Or, better yet, stop caring.

The first few sips burn going down, which is what he wanted to feel, anyway. Then his lips go numb, and a fire pools in his stomach, and he finally feels his taut muscles relax. The next cup tastes much better, and the third one gets tossed down so fast that taste isn't an issue. Something drips into the empty cup, plunking in the dregs of the amber liquid, and he realizes he's crying. Cardinal hasn't cried since Jakku. He hasn't had a reason to.

Sometime later, he blacks out on his bed. And it's a relief.

When his personal alarm announces the next shift, Cardinal has no idea who he is, where he is, or what's happening. Everything is sticky and unclear, and his head is pounding. It's a struggle to open his eyes, to stand, even to shower. Every other day on the *Absolution*, he's woken with purpose, ready to face the day and make the First Order proud. Today he doesn't even shave, just shoves his helmet down over beard scruff. He doesn't have time to polish his armor, just has to scrape it up off the floor and fling it on before the children's klaxon rings. He finds Phasma's knife by the half-empty bottle of booze and wraps it in a piece of cloth, tucking it into one of the ammo boxes on his belt, along with the beetle. He chokes out a sad laugh. It turns out evidence only works when you're allowed to present it.

At breakfast, he feels as if he's merely watching someone else's life unfold. The children greet him and smile and show deference, and he goes through the motions, all the while feeling hollow and sick inside. He gets his tray, and the cafeteria droid offers him an extra packet he hasn't received before.

"For the hangover," it says, its voice toneless.

Cardinal glares back at Iris, who bobs as if with a shrug, and he considers what it would feel like to take a droid apart with his bare hands. But instead of finding out, he simply takes the packet without thanks. He's about to remove his helmet to eat with the children when he realizes that his face is most likely a complete wreck. Instead, he takes his food to his room and finds it more tasteless than usual. The hangover packet is a powder, which turns his water orange and slightly fizzy. Once the liquid is down, the dull pounding in his skull lets up a bit, but the emptiness around his chest doesn't budge. There's an ache, deep down, that won't go away.

He gets to the training room before the children and surveys what he's always considered his domain. Spotlessly clean, perfectly maintained, everything exactly where it should be to maximize their training. He stands on the high balcony overlooking the fighting arenas on one side and the window to the cavernous sim room on the other. Five technicians sit at the computer banks, waiting for his word on which sim to run. It occurs to him that sims are not real, and he wonders what it's like for his new recruits, serving their first planetside tours under the watchful eye of Phasma. To go from Cardinal's well-run sims and patient training to holding a real weapon and taking human lives under Phasma's command. Many of his fellow soldiers seemed to enjoy such work, but Cardinal always found it distasteful, if necessary. Phasma probably relishes it.

As he watches the tiny children in their equally tiny armor arrive and pound on one another with riot batons, he realizes that he's going to find out, and soon, what it's like to fight when there's something very important at stake.

FORTY

ON THE *ABSOLUTION*

AS THE DAY GOES ON AND CARDINAL WALKS THROUGH HIS LIFE LIKE A ghost, trailed by a droid that now feels less like an accomplice and more like a nursemaid, he feels an increasing pressure in his chest. He takes his tray back to his room at dinner but has no appetite. Even the water is hard to swallow, as if there's a knot in his throat. Disgusted, he tosses it all in the garbage chute and heads for the shower.

Last night's shower was a slapdash, angry attack on his flesh. Tonight he moves through his First Order–outlined ablutions with a new sense of calmness, taking pride and comfort in every small step. He washes as they taught him at Brendol's academy, left-down-up-right. He uses the precise amount of cleanser. He dries off in the way that minimizes time. He shaves with absurd precision, taking satisfaction in the rasp of his razor. This time, he does not nick his skin. When he shaves his head, he feels as if a new creature has been revealed.

"My name is Cardinal," he says to the mirror. "Once CD-0922. Before that, Archex. But now my name is Cardinal. I am a decorated captain of the First Order, and I am a loyal soldier."

As he puts on a fresh bodysuit, he can't help noticing the muscles he's developed through years of hand-to-hand combat, running, and calisthenics. He's a man in the prime of his life, in top shape. He can outrun any of his charges, do pull-ups or push-ups until everyone else is winded. Just because he hasn't needed or accessed his power in several years doesn't mean he's helpless.

Before putting on his armor, he goes through it, piece by piece, and shines it until there are no scuffs, no rough places. He selects a freshly pressed captain's cape from the row in his closet and arranges it flawlessly over his shoulder. Once he's fully dressed, he checks the boxes of ammo on his belt, then each of his weapons, ensuring his blaster is primed, ready, and set to kill. Phasma's knife still sits on his table; he recalls inspecting it last night, holding it up to the light as if to discover some secret hidden in the blood-flecked blade. Now he returns the knife to the box with the beetle on his utility belt, un-wrapped and blade-down.

As he stands before his mirror, he sees a soldier that anyone would be proud to command. A leader and a warrior, flawlessly trained and adept at split-second responses to any situation. Brendol Hux once told him that together, they were training a new generation of storm-troopers that would far surpass the flawed troopers of the Empire. Cardinal believed him then, and he still believes him. Cardinal knows, in his heart, that he's unbeatable.

The only problem is that he now suspects Captain Phasma is much the same.

As he puts on his helmet, he realizes that it's become home. Yes, sure, the *Absolution* is home and these austere quarters are home, but Cardinal feels most himself when he's polished to a shine and seeing the world through the polarized lenses of his helmet. Is it strange, he wonders, that he's more himself in a uniform? In a costume? Up until yesterday, there was nothing strange at all, nothing to question. Now, staring at his fully dressed image in the mirror, he understands that his humanity has been erased. The violently red uniform is just the outward expression of what they've done to a small boy found half starving, alone, on a backwater planet. They've made him what he is, the First Order and Brendol and even Armitage. He's not the self-made man he's always considered himself to be. He's just another product, another perfect cog stamped out and plucked from a long belt of cogs to do his part in a larger machine.

He was happy as a cog. But now that he knows the entire machine is a fraud, that Phasma and Armitage are selfish killers who care more about their own advancement than about the First Order, what's the point? Those children he's training will just graduate to Phasma's care and be molded, in turn, into whatever sort of monster is requested from on high. It's sickening. It's awful.

And, as Cardinal sees it just now, it's all Phasma's fault.

Cardinal's eyes are locked with the reflective darkness of the helmet lenses. What color are his own eyes? Does he even remember? Before he realizes what he's doing, his fist shoots out and shatters the glass. This time, Iris does not beep in alarm. The droid appears unsurprised.

Turning on his heel, he marches out the door, and Iris follows. It's only a short walk to where he's going: the training room.

Phasma is known for her personal attention to every part of the stormtrooper training regime she oversees, and every time she leaves the *Finalizer* to visit the *Absolution* she fully dissects every component of Cardinal's curriculum, taking note of his students' performance and the battle simulations they've been running. Before, he's merely seen this as an intelligent way to transition the children's education as they age out of his barracks and into hers. But now he recognizes it for what it is: arrogant meddling and intrusive surveillance. It's just another reason to hate her, but at least it means that he knows exactly where to find her today.

The door slides open for him, so at least General Hux hasn't taken decisive action based on their little discussion earlier and locked him out of his own training room. After being excluded from the meeting, Cardinal has half expected to be marched out of his own quarters and tossed in the brig. If Cardinal knows Armitage, and he's known the weasel since he was a snotty and vindictive child, he knows that he won't be allowed to continue in his current capacity for long. Much as Cardinal gives demerits to recruits who tattle on other recruits, Armitage surely keeps a running tally of marks against him, and this is one scorch mark that can't be erased with a good polishing.

Not that it matters. Cardinal sees what he wants. Looking down from the balcony into the sim room, he watches Phasma. She's down there in full uniform, helmet and cape on, riot baton in hand, working through a simulation Cardinal personally programmed as the graduation test for his oldest recruits. She's destroying it, of course, smashing even his best students' scores. Taking the remote control as he so often does when interrupting a sim mid-battle to offer instruction or admonition to his students, he walks down the stairs and opens the door to the sim room. Phasma doesn't notice him at first, as she's in total immersion mode, all her senses fully focused on fighting a particularly agile Twi'lek in Resistance gear, so he hits PAUSE, freezing the scene mid-fight.

"And how do you find my program, Captain Phasma?" he asks. Even through the helmet's vocoder, he sounds mocking, and he doesn't care whether she senses it.

She unfolds from her fighting stance, lets her shock baton drop, and turns her head slowly, as if he represents zero threat and she's surprised to learn he can speak.

"You know how I feel, Captain Cardinal. Your numbers are superlative, but your clever simulations and Armitage's automated regimens are no match for real experience. No matter how pretty, such insubstantial simulations can't compare to a flesh-and-blood foe." Her hand brushes the Twi'lek's face, then slaps it. The droid underneath the holographic Twi'lek skin bobs from the hit. "You can't have a real reaction to a fake fight. You never know a soldier's true worth until they've stood on the battlefield, faced with death."

Cardinal clicks the remote, and the hologram disappears. Sand, beasts, droids, civilians, obstacles, and enemy combatants disappear to reveal a huge room filled with combat holo droids in standby mode. The walls are lined in weapons and lit coldly from far above. It's just them, now. Captain Cardinal, Captain Phasma, and their single witness, a floating droid silently recording their every word.

"So, you'd—what? Have me send children into real battle? Award them points for murdering civilians and possibly one another? My job is to make them soldiers. You're the one who makes sure they're killers."

Phasma steps closer, and Cardinal hates that she's taller than he is, forcing him to look up.

"Correct, Captain. I do make sure they're killers, because that's what the First Order demands. Courage, tenacity, and the ability to pull the trigger when the trigger needs pulling. That is how supremacy is won. You've never seen actual combat yourself, have you?"

Cardinal shrugs and casually pulls out his red blaster. *Pew pew pew,* and he's hit the bull's-eyes on three targets at the far end of the room.

"Of course I have, and I always received top marks. I consider it my duty to do as the First Order wills. I do as they command to the best of my ability, as Brendol Hux trained me to do. Even Supreme Leader Snoke speaks highly of my results and my skills. If you think my lack of recent experience is a problem, I suppose you could take it up with him. Or Armitage Hux. He does seem to appreciate a soldier with firsthand experience of murder."

The cold way Phasma cocks her head reminds Cardinal of some predator in the wild. He has her attention now, completely, and he's utterly sure that this is a predicament few people have survived. In the chrome of her helmet, all he sees reflected is a field of bright red.

"You seem to be hinting at something rather dangerous, Captain Cardinal."

Cardinal rams his blaster home in its holster. "A loyal soldier never challenges his superiors. But as we're both captains, I suppose I do have some questions about your commitment to upholding First Order ideals."

"You're wasting my time with these childish games, Cardinal. If you have something to say, say it."

The moment stretches out. It's impossible to lock eyes when both parties are wearing helmets, but Cardinal feels like whoever blinks first will lose. In the end, he isn't sure what to say. His training prevents him from directly accusing a fellow officer of murder, even if he's 99.9 percent sure she's guilty.

"That's what I thought," Phasma says, clipped voice dripping with disgust. "Coward."

Every wretched thought from the last day coalesces into rage. Cardinal snatches up her dropped riot baton, which flares to life the moment his magnetized gloves activate it. With a scream of rage, he swings for Phasma, desperate to feel the weapon collide with actual flesh, his enemy's flesh.

But Phasma is too quick for him, spinning out of range and darting to the rack of batons on the wall. Ripping off her cloak with one hand, she whips her baton into position and charges at him, shouting a war cry of her own. The ululating scream echoes off the high walls, and Cardinal's training kicks in.

He runs to meet her.

FORTY-ONE

ON THE *ABSOLUTION*

IT'S CLEAR FROM THE FIRST STRIKE THAT THE STAKES OF THIS FIGHT ARE different. Their batons clash, hard, the impact jarring up Cardinal's arms, making his bones ache. He spars regularly with SC-4044 and his other subordinate instructors, but it's always a friendly, relaxed experience. Not this . . . this madness. Phasma beats at him mercilessly, grunting and shrieking with each impact. As he parries, his body reacting half a second before his mind can keep up, he seems to separate into two selves. One is acting on autopilot, his muscles and nerves perfectly timed as if he's a droid running a program. The other is a purely emotional being filled with rage and fear and fire, and his lip curls as he merges those two selves, putting the power of fury into his strikes.

"You're weak, Cardinal. You strike like you're following directions someone else wrote," Phasma says, her voice a growl and her accent far less clipped.

"You're a killer." He goes for an uppercut, but she slashes his baton aside, making him stumble and recover.

"If you don't fight like it's a fight to the death, are you really fighting?"

She lands a hit on his armor, and electricity writhes over him but can't pierce his suit.

"They should write MURDERER under your poster, not EXEMPLAR. Those children look up to you, Phasma!"

"As well they should!"

His every parry is thrust aside. She's bigger, but she's fast, and each hit echoes through his nerves. He glances at Iris, but she's powerless to help him. He never programmed her to defend his life, and she couldn't harm a First Order soldier, in any case. She can only watch.

"You're only out for yourself. Your loyalty means nothing. Brendol should've left you where he found you!" he shouts.

Their batons clash and hold, and Cardinal pushes as hard as he can, his teeth bared as sweat drips down his forehead under his helmet.

"Your loyalty is disgusting," Phasma spits. "You were like a dog pissing itself at Brendol's feet. Do you think he cared about you outside of using you? Do you think he respected you? Do you think Brendol Hux was worthy of your allegiance, your adoration? If you think I'm a killer, then you should've gotten to know the real Brendol. Who he was off this ship."

The metal squeals as Cardinal struggles to hold her baton away. It takes everything he has not to fall back, but he's not about to let Phasma see any weakness.

"Oh, I've heard. I've heard all of it. I know you killed Brendol, and I know you killed your own brother, and I know you let everyone else you ever pretended to love die. As long as you survived, what did you care?"

Phasma steps back, causing Cardinal to stumble forward. Her baton sweeps up and cracks against his helmet, making the readouts buzz and glitch and his ears ring. In the moment that he's confused, she hooks his ankle, and he goes down on his back. But he's been trained for this, too; he rolls with the energy, right over his shoulder, and stands again, baton at the ready.

She wags a finger and *tsks*. "I know all your moves, Cardinal. I've studied your programs, run your sims. There is nothing you can do that would surprise me."

The only answer, it seems, is to step back and throw his baton at her head. As she ducks, Cardinal tackles Captain Phasma to the ground.

This is not a First Order–sanctioned move.

First Order stormtroopers are taught never to release a weapon. Dropping a weapon gives the enemy the advantage—and another weapon. And disregarding his training works, because Phasma goes down like a sack of sand, her chrome armor clanking against the floor. As she flails, Cardinal exerts his weight and reaches for her knife, pulling it out of his ammo box and aiming for the bodysuit peeking out from the armor at her neck. It's a dirty move, but that's the biggest gap in her armor, and he knows he'll only get one chance.

Before it sinks into flesh, the knife is stopped. He presses harder, but it just rasps against the slick metal on Phasma's forearm. She snakes her other arm around his neck, pulling him close and trapping him. Unable to move, Cardinal is stunned to find this is the closest he's been to another adult human. He's never embraced a woman, never put on his plain uniform to mingle in one of the ship's bars or taken leave off the *Absolution* to visit a backwater world's darker alleys. Even though their skin is hidden under layers of armor and thick body gloves, even though they're both wearing helmets, there's a strange intimacy here that Cardinal can't process.

"What are you going to do?" he asks. "Kill me?" His eyes flash up to Iris.

Phasma chuckles, a dark sound. "I've fought too hard and lost too much getting to where I am to risk everything by killing you," she says. "But if you were to bleed out after this terrible training accident, I doubt General Hux would investigate the incident too closely. We had a little talk about you at the assembly. You, and your recent . . . what did Armitage call it? Break with reality. It was put forth that perhaps the repetition of our programming might need to be tweaked to keep any other recruits from reaching your same sad end. There was some discussion of implementing my far superior training methods and phasing out your little game room here. Once you're gone."

"No," he says. "That would be the end of the First Order."

"Wrong. It would only be the beginning."

Phasma executes an escape that flips Cardinal onto his back on the ground. She's on top, in the position of power now, but the fight has gone out of him. What good will it do? If he kills Phasma now—if he's even able to do so, which is doubtful—his life is still over. If Armitage is against him, the entire First Order is against him. He doesn't know how they weed out the undesirables, but he knows it happens. He's watched children disappear over the years, or at least discovered their absence in the training room, their serial numbers erased from the records and scoreboards as if they'd never existed. They were always the slow ones, the clumsy ones, the ones who fought their programming or questioned the sims or pushed back when given commands. Almost like they were wired incorrectly. He's always known it has to happen, but he's never asked why or how. Maybe that's part of the training—to not miss what's gone, what's been taken away. To never question.

Now that he's questioning, of course he can't last here.

His head falls back, and his helmet clanks against the floor.

"They made me. I'm what I'm supposed to be," he murmurs, whether to himself or his enemy.

"Ah, Cardinal. That's your problem. You were only ever meant to be the tool, not the hand that wields it. You're what Brendol thought he wanted, a dull creature he crafted to do his will. But me? I'm what he didn't know he needed. I am your evolution. And that means you're deadweight. Extinct."

With that, he feels a hot, sharp pain in the side of his chest, just under his shoulder pauldron. He doesn't have to look down to know that it's her knife. She holds it up between them, considering the bead of blood on the jagged edge.

"I haven't seen this knife in a very long time. Where did you find it?"

Cardinal coughs and gulps.

"Parnassos."

"Then it sounds like I'll need to make another visit and see who survived. We can't have witnesses running around with evidence, can we?"

His feet and hands are starting to go cold. For all his years of training and fighting, he's never actually taken an injury anything like this. In his head, he hears a gentle voice intoning, *Use a belt or rope to make a tourniquet between the stab wound and the heart. If an artery has been punctured, you will require immediate medical attention from a First Order–authorized med droid. Try to keep the injury above your heart and your head raised. If you relax, you have a better chance of surviving. If you suspect that you will not survive the wound, attempt to kill the enemy combatant and alert your sergeant so that they may plan around your failure.*

Cardinal can't do any of those things. And he's pretty sure she hit a lung, maybe worse. It's all happening so fast.

"Recorders everywhere," he says. "They're always watching."

He lurches up as the knife plunges back in on the other side, even deeper.

"I've become quite adept over the years at shutting down cams and erasing extraneous feeds. Someone has to make the trash disappear around here."

The weight leaves his chest, and Phasma stands over him. She pulls out her blaster, shoots, and Iris falls to the ground, sparking. The droid rolls a bit and gives a sad beep as her red light flashes out.

"Nice try, Cardinal. But you never had a chance. There's a reason they put me on the posters instead of you. Oh, and look. You brought me an old friend." His helmet turns sideways just in time to watch her stomp on the specimen case that's tumbled out of his open ammo box. The beetle crunches amid the plastoid, the gold shards of its carapace glimmering in the gooey black of its guts.

He's got one last play. He reaches for his blaster.

FORTY-TWO

ON THE *ABSOLUTION*

BUT HE'S NOT FAST ENOUGH. SHE SEES HIS MOVE AND KICKS HIS HAND, hard enough to break bones. He never even touches the blaster. All Cardinal can do is lie there, suffering.

For all the time he's spent in the sim room, creating and running and practicing and instructing, he has never seen it from this angle: on the ground. Reaching up, he pulls the knife out of his chest and is rewarded with a fresh gout of blood. Only Phasma could slam a blade between the armor plates and deep into the meat of him with such fatal accuracy. He can barely breathe; she definitely got a lung. Not that it matters what she did or didn't hit. He knows well enough that the blade is poisoned. That's why he tried to stab her with it in the first place.

As his blood drains away, so does his anger. For all his talk of loyalty, integrity, obedience, allegiance, now he knows that when it comes down to it, words mean nothing in the face of power. It was his first real fight, and Phasma was right. He lost. All the sims and sparring in the galaxy couldn't match an entire lifetime spent fighting to survive.

At that last moment, the knife flashing down in his hand, did he flinch? Did he soften? Did he lack the instinct for such a personal kill? Or is she just that good at reading an opponent and controlling the fight? He still doesn't quite know what happened, whether he missed or she parried. All he knows is that his blade didn't find flesh. And hers did.

A noise reminds him that he's not alone. Phasma is looking down at him, and he sees a field of red reflected in her helmet, armor and blood mixed.

"Are you still in there, CD-0922?" she asks. "Still trying to understand how you lost?"

"Hypocrite," he mutters, although it's an effort.

"I'm not a hypocrite just because I don't believe the same things you believe."

"Liar."

"Yes, and who isn't? Armitage doesn't reward honesty. He rewards results."

He coughs, and wetness splatters the inside of his helmet.

"Monster."

Instead of answering this accusation, Phasma does the unthinkable: She takes off her helmet.

No one in the First Order has ever seen Phasma without her helmet, to Cardinal's knowledge—he wasn't lying when he told Vi that. When he still spent time among men his own age, it was a hotly debated topic, whether the tall warrior gleaming on the posters was actually hideous under her mask or terrifyingly beautiful. Now Cardinal knows, and he's actually quite surprised. There are those blue eyes Siv told Vi about, and a crown of soft gold hair haloing pale white skin. A deadly beauty, and he's the only one who knows. He can well imagine the dark green stripes under her eyes, her teeth bared to attack.

She kicks him, and when he can't do anything but groan, she kneels and pulls off his helmet, setting both of their helmets side by side like an audience, one shiny silver and one red.

"Everyone is a monster," she says, and her voice is so different without the vocoder.

"I'm . . . not . . ."

"Come now, Cardinal. Surely you've done something rebellious in your past. Something you regret. Besides attacking an officer tonight, of course."

"I did what I had to do," he sputters, "to get to you."

"And I did what I had to do to get to me as well. I don't regret it. That's the difference between us. I know what I am, and I embrace it. I'm proud of it. I fought for everything that I have, every bit of what I am. Now that you see what you are, you despise it. You're ashamed. And look where that's gotten you."

She shakes her head as if she's disappointed in him and puts her helmet back on. He watches, sideways and through a red haze, as she reattaches her captain's cape and slides the knife into her own ammo box. As she walks away, he feels a sudden desperation.

"You're just going to leave me here? Not even going to finish me?" he taunts, his voice a whisper.

"I did finish you," she says. "You just haven't realized it yet."

The door closes behind her.

Cardinal's world goes dark.

FORTY-THREE

ON THE *ABSOLUTION*

"OH, EMERGENCY BRAKE. I KNEW RED WAS YOUR COLOR, BUT NOT QUITE THIS much red."

Somehow, Cardinal is able to open his eyes, and he sees the strangest sight: a stormtrooper bending over him and speaking with the voice of Vi Moradi.

How did she manage it? He doesn't want to know. He'd hate to think that the *Absolution* has strategic weaknesses that could be so easily infiltrated by a half-dead spy. But perhaps she's not as damaged as she led him to believe. And perhaps he doesn't care so much about the *Absolution* anymore.

"Phasma's knife," he says. "Poison."

Vi's helmet shakes. "I hate to say I told you so, but . . ."

He gives a sad chuckle and feels hot blood spray his chin. "Told me so."

He wants to tell her to leave him alone so he can die in peace. His body, at least, has gone numb. There are worse places to die than his own training room, but he doesn't want the last thing he sees to be a

Resistance spy, especially not one gloating while wearing the armor he once wore himself.

"Go away," he murmurs, turning his head away. "We had a deal."

But instead of leaving, she puts his helmet back on him and rolls him over onto what he realizes is a hovergurney. They always keep a few in the training room in case emergency medical care is needed. Soon he's floating, in mind and body, as Vi pushes him . . . somewhere.

"What are you doing?" he asks.

"Saving you," she responds curtly. "Now tell me how to get to the hangar or shut up."

Even half dead, he knows his ship, and he's able to give her a few directions. The wounds don't hurt as much right now, but he can feel the fever heating up, hear his blood beating in his ears.

"Waste of time," he mutters. "Parnassos fever. Can't amputate my lungs."

"No, but I can put you in a medically induced coma and get you to a state-of-the-art medbay."

He wants to laugh but can barely breathe. It's like he's drowning in his own blood.

"Why?" is all he can manage.

She nods tersely as they pass marching troopers, then leans close.

"Because I am an infinitely hopeful creature, and I still think you can be flipped."

"Tough chance."

"It's one I'm willing to take. Thing is, I think you're actually a good man under all that vicious red armor."

He floats in and out of consciousness. The next time he looks up, they're in the main hangar bay. Then she's maneuvering him into a ship—not hers, something else. Something slightly bigger but still fast. Then they're in the air and she's barking into her comm. And then, blessedly, he sees the dark calm of space, and he's dumbfounded to realize she might actually get away with it.

"Where are we going?" he asks.

Hyperspace swirls overhead, and he struggles to stay awake for her answer. Vi stands over him and removes her stormtrooper helmet, giving him that wry smile he now knows very well. There are dark circles under her eyes, and the torture chair left a scorch mark across her forehead. What a pair they are, mortal enemies, each of them about half dead, stumbling into space.

"I made a promise," Vi reminds him. "I told Siv I'd come back for her, and you know I keep my promises. Turns out she and Torbi live in a station with an amazing medbay, so I don't think you'll mind. Now I'm going to put you out to slow down the infection, and you're going to do me a favor and go unconscious so you won't die."

Before he can protest, he feels the needle stab into his shoulder, and his body relaxes. From here on out, everything is out of his hands. Maybe he'll live, maybe he'll die. Maybe, one day, he can find a way to take down Phasma for good. But for now, all he can do is succumb to the anesthetic.

The world starts to go dark.

The last thing he hears is Vi sigh and mutter, "Wish I had some knitting."

FORTY-FOUR

ON PARNASSOS, 9 YEARS AGO

THE BLACK TIE FIGHTER LANDED, SETTLING INTO THE SOFT GRAY SAND. IT had been almost a year since Phasma had last seen her home planet, and Parnassos hadn't changed much. It looked just as inhospitable and wretched as she remembered.

She didn't immediately see the thing she came for, but then again she didn't expect it to just be sitting there, on the surface. Luckily, she had brought machines to find it. A quick scan revealed the hidden shape, and she was soon scraping sand away with her hands. For all her careful planning, she hadn't given enough thought to this part, hadn't brought a shovel or even a droid to do the dirty work. Even though she knew how things worked on Parnassos, how the elements conspired to whip away everything that was important or good, she had forgotten that a year in the desert would leave anything buried in sand. There must've been dozens of bodies here, the bones a few meters or even less under her white boots. But that wasn't why she had come. The dead were not her concern.

Soon her gloves scraped against something hard, and she began to find the shape of her prize. When the first glint of sun sparked off the metal, she had to look away. A year under the sand had done nothing to dull that spectacular brightness she had first touched a year ago, after dragging Brendol Hux across the endless desert, fighting for every step. It took hours to uncover the hidden prize, and she had to be careful of the beetles, which popped up from the sand every now and then, hungry for any kind of movement that could indicate liquid. She squashed each one she saw, knowing all too well their power. One of them, however, caught her eye, for no particular reason that came to mind. She recalled watching the sickness take over Carr, watching him fade into himself until he was practically transparent, far beyond help.

As the beetle crawled over her glove, its legs and proboscis hunting for the tiniest crack to invade and its golden carapace glinting like fire in the sun, she smiled under her helmet. Unclipping an ammo box from her belt, she opened and emptied it, dumping the energy cell into the sand. The beetle went in, and she clicked the top closed, jiggling it to be sure it was sound. The little beast might be useful, someday.

Returning to the real work at hand, she continued to dig out Brendol's ship, the one he called the Emperor's Naboo yacht. A silly name for a broken toy. She couldn't help remembering the first time she had seen it, a falling star burning through the sky and plummeting into unknown lands, farther away than anyone she'd ever known had traveled. Phasma had left a trail of bodies behind her, getting here. And she would leave a trail of bodies behind on the way back if that was what it took to erase every sign of the girl who had been born here on a forgotten, broken planet called Parnassos.

Tearing the ship apart took hours. Even with her various tools, it was an exhausting job, all done under the blistering sun in her full armor, and she had to take several breaks to sit in her TIE, drinking water, watching out for beetles, wiping the sweat off her forehead. Funny how, even on Parnassos, she didn't feel comfortable without her helmet. After she had joined the Scyre, she'd embraced their fierce masks and salve paint as her new visage, as a better way to face the world and terrify it, perhaps giving her a slight edge in any battle. Her helmet performed the same service. She'd first put on the fallen stormtrooper's armor in the middle of this very desert and had never looked back. No one in the First Order knew what her true face looked like, except Brendol.

She would remedy that. Soon.

But first, she had to complete her task. It had the feel of a ritual, what she was doing here. It felt right. Transforming valuable remains into protection was, after all, a very Parnassian talent.

Not that it was easy. But, then again, what in her life had been? As she dragged the chrome plates back to her ship one by one and loaded them in, she recalled using plates of metal as sleds and then as shields. To think that all those years she had lived in the Nautilus and then in the Scyre, she had had no idea what existed outside of their small territory. It had felt like a revelation that an entire group could sleep on one patch of dirt, as Balder's Claw folk did. And after she found the records and studied the colonization of Parnassos, she knew that, as Brendol had told her, there were indeed rich lands just out of reach that whole time. A few hours on a ship and life would have been entirely different, bereft of violence. She was going to visit one of those places of plenty now, in fact.

She only took as much of the yacht's chrome plating as she needed, leaving the rest to the desert, where it would soon be buried. Back in her TIE, she lifted off and zoomed into the blue sky and over the ocean. It had seemed so deep and dark when she was a child, this immense and yawning promise of cold death and monsters. From up here, it looked friendly and blue and balmy. A short while later, she landed the ship on a broad swath of green land. Once planted with crops to feed the millions of Con Star Mining Corporation workers, it was now a riot of wildly flowering grains. A short walk away was the exact thing she needed, the thing that Con Star had been kind enough to build nearly two hundred years ago: a factory. Not just any factory, but one dedicated to making mining equipment from local metals and ores. Cleo Station.

In the year she'd been with the First Order, Phasma had spent as much time as possible learning. She was accustomed to sleeping four hours or less in a day cycle, so while the rest of the stormtroopers and officers were asleep, she'd been catching up on tech, tactics, galactic history. And even a little slicing. She punched the right code into the datapad, and the abandoned factory's doors slid open as if they'd been greased only yesterday. Con Star hadn't known how to terraform a planet, but they'd known what they were doing when it came to constructing and programming their facilities to last.

Inside, the building was flawless. It was as if the miners had simply walked out, and everything had kept going without them. Which was almost what had happened. After Phasma found a small cart and rolled the heavy metal plates down the smooth hallway, she passed wide, shining windows looking down on the factory floors and into boardrooms. In one room, she found hundreds of deactivated droids, standing still and covered in dust. In another, she found several dozen people curled up on the ground as if they'd simply lain down to sleep and stayed there. Beside each of them was a cup still rimmed in poison. Funny, how people who had never had to fight to stay alive were so willing and eager to give up their lives when faced with a few challenges. Phasma had grown up eating sea urchins raw and drinking water from snail shells, while these folk had looked around at bounteous fields of grain and been unable to handle being abandoned by their overlords.

Phasma was happier with the First Order than she had been with the Scyre, but she would never be willing to drink poison for any master.

"Fools," she muttered, dragging the cart farther down the hall.

She had chosen this particular factory, out of dozens of Con Star factories, because it had specific machinery capable of replicating a very particular kind of process. Having downloaded the facility's map into her datapad, she knew exactly which room housed the equipment she needed. She didn't even have to flip the generator; everything hummed along perfectly when she powered up the synthicator.

Plate by plate, she fed the chrome sheets into the smelting chamber until they were all gone. Then, piece by piece, she removed her stormtrooper armor, placed it in the scanning chamber, waited until it had been properly coded, and replaced it with the next piece. They had built this costly machine so they wouldn't have to constantly ship in new parts whenever something broke; they could merely replicate an exact replacement. Phasma was happy to consider it one small piece of Con Star's payback for having made her early life a living hell.

The synthicator screeched back and forth as each new piece of armor took shape in glorious chrome. She had to carefully file the sharp edges and drill holes and place bolts here and there, but the printer's work was flawless beyond her wildest imagining. The helmet was the last piece and also the most time consuming. She had selected a prototype helmet design that Brendol had rejected but she had fought for, and she had to first remove all the intricate electronics within without damaging them, then reattach them inside the new helmet. It was a tricky business when working with plastoid and even more challenging when dealing with the slickness of the chrome. She sighed heavily and pulled out her datapad, studying the downloaded schematics to help her get all the fittings just right. To think: Just a year ago, she had never held a working datapad, and now she could build one from scratch, given the right materials.

Powering down the synthicator, Phasma left her old white armor on the ground. Piece by piece, she put on the chrome armor for the first time, lovingly fitting every shining plate. Her captain's cloak sat perfectly on her shoulder, swirling around the metal with a satisfying swish that it didn't have over the old white plastoid. Along with the chrome plating from the ship, she'd also hauled in a new chrome sidearm and matching chrome blaster rifle, both ordered secretly and already tuned to her gloves. The blaster slid into its holster with a decisive click, and Phasma smiled.

Standing before a plate-glass window, Phasma was, for once, satisfied. Just as she had constructed this shining suit, the first of its kind in the First Order and even more distinctive and commanding than that sycophantic fool Cardinal's red suit, she had also constructed a completely new Phasma. She spoke the updated Basic of the First Order fluently, her accent just as clipped and polished as Brendol Hux's. She fought better than any other stormtrooper, including Cardinal. And she took her orders directly from the general and no other, a position she'd reached in less than a year.

In part by getting rid of anyone who stood in her way, of course. But that was something she'd learned on this very planet. Kill or be killed.

So she killed. And still she rose.

Phasma rubbed a dull spot on the chrome helmet until it shone and carried it under her arm. Down the long hall, past the tomb of dead fools, and out the door she strode, her boots the only sound in the entire world. Her ship waited in a peaceful field, the kind of place her parents and then the Scyre folk had told her stories about as a child, a dream lost generations ago, of simply walking on solid ground without a starving belly. Placing the chrome helmet on her head, she took in a deep breath through the filtration system, tasting the air of Parnassos for the last time and finding it sweeter than ever before. She boarded her ship, took off, and blasted into the sky and back toward the *Finalizer* and her new life.

She swore never to return to this planet again, or to the girl who had once lived here.

There was only one more person alive who had seen her face, and she was on her way to end him.

She had become Captain Phasma of the First Order, and nothing could stop her.

ACKNOWLEDGMENTS

Long ago, in a galaxy far, far away, or maybe it was 2015, I bought a vanilla cupcake at the grocery store because it had a plastic Darth Vader ring stuck in the frosting. As I held the cupcake, I made a wish on it: I wanted to write a *Star Wars* novel. A few weeks after shoving that cupcake in my mouth and devouring it in two gigantic, messy bites, I was invited to write "The Perfect Weapon." A year later, I was offered the immense honor of writing *Phasma*.

Getting to write stories in the *Star Wars* universe is a dream come true for me, and I'm so grateful for the chance to be a part of something that's been so important throughout my life. I'd like to thank everyone who works on Del Rey *Star Wars,* including Elizabeth Schaefer, Tom Hoeler, Jen Heddle, Shelly Shapiro, Michael Siglain, David Moench, Julie Leung, the Story Group, and the publicity folks who take great care of us authors at cons (and everywhere else). Thanks to my agent, Kate McKean, for helping me navigate even when she isn't quite sure who Yoda is. Thanks to my best buddies Kevin Hearne and Chuck Wendig, who passed on their priceless knowledge about writing canon, as well as the support of Ty Franck, Daniel Abraham, Matt Stover, Christie Golden, Claudia Gray, Tim Zahn, Janine K. Spendlove, Beth Revis, E. K. Johnston, Kelly Thompson—heck, to all the amazing *Star Wars* writers, with extra hugs to the #StarWarsGirlGang.

I'm so grateful to everyone who reads my books and to those who review, podcast, retweet, blog, or otherwise take the time to spread the word. *Star Wars* fans are the best fans. Thanks to the 501st for inviting us to their amazing party at *Star Wars* Celebration Orlando— and for doing so much good in the world. And a shout-out to all the Bazine Netal and Captain Phasma cosplayers. I don't think I'll ever stop squealing when I see your amazing costumes.

Thanks to my husband, Craig, for always being my biggest fan and favorite person and for being just as nerdy about *Star Wars* as I am— but, again, you should feel very bad about killing me with Noghri. Thanks to my kids, both secretly name-dropped in this book, for being awesome. Thanks to my mom, Linda, for helping wrangle the Padawans while I was writing. And thanks to my much-loved plush Princess Kneesaa, who's been with me since Christmas 1983. I am and will always be #TeamMurderbear.

May the Force be with y'all, and thanks for reading!

ABOUT THE AUTHOR

DELILAH S. DAWSON is the writer of the Blud series, the Hit series, *Servants of the Storm,* and the Shadow series, written as Lila Bowen and beginning with *Wake of Vultures.* She is the creator of the *Ladycastle* comic and writes for the *Adventure Time* comic. With Kevin Hearne, she co-writes the forthcoming Tales of Pell series, beginning with *Kill the Farmboy.* Delilah teaches writing courses online for LitReactor and lives in Florida with her family.

whimsydark.com
Twitter: @DelilahSDawson
Facebook.com/DelilahSDawson

If you enjoyed *Star Wars: Phasma*, don't miss the
next must-read tale on the *Journey to the Last Jedi*.

Star Wars: Canto Bight

Visit a lavish new locale rich with opportunity,
but where the stakes couldn't be higher.

Featuring new stories and characters from
The Last Jedi.

On sale December 5.

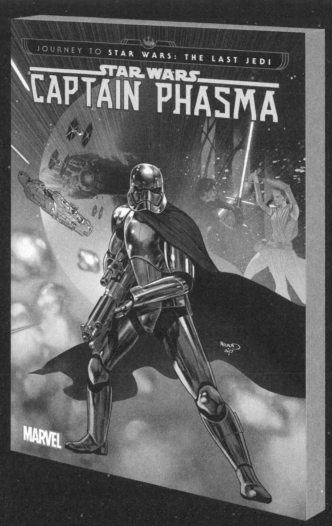